ABOVE THE CLOUDS

Book Three
THE CHRONICLES OF THE GOLDEN FRONTIER

ABOVE
THE
CLOUDS

~

GILBERT MORRIS
and
J. LANDON FERGUSON

CROSSWAY BOOKS • WHEATON, ILLINOIS
A DIVISION OF GOOD NEWS PUBLISHERS

Published by Crossway Books
   A division of Good News Publishers
   1300 Crescent Street
   Wheaton, Illinois 60187

Cover illustration: Tony Meers
Cover design: Cindy Kiple

First printing, 1999

Printed in the United States of America

Library of Congress Cataloging-in-Publication Data
Morris, Gilbert.
 Above the clouds / Gilbert Morris and J. Landon Ferguson.
  p. cm. — (The Chronicles of the golden frontier ; bk. #3)
 ISBN 1-58134-108-3 (pbk. : alk. paper)
 I. Ferguson, J. Landon, 1952- . II. Title. III. Series: Morris, Gilbert. Chronicles of the golden frontier ; bk. #3.
PS3563.08742A63 1999
813'.54—DC21   99-16862
                  CIP

15	14	13	12	11	10	09	08	07	06	05	04	03	02	01	00	99
15	14	13	12	11	10	9	8	7	6	5	4	3	2	1		

In Memory of:

Cassie Bernall

Kyle Velasquez

John Tomlin

Kelly Fleming

Isaiah Shoels

Daniel Mauser

Rachel Scott

Steven Curnow

Danny Rohrbough

Lauren Townsend

Matt Kechter

Corey DePooter

Dave Sanders

Students and Teacher of
Columbine High School
Littleton, Colorado
April 20, 1999

Contents

PART ONE

GOLD FEVER

CHAPTER

~ 1 ~

A Fire in the Heart

This will do," Jason Stone said, holding up the front page of the newspaper.

Jennifer DeSpain peered up from her work where she sat at her desk. "It looks very nice," she complimented, a slight smile adorning her lips before she returned to her work.

Having finished the first copy of the *Advertiser*—July 10, 1879, Jason Stone glanced over the small newspaper's headline: GILPIN MINING IN DECLINE. Placing the newspaper on his desk, Jason turned his thoughts to a more personal matter and strolled over to the front office window and glanced out. The streets weren't as busy as they had once been. Down a ways he could see an old prospector tugging at his stubborn burro's reins. Two nearby quartz mills had recently shut down, and the silence was both a relief and disturbing.

Jason's real problem sat at her desk not more than twenty feet away engrossed with an article she was writing. He looked over at Jennifer and noticed the distinct curve of her face, a sight he found rather satisfying. What bothered him was that they had been engaged for almost six months, and yet she refused to talk about setting a wedding date. He could see the little diamond flashing on her ring finger, as if it were signaling for its mate, a wedding band. He likened being engaged to having a trust fund in his name—money that gave him security for someday but not now. Waiting for Jennifer had proved to be another test of his patience. Whenever he found the anxiety to be almost overbearing, he would try to remember the lessons of faith, patience, and trust he'd learned in the past. However, his present impatience took his thoughts in a different direction, one that took his mind off Jennifer.

"You'd think that publisher back east would bother to contact me," Jason said impatiently. He had sent a book manuscript to an interested publisher many months before.

Feeling sympathy for Jason's discord, Jennifer put down her work and rose from her desk. She hadn't put her hair up that morning, and it rolled over her shoulders like an auburn waterfall. Her expression was one of concern as she approached Jason near the window. She found him physically attractive; his square shoulders and boyish blond hair made him appear youthful. At the moment his pale blue eyes looked worried, and she knew it wasn't about his book. She wanted to commit to a marriage date, but the failed romances in her past had left a bitter taste. She didn't want to make any more mistakes. And yet she knew that deep down she truly loved Jason. He'd helped her get through many tough times. She wanted to talk freely about these things, but, like Jason, she couldn't quite bring herself to do it. "I'm sure it'll take them some time to review a work of that size," she said encouragingly. She came closer, offering a sensitive smile.

Jason ran his hand through his hair and glanced at her. He couldn't help but notice that her green eyes changed color with her mood. She looked much younger with her hair down. He knew she felt his discouragement, and he found her compassion irresistible. "I feel like that book is part of me," he continued. "It's about my life and the trials we've been through and the wild boomtowns we've lived in. You'd think they'd have the decency to at least send me a letter and tell me *something!*"

"Don't worry," Jennifer said softly as she gently placed her hand on his shoulder. "You're an excellent writer, and I'm sure the people back east will find your stories exciting."

Jennifer's encouragement always lifted Jason's spirits. He smiled. "You mean like me getting in a gunfight? Or how about a westerner falling off his horse and getting laid up thinking he's paralyzed forever? Yes, it's been quite a venture. I'm not sure they'll believe my stories, even though they're true."

"Then again," she reminded him, "good reading is good reading. Look at how those dime novels sell, and there's hardly a speck of truth in them." She slipped her hand up to the back of his neck and gave him a gentle massage. "Sometimes you worry too much."

Jason put his arm around Jennifer and pulled her close. His lips met hers. He basked in her fragrance and the warmth of her feelings for him. It was moments like this that made him believe he had all that a man could ever possibly want. When they finished the kiss, he still held her close to him and looked deep into her eyes, now shining with affection. "Jennifer, let's get married. This waiting has been hard for me. Again and again I've protected and stood by you, and I always will. I love you as much as a man can." He stopped, his eyes pleading.

Jennifer dropped her glance; being put on the spot was always overwhelming for her. She'd heard these words before, but from different men, and those men had not turned out to be what they seemed and left her brokenhearted and betrayed. The shame and humiliation she'd suffered had almost ruined her ability to trust any man; strong doubt about herself was a persistent menace. But she knew Jason's words were true; even with his shortcomings, he'd always stood up for her and beside her in the most difficult of times. Accepting the engagement ring from him hadn't been hard, for she loved him; nevertheless, matrimony scared her. She knew he was a Christian and a good man, and she knew her decision to delay or accept was a matter of trust. She had to be honest with him.

"Jason," she murmured, her voice trembling, "I'm trying so hard. I've prayed about it, and my intentions are good, but the fear just won't leave me."

Hugging her, Jason whispered in her ear, "I'm sorry—it's my fault. I know what you've been through, and I don't want to pressure you. I'm being inconsiderate; forgive me. I'm sure you'll do the right thing in time." He smiled at her as he moved back a step so he could see her face. "Don't mind me, ma'am," he said jokingly, hoping he sounded calmer than he felt.

Her eyes moist, Jennifer's pleasant smile returned. Jason had such a marvelous way of pulling her away from the horrible fear that clung to her. She too felt that in time things would be all right and they'd be together. Sweeping away past hurts had been difficult, but every day she thought she noticed a little improvement, thanks to Jason and his persistent care. She took his face in her hands, pulled it to her lips, and gave him a healthy kiss. "That's for putting up with me," she said. Then she kissed him again. "And that's for being you."

Jason felt content for the time being. It was their ability to talk and share their deepest emotions that held them closely together. There was no doubt in his mind that they were truly in love. "We'll get through this together," he said. "I've put up with you this long— what's a little longer?"

Giving him a troubled smile, Jennifer pinched his square chin playfully.

What a woman! he thought, watching her graceful movements as she moved back to her desk. *Does she really understand how much I love her?*

~

Busying herself in the kitchen, Lita Washington prepared the midday meal. Her southern cooking drew no complaints, and she prided herself in being the best at it. But when she eased the door open to the front office, she saw Jennifer and Jason embracing, so she slowly closed the door so as not to be heard. After a while she tried again, this time sticking her round face in the door cautiously. When she saw them back at work she shouted, "All right, you lovebirds, ya'll come on back and eat. Everything's ready."

Jason gave Jennifer a knowing look. Lita never missed a trick. "Well, my lovebird," Jason said joyfully, "I guess we'd better go eat."

Jennifer turned as Jason approached. He took her arm in mock ceremony and escorted her to the kitchen door. "After you, my dear."

"Oh, you're much too kind, Mr. Stone," Jennifer responded, acting like royalty.

In the kitchen Abe Washington had just finished cleaning up and prepared to sit down at the table. Lita placed a steaming dish of her buttermilk biscuits on a hot plate on the worn but homey table. One last survey under her critical eye revealed that all was ready. The tender browned roast floating in its juice and surrounded by carrots and potatoes had its own beckoning aroma. Strong tea had already been poured in the tall glasses, and the black woman sat down to join the others already seated at the table. All eyes turned toward Abe as he bowed his head to say grace. "Dear Lord, we thank You for this food we're about to partake of, and we praise You for Your all-powerful glory. Help us not to stray, and forever look over us, for we sometimes under a lot of pressure. Amen."

"Thank you, Reverend Abe," Jason said as he reached for a biscuit.

"What you mean, under pressure?" Lita asked, glaring at old Abe.

Shaking his head, Abe searched for words that would satisfy Lita. "Well, you know, sometimes I don't know what to tell these folks that come to me—I has to ask them to wait a while until I can find an answer in the Bible. But sometimes God let me know right away, and I don't have to look for the answer."

"Ever since he become a preacher," Lita said, rolling her big brown eyes, "he think he got to always tell folks what's exactly right. Ain't nobody perfect!"

Big Abe hunched over his plate and ate so he wouldn't have to talk. Lita's strong words intimidated him.

Jennifer spoke up. "I think it's wonderful that he's a reverend who cares that much about people's needs. He felt called to do this work, Lita. Let him do it."

"To hear him bellowing behind that pulpit you'd done think he been struck by lightning," Lita said scornfully. But truth be told, she was proud of Abe's serving the Lord by faith. He still did some work as a blacksmith, but his primary focus now was on running the small church the black people of the district attended. Since Abe had become their permanent preacher, they'd reached a revival sort of state and often held prayer meetings and sang all Sunday long, with Abe preaching fire and brimstone in between.

"You've got my vote, Abe," Jason argued. He'd heard Abe preach, and at such times he sure wasn't the timid Abe that Jason had always known. The Abe who preached was an inspired man of faith. "I don't know how you do it, but you sure get everybody's attention."

"Unlike *our* church," Jennifer added. "Sometimes I can hardly stay awake. I wish that preacher would come back by here sometime—you know, Reverend John Dyer. He could sure get your attention."

Thinking back, Jason recalled the preacher. He'd personally pulled Jason through a major crisis in his life by encouraging Jason to have faith. "I hear he's over in South Park; evidently he helped move a church over there and rebuild it. He sure impressed me too."

"Maybe we can get over that way sometime," Jennifer said between bites. "I'd like to see him again."

"Ya'll do need to take a trip over yonder, and while you're there, get him to marry you!" Quick-tongued and opinionated, Lita didn't have any problem expressing her feelings on the subject. "Ya'll worry me the way you carry on."

"Aw, Lita," Abe mumbled, "let them young folks alone. They'll get married when the time is right."

The smile had suddenly disappeared from Jennifer's face as she looked down at her plate and pretended she hadn't heard Lita. *She's too much like a mother to me*, she thought. But she also knew that the subject of marriage was an uncomfortable one for her to talk about.

"Well, Abe," Jason said, taking a deep breath in hopes of changing the subject, "I hear you're going to preach at a tent revival."

"Sure am," Abe bragged. "Next week. Supposed to be a lot of preachin' goin' on, and they asked me to come. This town needs something to wake it up, what with folks movin' out the way they is just because some of the old mines shut down."

"Yeah, everybody thinks the grass is greener on the other side of the hill. Gold strike here—gold strike there." Jason set his fork down, readying himself to give a little talk. "I often wonder what goes through the heads of these miners. They have an abundance of mining experience, yet they let rumors pry them away from a secure job and off into the hills just 'cause somebody screams, 'Gold.' For the life of me I can't understand why intelligent men succumb to gold fever."

"Greed is one of Satan's best weapons," Abe said knowingly. "I've seen it more than once. It breaks up families—causes men a ton of grief."

"That much is certain," Jason agreed. "But I still don't understand how anyone could be that stupid."

After the fine meal Abe went back to the livery to shoe some horses before moseying over to the small one-room church he'd helped build. It was there where he felt most useful. Meanwhile, Jason and Jennifer went back up front to the office to run off copies of the next day's newspaper, then lazily fought off the slumber brought on by a satisfying meal.

Lita quickly cleaned up the kitchen. She worked afternoons with Clara Brown doing wash. Clara had become her best friend, and her unselfish efforts to help freed slaves come west was a noble purpose that Lita enjoyed being a part of.

～

The lazy July afternoon was pleasant enough, and customers dropped in now and then to run an advertisement. The *Advertiser* was doing fine, with most of the revenue generated by advertising, just as the name implied. Jason still enjoyed reporting newsworthy items or writing editorials, which were usually well-accepted. Jennifer reported on the social events, appealing to upper-class readers. She'd reported on the grand opening of the Central City Opera House in 1878, beginning a grand tradition of theater. She'd followed up with reports of performances by Buffalo Bill and P. T. Barnum. She showed her talent in writing about these social affairs. At times she secretly wished she were among the well-to-do, for they appeared to be so happy and far above the silliness of mundane worries.

A loud, annoying braying suddenly sounded just outside the office. "It sounds like somebody is torturing a donkey," Jason said, rushing to the window. Jennifer followed, just as curious. Right outside the front door they saw a little old man pulling on the reins of his stubborn burro. "C'mon, Pete!" he called as he tried to pull the animal a few inches closer so he could tie it to the hitching post. But Pete was not cooperating and opened his mouth, showing his big teeth as he hee-hawed at the top of his lungs. The donkey had a long, shaggy mane that hung over his eyes, but Jason could see the whites of the animal's angry eyes.

"What's he doing?" Jennifer asked, her expression one of concern.

"Trying to tie him to the post," Jason answered. "Looks like an old prospector to me. Wonder what he wants?"

Pete screamed in anguish as soon as his bridle was hitched to the post, then began kicking his hind legs until half his load had been deposited in the street.

The old miner patiently picked up his gear and tried loading it back on the animal's pack. "Your mother was a mule!" the old man spat.

The stubborn donkey kicked his legs high again, causing the gear to fall back off. "I give up—have it your way," the old-timer said as he dusted off his hat and came up the steps to the front door of the office. He walked with the aid of a crooked tree limb.

Jason and Jennifer quickly moved away from the window as if they hadn't been watching. The old fellow entered, took one look at the couple in the office, and saw a horrified look on both their faces. "Oh, don't mind Pete," the codger said, flipping his thumb back toward his burro. "His nature is a mite temperamental."

"Can I help you with something?" Jason asked, looking the old man over. A typical prospector of the day, the man had long white hair that blended so well with his long white beard, Jason couldn't tell where one started and the other stopped. His smile revealed that he was toothless, but his small eyes had a friendly twinkle. He wore an old corduroy suit that was about worn-out. He smelled like the outdoors.

Shuffling closer, the old man held his wide and stubby hand out to Jason. "I'm Emmitt Tugs."

Taking his hand, Jason could feel the rock-hard calluses. "How do you do, Mr. Tugs? What can I help you with?"

"I been tryin' to get up and down these streets all day, but Pete ain't havin' nothin' to do with it. Ornery sort, you know. But what I been a tryin' to do is locate a woman," Emmitt said, unsure how to get to the point.

Jason laughed uncomfortably, then turned to Jennifer to see if she was following this. "Well, Mr. Tugs, I'm afraid you're in the wrong district if it's a woman you're looking for."

"Naw, that ain't what I mean," Emmitt said a little impatiently. "I'm looking for a perticular woman." He fumbled in his coat pocket and drew out a piece of paper. He searched another pocket, produced a pair of tiny spectacles, and placed them on his nose as he read what was written on the paper. "I'm a-lookin' fer a Miss DeSpain."

"That's me," Jennifer said, surprised. She moved closer, her bright eyes searching Tugs for a clue as to what he might want.

"Mighty pleased to meet ya," he said, reaching for her hand and taking it into both of his and giving hers a good shake. "I been all over tryin' to find you, and Pete's been a handful today. Sometimes he's like that—don't want to do nothin' I ask."

"But how does that concern me?" Jennifer inquired, her lips forming a curious smile.

"Well, they tell me down at the clerk's office that you be the owner of the Wild Horse mine."

Jennifer glanced at Jason, who shrugged his shoulders. "Yes, I am," she said.

"Anyway, what I was aimin' to say was, would you be interested in grubstakin' me to work that mine?" Emmitt asked kindly.

Jennifer couldn't help but laugh, and Jason joined in. "Mr. Tugs, everyone knows that mine is barren. Why, it's probably even dangerous, it's been so many years since it was worked. Besides, I'm not in the business of grubstaking miners. You might try the general store for supplies, but I believe that all the claims around here are already spoken for."

Emmitt rolled his eyes, obviously irritated with himself. "That ain't what I mean," he said. "When I said grubstake, what I meant was, you let me work that old mine, and I'll give you half of what I get. How's that sound?"

"I don't know," Jennifer said, her expression suddenly changing. She knew of most of the flimflams and shenanigans pulled in the mining business, but she wasn't sure what Emmitt Tugs was up to.

"Ain't no sweat off your back," he continued. "You ain't makin' nothin' from it right now."

"What makes you think that mine is worth working?" Jason asked firmly. "Every experienced miner in town knows it's worthless."

"They didn't look close 'nough," Emmitt said, his eyes twinkling again as if he had secret knowledge. He hobbled over near Jennifer's desk and found a chair. Sitting down slowly, he groaned as he took the load off his feet. He noticed a rock on Jennifer's desk, picked it up and smelled it, then stuck his tongue out and tasted it. "Where'd this come from?" he asked, looking at Jennifer.

"I don't remember," she said. "I think I picked it up in the street. I thought it was pretty."

"That's fool's gold," he said. "It ain't worth nothin'."

"What do you mean, they didn't look close enough?" Jennifer inquired.

"I was in the mine a few days ago, went way on back," Emmitt began. "It don't go too far. Whoever was running that operation didn't know what he was doin'." He slowly got back to his feet, not wanting his leg muscles to tighten up from sitting too long.

"What . . . Did you find some color?" Jason asked, his interest piqued.

"Well, no," Emmitt said. "Are you related to Miss DeSpain?"

"I'm her fiancé," Jason told him. "We're engaged to be married."

"That's mighty fine, son," Emmitt shouted, slapping Jason on the back. "She's a real looker, shore is, and you ought to be proud."

Growing impatient, Jason said, "Yes, well, what makes you think this mine would be worth working if you didn't find any sign?"

"I didn't say that," Emmitt said. "I seen rock formation in there, and it's the right kind of rock if'n what yer lookin' for is gold."

Slumping, Jason informed Emmitt, "Almost all of the rock in Gregory Gulch looks like that. Everybody knows that."

"Yeah, but there could be gold right behind the next drift!" Emmitt said excitedly. Then he turned back to Jennifer. "Don't you see, it could be right there, just a waitin' to be snatched up!" His excitement failed to entice either Jennifer or Jason. They'd heard talk like this before.

"What do you know about mining?" Jennifer asked. Her patience was growing short.

"I'm a Cornishman, and my family's been miners since way back. I come to America and joined in on the Californy rush of '49. Course there wasn't much to that—just some fellers panning out yonder. So I done left there to work the Comstock Lode in Virginny City. I worked for a mining company there and done right good—I was a foreman. Saved up 'til I bought a claim of my own and hit it good!"

"So you got rich?" Jennifer asked.

"I did."

"Then what happened? Don't you have anything to show for it?"

"No, ma'am. I spent all my money on whiskey and women. Of course, I was a lot younger then. Now I just speculate here and there, but me and old Pete, we get by."

"We formerly lived in Virginia City," Jason said. "Ran a newspaper there called *The Miner's News*."

Emmitt's mouth fell open. "You don't say! Wait a minute—I remember you!" He glanced at Jennifer, his little eyes wide open. "And you be that woman! Why, shore, you caused quite a stink there, takin' on them mining owners!"

Emmitt held his hand to his chin. Jason figured Emmitt could think or talk but not both at once.

"You ain't the one that got in a gunfight with that mean and ornery Big Ned, are ya?" he asked Jason. "Then later you took a pick handle and whooped him up somethin' good. Was that you?" Emmitt was excited.

Jason nodded.

"Glory be!" Emmitt wailed. "I be in the presence of some good people today. I got a bottle outside—we can have us a nip to celebrate." Emmitt turned for the door, but Jason grabbed his arm.

"No need," Jason said, now smiling. "Neither of us drink. But you're right—it's good to talk to someone who was at the Comstock. Not many people would ever believe what that place was like."

"It was shore somethin'!" Emmitt agreed as he pictured the old days in his head. But after a minute he came back to the present and paused, trying to remember the reason he'd come there. "Anyway, like I was sayin', I think that mine of yorn shows promise. I'm a man of my word—half of what comes out is yours, and you ain't got to do nothin'."

His hands in his pockets, Jason shrugged and looked at Jennifer. His expression suggested, *Why not?*

"Mr. Tugs," Jennifer said, now all business, "we'll have to draw up the right papers—we can't settle any debts you might leave on our doorstep or be responsible for your actions up on that hill."

"I'm familiar with contracts, Miss DeSpain," Emmitt said excitedly. "You go right ahead and draw up whatever's in your pretty head. Be sure and say somethin' about you gettin' half, and I'll be back by to sign it. It's mighty fine to know you folks," Emmitt said, smiling, his toothless mouth a black hole in his white beard. He made his way to the door and turned to wave good-bye. "Be seein' ya."

"What do you think?" Jennifer asked Jason. "He seems nice enough."

Chuckling, Jason admitted, "You have to like him. What's not to like? As for gold, I wouldn't hold my breath. An old man and a pick—I doubt the odds are very good. I imagine he spotted the old toolshed near the mouth of the mine and decided it makes a free place to stay for a while. I don't guess he could hurt anything, the poor old dolt."

"Reminds me of the old days," Jennifer said almost sadly. "You don't see that kind of spirit anymore—at least not around here."

Adolescence

Abby DeSpain was at that challenging point in life when a child inhabits an adult's body. Her long, wavy brown hair and penetrating blue eyes were natural assets of beauty. She had already taken an interest in boys, and they had definitely taken an interest in her.

"This town is a pigsty!" Abby mumbled with irritation as she sorted through her clothes, searching for anything that might attract more attention. "How come we can't be rich and have nice clothes like so many others?" Her only pretty dresses were for church on Sunday, and they were high-necked and revealed nothing of her recent physical development. She was packing and intended to move away, though her plans were vague. "I'll find someone who'll take care of me, some rich fellow who'll buy me whatever I want and take me to decent places. There has to be a better life out there somewhere!"

A gentle knock came from her closed door. Abby jumped, fearing it was her mother. "Who is it?" she called.

"It's me, Abby—Grant."

Moving over to the door, Abby opened it slightly and looked at her brother through the crack. "What do you want?"

"Can I come in?"

Abby made a face of disgust but opened the door to allow Grant to enter. The fifteen-year-old with greenish eyes and wavy short auburn hair was getting tall and was already shaving. The resemblance to his mother was apparent, though he had the masculine look of a healthy young man. Always casual but also given to deep thought and careful decisions, he might have passed for a law student. His concern for his sister had grown intensely, mainly due to the fact that she had developed into a rare beauty, and he didn't think she realized what kind of mischief that could lead to.

"Looks like you're packing," Grant noticed as he sat down on her bed. "You're not going to run away, are you?"

"Yes!" Abby snapped. "I'm sick of this place—sick of everything!"

Nodding, Grant pondered the situation. He never made quick judgments but considered all the facts. "Have you thought about where you'll go or what you'll use for money or where you'll sleep or what you'll eat?"

"I'll get by," Abby assured him as she continued to fill the large carpetbag. "There's always some sucker who'll give me money."

"Have you considered what one of these suckers might want from a fourteen-year-old girl in return?" Grant asked solemnly.

Abby didn't answer at first. She knew exactly what Grant was hinting at. "Well, I don't have to be like that," she said. "I'll be a lady!"

"Desperation leads to some awful things, Abby," Grant reminded her. "We've seen it here and back in Virginia City. Do you remember the young and pretty girls like you who used to arrive in town with such high hopes and dreams? Later we'd see them after they were forced to work in the dance halls just to have something to eat and somewhere to sleep. Remember how they looked? They had dark circles under their eyes—they looked terribly tired. Is that what you want?"

Stopping what she was doing, Abby turned to Grant, then came and sat beside him on her bed. "No," she mumbled. "But I'm so unhappy. I only want to do something about it."

"Happiness comes from within," Grant said. He loved studying people, especially the citizens of the boomtowns, and he'd picked up a lot of practical wisdom along the way.

"You sound like you're preaching," Abby said with distaste. "You know I don't like to be preached at."

"Are you afraid of it?"

"God never did anything good for me!" Abby flared. "He took my father away. And every time it seems like I get to liking some fellow, God takes him away too!"

"But you do believe in God," Grant suggested.

"Of course!" Abby almost shouted. "I hate Him! I don't know why He picks on me."

Grant nodded again as if he understood. Actually he wasn't so sure about God and the things he'd read in the Bible himself, but part of his search would be to find out more about it all. His curiosity about people and what made them do what they did in the boomtowns was a driving factor that never let him rest. Since some of these people were religious, that played a role in his search.

The discord he saw in his sister was all part of the big picture. However, he seemed to understand her frustration to some degree and often sympathized with her. The difficulties of their growing-up years had brought them closer together. He loved and cared about Abby very much.

"I have an idea," Grant suggested enthusiastically. "I'm making a little money now working at the assayer's office. Let me be the sucker for a day and buy you something. What would you like?"

Abby's eyes lit up with an intensity that almost scared Grant. "A new dress!" she exclaimed. "Not one of those stupid dresses either, but a *real* dress!"

"You've got it," Grant said, standing. He smiled, pleased he'd given Abby something to look forward to. "We'll do it this Saturday. How's that?"

Unable to resist, Abby gave her brother a big hug. "You're the only one who cares about me," she murmured.

"That's not true," Grant said, holding her away. "Everyone in this house cares about you. It's just that at times you can't see it. But things will be all right. I just know they will."

Grant left, feeling better himself. He liked being able to soothe Abby's ruffled feathers.

And Abby admired her brother's negotiating abilities; he was so diplomatic, easygoing, and logical, traits she lacked. It was kind of him to let her vent her anger and then offer sound advice. All and all, she was glad she had Grant for a brother.

~

Grant had found his job kind of by accident. Strolling down Chase Street one afternoon, he saw a little old man, bald as a cue ball, hunched over a broom and sweeping out his shop. It was obvious the man was disgruntled by the jerking way he handled the broom. As Grant happened by, he said, "I'll do that for you."

"It don't pay nothin'," the man spat from under his walrus mustache.

"Just trying to help out," Grant remarked.

Handing him the broom, the proprietor complained, "Everyone who comes in here tracks in wagon-loads of dirt and mud and horse manure. These dirty miners wouldn't know how to wipe their feet if their life depended on it! This whole place ain't nothin' but a mud pit!"

Taking the broom, Grant swept the pile of dirt out the front door and then swept the boardwalk in front of the shop. He took the broom back inside the strange little shop and handed it to the grouchy old man.

"You didn't have to sweep the boardwalk," the man said.

"Oh well," Grant apologized, "I figured if it was clean they'd track less in here."

"You're a thinker, aren't you?" the old man said bitterly.

"I suppose."

"How old are you?"

"Fifteen."

"How'd you like to come by here and sweep this place out in the afternoons? I'm much too busy to tend to the worries of house-keeping."

"Sure," Grant agreed.

"My name's Potter. I'll give you a nickel a day."

Grant jumped at the opportunity and soon discovered the strange little shop full of glass bottles, small forges, and balance scales was an assayer's shop. Grant's curiosity led Mr. Potter to show him more and more about assaying, and soon Grant was actually doing some of the primary skills such as grinding rock samples. Later he began to do a few of the basic chemical tests to determine the nature of certain samples.

"You have a genuine interest," Mr. Potter said. "I like that. Most kids don't care about nothin' nowadays." Mr. Potter had turned out to be a good man even though he had some quirky ways. One thing Grant noticed was that Mr. Potter liked to take a break from his work every now and then and go stand in the back door and gaze up at the sky. When he did this, he had a cigar he liked to gnaw on slightly, though he never struck a match to it. When he was done with his break, he'd put the cigar in its little place on a shelf until the next time. Grant noticed Mr. Potter could stretch several weeks out of one cigar, but even more interesting was the look on Mr. Potter's face when he stood on the back porch gazing. He looked as if he was thinking of something very far away.

"More samples over there," Mr. Potter said one day as he looked up from his magnifying lenses. You need to grind them to powder and label the jars they're in. After you've done all that, I want to show you how to handle mercury and how to use it safely."

Grant rejoiced at that news but showed little of his enthusiasm. "Yes, sir," he answered calmly. The way chemicals could reveal what was contained in various rocks was astonishing. Mr. Potter could take one small rock and get more information out of it than a man could get out of a dictionary.

"You're good with your hands," Mr. Potter told Grant one afternoon as if he were talking to a young surgeon. "A sharp mind isn't all that's needed in this profession. Dexterity is of the utmost importance. You've developed good lab technique, and that takes a good pair of steady hands. A laboratory is no place to fool around." He pronounced it la-boor-a-tory.

"I wish I could learn all there is to know about this," Grant said.

"You'll never know that," Mr. Potter warned. "Modern science and chemistry are always making new discoveries, and sometimes it makes your old theories invalid. But I like a hungry mind. It will enable you to keep up with the changes. Assaying is a good business, but it takes a bit of politicking as well, and that's something else you'll have to get a knack for."

This was not news to Grant. He'd seen miners come in acting shifty and produce a piece of ore they'd found. "I don't want nobody to know about this here rock, Mr. Potter. You just tell me what it's worth by the ton and keep it under your hat, and I'll pay you for your services."

More often than not, Mr. Potter not only could tell the percentage of gold and silver by the ton but also precisely which mine the rock came from, or at least within a few hundred yards. And sometimes it was his responsibility to report mining intrusions, including when an underground shaft had ventured into another claim. This could be a very touchy if not dangerous business, something else that intrigued Grant.

"How do you know when to report a crook? Aren't you afraid they'll come after you?" Grant had asked.

"You watch me, and over time you will see how to handle these delicate situations," Mr. Potter advised. "It's not always in your best interest to run to the law. Sometimes these are honest mistakes. When I tell a man I know what he's up to, then it's his burden to make things right, and he usually has to make a choice—he knows his secret is no longer a secret."

Grant's fascination with assaying was only paralleled by the people he watched. The rocks were certainly a key to the search that inspired him to find out why men and women in boomtowns acted normal sometimes and insane at other times. The rocks represented something dear to these people and led to wealth and greed, even gambling. Grant realized the newspaper business kept him in the thick of things, which helped him understand the people of boomtowns; but now the rocks attracted him more.

One day Mr. Potter showed Grant one of his prized possessions.

"Ever seen anything like this?" the man asked, handing Grant a piece of gold about the size of a hickory nut.

Struck with awe, Grant's mouth fell open. He'd seen gold nuggets and gold jewelry and gold coins, but never any color like what he was looking at now. It was a sort of iridescent, burnt-orange gold that actually changed hues as he rotated it in the light. It could vary from a high-polished brass color to almost a red. "Wow!" he said, delighted with the weight of the rock in his palm. He suddenly felt an uneasy and queasy feeling in his stomach. He figured that feeling must be what the discoverers felt when they struck gold.

"That's pure 24 karat gold," Mr. Potter said admiring the stone Grant held. "As you can see, gold can come in many colors."

"Where'd it come from?" Grant asked, almost hypnotized by the nugget's beauty.

"Nobody knows," Mr. Potter said sadly. "Back in California an old prospector brought that to me to inspect. Said he'd found the Eldorado and was going to file a claim, said there was a lot more where that came from. But he was killed in a saloon brawl that very evening, and nobody knows where he found it."

Stories like this drove men mad, and now Grant had a better idea why. The nugget was precious and held a certain beauty of its own. He could only imagine the effect it would have on men seeking riches and glory.

Grant loved his work, and Mr. Potter paid him well for a fifteen-year-old. Assaying involved solving mysteries, a thing Grant found he loved.

～

A gusty summer wind whisked clouds of dust down Merchant Street, lightly coating everything with a fine grit. Jason went over to the office window to close it. "This place is as dusty as Virginia City," he said to Jennifer as he tried to force the old window shut. Then he thought he heard a muffled whimpering, like some poor old dog in pain. "Do you hear that?" he asked Jennifer.

"Hear what?" she said, coming over to his side. She listened. "Why, yes, I do. What is it?"

Jason went to the front door and stepped out onto the front boardwalk. There he saw a woman sitting on the wooden bench, her head in her hands as she cried softly. He turned to Jennifer who was right behind him, alarm evident in his expression. He whispered, "Isn't that Lizzie Doe?"

Jennifer peered over Jason's shoulder at the forlorn woman, then glanced back at Jason and nodded. "Maybe we should ask her in."

Slowly Jason approached the unsuspecting woman. "Mrs. Doe, are you all right? Is there something we can do?"

Lizzie Doe, often called Baby Doe, was known about town for her bold and different ways. She'd been seen wearing men's dungarees as she headed to work in the mine owned by her husband, Harvey Doe. It was well-known that Harvey wasn't the ambitious sort and often avoided any form of physical labor, but Baby Doe was certain that riches lay just beyond the next charge of dynamite. She ran the crew and worked like a man while the miners ridiculed Harvey behind his back.

When she was relatively new to Black Hawk, Lizzie Doe caught the eyes of many a miner as she strolled down the boardwalk. "Hello, there, Baby! Want a ride?" a robust freighter driver would call. "You're much too pretty to be walking!"

"You're too fresh! My name is Mrs. Lizzie Doe!" she would reply as she tromped on up the hill with a great show of indignation.

"Well, all the miners know you as Baby," the driver would reply, tipping his hat. "A pretty woman like you walking down the street—you better tell that husband of yours to watch out."

Though she wouldn't admit it, Lizzie was flattered by such remarks. Though the miners talked like that continuously, they were a friendly lot, just a little short on manners.

But lately it had been no secret around town that Baby Doe and her husband were having their share of troubles. Jason reached to take Baby Doe's hand. "Come inside and have a cup of coffee. Perhaps we can help. I'm Jason, and this is Jennifer."

Rushing around to help Baby Doe up, Jennifer took her other hand. Struggling to her feet, Baby Doe was so pregnant, she looked as if she might have her baby any moment.

Later Lita scurried around the kitchen table serving coffee and leftover powdered donuts she'd made earlier that morning. "Can I get you anything else, honey?" Lita asked Baby Doe.

"You're too kind, all of you," Baby Doe cried shakily.

"Shall we call Doc?" Jennifer asked, touching Baby Doe's hand.

"Oh no. I'll be fine, I'm sure." Baby Doe took a sip of the hot coffee as she slowly regained her composure. "It's just so hard right now. I don't know what I'm going to do."

"Maybe it would help to talk about it," Jason said.

"Well," Baby Doe whimpered, wiping her eyes with a lace handkerchief, "Harvey has disappeared, and I have no idea where he went. We're deeply in debt, and the landlord has just evicted me from our room. I have no money and nowhere to stay, and I'm due to have a baby anytime now."

Lita stared at the disheveled little woman. "This calls for prayer to Almighty God," Lita blurted out.

"God?" Baby Doe asked, surprised.

"That's a good idea, Lita," Jason agreed. "Baby Doe, if you only knew what I've survived thanks to answered prayer . . . God works in magnificent ways." Without hesitation, Jason led the small group in prayer for Baby Doe.

"You are good people," Baby Doe said. "It must be nice to have things under control and be content with your life."

This caused Jason to give Jennifer a quick glance. Things had a long ways to go before he'd be content. Jennifer disregarded his stare and resumed her concern for the young lady sitting with them. "We have an extra room upstairs. You're welcome to stay here as long as you like."

"Oh thank you so much, but I can't impose like that. I'll find a way to get by," Baby Doe said wearily.

"Nonsense," Jason insisted. "We want to help—it's the right thing to do."

Baby Doe smiled through her tears. "I'm so embarrassed. You're really much too kind." After taking a moment to think, she realized she had little choice. "I have some things in the lobby over at the boarding house—a few trunks full of my clothes. It's all I have left."

"I'll send someone over to get them," Jennifer said comfortingly. "Would you like to go upstairs and lie down? You look like you could use the rest."

"Yes, I would. I don't know what to say, Jason. You and Jennifer are the nicest people I've ever met."

Lita helped the young, pregnant woman upstairs and showed her into the empty room where Abe used to sleep. She fluffed the pillows and helped Mrs. Doe onto the feather mattress covered with cotton quilts. "You lie here and take a nap," Lita instructed. "I'll check on you later in case you need anything."

"Thank you." Baby Doe sighed as she closed her eyes and drifted immediately off to sleep. She was drained from her ordeal.

Downstairs Jason discussed the unfortunate situation with Jennifer in the front office. "I'm not sure what we can do for her," he said, shaking his head with dismay. "Looks like she's ready to give birth any minute."

"If she does, then she does," Jennifer said. "Nobody but God can control that."

"Poor girl," Jason said. "So many venture out here expecting to find riches and wealth and end up heartbroken and poor and desperate. It's a repeating saga. Mr. and Mrs. Doe should have stayed wherever they came from."

"They came from Oshkosh, Wisconsin." Jennifer answered. "Her father-in-law used to live here. You remember Colonel Doe? He was here in the early days but returned to Wisconsin. He owned some mines here and was quite successful. He left Harvey and Lizzie a mine to work, but I don't think it was productive."

"The usual scenario," Jason admitted. "Isn't Jake Sandelowski a close friend of the Does? I've seen him with Baby Doe on several occasions. Maybe I should run over and get him—I'm sure he'd like to know about Lizzie's condition."

Jennifer rolled her eyes. "From the talk I've heard around town, I think Jake and Baby Doe are *quite* well acquainted, if you know what I mean. I certainly don't approve of that kind of behavior. But then again, she is in need."

"You shouldn't make judgments based on rumors," Jason warned.

"I've heard the same thing, but a friend is a friend." Heading for the front door, he said over his shoulder, "I'll see if I can round him up. I'll be back shortly."

Jason found Jake Sandelowski in his clothing shop. After he told Jake about the morning's episode, the two returned to the newspaper office.

"How are you?" Jake asked as soon as he stepped into the office and saw Jennifer. He was well-dressed and looked like he was ready for a night out. His perpetually present and pleasing smile was hard to ignore; his blue eyes, wavy brown hair, and tall frame made him unusually handsome. "I hear Lizzie had a bad morning and is asleep upstairs."

"Indeed," Jennifer agreed, looking to Jason who'd followed Jake inside. "I'm worried about her condition. She should be resting and have someone looking after her with a baby coming and all."

"I couldn't have said it better myself," Jake added. "I had no idea she was in such despair. I heard about her dilemma, and I don't know why she didn't come to me in the first place. I have a spare bedroom that's most accommodating, and the doctor's office is right above me. It would be my pleasure to look after her."

It was apparent that Jake had more than a passing concern for Baby Doe; it sounded as if he was talking about his sweetheart.

"She didn't exactly come here begging," Jason said, not wanting Jake to get the wrong idea. "I think she had taken a walk and grew despondent. We found her sitting right outside on the bench, weeping."

"Should I go up and see her? Perhaps she feels better now," Jake suggested, gesturing with his hands, obviously eager to talk to Baby Doe.

About that time Lizzie opened the back door from the kitchen. She looked somewhat refreshed but still troubled.

"Lizzie!" Jake said, rushing to her and putting his arms around her. "You poor thing. Let me take you over to my place where you can relax. No need to worry—I'm here."

Jennifer and Jason both felt like they were intruding on something very personal, and a glance between them confirmed that the feeling was mutual.

"I'm indebted to you," Baby Doe said meekly, quickly glancing at Jason and Jennifer. "I feel like a fool. I don't know what came over me. Thank you for your kindness."

"It's nothing," Jason said, glad to be helpful. "Anything we can do anytime, feel free to come right over."

Placing her hand on Bay Doe's shoulder, Jennifer also offered her consolation. "We'll be glad to do anything to help. We'll be excited to see the new baby too!"

Baby Doe nodded as she hung onto Jake. "Thank you again," Jake said as he helped Baby Doe toward the front door. "We'll be in touch."

In a moment they were gone. Jennifer stared at the door, her expression one of wonder. "I don't know why, but I feel so sorry for her. Her situation certainly doesn't appear very moral, I mean with Jake and all, but . . ."

"I'm glad Jake is around to help her. He's done well with his clothing shop, and he can certainly afford it. But I do think you're right—there's more to the situation than meets the eye. Did you see how he looked at her? How he acted when she came in?"

Smiling knowingly, Jennifer looked at Jason as if he were a tenderfoot who'd just gotten off the train. "He's in love with her, silly! A blind man could see that!"

"Of course . . . I knew that," Jason mumbled, though of course he didn't.

Gold!

It was a typical July Saturday morning in Black Hawk, the sky a shocking blue and the sun golden on the mountaintops. Jennifer had finished breakfast and returned upstairs to her room to freshen up for the day ahead. When she left her room, she strolled down the narrow hall. It occurred to her to check in on Abby, who was probably still asleep, for she hadn't seen her earlier at breakfast. Opening Abby's door without knocking, the immediate shock of what she saw didn't register. She stood motionless, her mouth open.

Abby jumped, startled by the intrusion. "What are you looking at?" she yelled defensively. "Can't you knock?"

Jennifer didn't know what to say. Abby was standing there in a beautiful dress designed for someone much older, her hair an array of brown curls, her eyes a deep deceptive blue. The dress was red and trimmed with white lace and had a revealing neckline. She looked stunning in red. The shock for Jennifer wasn't just the dress, but the sudden dawning that Abby was no longer a child but a young woman. Abby's disgruntled face had a hint of makeup, making her appear more mature than her years.

"Abby, where'd you get that dress?" Jennifer questioned slowly. It was hard to force the words out.

Abby stomped over to her bed and sat down with her arms

crossed. "Grant bought it for me!" she snapped, certain she was in trouble.

Jennifer knew this was a situation she had to handle delicately, for Abby could instantly become unreachable. "Well," Jennifer sighed, closing the door behind her, "I wasn't sure I was in the right room. You look . . . you look absolutely beautiful!"

Jumping to her feet, Abby flashed the wonderful smile she so rarely showed, a smile that made her gorgeous. "You think so?" she said happily as she turned so her mother could get a better look at it. It was an expensive dress made of the finest materials—definitely an evening dress, the kind of dress a young woman might wear only to a gala event.

Feeling a little weak, Jennifer came over and sat down on Abby's bed. She still couldn't believe she was looking at her own daughter. "What possessed Grant to buy you such a nice dress?"

"I asked him to," Abby admitted without guilt. "He makes good money. Did you know that?"

"No, I didn't," Jennifer said shamefully. She felt a terrible guilt for being so out of touch with her children. "Why didn't you ask *me*? Maybe I would have liked to buy you a dress."

Her features suddenly changing, Abby went back to a defensive attitude. "You'd never let me buy a dress like this! You'd say maybe when I was older or something like that. Anyway, you always say we don't have the money."

Jennifer felt like she'd had a rug snatched out from under her, but she was determined to communicate with Abby, who always had the grandest notions about how she wanted to live her life. "You look like a lovely young woman. I can't get over it. I don't know," she mumbled, placing a hand to her forehead, "it's like you grew up all at once."

Sensing her mother's despair, Abby sat down beside her on the bed, looking up at her. "I only want to be pretty," she acknowledged.

Taking her daughter into her arms, Jennifer gave her a warm hug. Her eyes a little glassy, she desperately wanted to be part of Abby's mysterious world. After a moment she decided on the right words. "You know, a lovely dress like that is for very special occasions. You must always be accompanied by a gentleman. Do you know why?"

"Why?"

"Well, the dress is very attractive, as are you. A red dress like this sends a message to men. It tells them you are . . ." Jennifer had to stop. She knew good and well it was time to inform Abby a little more about the birds and the bees, but she found it far more difficult than she had ever anticipated. "It's only natural for men and women to be attracted to each other, and the things they do offer subtle messages. Your lovely dress says you're coming of age and you want to court a man. This is a way of attracting them."

Frowning, Abby thought about what her mother was saying. She *was* interested in boys, and the dress was one way of getting their attention. However, she didn't realize the dress was as bold an announcement as her mother had indicated. "Do you think my dress says too much?" she asked with respect for her mother's opinion.

"Let's put it this way—you must be careful when and where you wear it. As I said before, if you're accompanied by a gentleman, like Grant or Jason for instance, then it says you're spoken for for the moment—you have an escort."

"But when would something like that ever happen? We never go out anywhere nice or do anything like that," Abby complained. "You say we're too poor."

Again feeling guilty, Jennifer wanted to do something special for Abby, a sort of coming of age outing. "We'll make an exception," Jennifer announced, a new smile on her face. "I'll ask Jason—maybe we can all go out for an evening and have a fine time, and you can wear your new dress."

Abby threw her arms around her mother's neck, overcome with joy. "I can't wait! Oh, Mother! I can't wait!"

Later Jennifer couldn't get Abby's appearance out of her mind. *It's hard seeing your daughter grow up*, she thought dejectedly, *and Abby is eager to grow up too fast! I wish she trusted me more.*

∼

Jason couldn't help but notice that something was bothering Jennifer as he inked the press, ready to run the weekend copy.

"Something wrong?" he asked from across the office, fearing he'd done something to upset her.

With a jerk Jennifer looked up from where she sat at her desk. She had often been guilty of retreating into her private world of loneliness, where she fretted over personal matters. She secretly feared what was happening to Abby, the possibility of her getting mixed up with the wrong men and finding life to be one long heartbroken memory. And the girl had clearly been toying with the idea, something out of character for her. "Do you think we could go out one evening?" she blurted. "I mean you and me and Grant and Abby— go to dinner and then the theater, only the finest!"

Speechless, Jason stared at her as if she'd lost her mind. He couldn't believe this was coming from Jennifer, for she hadn't indulged in such social frivolity since the days of Lance Rivers, a former suitor who'd broken her heart. "Are you feeling all right?" he asked without thinking.

Jennifer stood up, her green eyes sensitive and half hidden behind narrowed lids. Sad memories of painful losses had affected her for so long, but now hopes of what might be were finally emerging. Was she finally taking a giant step out of her world of long thoughts and painful images? "I think I'm feeling better than I have in a long time."

"This is a cause for celebration!" Jason quickly wiped his ink-stained hands and came over to face Jennifer. "I think it's a grand idea. We can't afford it, but who cares." He used this special moment to draw close to her. Taking her into his arms, he kissed her.

The revealing conversation with Abby had awakened a burning desire in Jennifer, and she suddenly realized the world she was missing and the excitement it could bring. She responded to Jason's kiss, pulling him closer.

After a long moment Jason backed away with a new kind of look in his eyes. "I don't know what happened to you, but I wish it would happen more often."

Smiling happily, Jennifer turned her head away, her hands still resting on Jason's shoulder. "It's hard to explain, but it all started when I saw Abby in a rather revealing dress."

"Abby in a revealing dress?" Jason retorted, now thoroughly confused.

"Yes," Jennifer said, slightly laughing as she removed her hands from Jason. "It's certainly not what you'd call a Sunday school dress. Grant bought it for her. She's growing up, Jason." She swung her soft eyes back to Jason, her eyes a color that showed her tender mood. "I wish we were better off financially. I wish I could do more for Abby, give her things I never had, the finer things of life."

It was apparent to Jason that what had happened had moved Jennifer deeply. "We'll take it a day at a time," he said. "From now on we'll make some plans so all of us can have something to look forward to. For right now the plan will be a grand evening on the town, and you and Abby will be the special guests."

Jason's understanding made him irresistible as Jennifer moved back into his arms and laid her head on his shoulders. No words were needed for the time being.

Lita opened the back door to announce the midday meal, saw Jason and Jennifer embracing, and simply shook her head, then closed the door without uttering a word.

～

Saturday afternoon passed smoothly at the newspaper office. Jennifer's new outlook helped her forget the sorrows of the past that had frequently tormented her. "I'm so thankful!" she murmured. "Father in heaven, only You understand how much better I feel, and You are the One who brought it about."

"You say something?" Jason asked.

A pleasing smile greeted him as Jennifer glanced his way. "I was just saying a prayer, thanking God."

Jason smiled too. He knew all about God's miracles, and the change he saw in Jennifer was itself a refreshing gift from heaven.

The peace of the lazy afternoon was rudely broken by the unmistakable screaming of a burro, a loud and distracting nuisance.

"What on earth?" Jason cried out irritably.

Just then the front door was flung open, and Emmitt Tugs tromped in with a heavy canvas bag over his shoulder. His old, worn corduroy suit was filthy with grime as he tracked dirt straight over to Jennifer's desk. He said nothing, a huge smile making his small eyes squint. When he got to her desk, he hoisted the bag from his shoulder and rudely dumped the contents all over her paperwork.

"Are you crazy?" Jennifer shouted, angrily jumping to her feet to avoid the pile of dirt and rocks spilling over her desk.

Jason quickly came up behind Emmitt and, grabbing his arm, spun him around. "You old coot! What's the matter with you?" Jason shouted angrily.

Emmitt just smiled a toothless smile. "Gold!" he screamed hoarsely. "Look at that," he exclaimed, waving his arm over the desk. "And there's lots more where that came from!" He laughed heartily, his big belly shaking.

Bending over what at first resembled a pile of rocks and dirt from the street, Jennifer and Jason looked over the debris. Jennifer picked up a stone and studied it closely. It was milk-white quartz with black streaks and was speckled with reflective little particles of yellow gold. She gulped, trying to swallow the huge lump in her throat.

More skeptical, Jason picked up a piece of quartz and examined it. "That's fool's gold," he said, relatively sure. However, the thumping in his chest persisted. He turned to Emmitt, who couldn't clear the smile from his face, and asked, "It is fool's gold, isn't it?"

Emmitt reached in his pocket, pulled out his wide hand, and opened it in front of Jason's face. In his dirty fat palm stood a golden nugget almost as big as a chicken egg. "That's pure gold," Emmitt boasted. "And the vein is wide." He paused as Jason took the heavy gold nugget and stared at it completely mesmerized. "We're rich!" Emmitt announced with authority. "We're filthy, stinkin' rich!"

A dead silence fell over the room. Neither Jennifer nor Jason could fathom what was taking place. It was like winning the biggest prize one could imagine, the dream so many dreamed of but so few achieved. But as the truth sank in, many questions also came to mind.

"Does anybody else know about this?" Jason asked frantically.

"Just us," Emmitt smiled.

"There are so many things to do," Jason spat, almost stuttering.

Jennifer thought about the simple little contract she and Jason had drawn up with Emmitt. She nervously found it in her desk and read over what was now a very important document. Emmitt recognized the paper. "Don't worry your head none, ma'am," he said assuredly. "I done read it over, and it'll do just fine. I'm a man of my word. What's yours is safe."

"Oh my!" Jennifer sighed, finally able to get her breath. Instantly the pile of rocks and dirt on her desk became far more important than anything else there. "What should we do next?"

"You happen to know an honest assayer?" Emmitt asked. His mining experience was not forgotten in that moment of bliss.

"Uh, yes!" Jason said. "We do." He feverishly looked at Jennifer. "The man Grant works for."

"That there ore on your desk is a good sample," Emmitt said. "Have him assay it. I'll bet it's over $3,000 per ton."

Jennifer's heart almost stopped. That was more money than the newspaper had earned the entire past year.

"Here," said Emmitt, "you take this." He gave her the heavy gold nugget. "That can be a keepsake to remind you of the greatest day of your life."

Jennifer was speechless. The nugget seemed much too heavy for its size and color. It had far more character than a piece of jewelry. It changed its appearance as the light danced on its surface forming a multitude of deep golden colors, some almost red, others an iridescent blue, and some looking black.

"You care to see the mine?" Emmitt asked.

Quickly glancing at Jennifer to make sure she was as anxious as he was, Jason said, "Sure, let's go."

Checking an old silver pocket watch he plucked from his dirty vest, Emmitt suggested, "It's a mite late—could be dark before we get there and certainly dark on the way back. How about first thing in the morning?"

"Sure," Jason said, finding it hard to restrain his voice. "That's not a good road going up there. First thing in the morning, of course."

Jennifer simply nodded. She felt like she was being rushed through a tunnel where she couldn't find anything solid to cling to. The effect was dizzying.

"First thing!" Emmitt chuckled as he went to the door. "We're all rich now!" he needlessly reminded them.

"I can't believe it!" Jason said after Emmitt left. He hovered over the ore samples, inspecting each one as if he knew what he was looking at.

It was hard for Jennifer to keep from crying for joy. A pile of dirt on her desk had just changed her life drastically, even more than she knew.

~

That night both Jason and Jennifer were unable to sleep. For Jennifer, the situation was almost as scary as it was exciting. There were so many more things to consider now, things she'd never thought of before, like how to safeguard their newly found wealth, how they would spend it, whether they should move to a better place. She could now afford more stylish clothes for her and Abby. She found there was no way to keep her thoughts in anything remotely resembling an organized pattern. Her mind danced from subject to subject until she fell into a sleep filled with crazy dreams. In all the excitement she forgot to pray.

For Jason their new wealth seemed to offer resolution to immediate problems. His first thought was that once they got things in order and under control, maybe Jennifer would consent to a marriage date. He approached this from every angle imaginable. Certainly the discovery would ease Jennifer's worries so she would finally give Jason her hand in marriage. Of course, the new fortune wasn't his yet, but that detail didn't keep him from planning. He wasn't just thinking about the wealth either. He loved Jennifer more than anything or anyone else, and he looked forward to their life together. These thoughts twisted and turned until he was dizzy with it all, and he fell asleep in the early morning hours. His habit of bedtime prayers had slipped his mind.

The next morning everyone in the house was up before dawn. Too much excitement and too many ideas produced unorganized chaos. Jason had cleaned up the mess on Jennifer's desk, saving every little scrap of dust, and placed it all in a heavy pillowcase. His first line of business involved talking with Grant over breakfast, which nobody took an interest in except Abe. "I need you to take this down to Mr. Potter and have it assayed," he said, holding a few good samples of the ore.

Grant had glanced at the rock the night before, but this morning he studied it more closely. "Doesn't look like anything I've seen from around here," he stated.

"Does it look good?" Jason eagerly asked.

"From what I've learned, it's good all right!" Grant affirmed. "It's too good—makes me suspicious."

Jason didn't like hearing that. Jennifer raised an eyebrow as well. "What do you mean?"

"I mean it's not typical for ore found around here, that's all," Grant insisted. He didn't believe their mine held any riches. He recalled the times he went there with Lance Rivers when it was a working mine with a crew of twelve or fifteen men, and it never produced any sign.

"Are you saying it came from somewhere else?" Jason drilled.

"It's possible," Grant assumed. "But I'll go over and get Mr. Potter even if it is Sunday morning. I'm sure he'll be very interested in this new find."

With that Grant was off, almost running from the table. Abby ate her hot cereal and wore a smile that was not at all typical for her. Her mind dwelt on the things riches could buy. She would not accept her brother's skepticism. She was sure her family deserved to be rich, so it must be so.

Since she had no appetite, Jennifer went up to her room to dress appropriately for entering a mine. She'd only been in one in her life, in Virginia City years before. Escorted by a fiancé who later broke her heart, she'd seen part of the steamy cauldrons a thousand feet down into the Comstock Lode. Her memories of that trip were vivid. How any man could work long hours in a mine was beyond her. She found a rugged old dress and some old high-top shoes that would serve as boots. She wasn't sure what to expect, since the mines in the mountains were said to be different from the others.

Jason had rushed outside to hitch his horse, Dolly, to a buggy to take Jennifer up the winding road to the Wild Horse mine. Only Abe remained at the table, taking his time with his breakfast.

"Hardly nobody ate nothin'," Lita said.

"They too excited," Abe mumbled with his mouth full.

"If it's all true, might be some rich folks runnin' around this house," Lita said, thinking out loud.

"Lita, I love these folks, every one of 'em, but I'm afraid for 'em."

"What you mean?" Lita asked, not understanding. "There was a time not too long ago we was all so poor, we was almost on the street in the middle of winter. Maybe some money comin' is good."

"Maybe," Abe mumbled.

"Or what?" Lita pried.

Abe stopped eating and turned his big brown eyes up to her. "Being poor was a true test of our faith and a hard one," he said. "Two of the biggest tests on earth for folks is to be poor or to be wealthy. I'm afraid my friends is getting ready to be tested again."

Lita stopped what she was doing and looked over at Abe. Her dark face was lined with worry.

~

The trip up to the mine seemed much farther than Jason remembered, or was he just eager to confirm Emmitt's news? He couldn't get comfortable in the driver's seat as he squirmed and glanced at every face they passed in town. He feared that just by looking at him someone might be able to tell they'd struck gold, and he wasn't ready for the secret to get out and somehow cause them to lose their stake. Old Emmitt rode in the back in the warm and sunny morning light, as peaceful and serene as a newborn calf. Riding up front with Jason, Jennifer sat with her shoulders back and her head held high, refusing to believe that anything could possibly go wrong. And yet at the same time she couldn't entirely set aside the fear that the odd prospector had simply made a big mistake.

At the mine Emmitt jumped out with the energy of a young man, grabbed Dolly's reins, and tied them to the old toolshed where he lived. He'd been up before sunup and walked to town, a short walk for him.

"Come on down, Miss Jenny," he said, reaching for her arm. She noticed his hands were rough and strong.

"Let me get a lantern lit," Emmitt said, fussing with the old coal oil lamp.

Eagerly following Emmitt, Jason and Jennifer entered the mouth of the tunnel. "You'll have to watch for these ore cart tracks," Emmitt said, swinging the lantern so the yellow light exposed the rusty old tracks.

In no time at all the cold breath of the tunnel had seeped through their garments, causing Jennifer to shiver. They splashed through puddles of water and smelled the stale air. All light had vanished except for that coming from the dim lanterns. The only sound was their echoing footsteps and the ghostly sounds of dripping water. Before long they'd gone a hundred yards, all horizontal.

"Them fellows that was working this mine before," Emmitt said into the darkness as he led the others, "I don't know why they never dropped or raised a shaft. Looks like they were lazy—just tryin' to make a paycheck and didn't care if they found nothin' or not."

"Could be," Jason said, thinking of the late Lance Rivers who had once owned the mine. He had been wealthy, and Jason doubted if any miner working for him cared to see him earn even more money.

The tunnel soon became narrow, close, and wet, and Jennifer's delicate shoulders brushed against the cold rock walls. This wasn't anything like the Comstock; it seemed more like a forgotten tomb. It was lonely and silent, and the hard granite walls seemed totally immovable, unrelenting, and unforgiving.

Finally they neared the end of the shaft, still traveling horizontally. "Right here's where I thought I seen sign," Emmitt said, holding the lantern up high. "So I put a charge going up yonder, and when I blowed out, I knew I'd found it." He leaned over and picked up some of the ore. "See—this here's it."

Taking the rock, Jason could see it was like the others. But he knew any man could plant a rock; Jason wanted to see the ore on the face of the drift where Emmitt had placed the charge.

"I blasted again, and there she was," Emmitt said, moving a few feet ahead to an old ladder made of aspen tree trunks. "Here, take your lantern and crawl up that ladder and look at the rock," he told Jason

Climbing up the makeshift ladder, Jason held the lamp up high. There before him quartz garnished the wall with sparkles, and he saw gold in every form from fine particles to nickel-sized nuggets in the frosty quartz. It was magical, almost unbelievable. "Dear God, it's true!"

Shivering in the darkness, Jennifer's curiosity brought her closer. Jason came down the ladder and handed her the lantern. "Go on up. Don't be afraid." He couldn't hide the excitement in his voice.

Nervously, Jennifer climbed the shaky ladder and had a look for herself. What she saw made her heart skip a beat, and momentarily she thought she might fall, she felt so light-headed. The gold was golden, crystalline, and beautiful. Despite the stale, still air, this was a sight she'd never forget.

"This vein runs up and down," Emmitt pointed out. "So I'll have to shaft up and down. It'll take a crew to work it, Miss Jenny. We got to hire a crew."

"We'll have to hire some guards too," Jason figured. "A man could get rich high grading out of here."

"That's a fact," agreed Emmitt.

On their way out Jennifer and Jason could hardly contain their joy. It was true! They really were rich! "A couple of tons of this ore should pay for getting any help we need," Jason said.

"And more," Emmitt added. "You get a big wagon up here, and we'll fill it and take the ore down to a mill. From then on we'll have enough money to operate. I guarantee it!"

The three discussed the situation on their way back to town. Suddenly their world was filled with challenges. They knew that even getting rich would mean hard work. For the time being Jason would labor with Emmitt at the mine, and Jennifer would tend the books. All of this was fine with old Emmitt. Saturday's edition of the *Advertiser* sat in forgotten piles back in the newspaper office.

CHAPTER

~ 4 ~

A New Kind of Life

Grant saddled up his thoroughbred stallion, Midnight, and pranced up to Central City until he came to the point where the streets lined Gregory Gulch in stair-step fashion. Midnight grunted as they climbed high above the gulch to Mr. Potter's house. An assayer's earnings might be meager, but what man would know better which mines to invest in? Mr. Potter's investments had paid handsomely, and it showed in his three-story home perched high above the town.

A bachelor, Mr. Potter employed an Irish woman as housekeeper. Grant found Mr. Potter enjoying the morning sun on his front porch. Tying Midnight to the hitching post, Grant flew up the front steps two at a time.

"Mr. Potter, something has come up—you've got to help," Grant spouted, out of breath.

"And what could be so important on a Sunday morning that you have to come all the way up here?"

Producing a handful of rocks, Grant showed Mr. Potter the ore.

Adjusting his glasses, Mr. Potter rotated an ore sample in one hand. Just then the housekeeper came out the front door with a coffeepot in her hand to refill Mr. Potter's cup. She was short and round, and her face reflected sincere joy. "Why, who's this handsome young lad, Mr. Potter?"

"Grant works for me, Glenda." But his attention was on the stone.

"If I was younger I'd be hot on his heels," Glenda said, eyeing Grant closely. "He's a fine specimen!"

Grant felt his face blush. It hadn't been the first time some older woman had remarked about his looks. Such flattery always embarrassed him.

"Does he talk?" Glenda asked Mr. Potter.

"Of course, he talks." Potter answered coldly. "Glenda, could you give us some privacy?"

As Glenda left, she turned back before she entered the front door and winked at Grant. He was glad when she was gone.

"Where'd this come from?" Potter asked seriously.

"My mother owns a mine. Everyone thought it was barren, but an old miner found a vein. This is a sample from it."

"The mine must not be around here," Potter said.

"Oh, but it is," Grant added. "It's the old Wild Horse mine."

Potter shook his head as if he were trying to recall something from the past. "Wild Horse," he muttered. "Seems like years ago somebody who thought he was important owned a Wild Horse mine. He was constantly bringing me rock to analyze. If I recall, the rock never showed a thing."

"Yeah, I knew him," Grant said rather solemnly. "His name was Lance Rivers, the kissing bandit."

"That's right!" Potter said, perking up. "I remember now. Your mother was to marry him."

Grant turned his eyes down to the porch. These were not pleasant memories.

"Yes, well, anyway," Potter continued, seeing the boy's anguish, "I've never seen a formation like this around here. I'll meet you down at the laboratory in an hour so we can take a closer look at this."

Springing to his feet, Grant said, "Thanks, Mr. Potter. My mother would be most thankful too."

Flying down the residential streets, Grant only slowed for the hairpin curves as he zigzagged back down to the main avenues of the gulch. He went straight to the assayer's office, tied up Midnight, and waited out front for Mr. Potter. After what seemed like several hours, Mr. Potter trotted his walker behind his modest carriage and parked the rig in his special place in an alley beside the building. He soon appeared on the boardwalk, searched for his keys, and unlocked the front door.

The chemical smell had been closed in overnight and gave out a strong odor as Grant and Mr. Potter entered. "Fire up the forge," Mr. Potter said.

Doing as he was told, Grant fired up the small forge and tended the fire, using the bellows until the coke was soon glowing red-hot. In the meantime Mr. Potter had pulverized one of the ore samples and had begun to mix some chemicals.

"If I'm right," Potter said, "I think we'll soon find this is an extremely rare gold sample, like that nugget I once showed you, a very high grade of gold ore, no matter where it came from."

Both eagerly worked the sample, and before long Mr. Potter extracted the gold and weighed it. He then worked with his figures from the original weight of the ore sample. "Must have made an error," he said with minor disgust. "I'm afraid we'll have to try it again with another sample."

Handing over another piece of ore, Grant watched Mr. Potter very patiently take care not to make any mistakes. But the results were the same.

"I'll be!" Potter said. "I figure six or seven thousand dollars a ton in gold alone. There's some silver in there, but with that kind of gold I'm not sure you'd even calculate the trace amounts of silver. You're sure this came from around here?"

"Pretty sure," Grant said. "My mother and Jason are looking at the mine right now."

"If it's true, this is one of nature's anomalies," he said on the basis of years of experience. "I've seen it once or twice before, and the man who finds it is certainly a lucky man."

"Thanks so much!" Grant said, exploding from his chair and running for the door. "I'll see you tomorrow."

Grant didn't have to wait long at the office before Jason and Jennifer appeared at the end of the street, heading his way in the small carriage. He walked out into the street and waited impatiently as they drew near. Catching Dolly by the bit, Grant halted the carriage in front of the office and pulled Dolly over to hitch her up. "Did you see it?" Grant asked as he handled the horse. "Did you see any more rock?"

Jason leaped from the carriage and went around to help Jennifer down. "Did we see it! I've never seen anything like it! It's real, Grant, just as real as you and me standing here."

Looking at his mother, Grant didn't need to ask before she spoke. "I saw it too! It's beautiful," she said proudly.

Hesitating, Grant glanced around to make sure nobody was in hearing range, then said, "It's worth six or seven thousand dollars a ton in gold alone. We didn't bother to test for anything else."

Jason quickly took Jennifer's hands and started dancing with her in a circle in the street. He could no longer hold back the boyish animation erupting through his happiness. She wasn't offended and did not hold back as she laughed heartily at Jason's antics. This attracted some unnoticed attention from a few curious onlookers. Certainly it was too early to be drunk, and on a Sunday morning! Most disregarded it all as foolishness and went on their way. One or two others watched curiously from a distance.

"Let's get inside," Grant said, finally noticing the unwanted spectators.

Jason hurriedly escorted Jennifer indoors, and once inside he resumed the dancing, bowing her backwards so far that her head almost touched the floor. He kissed her, then pulled her up with an amazing amount of grace. Grant watched, the corner of his mouth pulled tight. He didn't care for such public exhibition of emotions of any kind.

For the moment Jennifer had discarded her usual self-consciousness and enjoyed playing along with Jason. She didn't care who was watching. But finally she said, "Jason, you've winded me."

"And I promise you a lot more winding, my dear," Jason joked.

"What's all the racket in here?" Lita asked, standing in the back door. "Ya'll come eat. Even rich folks has got to eat."

Lita's fulfilling meal settled their rambunctious attitudes, though it didn't keep Jason and Jennifer from sharing all the details about the gold strike. Afterwards Jason obtained sufficient provisions for staying up at the mine with Emmitt. "I'm going to rent an ore wagon and mule team," he told Jennifer as he prepared to depart. "I don't think it'll take us long to fill the wagon and get a load in—a few days maybe. I'll see you then."

The delight had left Jennifer's face. She knew the dangers of mining. "Do be careful," she pleaded, placing a soft palm on Jason's cheek.

Leaning toward her, Jason gave her a hurried kiss. "I'm excited, Jennifer," he said, "not about the gold but about what it can do for you. I want you to be happy and stop worrying." He paused. His pale blue eyes appeared deep and liquid. "And there's more—I want you to be Mrs. Jason Stone."

The idea did seem more reasonable than ever, and its appeal showed in her face. Yet with past mistakes still intruding into her mind, she couldn't quite say yes. "We'll see," she said softly.

Jason smiled a good-natured smile, one that was full of hope. He picked up his gear and left.

~

Jason discovered how soft he had become, for the mining work quickly took its toll on him. The distance was too far to tote the gold ore in bags; so they had to fix the ore cart and the small tracks. This meant swinging a sledge and moving timber and straining muscles Jason had forgotten he had. This took almost two days, and camp beans didn't come close to satisfying his new hunger.

"You'll toughen up," Emmitt promised. "Won't take long neither, young man like you. Now you take me, I was born tough, and no matter what I do I stay tough. That's 'cause my mother was the toughest woman that ever lived, God rest her weary soul. She raised four of us boys cause my father was kilt in a mining accident. She smoked cigars and drank whiskey like a man—taught all us boys how to. It's a good thing I had a tough mother," he said, reminiscing.

Jason groaned. He was tired and felt the pain of hurting muscles. Campfire stories didn't impress him much at the present.

The next morning Jason was awakened by a loud cry. "Fire in the hole!" Just as he sat up, a loud boom and and cold air rushed from the mouth of the mine, followed by dust and dirt. He jumped up to discover Emmitt had been standing right behind him the whole time.

Jason searched for his boots and angrily asked, "Is that how you wake people up?"

"It works, don't it?" Emmitt said in a jovial tone.

"What about breakfast?"

"I already et, but you can find some grub and coffee right beside the campfire coals," Emmitt said, pointing with his stick. "It'll take a while for the dust to settle before we can go back in anyway."

Hungrily, Jason went for the coffeepot and poured some of the black mud. His muscles were sorer than ever. When he opened the lid on the cast-iron pot, he found, again, campfire beans. "Is beans all you ever cook?"

"Keeps a man goin," Emmitt said,

"I bet it does," Jason said, thinking of their working together in the close confines of the shaft.

The next few days proved even more tiresome, but very profitable. Jason and Emmitt mucked up the ore, loaded it into the little ore cart, and pushed it out to the ore wagon until finally it was full. The ore wagon groaned as they pulled away from the mine. The two blue-nosed mules strained without complaint under a brilliant blue sky.

At the mill Jason and Emmitt accepted a ticket after their load was emptied from the wagon and weighed. "We should be able to settle up by tomorrow," the burly supervisor said. "Been kind of slow lately." He hadn't even glanced at the ore.

"I'll take the wagon back," Jason said.

"We'll be able to buy our own tomorrow," Emmitt announced happily. "That and hire some help."

Jason returned to the mill the next day with Jennifer. Emmitt was already there waiting. When the supervisor saw them, he quickly rushed over. "You'll have to go up to the main office—we don't give vouchers that size down here at the window." He eyed them carefully as if there was something strange about them.

Up in the office the manager was most courteous. "Please sit down." Introductions were formal. "Mrs. DeSpain, do you have a contract with these men?" the manager asked. He was a small man with a strange smile and a receding hairline shaped like a V.

"I have a contract with Emmitt." She looked at Jason. "This is my fiancé, Jason Stone."

"I see," the manager said. "Normally we have some kind of agreement when we're dealing with bank vouchers of this size. I've already checked the authenticity of your ownership of the mine through our company lawyer, Mrs. DeSpain. It would be prudent for you to give these men authority to run the mine, unless you're going to do it yourself; otherwise you'll have to be present for every transaction. We do appreciate your business, and we hope there will be many transactions. Let me be the first to congratulate you." Smiling intensely now, the manager came around his desk and handed Jennifer a bank voucher on the mill's account—for $32,500. Her bottom lip quivered as she looked up.

"Th-thank you," she stuttered.

"Thanks," Jason said. "We'll be back. C'mon, Jennifer." He took her by the hand and led her out. Emmitt followed with his hat still in his hand, ecstatic at the amount he'd seen on the voucher.

They all went to the bank and settled up, Emmitt getting his half. "I'm reinvesting this in the mine," Emmitt said. "It'll more than pay for itself. I'm going to get some equipment and hire some men and guards—I can get that all done today." Before he walked away, he said, "And, Jason, I 'spect you'll be up there to help me for a while—one man can't oversee everything inside and outside the tunnel."

"I'll be there," Jason promised.

After Emmitt had gone, Jason and Jennifer slowly strolled down the boardwalk and headed home. It was a glorious day of fine weather and new riches. The word had spread about town like a wildfire in a windstorm, and people stared at the couple.

"All of this is just now registering with me," Jennifer said, walking along slowly, holding Jason's hand. "The balance in the bank account is staggering." They walked a little farther before she pulled

Jason to a stop. "Jason, I want half of my earnings to be yours. We'll be business partners. You deserve it after all we've been through together."

Jason expressed his appreciation with a large grin. "I have an even better idea—we'll be marriage partners. Marry me, Jennifer. We don't have to have a big wedding."

Still not ready to make the decision, she turned her gaze down the street and for the first time noticed the many people looking at them. "Let's get all of this mining business in order, then we'll discuss it," she stated. She knew her words hurt Jason's feelings, but she felt she couldn't help it.

A bit put out, Jason patiently remarked, "Whatever you say, Jennifer. I only want your happiness."

Jennifer meant what she'd said about making Jason her partner in the mine. Knowing she'd need an attorney, after Jason left for the mine the following day she contacted Mr. Smith, who'd done some work for her before, and had everything put in order. Jason and Jennifer owned half, and Emmitt owned half, a three-way partnership they all believed would be long-lived.

～

After several more wagon-loads of ore, Jennifer found the bank balance growing at an incredible rate, quickly reaching over $60,000. Unfortunately, along with the wonderful news of the Wild Horse strike came, on July 13, the sad news of Baby Doe's stillborn baby boy. The baby had big blue eyes and wavy brown hair, not unlike that of Jake Sandelowski.

"I feel so sorry for her," Jennifer said. "She seems so young and innocent, a very nice girl who was led astray."

"I hear she's recovering all right, working over in Jake's store. I understand Harvey Doe has left her for good and left her in heavy debt as well, with bank notes and whatnot she wasn't even aware of." Jason thought about it some more. "Why don't we pay them a visit. We need to buy some clothes for all of us anyway. Things are under control at the mine, and we certainly can afford to spend the money now!"

Jennifer didn't know what to say. She'd been a penny-pincher for so long that she couldn't spend money without feeling guilty. Then she thought about the rapidly growing bank balance. "You're right," she said. "We can all use some nice clothes. I'm ready to throw away all of these faded, worn-out dresses that Lita's been mending for years. And Abby's closet looks more like a rat's nest than a wardrobe. I'll round up the children so we can go right away."

More of the stones in the wall Jennifer has built between us are falling away, Jason thought. *Perhaps the gold strike was just what she needed to bring her out of her shell! God, thanks for Your help. After all this time I think she's finally healing.*

It wasn't hard to convince Abby or even Grant to go shopping for the new clothes they so badly needed. Like a small family, Jason and Jennifer and the children walked all the way to Jake's store in Central City, thanks to the pleasant July weather. On the way they were greeted by almost every passerby with words like "Congratulations on your strike!" or "You've brought the luck back to a dying town!" or "May your prosperity be long!" All were friendly toward the group as they walked up the steep incline of Gregory Gulch. For a change it seemed they were *somebody*.

At Jake's store, they offered Baby Doe whatever consolations they could, letting her know they felt her grief with her. Evidently trying to assuage her sorrow through hard work, Baby Doe was most humble and perceptive, helping Jennifer and Abby pick out new clothes. "What a pretty girl!" Baby Doe said, referring to Abby. "I believe she's the most attractive young lady I've ever seen."

Poor Abby was still finding it difficult to accept the reality of their new wealth. It was a fairy tale come true, a dream she always thought she'd have to make happen herself when she was older. Now here it was, and she couldn't believe it.

For Jennifer, Baby Doe picked out clothes that only the wealthy could afford, made from the finest imported materials. The fashion of the day had a heavy European influence, and Jake had plenty of that kind of item in stock. Jennifer made every dress she tried on look the way it was intended to look—gorgeous!

Jake took it upon himself to help Jason and "Master Grant" as he called him. Jason's angular frame fit the nice suits as if they'd been tailored just for him. Grant had a slightly different cut in mind, preferring a more functional outfit, something a little more rugged. One dinner suit was fine, but the rest had to be clothes that would endure.

After several hours the group seemed well-satisfied with their choices. "We're planning a night out this evening," Jason announced. "First a fine dinner and then the theater." He paused and looked at Jennifer, who encouraged him to continue. "Jake, we'd like you and Lizzie to be our guests. It's a celebration of sorts, of the new strike and all."

"I'm certainly game!" Jake said. "It sounds lovely. How about you, Lizzie—are you up for it?"

Slightly embarrassed, Baby Doe already knew she was the gossip of the town. But she had a brave heart, and she had no intentions of hiding from the public for very long. Perking up, she said, "It does sound lovely. It might get my mind off my loss. I'd be happy to accept."

"Good. We'll come by here around 7," Jason added. He was enjoying being able to do things he had only observed the wealthy doing before. "I'll hire a driver and coach, and we'll have a fine evening."

Jake reached over and shook Jason's hand. "Thank you for the business. And thank you for your concern about Baby Doe. We'll see you this evening."

~

A superbly crafted black lacquered carriage with a tall driver dressed in a black suit and top hat picked up Jennifer's family and Jason at dusk. The setting sun peeked over the mountaintops with its last ridge of light; a hue of warm orange mixed with the clear blue sky made colors of magenta and violet.

Jennifer and Abby could have passed for aristocracy, and Jason and Grant looked handsome in their new outfits with their hair slicked down. Of all the things Abby had to choose from to wear, she'd chosen the red dress Grant had bought for her earlier. With her hair up like her mother's, she appeared to be every bit of eighteen years old, the beauty of youth shining from her young face. The carriage stopped to pick up Jake and Baby Doe, who were dressed in their finest as well. Already known for her grand radiance, Baby Doe wore a shoulderless flowered dress that was sure to catch the eye of any man who wasn't blind.

They first entered an outdoor beer garden up on Eureka Street where they ordered expensive delicacies. Baby Doe ordered her favorite, raw oysters on the half shell, and ate them in front of the curious Grant and Abby. "Waiter, bring me another beer and more water for my water-drinking friends," Jake called joyfully. His drinking brought Jennifer troublesome memories, but she was so enjoying their celebration that she thrust her thoughts aside.

Soon they rode over to a second restaurant, a new one owned by relatives of Judge James Belford, Colorado's first congressman. The place was lavishly decorated and overflowed with works of art. The subtle candlelight flashed in the women's eyes, making them appear enchanting. The new establishment had few guests, for few could afford to eat at a place where the menu did not even list the prices.

"Take us the route!" Jason ordered the headwaiter.

This meant a sample of everything for everybody. The first round consisted of roast duck in a sweet apple sauce. Next came cuts from a broiled rack of lamb. Then came an aromatic smoked salmon treat. This continued on and on until the guests were looking rather stuffed. Jason removed the white linen napkin from his lap and waved it like a flag of surrender. "No more," he claimed.

"But, sir," the well-mannered waiter pleaded, "you must try some of our dessert, a light soufflé."

Jason declined. "I have had enough." Everyone nodded in agreement.

When the bill arrived, Jason didn't even blink at the $200 charge. It was common knowledge that the escalated prices of Central City were among the highest in the country. He was proud to be able to pay it without a second thought.

They then strolled over to the Belvidere to take in an evening of entertainment. Although the play had failed dramatically in

Denver, it had seen great success among the upper crust of Central City. The play was a singing enactment of Little Red Riding Hood, with the starring role being played by the young and beautiful Miss Marie Kelly.

All enjoyed the show, but Abby was the most impressed. Her first experience with the theater left an indelible image in her memory.

After the show the group returned to the pleasant night atmosphere of the beer garden where they could sit and converse. Jennifer and Baby Doe talked about the play and the costumes the actors and actresses wore while Abby listened intently. "And that Marie Kelly!" Baby Doe said rolling her big blue eyes. "She's such a tease. Did you see the way the men drooled over her? I loved it!"

Jennifer found the play delightful and realized she didn't think about anything else the whole time she was there. It had been a welcome escape.

Meanwhile, Jake cornered Jason for a little business talk. "You know advice is cheap, but sometimes it's the best bargain," Jake began. "Now that you're in the money, I mean real money, you'll soon realize that you need to invest, and I've got the perfect idea." He smiled arrogantly and took a swig of his beer. Jason nursed his glass of cool water as he listened, for Jake had been very successful in his financial ventures.

"It's the new El Dorado!" Jake whispered forcefully.

"What?" Jason ridiculed. "I must've heard that a million times. Every new boomtown is the new El Dorado."

"No, I'm serious, this is really it!" Jake stressed.

"And where's this supposed to be?" Jason asked, a sarcastic tone in his voice.

"Leadville!" Jake whispered again. "I'm moving there myself soon, opening a new store there. I have to return to New York to buy my inventory first, then I'll be going. This place here is on a decline—except for your discovery of course. Listen to me, Jason— I've seen strikes like yours before, and they're big, but that kind of rock plays out quickly. You need to stake some claims in Leadville before it's too late." Jake slammed down his mug to drive home the point.

Smiling, Jason tried to humor Jake. "I know all about Leadville. Big gold town, then it died out back in the sixties."

"It's at its prime right now," Jake said, ignoring Jason. "It's a big town, not for gold, but for silver! You know how it works—the discoverers do their best, but most of them can't run a mining operation either due to lack of knowledge or lack of money, so they sell out. That's where you come in—you've got the money. You could buy a claim and afford to have it worked and make a lot of money— millions!" The word *millions* and the way Jake said it was music to Jason's ears.

"Look at Horace Tabor. He was a simple merchant who grub-staked two miners, and now he's a multimillionaire and making millions more!" Jake stared at Jason intently.

"You're crazy," Jason chuckled. "I've just hit it big right here in gold, not silver! Why would I be crazy enough to go to Leadville?"

"You'll see, my good friend," Jake concluded. "You'll see."

CHAPTER
~ 5 ~

The Dawn of a
New Perspective

August was a lazy month in Black Hawk and Central City, except for the news about the Wild Horse mine. As reported to the curious public in the *Advertiser*, the gold-laden ore of the surprising find was now $63,000 per ton since workers were now mining what was believed to be the heart of the vein. Newspaper sales were again at a record high due to this single subject. The friendly citizens of the community tended to frequent the newspaper office in hopes some of the good luck would rub off, or perhaps some of the wealth would at least carelessly spill in their direction. Between keeping an eye on the work at the mine and the busy newspaper, Jason and Jennifer were rushing toward exhaustion.

Jennifer huddled at her desk, keeping her head just below a cloud of heavy cigar smoke, her mind racing with a busy agenda. Ben Crockett and James Lyon had just left the office, smoking their cigars and laughing about their new claims adjacent to the Wild Horse mine. It wasn't uncommon for speculators to rush to the find and buy up the surrounding claims. They had visited the office in hopes of gathering more information from Jason but had discovered he was at the mine.

"Is this from your mine?" Lyon had ventured, picking up a piece of rock from Jennifer's desk.

"Yes," Jennifer said. "It was found the day before yesterday."

"By golly this is the prettiest ore I've ever seen," Lyon said, waggling his heavy mustache. "Look at this, Ben."

Ben Crockett inspected the rock. "It's got a good heft to it," he had said, weighing it in his hand. "I never seen gold out of the ground that color. Mighty nice. I hope we do as well. We're already dropping a shaft." He carefully placed the quartz gold back on her desk.

"Thank you, Mrs. DeSpain," Lyon said gratefully around his cigar. "We'll head on up to your mine and find Jason. We're interested in the angle the vein runs—might give us a clue as to which way to tunnel. Good day, ma'am." The men were obviously confident of their abilities.

So many people were visiting lately that Jennifer found it interrupted her work schedule. *I guess I need to hire someone to help me with this newspaper,* Jennifer thought, rubbing her forehead. *Jason is always up at the mine overseeing it with Emmitt—I can't run this newspaper all by myself.*

Jennifer hadn't yet realized that the *Advertiser's* income was trivial compared to the half a million dollars in her bank account. She weighed the newspaper budget versus the payroll of an additional employee. The big money in the bank scared her; despite their expensive celebration that first night, she was almost afraid to touch it.

As Jennifer spun the flywheel on the press cranking out the new edition for the next day, she was unaware that the afternoon had grown late. Her face was like that of a contented child playing silently with a new toy. The riches from the Wild Horse mine had placed her in a new category, that of the elite and wealthy. Yet her daily routine had remained much the same. She approached the large sum of money with caution, observing it from a distance. There wasn't much in the way of possibilities that she could not pursue, but she wasn't sure what to do first or which way to go. "Dear God, what am I to do?" she mumbled. "Such a large blessing, yet it requires so much attention and consideration. Dear God," she repeated, "You're going to have to help me make the right decisions."

Prayers like these often comforted her, but not this time.

"Miss Jenny," Lita called from the back door of the office, "could you come help me a minute?"

Shaking like one awakening from a vivid dream, Jennifer took a moment to get her bearings. "Yes, Lita. I'll be right there."

In the kitchen Lita was tending a huge pot of apple juice, which had been boiled and cooled until it reached a thick molasses-like texture. The candy fragrance was sweet and delicious. "This old pot is missing the handle on one side, and I can't pour it by myself," Lita said, handing Jennifer a heavy towel as she approached the stove. "I need to pour it into them quart jars on the table."

"Apple jelly?" Jennifer guessed.

"You know it is, Miss Jenny. Ain't nothin' else smells like that."

"It sure smells good," Jennifer said as the two women lifted the pot and began pouring it into the lined-up jars. Steam was rising from the thick liquid. Lita's grip suddenly slipped, and before she could catch the big pot, a portion sloshed on her arm, scalding her.

"Set it down!" Lita shouted, and they quickly put the pot back on the stove. She grimaced, holding a towel over the burn on her arm.

Thinking fast, Jennifer dunked her small kitchen towel in a water bucket and placed it over the minor burn on Lita's arm.

"Mercy!" Lita sighed. The pain was evident in her squinting eyes.

"We need to put some grease on it," Jennifer said with a bit of panic as she searched for the cooking grease.

"I know that," Lita said, rocking back and forth in the chair she'd sat down in. "It be over the stove in that lard can."

As Jennifer tended the burn, the emotion of the situation moved into the kind of despair one experiences when seeing a loved one injured. She felt deep and throbbing remorse.

"If you ain't never got burned, then you ain't done no cookin'," Lita said as she calmed down. The sting waned as Jennifer gently smeared the grease over her forearm. Fortunately, it wasn't a serious burn.

Sudden guilt rose in Jennifer. The old pot only had a handle on one side. Her eyes roamed over the rest of the kitchen. Everything was about worn-out, including the leaky old stove. It was a wonder Lita managed at all. "I've got to do something about this kitchen!" she threatened.

"Like what?" Lita questioned.

"I don't know . . . I just," Jennifer began. "That smoky old stove, all these worn-out utensils—all I have to do is give the word and the hardware store would be down here replacing all of it. I won't have you getting burned when I can do something about it."

Lita's eyes grew big. She saw something developing, and it frightened her a bit. "I be all right, Miss Jenny. Accidents happen."

"Not if I can help it." Jennifer had a determined expression on her face.

The next afternoon Lita was run out of her own kitchen as a crew from the hardware company came in to make everything new. Part of the condition, Jennifer had made clear, was that the job be done without haste, and it was. The new cookstove, complete with nickel-plated trim, was the best money could buy.

Lita thought the new stove sat kind of haughtily where her old friend used to sit. The new kitchen would take some getting used to, as would the new Jennifer.

~

Richard Morgan was an astute scholar of banking and investments despite his young years, a wiry man with constantly present bifocals perched on the end of his nose. He had worked his way up from teller to loan officer and even sat on the bank board. His greatest accomplishment to date was landing the accounts of Jason Stone and Jennifer DeSpain. Meticulous with numbers, he treated them as the one and only true language, and he never made an error. Everything was in place in his life, always. Even the coffee cup on his perfectly organized desk sat on a laced napkin. His attire of pressed fabric shone, his dark hair slick and in place. Only one thing currently threatened his well-ordered life. It had come to his attention that the deposits of his new clients by far exceeded what the bank could insure. He'd have to pay a visit to Mr. Stone.

Driving his black buggy, Morgan whipped his horse into a gallop up the winding road to the Wild Horse mine. There he found a new office constructed of fresh lumber. The fresh August summer day reminded him of new money.

"Mr. Stone," Morgan greeted as he let himself into the little office. He saw Jason sitting at a desk, busy with the kind of paperwork a mine manager would have.

"Hello, Richard," Jason said, standing. "What brings you up here?"

Morgan carried his satchel as if it were part of him. "Do you have a minute?"

Jason still dressed in a normal workday fashion, although his denims crackled with newness. One look at Morgan in his dark business suit and Jason could tell he was sniffing and circling, always on the prowl for new capital investments. "Certainly. What can I do for you?"

Dragging over a chair, Morgan sat in front of Jason's desk, placing his satchel before him. He removed a folder full of documents and opened it. "I'm afraid your deposits, as well as Mrs. DeSpain's, have grown so rapidly that there's no way the bank can guarantee it all. What I mean is, we can only insure so much, and as you know, together you've reached over a million dollars in deposits." He rested, waiting for Jason to ask what he should do, like dangling a worm in front of a fish.

The sound of the term *million* still caused Jason's spine to tingle. He remembered the countless times he'd begged bankers, and now they were coming begging to him. "And?" he said.

"Well," Morgan began, eager to give Jason ideas that would guide him into a director's spot at the bank, "as you might know, we are equipped to make long-term investments with your money, and the interest is very handsome, much more so than a simple account."

"What kind of investments?" Jason inquired. He held a poised pencil as he leaned back in his new office chair.

"Much of it goes right here to the community," Morgan reported excitedly. "We make long-term loans for homes and businesses mostly. There are also some speculations in major stocks, but only those with great promise. And the bank has many lucrative silver investments. What could be more certain than a precious metal that backs the country's currency?"

"I see," Jason said. "What do Jennifer and I get out of this?"

This is where Morgan was at his best. He produced his careful calculations. "As you can see, I've made a prospectus here, showing your investments spread out over a ten-year period. *Safe* investments! For instance, if you and Mrs. DeSpain invested a million dollars, you could live quite well off the interest alone." He pointed at the figures with a needle-sharp pencil.

Taking the paperwork, Jason studied the columns of figures like he knew what he was doing. He might as well have been trying to read Greek. "Wouldn't a move like this put me on the board of directors at the bank?"

"Of course," Morgan smiled. "You'd have a voice in the bank's business."

Nodding, Jason for the first time realized he had a problem—he had too much money. He'd have to figure out what to do, for Morgan wasn't lying about the bank not being able to cover their deposits in case of a robbery or fire or economic collapse. "Let me talk to Mrs. DeSpain about it, Richard. I'm sure whatever we do, we'll do together."

"Very well," Morgan said, coming to his feet. He reached over the desk with his thin hand to give Jason a handshake. "I'll be looking forward to hearing from you." Turning, he let himself out. Mounting his buggy, he glanced up at the clear summer sky. *I'm too good at this*, he thought happily.

Inside, feeling uncertain, Jason had no idea what to do. He did know one thing—Black Hawk and Central City were beginning to show a loss of citizens and businesses. The area showed all the signs of a boomtown going dry, a poor place to invest in. Then he remembered Jake's Sandelowski's talk about big promise in Leadville. In fact, Jake had already gone to Leadville to open his new store— Sands Clothing, he called it. Jason decided to write to Jake and inquire about the investment opportunities there. Jason was especially skillful at writing outstanding business letters.

~

Grant was affected less by the sudden wealth than anyone. He considered himself an observer as he watched his family's values change. The thing that had intrigued him most during his entire life was watching this transfiguration of people in boomtowns, all because of minerals, mere rocks, some of which were pretty and some of which were not. They drove men and women crazy and made them do things they'd never have considered before. He was determined to get to the bottom of this someday.

As for his own needs, they were unchanging. He liked his job because learning about assaying meant learning about the rocks that made people go crazy. He had reasonable clothes, a place to eat and sleep, a decent job, and a good horse and saddle. He was well satisfied.

Mr. Potter continued to be amazed with the ore that came from the Wild Horse mine. It just kept bearing more and more gold and profits. "I have no idea why you persist in working for simple wages," he said one day. "I have a hard time explaining to my friends how I can employ a young man who could buy me out ten times over."

Grant shrugged. "Money don't mean that much to me."

"Humph!" Potter grunted. "It will someday as your tastes and interests grow. You're a most peculiar young man. You don't care about getting rich, but you always seem to be searching. What is it you're looking for, Grant?"

"I don't know," Grant mumbled. He admired Mr. Potter, for he was not only an intelligent man but patient and a good friend. "I guess it's kind of like you, Mr. Potter, when you stand at the back door and bite on that cigar and stare out like you're in another world. What are you thinking?"

Mr. Potter's little head seemed to shrink into his shoulders. His expression was somewhat forlorn. "That's something I rarely talk about," he began. Turning to Grant, his eyes looked huge and watery through the thick glasses he used when laboring at the workbench. "Not too long ago, back in Delaware, I was married to the loveliest woman in the world. Her name was Charlotte, and she was a real beauty. I taught chemistry at a university, and we had a nice little home with everything a man could want. It was like a dream come true for me.

"My father owned a huge lumber company, and it was thought that when he died my brother and I would inherit the business. Well, he died all right, but the business was in debt—there was nothing to inherit. I came home from the university soon after that and found a note on the kitchen table. It was from Charlotte. She said she was never coming back. I can't help but wonder what happened to her, where she went, or what it was she needed that we didn't have. It was like half of me had died. I've recovered to some degree, but the questions remain. I'll never figure it out."

Mr. Potter's story was very personal, and Grant knew it. But there were no tears in Mr. Potter's eyes, only a destitute loneliness. The hardness he'd developed apparently protected him against the emotional pain of his loss. Grant felt sad that his employer had had to endure a lost love and live with unanswered questions. It did sound like the woman had left him because the expected wealth didn't come. This only added to the mystery of people and money that Grant was determined to solve. Above all, he wanted to be careful not to be corrupted by money himself, for then he would never find the answers he was seeking.

Often Grant tried to relate passages from the Bible to everyday life and its questions, but he found that difficult to do. A few things were clear enough, the do's and don'ts, but otherwise . . .

～

"What's the matter with these eggs?" Abby shouted from the breakfast table. "And the bread is burned too! Lita!"

Frustrated and distraught, Lita turned to Abby, shaking her head in disgust. "That new stove!" Lita said vigorously, shaking a dishrag at it. "It either get too hot or it don't get hot at all. I don't know what I'm going to do."

Abby had never seen Lita so distressed. It was as if something very personal had happened to her. The scrambled eggs were dry and hard, so Abby drank down her large glass of milk, savoring the cream floating on top. "That's all right, Lita. I wasn't very hungry anyway." She rose from her chair and went through the door to the front office.

Lita felt like crying. She couldn't seem to cook a thing. Surely everyone would start getting sick if she didn't figure out the new stove soon. Even Abe had skipped meals lately. Her first meal from the new oven had shocked everyone. She'd decided to cook a fine roast full of good fat for gravy drippings. But by the time she looked in the oven, there was a small black rock where the roast used to be. A group of surprised faces waiting at the table stared at her. The meal that night had to be cold leftovers prepared on the old stove. She wrung her hands, her eyes sorrowful.

Abe had developed a simple solution for his meals. He would put eggs or bacon or whatnot in his coat pockets and take them to work. He had found that the coke forge at the smithy cooked meals faster than any stove. After all his years as a blacksmith, he was shocked that this fact hadn't occurred to him sooner.

In the front office Abby approached her mother who was busy greasing the press. Her hands were a mess, covered with thick black grease. "Why do you do that?" Abby questioned disapprovingly.

"The press has to be greased or it won't work," Jennifer answered, a strand of hair falling across her face as she bent over. Unconsciously she pushed the strand back into place, leaving a black grease mark across her forehead.

"You don't understand, Mother," Abby persisted. "What I mean is, why do you even bother with this stupid old newspaper? Everybody in town knows we're millionaires. Isn't it kind of dumb to keep doing your old job?"

"Just because we have money doesn't mean we should be lazy," Jennifer lectured. "We all have work to do and should do it."

The front door opened, and a store clerk from a nearby business came in. "Good morning, Jennifer," he said. "I want to . . ." Then he stopped, looking at the black smear on her forehead. His stifled smile caught the corners of his lips, but he controlled himself and continued, "I dropped by to let you know to keep running that ad. I didn't sell the brass bed frame yet." The smile had a mind of its own and appeared in his eyes even though the mouth held firm.

"Of course, Mr. Devers. I'll be glad to continue the ad."

"Got to go," he said, and the smile appeared. As he left, the smile erupted into a chuckle.

"Wonder what's wrong with him?" Jennifer said, dumbfounded, for Mr. Devers was usually a very serious man.

Abby stood staring coldly at her mother, her arms crossed as she stood leaning back on one hip, tapping her foot impatiently. Then she dashed off only to return holding a hand mirror. She gave it to her mother.

Taking the mirror, Jennifer was confused. "What?" she inquired.

"Look in the mirror, Mother. I want you to see what a dumb millionaire looks like."

The streak of grease made her look like a common workwoman too busy to worry about her appearance. "Oh, Abby! Why didn't you tell me that was there?" She searched for a cloth to wipe it off.

"What if I hadn't walked in here? You might have worn that all day, and people would be laughing at you and wondering why you do this when you could be doing better things."

Jennifer scrubbed at the persistent grease while looking at the mirror. "What do you mean, 'better things'?"

"Go look at our bedrooms. It looks like we live in poverty. Old dingy curtains, torn quilts with the cotton stuffing hanging out, worn-out rugs. That's why we don't have mice—*they* refuse to live such a miserable life." Abby pursed her lips, a bit of a stubborn pout that no longer looked childish but rather utterly convincing on a pretty young woman.

"I never really thought of it," Jennifer said, dismayed at a clumsy oversight. "I suppose we could use some new things."

"You suppose?" Now Abby laughed. "You're a millionaire living like a pauper! I wish you'd wake up!"

"Well . . ." Jennifer said.

"Well nothing! Let's go," Abby said. "It won't take long—we can buy some things we need and at least move up to the middle class."

There was no denying it—Abby was brazen, but she was smart too. Jennifer had no doubt about what she should do. "Let me grab a few things and tell Lita and we'll go," she said.

The mercantile had exactly what they needed, and a plentiful selection as well. It was a big store with long, deep aisles piled with goods to the ceiling in some places. The strong smells from the new materials were enough to make the women's eyes water, but they steadily picked through the brilliant colors and designs, losing track of time.

"Don't you love this quilt?" Abby said delightfully, holding up the corner for her mother to see. "Look, it has little red hearts sewn into it."

"It's probably expensive," Jennifer answered, noticing the fine needlework. There was so much to look at. Never before had she come into a store just shopping. She usually knew exactly what she needed, and that was all she looked at before she purchased it.

"So . . . ?" Abby chided.

Jennifer cocked her head to one side. She was finally understanding what Abby was trying to say—she could buy the entire store if she wished and still have a fortune left in the bank. "Yes, I like that quilt. It would look lovely in your room."

The better part of the day slipped away as Jennifer and Abby spent it happily shopping. They bought so much that the clerk insisted he have it delivered, for it was far too much to carry.

Every gentleman they passed tipped his hat and greeted the lovely, obviously well-to-do ladies. Abby relished the attention. Jennifer began to relax, the sun's warm rays feeling good on her face as they walked down the boardwalks between stores. Everyone who walked by them acknowledged they knew who they were, for it was always beneficial to stay on good terms with those of affluence. Jennifer couldn't remember ever having so much fun in one afternoon as she shopped with her daughter and spoke to all the friendly people. The entire aura of the town was warm and becoming. Before she realized it, the clear blue sky paled into the burnt orange of a western sunset.

"We should get back," Jennifer announced. "It's getting late."

Abby took her mother's hand happily in hers as they strolled side by side. "You see, Mother, that didn't hurt a bit, did it?"

CHAPTER

～ 6 ～

The Best-Laid Plans

It seemed that Jason and Jennifer now received ten times as much mail as previously. It consisted mostly of strangers offering potential investments or giving them advice. The best time for Jason to sort through this mail was early in the morning before he went up to the mine. Naturally Jennifer liked to be present to see what information and curiosities the mail held. She loved being up early and having coffee in the front office at the big desk with Jason, for this seemed to be their only private time together. Some of the mail came from fawning old ladies who boasted about once being wealthy themselves and always had plenty of free advice.

One glance at Jennifer gave Jason's morning a surge of joy. It was early enough that she hadn't had time to fix herself up; her hair was down and unruly, and often an auburn wisp fell across her face. This is when she thought she was unattractive, but the sight of her made Jason proud to have this woman for his fiancée. Her face and lips still had a slight puffiness from sleep, but she looked beautiful to him.

"Are you going to read the mail or look at me?" Jennifer remarked one morning.

"I could look at you forever," Jason said. Then, needing to divert his attention elsewhere, he grabbed his mug of coffee.

"Well, don't look at me. It's too early."

Why are women like that? Jason wondered. *She thinks she's ugly, but I can't take my eyes off her!*

Turning his attention to the mail, he sorted it into piles. Jennifer liked to read the mail from curiosity seekers who had read about them in newspapers. Most of these letters were from Denver, but some from as far away as Europe.

"What's this?" Jason said, tearing into an envelope. "I think it's from my publisher."

Jason removed a letter, and a bank check slid out and onto his lap. He picked up the check—it was for $500. "How about that . . . it says here they want to publish my book, and this is an advance." He smiled real big and then began to chuckle. Quickly the chuckle gave way to laughter.

"What's so funny?" Jennifer asked.

"How ironic!" Jason choked out as he gasped for air. "All these years I'm starving and needing a check from a book, and I work and I work, and finally . . ." He had to laugh some more, and by now Jennifer was laughing. "And finally," he said, "finally they send me a check for $500 when I'm a millionaire!" He tossed the check onto the desk.

Jennifer was laughing more at Jason himself than at his words, but she caught herself and picked up the check. "But $500 is $500," she reminded him.

Waving it off with a flick of his hand, Jason wiped the tears from his eyes. "Cash it! Have yourself a good time!"

Reaching over, Jennifer squeezed Jason's forearm softly. "You know, you're a sight when you laugh like that. It's not something I've seen very often."

Leaning over in his chair, Jason hugged Jennifer. He loved her more than ever. But he also had more to do than sit and chat. Business was business, and he had to get through the mail so he could get off to the mine. The letters were all different shapes and sizes, some appearing old and weather-beaten.

"Here's one you missed," said Jennifer, holding it up.

Jason grabbed the letter and looked at it closely. "It's from Jake Sands, up in Leadville. I wrote him asking about possible investments there." After slicing the letter open with a penknife, Jason read it quickly as Jennifer watched his pale blue eyes dart across the page. An ever-increasing smile covered Jason's face.

"He says I'm a madman if I don't get right up there—says there's more money to be made than I could ever imagine." Jason stopped and excitedly read further. "He says not to listen to that weasel from the bank who was out at my office gawking over his stupid ideas. Jake says there are producing mines for sale there that I could easily afford, and the returns would be astounding!"

This troubled Jennifer, and her apprehension showed on her face. "But would you know how to go about it?"

"It's easy—money makes money! Like our bank said, they can't cover our deposits anymore unless we let them invest it in something long-term. Why do that for some measly percentage when we're capable of investing our money ourselves and doubling or tripling our investment?" Jason was so excited, he was gasping for air.

"You can do it with your money if you want, but I'm not sure I want to gamble on Leadville mining," Jennifer said worriedly. "I don't know anything about Leadville."

"I'm only trying to do what's best," Jason said, realizing that Jennifer might be identifying an actual problem. He didn't want them to have separate accounts either; he wanted everything to be joint. And yet . . . "Do you remember Jesus' parable in the Gospel of Matthew about the talents? The slaves who invested their master's talents and earned more were rewarded, but the slave who buried his one talent in the ground was punished and sent out into the darkness."

Jennifer answered, "I guess I'm like that one slave—I just want to sit on my money. I'm afraid to do anything with it."

"You figure out what you want to do, Jennifer. I'm going to make plans to go to Leadville soon and see what investment opportunities are there." Jason waited.

"I'll have to think about it," Jennifer said. "I've never been in a situation like this, never dreamed I would be." She raised her eyes to meet Jason's and took his hand in hers. "Don't force me to make a quick decision—let me give it some thought."

Suddenly Jason felt as if he'd stepped out of line. "I'm sorry—I get ahead of myself sometimes. With all this money pouring in, I only figured we need to do something wise with it, that's all. I never meant to pressure you."

Despite their disagreement, moments like these brought them close and built trust.

～

The winds of summer blew the breath of life into Gregory Gulch and greened the nearby mountains. The Wild Horse mine poured forth incredible wealth. Its crystalline-encased gold nuggets became the topic of every local conversation and even found their way into whispered prayers. The story was picked up by the local newspaper in Central City, the *Register*, and even spread throughout the Rockies. The stories coaxed those far away to come there in hopes of reestablishing the glory days Central City and Black Hawk once knew. Printed articles declared this was a mother lode, and surely there would be more. It wasn't the first time a boomtown exaggerated its success in hopes of drawing in more people, businesses, and of course money.

The Wild Horse mine had the best equipment and the most skilled and experienced men; after all, the partnership could afford it. Three shifts worked day and night every day of the week. Emmitt superintended the internal workings of the mine, while Jason worked in the office just outside the shaft. But with money freely at hand, it was soon discovered that even these jobs could be delegated to qualified men. Emmitt found that at his old age he was better suited to oversee work from the superintendent's office, where he functioned in the capacity of owner/consultant. Clad in a tailor-cut, pin-striped suit, he was now addressed as Mr. Tugs.

Emmitt Tugs had known lavish wealth once before, as a young man, but he had squandered it without a thought, always believing, as did most who made fortunes from mining, there was more where that came from. Now older and wiser, he realized few were blessed with a second fortune in one lifetime, and he planned on using this one more wisely. It occurred to him to call a meeting of the partnership, so he could share his valuable experience with his younger partners.

"You look like a congressman!" Jennifer said, her face lighting up at the well-groomed Emmitt Tugs. His white hair and beard were slicked down, every hair in place. The old walking stick was now gone, replaced by an ebony-lacquered rod with an ivory handle in the shape of a horse's head. A brightly colored blue satin kerchief protruded from the coat pocket of a shiny new suit. From the vest drooped a heavy gold watch chain, and on top of his head was a fine gray bowler with the brim trimmed in black.

Removing his hat, he smiled, the twinkle in his small, old eyes brighter than ever. "Miss Jennifer, I know you meant that as a compliment, but I'd rather be a mule than a politician. You know how to tell the difference, don't you?"

"Why no, I don't, Emmitt. What is it?" Jennifer asked.

"Don't feel bad," Emmitt smiled. "Most folks is just like you— they can't tell the difference either. A mule is a much more dependable animal—that's the biggest difference."

"Hello, Emmitt," Jason called as he entered the front office of the newspaper. He was tying his necktie, something he wore every day now. It was late morning, and the newspaper works sat idle, as they had been for days straight. "I think it's a good idea you called this meeting. I have a lot on my mind."

"Good," said Emmitt, "I do too."

The back door to the kitchen opened, and Lita backed through holding a large silver tray with a silver coffeepot, cream and sugar pitchers, and three coffee cups of fine china. She was wearing a new white dress, the kind a servant wears.

"Good mornin', Mr. Emmitt," Lita said happily. "You look fit to give a sermon."

"I'd planned on doing exactly that, Lita," Emmitt chuckled.

"We got plenty to be thankful for," Lita said humbly as she moved on back to the kitchen.

Scooting a chair up, Jason sat down next to Jennifer at the big desk. Emmitt sat also, resting both his hands in front of him on top of his stick.

"Just to run over things," Jason began in a businesslike manner, adjusting his glasses as he reviewed some documents in front of him, "it looks like you've made about a million and a half dollars, Emmitt, and Jennifer and I have split the same. According to these projections, if the current rate of production from the mine continues, it will produce about three million a month. After overhead and the mill's cut, we—"

Emmitt was waving a hand for things to halt. "I don't care about all that, and that's not what I came here to talk about," he interrupted. "There's lots of money that's been made and lots more to be made from that old shaft, but that's not what's important. Jason, I hear you're going up to Leadville to look at mining investments there. Is that right?"

"Yes. I have some good reports about the silver found in the carbonate of lead. I'm told you can run a shaft down about anywhere and hit the stuff, and with the price of silver, I expect some good returns for my investment." Jason glanced at Jennifer, who listened with a straight face. "She's decided to let me invest a good portion of her money as well."

Nodding, Emmitt maintained his kind smile. "I'm sure you'll do well. I've heard the same thing."

"Why don't you get in on it?" Jason asked. "You know as well as I do that the little banks here can't guarantee our money any longer unless we practically go into the banking business with them."

"I know," Emmitt agreed. "I've had a second blessing, this being my second strike. I'm satisfied with that. As for my money, I've got some ideas about buying some land."

"Mining claims?" Jennifer questioned since that seemed like the only thing to do with mining profits.

"No. I'm looking at Denver." Emmitt pulled at his beard, his eyes cast downward as if he were looking into the future in a crystal ball. "Now *there's* a growing city, and it don't depend on mining. If you think about it, it's the only real city on the front range. I honestly believe it will be the gateway to the West, and any real estate bought there can only do good." He grinned. "Yep, real estate. It may not pay nothin' back for a while, but your money is always there."

This sounded fine to Jason and Jennifer, but anyone knew unless it was developed real estate so one could collect rent, returns were questionable. "Well, that's good, Emmitt," Jason confided. "Based on your knowledge of hard-rock mining, what do you think about the vein in the Wild Horse? How far do you think it runs?"

"Only God knows," Emmitt said. "It could run out just like it started—all of a sudden. Or it could run strong a long time. Who knows? If I was a wagerin' man, which I used to be, I'd say we haven't even hit the fattest portion of the vein yet. Now that's only a hunch, mind you."

This information made Jason even more confident in his plans. It made Jennifer tingle with delight as well.

"I had a few things I wanted to tell you about all of this," Emmitt said at last. "That's why I called this here meetin'. You folks is God-fearin' folks, ain't you?"

"Yes indeed," Jennifer proudly admitted.

"I've had a hard life, and I've made more than my share of moral errors, but thanks to Jennifer and Lita, I came to know God too," Jason added.

"I figured you was," said Emmitt. "I was raised in a Christian family my own self, but when I hit it big at the Comstock, I'm afraid things changed. I forgot all about God. Money was my god, and that's what I wanted to warn you young folks about, 'cause I like you a lot. Riches like we've found can be good if you can keep your head about you, but let me tell you from my own experience, it sure can corrupt too. I gambled, drank, threw parties, chased women, you name it. I was a sinful creature, I was. I knew there'd always be more money, and I depended on it, and I weren't shy about parting with it. Everybody was my friend, and the ladies loved me. But I want you to know, I worked hard for something I never could quite find."

"What was that?" Jennifer asked, listening intently.

"Happiness. Never could get a grip on it. I'm a lot older now, and I know happiness comes from within—it's a spiritual thing. And if your spiritual world ain't right—I'm talking about the Almighty—then nothing will bring you happiness, not even a bunch of gold. That's where many a man has made a big mistake. Money ain't a good god; it'll let you down every time. Been a lot of good folks like yourself hit it big, and it ruint their lives. I've seen it happen, even happened to me once. And you don't even know it's happenin' 'til it's too late. Keep readin' your Bible, and keep your flanks guarded against the devil's forces. He's lookin' to step right in."

Producing a white handkerchief, Emmitt dabbed his forehead. "I must sound like a Bible-thumpin' preacher, but all I'm tryin' to do is give you some good advice. Funny thing, one of the best things in the world is good advice, and it can be free, but folks won't take heed in it."

Smiling, Jennifer stood and flattened her new calico dress. "You're a good man, Emmitt. If you only knew what Jason and I have been through—it's like we've already been tested by fire." She looked down at Jason and smiled. "We've been through so much together, and we've made God first and foremost in our lives. I'm sure He won't let us down now."

"He never lets nobody down," Emmitt agreed. He reached in his coat, pulled out a cigar, and offered it to Jason.

"No thanks," Jason said. "I don't smoke."

Emmitt took his time lighting the expensive cheroot, inhaled, and watched the smoke as he blew it into the air. "Nothing like a good cigar," he muttered to himself. "I reckon that's all I wanted to make clear. Great wealth can be a dangerous thing."

Jason reached over and took Jennifer's hand. "I think as long as we have each other and God on our side we'll make it."

Standing, Emmitt leaned on his walking stick. "Could be I wasted my time," he said as he cast his smiling eyes at Jason. "I'll be watchin' over things while you're gone, so don't worry none. This has been one fine summer, I'm here to tell you! Now August is about over, and old man winter is waiting just over the mountain. At least I know I can stay warm this winter—got me a room over at the Teller House. Got Pete the best stall in town, and he don't complain so much anymore."

Jason and Jennifer followed Emmitt to the door. As they stepped onto the front boardwalk, Emmitt shared a little of what was on his mind. "You know, I've done a whole mess of dumb things, and I might be just an old fool, but I ain't stupid. I never seen two young folks so much in love. How come you ain't married?"

Hot blood flushed Jennifer's face. She started to say something, but the words wouldn't quite come. Jason spoke to cover her embarrassment. "We're engaged," he blurted out. "We plan on getting married soon."

"Uh-huh," Emmitt said. "Take it from an old coot who knows what he's talkin' about—you ought to get married real soon!" He puffed on his cigar and rambled on down the boardwalk as the couple watched him disappear into the groups of people crowding the walkway.

"How about it?" Jason asked, turning to Jennifer. "He said good advice was often free, and that sounded like excellent advice to me."

Reacting to the confrontation, Jennifer quickly suggested, "Why don't we talk about it over dinner tonight—I'm buying!"

"Great!" Jason said. "I don't think I've ever been asked out to a dinner by a lovely woman before, and certainly not a paying one!"

Little did he know that she would be a perfect date in every way, or that she would successfully manage to evade the subject of setting a wedding date.

～

October was just like August—at least it started out that way. Things couldn't have been running more smoothly, with money pouring in faster than it could be counted. With her escalating bank account, Jennifer felt even more confident about investing in a silver mine in Leadville. She asked everyone she knew what they thought, and not a soul discredited the plan. "If I had the money, I'd already be up there trying to buy into one of those claims! Did you hear about Horace Tabor? Every claim he's bought has made him the money!"

Jake Sandelowski, now known as Jake Sands, was running a successful clothing store and had sent for Baby Doe, who left to join him immediately.

With his things packed and sitting in the front office, Jason went over his list to make sure nothing was forgotten.

Jennifer hovered nearby. "We've neglected the newspaper for so long, I'm sure people think we've closed the business up."

"And rightfully so," Jason said confidently. "Why would we mess with any nickel-and-dime business when we have millions to worry about? No way I feel bad about it. How about you?"

"I guess not," Jennifer admitted weakly. "But while you're gone I'm not sure what I'll do with myself. The paper was my job, and it kept me busy. Now, even with all this money, I don't feel like I have a profession. A person needs to stay busy with something."

"That's right," Jason said. "Things have changed. Your job now is more important than ever. Let's see, look around—you've bought this building and have done a wonderful job of fixing it up. There's more that could be done with it, but I'm sure we won't live here forever. Think of it as fixing up future income property. You know you'll rent it after we leave. That's one job you've been doing well that's unfinished. Also, now that you have the time, don't forget the church. Just because we're rich doesn't mean we can't help by doing some volunteer work. Lita likes to cook for those kind of things—you could help her with that. I'm sure she'd appreciate your company. I think she's having a hard time adjusting to her new kitchen. There are also the books on the Wild Horse—you like to keep track of the accounts, and that takes time. I'm sure I could think of some more things too." He smiled.

"You're right," Jennifer said, regretting her useless worry. "There's plenty to do." Then a sudden change came over her.

Jason was puzzled by what he was seeing. It was as if she changed seasons right before him.

Her face was alluring as Jennifer came close. She carefully placed her arms around him and looked him straight in the eye. "I don't recall us ever being apart for very long, not since we first met," she whispered. "I'm not sure how I will handle it—I've come to depend on you so much." Her expression softened. "I'll miss you." She paused as she held him close. "I don't suppose you have any way of knowing how long all this will take?"

Jason felt like an important man in an important woman's arms. "We've been over this—I'll stay in touch. If I get too involved in

business, overseeing a mining effort or whatever, I'll send for you!"
He hugged her and whispered in her ear, "Jennifer, I love you. I
always have—I always will."

She turned her head and accepted his passionate kiss. She knew
it would be a long time before she would enjoy this kind of closeness
again. "Jason, I love you too."

PART TWO

A WORLD AWAY

~ 7 ~

Treacherous Travels

A small group had gathered to see Jason off under a cloudy October morning sky. Abe held Lita as they watched the stagecoach hands throw luggage on top of the big coach. Grant and Abby stood idly, neither wanting to see Jason leave, but neither knowing what to say. Jason held Jennifer in his arms, their faces close as they said their good-byes.

"I'll do the best I can and watch for the crooks trying to sell salted mines," Jason assured Jennifer. Her face showed worry as well as a hint of regret.

"It's not the money I'm worried about—it's you," Jennifer said. "I've heard plenty about Leadville and its wild ways. Sounds like a good place for a person to get hurt or something worse." She slipped her arms around Jason's waist and pulled him closer. "Promise me you'll look out for yourself."

"I'm a big boy—I can take care of myself. But I'll miss you so much—it will be the hardest thing I've done in a long while." He kissed her softly on the lips. "I have to remind myself it's for a good cause. If things go like I expect, we'll be set for life, able to do what we want when we want."

Jennifer suspected they were already set for life financially, but she was well aware they needed to invest, and investing mining prof its in other mines seemed to be the best option. With the money rolling in from the Wild Horse, she knew they had to do something. The drawback was obvious. Now that the time had actually come, she couldn't stand to see Jason leave. "Maybe you can come back in a few weeks, even if it's only for a short while."

"I will," Jason said as he kissed her quickly again. He then turned to Grant and Abby and shook Grant's hand. "Take care of things, Grant. Take care of your mother and your sister."

Nodding, Grant said, "I can do that. You take care of yourself."

Jason smiled and glanced at Abby. "Young lady, if you keep getting any prettier you'll have to chase the boys off with a broom."

Blushing, Abby hugged Jason. She secretly wished all men were as nice and considerate as he was. Knowing he could be gone for weeks or months, she wanted to tell him how much she'd miss him, but the words wouldn't come.

"Here," Lita said, handing Jason a paper bag. "That's lunch. You'll be getting hungry before the mornin's out."

"Thanks, Lita," Jason said, leaning over to hug her. He looked over at Abe. "Watch over these women, Abe"

"Oh, I will. And you watch out for them loose women and pickpockets and thieves. You know how a town like that is." Abe believed from what he'd heard that Leadville might be the wildest place on earth—the devil's own den.

"And read your Bible!" Lita ordered.

Turning back to Jennifer, Jason reached around her neck and kissed her again, then turned to climb into the coach. "I'll write you as soon as I get settled in."

Climbing in the already crowded coach, Jason shut the door behind him. Jennifer could see him waving from inside as the driver cracked a whip and the rig lurched into motion. She could feel a sinking feeling in her heart, like she was losing him. Reminding herself of past trying circumstances that worked out well did no good. She felt a lump in her throat, and her eyes brimmed with tears. She pulled a kerchief from her bag and dabbed her eyes.

"He'll be all right," Lita comforted as she came over beside Jennifer and took her arm. "The Lord has plans for that man."

"I don't know what's wrong with me," Jennifer whined. "I just have an intuition about all of this that scares me."

"Fear is not from the Lord," Abe reminded her as he listened in. "Fear is of Satan."

It was a sad morning for all, but Grant had an idea to brighten things up. "How about I take everybody to breakfast?"

"Whoopee!" Abby shouted. "I want pancakes."

Stopped in her mournful tracks, Jennifer was astonished at Grant's bold behavior. "You make good enough money to afford to do that?"

"Of course not," he replied casually. "But you have plenty of money, Mother."

They all laughed, feeling a little brighter as they moved on down the street discussing which place had the best pancakes.

~

Jason wasn't gone five minutes before he was feeling nervous. He was sad about leaving Jennifer behind. The gray skies matched his mood. The long, bumpy trail curving over steep cliffs wound down and down toward Idaho Springs. The big Concord coach was full, which was good, for the passengers were squeezed in tight and cushioned each other against the rocking motion of the coach. The passengers were all men, three wearing suits and the other five wearing the rougher clothes of working men. For a long time the travelers stared silently from the coach at the long distance below. The driver constantly applied a squealing brake.

"Whew!" a heavyset man wearing a dark suit and derby hat exclaimed. "A man might die of old age before he hit the bottom if this coach was to go over one of these cliffs."

A few chuckled, but for most, their stomachs were in their throats. The fat man pulled out a satchel he carried with him, reached inside, pulled out a bottle of whiskey, and took a couple of swallows. "Ah! That's mighty fine, mighty fine. Helps steady the nerves and settle this old stomach." He glanced at the old man beside him. "Care for a snort, partner?"

"Shore would," the old man said, grabbing the bottle and putting it to his lips.

It wasn't long before the bottle had made its way around the coach until it was empty. Jason declined. He noticed how the liquor loosened the tongues of the group.

"I'm a goin' to pick up my future wife at Georgetown," a young man said sprightly. His eyes were fairly glazed over.

"Congratulations," the fat man said. "When are you getting married?"

"I don't know. Soon, I reckon."

"How'd you come to meet your wife?" the other man questioned for conversation's sake as the coach rolled from side to side.

"Well, I ain't met her yet. She's a mail-order bride, come here from Californy."

There were some laughs, but for the most part the men considered it a good deal. The scarcity of women in the mining camps and nearby boomtowns made the idea seem useful and practical. Most considered an ideal woman to be big and strong so she could share the workload and handle childbearing with no problems. The peddlers of these women knew that and did their best to fill the order. The reason there were laughs in the coach was that the young man was somewhat frail. Every man present pictured a woman the size of a boxcar picking up this young man and hauling him off like a sack of potatoes.

The whiskey-induced talk shifted to women, with a few inappropriate jokes about them. Jason couldn't help but laugh at the men, though he couldn't bring himself to participate in the vulgar insinuations. His mind too was on a woman—Jennifer; he couldn't think about anything but her.

Before long the driver called over the side, "We made it, gents— bottom of the hill—Idaho Springs!"

"Good. I need to stretch my legs," Jason said as the stage pulled into the small town. Rather than eat at the layover, Jason took a walk and munched on his sack lunch—fried chicken and cornbread. He couldn't believe how good it tasted, even though it was cold and coming out of a paper bag. A twinge of regret caught him by surprise when he realized he wouldn't be eating any of Lita's cooking for quite a while. It had taken her some time to get used to the new stove, but now she was back in her prime at her kitchen duties. Disheartened, he realized he would miss them all; they were like family.

Passing in front of the Beebe House, Jason glanced inside. It was a truly splendid establishment with thick carpets and horsehair-stuffed sofas surrounded by mirrors. Jason had heard it was one of the finest hotels in Colorado, with a dining area that sat 125 people. He looked up at it as if it were something out of his reach, and then he remembered that was no longer true. He was rich and could certainly stay in a grand place if he so desired. He smiled, pleased with himself, and walked on back to the stage. It would be leaving soon.

Most of the same men were on the stage when Jason arrived and climbed in. He took a window seat and hung his arm out the window. The rude talk was already off and running, for the gents had obviously indulged in more drink for lunch. Hearing a commotion, he turned and looked to see a group of men toting trunks and luggage and hurrying beside a well-dressed lady as she walked toward the stage. The men were quick to help her with every little thing. Two of them saw to it that she climbed up and into the coach without strain. "Yes, ma'am," they repeated over and over.

As she climbed in, she surveyed the passengers, appraising them quickly, then squeezed into the seat beside Jason. She glanced at him and gave him a knowing smile that insinuated she was a lady accustomed to having her way. Her body pressed against his, and he blushed. The rude talk ceased; in fact, all talk did. All eyes were on the lady.

The woman was apparently used to such stares, for they seemed to bother her not in the slightest. The stage jerked into motion and was off, the horses now able to make quicker time on a better road headed west.

"Are all of you gentlemen deaf and dumb or haven't you seen a woman before?" she spat out boldly.

After embarrassed coughs and gasps, the fat man introduced himself. "I'm Thomas Hutchinson, mining speculator and investor. I'm going to Leadville to see if these big stories are true, and if they are, by golly, I'll be wealthy in no time."

"I see—the plan of all speculators," she replied, ending the conversation abruptly. Now able to turn and look at her very close, Jason noted that the woman was unusually beautiful, though her attitude was superior and insulting. She appeared to be about twenty-six or twenty-seven; her peachy complexion was clear and soft. She smelled like a rose; her jet-black hair lay under a fashionable hat, and her almond-shaped, turquoise-blue eyes drilled holes in whoever she stared at. Her mouth was small with plush lips, her nose curved up a little. A slight eastern accent lilted her voice, a voice perhaps for singing. She was rather short, but certainly no man could miss her presence. *She's probably used to ruling men,* Jason thought.

"I'm Marie Kelly," she said. "I'm an actress trying to catch up with my theatrical company, already in Leadville."

Suddenly Marie turned to Jason. She was direct, her sweet breath right in his face. "And who might you be, sir?"

"I'm Jason Stone." There was a vague shakiness in his voice he hoped nobody noticed.

"Jason Stone!" Thomas Hutchinson shouted. "Why, you're the one who owns the Wild Horse mine back in Central City. What a find that was!" He grunted as he leaned over and reached to shake Jason's hand.

Jason shook the man's hand but said nothing.

"You've been so quiet on this trip I had no idea," Hutchinson persisted. "The prettiest gold ore I ever did see," he continued, now talking to Marie Kelly. "And this man here owns that mine, one of those western success stories I'm sure you've read about."

"Is that right, Mr. Stone?" Marie said, a devilish sparkle in her eyes.

"Yes," Jason said. "It was a crazy accident, you might say. We've had that old mine for years, and everyone thought it was barren— we couldn't give it away."

Marie was a dedicated student of people, especially men. She would store away all the information she took in, like a row of reference books in a library; and at any given time she could recall a name, situation, person, or place to be used to her advantage. She caught the "we" in Jason's statement and leaned forward. "You said, 'we.' Did you mean your wife?"

"My fiancée," Jason said, "Jennifer."

"Sweet name," Marie said with a most subtle hint of sarcasm. "I played in Central City recently," she went on to say in order to change the subject.

Jason knew he'd seen this woman somewhere before, but he hadn't been able to remember where. The last time he saw her, she wore a red frock down to her ankles and had on a wig of giant blonde curls—Little Red Riding Hood. "That's right!" Jason said, happy to find a common subject they could talk about freely. "I saw your play—you were marvelous, and you sing very well."

Marie batted an eye, feeding on the flattery, though she already knew she was wonderful. "Why, thank you, Mr. Stone. I'm pleased you liked my performance."

With the ice broken, Jason and Marie discussed a number of subjects while the others sat disgruntled at not being invited into the conversation. However, this didn't stop their eyes from gazing upon Marie Kelly.

In what seemed like minutes the driver was calling, "Georgetown comin' up, folks!"

"That was fast," Jason said, sincerely surprised.

"We stay here overnight," Marie said. "I have friends I'll be staying with. Do you suppose, Mr. Stone, that you'll be on the morning stage for Leadville?"

"Call me Jason, please. And, yes, I'm riding all the way through to Leadville."

The passengers unloaded, and Marie turned to Jason again, her eyes captivating him. "I'll be looking forward to our trip together. Good evening."

"Good evening," Jason said, touching his fine black derby. *She's either the sweetest thing I've ever seen or she's an absolute monster.* He smiled and went to find the nicest place in town to stay.

~

Georgetown had become an elegant town with pretentious Victorian houses and hotels equally lavish. Though founded as a gold camp, Georgetown had emerged as a silver town, sometimes referred to as the Silver Queen due to the rich silver mines in the vicinity. Ironically, the first prospectors had encountered silver, but since they were looking for gold, they failed to recognize the fortune at hand. All considered, Georgetown was relatively tame compared to other silver mining boomtowns like Leadville.

Jason found a most extraordinary hotel to spend the evening, the Hotel de Paris. It was like a French country inn furnished with heavy walnut pieces. Dinner at the inn was most impressive; not only did it have an indoor fountain full of small trout, so that guests could have truly fresh fish, but the hotel bottled its own wine. The floor of the dining room was walnut and maple laid in alternating strips. *This is the life!* Jason thought as he enjoyed a dinner of quail. *It's nice to be treated with such respect.* However, as he sat alone at his table enjoying a cup of strong coffee after his meal, his thoughts ran through the same circle over and over—what he intended to do in Leadville—and the long trip ahead with that utterly beautiful woman.

He felt ashamed and guilty; thinking about Marie Kelly was like betraying Jennifer, the farthest thing from his wishes. But the actress was dangerously attractive, her scent overpowering and her personality mysteriously seductive. He'd seen women like this before, explosive and domineering, using their beauty as a weapon. The hungry men of the mining camps were easy targets for this kind of woman and usually ended up heartbroken and broke. The strange magnetism was hard for any man to resist.

～

The next morning Jason was up bright and early and had a good breakfast. Outside the wind rushed by as dark clouds made ominous outlines in the gray overcast sky. The threatening clouds scooted past like schooners with billowing sails.

The stage sat ready and waiting as a crew hitched up an eight-horse team of sleek, muscular horses. Jason went inside to be sure everything was in order. The elderly man at the stage house was most accommodating. "Got a full load goin' over the divide," he said, still wearing his undershirt, which he'd apparently slept in. Wide suspenders held his pants up, but nothing could hold up his droopy eyelids still heavy with sleep. "But that's good, keeps everybody squished in their place—don't jostle around so."

"Yes, I know," Jason said. "The coach leaving soon?"

"In about half an hour," the old man replied, scratching under his arm. "Looks like we might have a spell of weather blowin' in, but don't worry, you got one of the best drivers in the Rockies, Broken-nose Scotty."

Jason walked outside and studied the sky again. The old man was right. It did look like something fierce was blowing in.

A small group waiting to board the stage watched Marie Kelly walk over. Although she had herself fixed up pretty as a picture, she was quiet and reserved, the opposite of the day before. She seemed rather tired.

"Good morning, Jason," she mumbled as she boarded the stage. Several others boarded before Jason.

"Sit here," Marie said, patting the seat next to her. It was roughly the same arrangement as the day before, Jason at the window and Marie by his side. He smiled and did as he was told.

Once underway, the horses galloped harder and harder until Jason noticed his ears were popping from the altitude. The coach stopped briefly in Silver Plume so the horses could drink some water, and then the stage was again on its way at breakneck speed. By now the dark clouds appeared even more imposing.

Unable to hold her eyes open, Marie kept nodding off until finally her head rested on Jason's shoulder. The other male passengers were amused and smiled knowingly at him but kept conversation to a minimum out of respect for the sleeping lady. A little embarrassed, Jason said nothing, always a gentleman.

Marie awoke as the stage was laboring to get over the Continental Divide. The temperature had dropped considerably. "It's cold in here," she said, cuddling closer to Jason for warmth.

Pulling back his window shade, the fat man, Mr. Hutchinson, said, "Why, it's snowing."

The nine passengers all strained to see out a window as the big lazy snowflakes drifted down. This made it seem even colder. Though Jason felt uncomfortable about Marie being so close to him, he didn't mind because he was cold as well. He thought about how young Grant had made the decision to buy more functional, practical clothing for Rocky Mountain weather. Now Jason was dressed as fancy as any city dude in expensive clothes and was freezing.

The coach rambled on, Broken-nose Scotty as good as any at handling the horses in winter weather.

It was almost dark when the big Concord stage rolled up to the Half Mile House on Weston Pass. There they would change horses and serve the passengers an evening meal. Broken-nose Scotty looked over the coach with extra care, making sure everything was all right before he went inside for hot coffee and a warm meal. Restless and worried, Scotty ate very little. After a while he went outside and looked for the pass but couldn't see more than twenty feet—the snowstorm had turned into a blizzard. He went back inside the station house to talk to the passengers.

"It'd be a mite reckless to continue on, seeing the way this storm has set in. It'd be best to wait 'til mornin'." He removed his hat, shook the heavy snow from it, and scratched his head. His bent nose seemed to be looking a different way than his eyes. "Could be treacherous," he added, "but it's up to you folks."

Mr. Hutchinson waved his fat hand in the air for attention. "I don't know about the rest of ya'll, but I think I'll sit it out."

The other men joined in as well, agreeing with Hutchinson.

But Miss Marie Kelly jumped to her feet, almost in a rage. "I have to be in Leadville! Your company guarantees delivery of passengers!" she shouted, daring Scotty to deny it. "My show opens tomorrow night—I *have* to be there!"

Jason didn't mind staying overnight in the crowded station house with all the snoring men, but he also wanted to get started on his new business ventures immediately, for Jennifer and himself and their future. "Surely you've driven in a snowstorm before?" he asked the experienced driver.

"Well, yeah, I have," Scotty admitted.

"Ever been lost?" Jason pressed.

"I've been a mite bewildered, but I've never been lost!" he

bragged. "I can do it, though I have to admit I'm a little worried. This storm seems stronger than the ones I fought before."

But the protestors prevailed, and soon the stage was again on its way, the blizzard howling as Jason and Marie sat wrapped in buffalo robes. None of the other passengers dared to continue and said they'd be glad to wait for the next stage. Traveling was slow as Scotty refused to rush the horses over snow-drifted roads. The stage finally reached the top of the pass with no trouble, and Jason and Marie breathed a sigh of relief. Not long after they started their descent down the west side of Weston Pass the stage came to a stop.

There was no word from the driver, so Jason flipped open the window flap and yelled up, "What's the matter—are you lost?"

There was silence as he glanced at Marie in the darkness of the coach. Her eyes reflected the outside lamplight like a cat's. An answer rang out from above. "No, I ain't lost! It's the horses that's lost!"

"Great!" Jason replied.

Moments later the stage was again rolling like a ship in rough seas, lurching from side to side and bumping over small boulders that at times made it feel like the coach would overturn. Marie slid back and forth in the long seat opposite Jason, trying to hold her robe around her and hang onto the leather strap as well. She jumped up, landed in the seat beside Jason, and grabbed hold of him.

Out of decency, Jason placed his strong arm around her to hold her in place while they endured the rough ride.

Up top, Scotty couldn't see past the lead horse. The blizzard had piled deep drifts in the road, and it was hard to determine exactly where it ended and the mountainsides began. He pushed on, his hat brim mashed flat against his forehead and his beard white with snow. Suddenly the outside wheels went too far over the edge of the road, and the stage started to roll over. Marie let out a hysterical scream.

Scotty shouted, "Brace yourselves!" He cracked the ten-foot whip at the horses, trying to get the coach back onto the road.

The coach struggled, and there was a loud pop as the pin broke loose and the horses came uncoupled. Frightened, the team dashed into the darkness, snatching Scotty from his perch. "Whoa! Whoa!" he cried over the howling wind.

Jason stuck his head out the window and caught the last glimpse of Broken-nose Scotty holding the reins as the horses dragged him off into the darkness. The coach sat at a perilous angle. "We're not out of danger," he mumbled, fearing any movement might send the coach over the cliff.

A startled look on her young, worried face, Marie moved closer. "Oh, Jason, I don't want to freeze to death! I don't want to die!" She clutched him as if her life depended on it.

A long silence followed, the wind outside strong enough to rock the stage. The cold seemed to steal in from the night, causing the passengers to shiver uncontrollably.

Unwrapping her robe, her teeth chattering and her lower lip quivering, Marie said, "I bet if we cuddle together, we'll stay warmer." Without asking, she moved to get inside Jason's buffalo skin with him, and he fearfully complied.

What better way to die than in the arms of a beautiful woman? he thought. Brief images of Jennifer and short reminiscences of his Christian commitments came to mind, but he pushed them away, not daring to ignore the immediate dangers. Their shared warmth helped them both, and Marie soon quit shivering. She warmed her hands in Jason's, moving as close to him as possible.

"Jason, you won't let me die, will you?"

"We're not going to die," he said courageously even though he wasn't so sure. "We'll just have to sit it out. We'd be crazy to leave our shelter in weather like this."

Marie, now warm and comfortable, held her face against Jason's neck; her touch was cold at first but was soon warmer. She let her lips drift to his neck, and as he turned to say something, he felt her lips on his in a passionate kiss.

Jason enjoyed the kiss, but then he remembered his commitments and pulled away. "Marie, you're lovely, but I have to remind you, I'm engaged to a wonderful woman I love very much."

"But you're not married," she whispered softly, then took his face in her small hands and pulled him back into her kiss.

Jason knew the gorgeous little vixen was taking advantage of him, and he both hated it and loved it. He was scared of his own willingness and his own helplessness. Never had he dreamed anything like this would happen. He felt he'd failed Jennifer and the Lord, and the guilt was eating at him. "Stop it, Marie!" he demanded forcefully.

But Marie wasn't the least bit intimidated. She knew exactly what she was doing. "You aren't scared of me, are you?"

"Yes!" he admitted. "Your beauty and my weakness scare me plenty!"

"Good," she said. "I admired you from the moment I met you. You're a handsome and well-mannered man, unlike most. I was happy to hear you weren't married, at least not yet. To me that meant I still had a chance." She softly massaged his shoulders, then said, "You can't blame me for trying, can you, Jason?"

He shook his head. It was nice to be wanted by an attractive woman who might have her choice of any man, but he was determined to do what was right.

~

Broken-nose Scotty had held on to the reins for some 300 yards before being too battered and bruised to hang on any longer. The horses galloped away. He stood up and dusted the snow off him, cursing at the wind. Glancing around, he wasn't sure where he was but decided to follow the horses' tracks as far as he could. Fortunately, they'd left a fair-sized rut that was easy to see.

Before long he came to a group of teamsters who'd caught the horses. Scotty explained the problem and climbed aboard the big, heavy wagons so they could take him back to the coach.

It was only an hour before the freighters reached the lopsided stage. "You all right in there?"

Before Jason could answer, Marie cried out, "Never been better!"

Jason made a face at her—she was a bold, daring woman.

The men took long poles and soon had the stage upright again and the horses hitched up with a new pin. Broken-nose Scotty talked to the men a moment and then whipped the horses into a cautious descent. The road would be easier to follow thanks to the wagon ruts.

Marie held tight to Jason, and he again began to weaken, enjoying the comforting touch. He only wished Jennifer would freely express such emotion and affection. He figured it wouldn't hurt to let Marie hang on to him for a while.

They rocked along in silence for a few more hours before the storm finally let up. They'd been over 11,000 feet high in a blinding blizzard over Weston Pass but finally spotted the twinkling lights of Leadville dispersed in the distance like shining specks of silver.

CHAPTER
~ 8 ~

Leadville

The boom of Leadville in 1878, big as it was, seemed small by comparison to the rush of people in 1879. That summer of 1878 new arrivals, coming from all over the world, had averaged 100 a day. A record was set on July 15 with, according to some, 236 in just one day. Each hour a Concord Coach arrived with eighteen to twenty persons aboard. The throng of people that patronized the more than 200 business establishments on Chestnut Street was so thick that many took to the streets to avoid the crowded sidewalks. The post office handled a larger amount of mail than Kansas City or San Francisco. At first people built whatever they wanted wherever they wished, but by the fall of 1878 thoroughfares had been laid out, and the following year the city gave those who had shanties obstructing street developments ten days to remove them. The city grew so rapidly there were thirty sawmills running day and night to turn out an estimated 3,600,000 feet of lumber weekly.

Despite the progress, the town was also a dangerous place. In fact, Leadville was the most lawless place in the West at the time. Whiskey incited many to drastic actions, and daily quarrels and general turbulence cost many a man his life. The diversity of languages and ethnic identities contributed to the problems. Since the French, Germans, Slovaks, Italians, Greeks, and others often couldn't understand what others were saying, conflicts were inevitable. Each dark alley had its own riff-raff, and one had to be on guard at all times. A gentleman walking the streets alone at night often carried a cocked pistol. Vigilantes and hired guns were the only form of anything remotely resembling justice.

But there was also unequaled gaiety and celebration. Hundreds of beautiful girls of all nationalities and all ages were decked out in fancy dresses and adorned with various colors of feathers around their head and body. Frequently a girl would get a man drunk, lead him to a room or an alley, and rob him of whatever he had of value. The strains of music and laughter poured from the dance halls, saloons, and gambling houses twenty-four hours a day. Appearing at first glance like a magical scene from a fairy tale, it was in reality a city of robberies, killings, prostitution, gambling, and thievery ranging from small stakes to grand schemes to pilfer another's fortune.

～

It was 11 P.M. when the stage rounded the corner on Chestnut Street, where it came to a stop in front of Tom Walsh's Grand Hotel. Jason climbed down from the coach, every bone in his body aching from the rough trip, then turned to take Marie's hand and help her down.

"Would you look at this?" Marie stated in amazement as her eyes reflected the firelight of the many fires and lanterns. "Looks like some kind of Fourth of July celebration." The enticing music flooded the street from a nearby dance hall, and the hustle and bustle of the number of people in the street seemed far more than the town could handle.

Noticing the ruckus, Jason said, "I've seen something like this before, back in Virginia City." He turned to Marie, staring into her captivating eyes. "You'd best be careful, Marie. This place looks to me like it's awful dangerous, in more ways than you might know."

Clinging to his arm, Marie pleaded, "Jason, don't be mad at me for what happened. Please don't leave me! Help me get situated."

Realizing it was the only courteous thing to do, Jason agreed. "All right, but I want you to understand—I am in love with another woman. I'll help you all I can, but you'll soon have to find your own way." He'd said it, and he was glad. "Now let's go into the hotel and find us some rooms."

On the way in Jason noticed that every man practically stumbled over his own feet staring at Marie; then their eyes would focus on Jason to see what kind of lucky man would have the company of such an incredible woman. Jason did his best to stay humble.

"I'm famished," Marie said as they waited for the desk clerk to wait on them. "You won't make me have dinner by myself, will you?"

Jason was half-starved himself. "We can have dinner here," he said. "After we get our things up to our rooms."

Marie managed to get a room by herself, although she had to pay double since all rooms were for two. Jason would have to share his with a complete stranger. When Jason went to his room, he opened the door and heard loud snoring. The place smelled like an old dog. Disgusted, he immediately closed the door and went back down to the dining room, leaving his luggage at the desk. He'd tend to the room's challenges later.

Jason was shown to a formal table where he sat waiting for Marie. Several distinguished gentlemen sitting nearby were dressed as if they were attending an inauguration; they were obviously involved in important talk.

A half hour passed, and still Marie hadn't shown up. Jason was about to give up on her and order when she appeared in an evening gown, her appearance as refreshing as a flower after a gentle rain. The rumble of talk went silent as all eyes turned toward her. She took the attention graciously while the waiter brought her to Jason's table and seated her.

"Looks like you already have an audience," Jason remarked, determined not to be too kind.

"I'm used to it," she said, her delicate tongue moistening her lips. "You act like you've just been slapped with a cold fish. Is something wrong?"

Tightening his lips with disgust, Jason said, "I'm going to have to do something about my room. The fellow sleeping in there sounds like a sawmill and smells like an outhouse."

Quick laughter lit up Marie's face. "You can stay in my room," she teased.

"I may have to stay on the street," Jason said angrily.

"Jason Stone! You mean to tell me you'd rather sleep in an alley than in the luxury of my company?" Marie had intentionally said this loudly enough to turn the heads of the nearby gentlemen, who all stared at Jason in disbelief.

"C'mon, Marie!" Jason whispered coarsely. "You're making me look like a fool! Pipe down!"

Marie smiled her wicked little smile, the kind that's half tease and half mischief.

A tall gentleman in a tuxedo approached and bent over to Jason. "Pardon me, sir, but I couldn't help overhearing your conversation. Did I understand this lovely woman to address you as Jason Stone?"

Looking up, Jason said, "Yeah, I'm Jason Stone. What about it?"

"The same Jason Stone of Black Hawk who made the gold strike?"

"Yes."

"I read all about it in the newspaper," the gentleman said. "Please . . . allow me to introduce myself—I'm Horace Tabor. Would you and your lovely guest be kind enough to join me at my table?"

"We'd love to join you, Mr. Tabor," Marie said quickly, answering for Jason and again irritating him.

Once they sat at Tabor's table, the man began talking again. "I suppose you've come to Leadville looking for investments. Well, let me tell you, you're in the right place. I believe a man could dig a hole right where we're sitting and strike it rich. A wealthy man like yourself who can develop a mine properly—why, I suppose you'd have at least three of them running in no time." He paused and sipped his champagne, his eyes also drinking in Marie. "And who might this lovely lady be, Jason?"

"Uh, this is Miss Marie Kelly. She's an actress and will be joining her company at the theater tomorrow, won't you, Marie?"

"Yes," she said, smiling at Tabor but giving Jason a stern look. "Our production is to start tomorrow night."

"I can't wait—that's my theater," Tabor said. "Why don't we make plans to go together, Jason?"

"I don't know. Seems I can't even find a room, so I'm not sure . . ."

"Nonsense. Move into my suite with me—there's an extra bedroom." He reached his hand high in the air and snapped his fingers, and a waiter appeared instantly. "John, see to it that Mr. Stone's things are moved up to my suite."

"Yes, sir, Mr. Tabor. Right away." The young man hustled off.

Astounded, Jason sat stupefied until he could think of something to say. "That's very kind, but—"

"No buts!" Tabor said, holding up his hand. He was a handsome man with a balding head, a walrus mustache, and long sideburns. His bushy eyebrows danced over his excitable eyes. He gave the distinct impression of a man who'd been imprisoned all his life and was suddenly set free. "I would like to show you my mining works and perhaps guide you with your investments. We can do that as soon as you like."

Soon several waiters showed up carrying platters of food. "I took the liberty of ordering for you," Tabor said, proud of his generosity.

Marie winked at Jason. Her expression clearly indicated that Jason should relax. She did everything possible to flirt with Jason and made sure every man present caught every insinuation.

～

Horace Tabor's suite was plush, and Jason slept well and woke up feeling fantastic. He decided to take Marie's subtle advice. He hummed as he shaved over the washbowl and gazed at himself in the mirror's reflection. *What's to worry about?* he thought joyfully. *I have plenty of money, and I can make a lot more! I'll make Jennifer proud.*

Jason searched the suite only to find it empty. Tabor was nowhere to be found. Locking the room, he ventured outside to see the town. It was a clear morning, and he couldn't help but notice the towering white peaks of Mount Elbert and Mount Massive to the west, as well as the hundreds of people lining the streets from curb to curb. The blanket of snow had already been reduced to packed ice and hard mud. Unlike most other mining towns, which were located in a valley or a gulch, Leadville sat right on top of a mountain at an altitude of 10,150 feet, where the air was thin and sharply crisp and cool. "So this is the city above the clouds," he muttered to himself. It indeed had an air of its own and sat in a most impressive setting. The excitement in the air felt like an electrical current.

Jason slipped his gold pocket watch from his fancy vest pocket and checked the time. It was 9 a.m. His first order of business would be to locate Jake Sands. Breakfast could wait.

A clambering noise came from around the corner, and before he knew it Jason stood at the curb watching a loud brass band file by in a small parade. The man leading the band wore a fur coat covered with diamonds glistening in the morning sun. "What in the world is that?" Jason asked, leaning over to the gentleman beside him.

"Sir, I'll have you know that's Ben Loeb of Loeb's Theater." Ben marched by strutting and whirling a baton. "He has twelve performances a day, and before each performance he has a parade. Many customers follow him back to see the show."

Jason watched in disbelief. He hadn't seen anything like this in a long time, and in a way the memories made him feel younger, like when he'd first arrived in the West. Smiling as he watched the band retreat, he resumed his search and soon found Jake Sands's clothing store on Harrison Avenue. Jason could see the store was by no means a small affair. Jake had outdone himself. A tall façade with a sign announcing *Sands, Pelton & Co.* welcomed him.

Jake Sands was the kind of person who made people like him look important, and that explained the success of his business. Tall and naturally well-dressed, he ran over to his old friend. "Jason! You finally took my advice!" He threw an arm around Jason's square shoulders. "My good man, so glad you could make it!"

The store was crowded with customers and merchandise, but Jake had a staff to wait on the many people. The smell of fine imported cloth left an unforgettable impression. Wooden mannequins displayed the most popular attire. Smiling in return, Jason responded, "It's good to be here. Looks like you're doing quite well, you rascal."

"Couldn't be better. Leadville is everything I told you and more. When did you arrive?"

"Last night—after a terrible coach ride through a blizzard."

Jake laughed. "Funny weather in the high country. Who'd ever imagine we'd have a blizzard in October? They say just wait a little while if you don't like the weather—it'll change. And look at today—just beautiful. Come to my office, and we'll talk over a cup of tea."

Upstairs, Jake had a roomy office of exquisite English furniture imported from London. The room smelled of mahogany and fine tobacco.

As they drank their tea in thin porcelain cups, Jake asked, "Cigar?" and held out an open humidor for Jason. The high-quality cigars were lined up neatly.

Taking one, Jason examined the hand-rolled product and held it under his nose. "I don't smoke, but these sure smell good."

"Well, start!" Jake insisted, always the salesman. "These cost a dollar apiece, and a wealthy gentleman always smokes a cigar."

Eager to fulfill his role, Jason accepted a light from the match Jake struck for his friend. The tightly wound cigar immediately filled the room with an odor of importance.

"So, are you here to invest in some mining works?" Jake questioned as he leaned back in his tall leather-covered chair.

"Certainly," Jason said around the cigar. "I thought you might have some leads."

"That I do," Jake answered as he bent over and opened a drawer in front of him. "Here's some materials you might look through—some advertisements and a list of names including bankers, lawyers, mining superintendents, and assayers—all trustworthy men. Sometimes the best way to approach a mining purchase is through the back door—for example, by going to an assayer or attorney and finding out who might be interested in selling. Sometimes a superintendent can give you some leads too."

Taking the papers, Jason studied them. Jake Sands had done Jason's homework for him. "This is good, Jake. I appreciate it—it gives me somewhere to start."

"Anything for a friend," Jake said, leaning back in his chair and touching his outstretched fingertips together in front of his face. "I'm sure it won't be long before you'll be among the elite mining owners here. Sort of makes Central City look like a one-horse town, doesn't it?"

Setting the papers down, Jason smiled. His dreams of wealth and power were about to become reality. "This place is something to behold—might be a good place to make a fortune, I suppose."

"My friend, that is a certainty!" Jake affirmed.

Jason felt nervous about the new and glorious life in front of him. He decided to change the subject. "So how's Baby Doe? She's here, isn't she?"

Jake waved a hand and smiled uncertainly. "Yes, of course. She's staying in a nice boarding room I found for her, and she's as pretty as ever!" He hesitated, then said, "I asked her to marry me when her divorce is final. She's the sweetest thing, and I know she adores me as a dear friend. But, Jason, she doesn't love me. What am I to do?"

"I can relate to that," Jason admitted. "I've been trying to get Jennifer to marry me for so long I'm starting to think it will never happen. As for her loving me, I think she does, but I'm not sure. She won't commit to a wedding date."

"Women!" Jake retorted with his pleasant smile.

Jason marveled at the misfortune they had in common. "I'm beginning to think women are in control of everything, and there isn't much we men can do about it."

Jake slapped his knee in uncontrollable laughter until tears appeared in his eyes. He straightened up in an effort to regain his voice, and it was several moments before he could speak. "My good man, are you just now discovering that?"

A wave of nausea suddenly swept over Jason, and he felt like he was spinning in a cloud of smoke. He hadn't figured the cigar would affect him so strongly.

"Why, Jason, you look green!" Jake jumped to his feet, came around to Jason, and took his arm. "I think you should lie down." He led Jason over to the expansive leather couch and stuffed a pillow behind his head as he lay down. Jake took the cigar and placed it in an ashtray. For the moment all Jason could do was groan.

~

Up in her room, Marie Kelly prepared herself for the day. Her mind ticked like a Swiss watch as she calculated everything in great detail. She was well aware of having a face so beautiful she could manipulate men like soft clay and a figure that turned heads wherever she went. She'd learned how to be a seductive temptress at a young age. Her persistence knew no boundaries and pushed any opposition out of her way. Her immediate attention was focused on Jason Stone.

Marie smiled at herself in the mirror's reflection while she applied a light tint of red rouge to her cheeks. Her wide-set, almond-shaped eyes had a sweet wickedness about them, the turquoise light in them hypnotic. The delicate expressive lips formed an irresistible smile. Her presence made men feel confused, like a bee trying to choose between many flowers.

She saw Jason Stone as a desirable man with a handsome face and solid build. His strong shoulders and square jaw appealed to her, though his bashfulness made him seem like he hadn't been out of the woods for very long. His newly found wealth made him even more attractive to her. Jason Stone would be easy pickings—a rare and sweet find. She was determined to devour him like a ripe plum.

"I'll show him how to live!" she mumbled with amusement. She giggled at herself.

Certain every glorious black hair was in place, she carefully placed a large-brimmed red hat on her head. Since red accented her beauty so well, she almost always wore it. The dress was tight-waisted and rather revealing, but of course nobody expected anything less from an actress.

In her case acting didn't mean portraying a character other than one's self. Onstage she was very much herself and in control. Being the center of attention pleased her just fine and had men drooling at her feet. If there was any real acting in her life, it was offstage, and she was a perfectionist at that too. She was able to mix lies with truth so skillfully that no one ever suspected.

Not long before noon Marie ventured downstairs to have breakfast. Since she was nocturnal, this was perfectly normal for her. She wasn't worried about getting to the theater late because they never started without her. She *was* the show; everything and everyone else was merely a prop.

Jake Sands and Jason Stone sat downstairs in the dining room. Jake had kindly convinced Jason that his spell had occurred because he hadn't eaten. Jason did indeed feel terribly hungry and insisted upon returning to the hotel where he'd had dinner the night before. Jake was more than agreeable since the hotel had a reputation for good food and good service. The men discussed business possibilities with great excitement.

When Marie entered, she immediately spotted Jason sitting with another handsome man and decided this would be the table she would sit at. *Timing is everything*, she thought happily as she approached.

Jake's eyes opened wide when the extraordinarily beautiful woman came up behind Jason, put her small hands on his neck, and caressed him. Jason turned sharply in surprise.

"Good morning, my dear," she said, as if she and Jason had an intimate relationship. "Who's your friend?"

Again caught off guard by her tactics, Jason turned to Jake, who looked like he'd just swallowed a chew of tobacco. "This is Jake Sands, owner of the clothing store over on Harrison."

"How are you?" Jake said, coming to his feet.

"May I join you?" Marie asked ever so politely.

Instantly Jake had the chair out for her and seated her. He returned to his seat like an eager puppy.

"This is Marie Kelly, Jake," Jason said. "I had the pleasure of riding on the coach with her." He gave Marie a knowing glance, reminding her of his disapproval.

"Marie Kelly," Jake repeated as he searched his mental records. "Aren't you the actress? Say, Jason, isn't she the one who was in the play in Central City—*Little Red Riding Hood* it was!" He turned back to Marie. "You were simply marvelous. I've never had so much fun at the theater."

"Thank you," Marie said, pretending she was a little shy about accepting praise.

"So, Miss Kelly, are you here with your acting company?" Jake settled down and concentrated on making conversation with the lovely young lady.

"Yes, I am," Marie twinkled. "I'm sure we'll be doing a show tonight, but I haven't located my manager yet. He won't make any plans without me."

"I can't wait to see the performance," Jake said admiringly. "Do you plan on staying in Leadville long?"

"Indeed I do. Such an exciting town, with such great events transpiring." She scooted around in her seat to get more comfortable, a gesture Jake found flirtatious.

"Do you have any idea what you will be performing?" Jake was enjoying Marie's company and her intoxicating presence.

"I'm not sure yet," she answered. "Could be we'll do some drama and perhaps some singing as well."

Turning to Jason, Jake said, "We'll have to get tickets as soon as we find out where Miss Kelly is playing."

"Sure," Jason mumbled. He was somewhat interested, but he didn't want to show Marie that he had any interest in her after what had happened in the coach. Little did he know that she assumed he was playing a game with her, motivating her to try harder.

"Are you married, Miss Kelly?" Jake asked, hoping this glamorous woman might take some interest in him.

"Why should I get married when I can always borrow me a husband?" she replied sharply.

Jake's neck and cheeks flushed red. A woman like this excited him. He chuckled in embarrassment. "I guess I was trying to ask if you are available—I'd love to show you the town."

Getting irritated, Marie looked at Jason. Throwing her eyes toward Jake, then back at Jason, she said, "I thought you said he owned a clothing store. It'd be my guess he works for a newspaper, asking all these questions!"

Jason was laughing inside. Marie had succeeded in whittling down Jake, well-known as a lady's man. He was beginning to find this forward, audacious, and witty woman seductive and charming. He'd have to be careful of this venomous vixen.

When they were through dining, Marie stood to her feet. "I must be going," she apologized. "I have to find my troupe and get things in order." To both Jake and Jason's surprise, she bent over and kissed Jason on the cheek, then quickly departed. Both men watched her leave, her fragrant perfume lingering behind.

"I sold you short!" Jake said with a grin. "You have an amazing and varied taste in women."

Anger appeared on Jason's face, but before he could speak, Jake held his hands in front of him in surrender. "Don't worry—I won't tell a soul!"

"It's not like that!" Jason snapped. "I wouldn't have anything to do with a woman like her!"

A conspiring smile covered Jake's face. "Yes, of course. I understand. But I do admire your taste in women—they're always very beautiful."

Exasperated, Jason sighed. "She left it up to us to pay for her lunch."

"Who cares?" Jake said jokingly. "She's worth lunch any day."

Jason shook his head in disgust. This Marie Kelly was the boldest female he'd ever come across, and he was sure she had impure motives. But at the same time, secretly, under the hard shell of denial, he liked her aggressiveness and the sweet smell of her perfume. Engaging her wit was like playing with fire, but he was sure he could handle her.

CHAPTER

～ 9 ～

Daily Affairs

Black Hawk, by comparison, wasn't the place where wealthy people lived. It was the working man's town of mills and taverns. But Jennifer busily fixed up their old home until she could do no more. Lita had even allowed Jennifer to buy new furniture for the bedroom she and Abe lived in. A tall brass-posted bed now sat where the old and worn wooden frame bed had once sat. Abe had told Lita, "It all looks mighty nice, Lita, but it don't seem like home." Like the remodeled kitchen, the newly furnished bedroom would take a bit of getting used to.

"Why do we stay here?" Abby asked one day, the bright afternoon sun shining on her face. She and her mother were walking home from a brief shopping spree. Abby was now almost as tall as her mother.

Her daughter's question made Jennifer apprehensive. She'd already moved twice, but moving again seemed like an expedition into the unknown, a place she feared. At least things were familiar where she was now. "I don't know—where would we move to? Leadville?"

"No!" Abby said vehemently. "Who wants to live in a stinking mining camp? How about Denver? It's big and nice now. We could move there and still be close enough to Black Hawk for you to tend your gold mine and get the money from it."

"Well, I'm waiting to hear from Jason. What he says may have a bearing on any decisions we make."

Abby thought about the relationship between her mother and Jason. She couldn't understand why Jason remained faithful and patient with so little in return. He was a good fellow—true blue and handsome as well. But it irritated Abby that he wasn't a little more aggressive. If he'd just sweep her mother off her feet like Lance Rivers had, everything would be all right. But in her opinion, both her mother and Jason were scaredy-cats.

"Why don't you marry Jason?" she blurted, surprising even herself.

Unexpected, even inappropriate questions were normal for Abby, but this one bothered Jennifer because she didn't know the answer herself. "We are engaged!" she offered defensively.

"That's not what I asked," Abby shot back, "and that's not an answer."

This girl! Jennifer thought. *I keep forgetting she's growing up and talking and thinking like an adult. Why does she ask me such questions! She's relentless!* "We'll be getting married soon enough, Abby."

Despite her impertinence, Abby felt sorry for her mother. Now that they were closer, they often talked openly and revealed more of their feelings. It was obvious to Abby that something held her mother back and kept her from having fun. She wasn't sure what that was, but she was sure of the heart-felt advice she wanted to express. "I think you should marry Jason *soon*—first chance you get."

As they walked along, people scurried by, sometimes speaking, sometimes not. The October weather was ideal, the days continually growing shorter. Jennifer wondered what Jason was doing these days. She expected a letter any day; her life was empty without him. She found it hard to put her feelings into words, and that made Abby's questions even more disturbing. What *was* holding her back? Was it doubt? Love? Guilt? She could no longer blame her problems on poverty, for she was the richest woman in Black Hawk and Central City. She couldn't identify whatever was holding her back. She decided she would pray about it and put it in God's hands.

~

Evening brought with it a reminder that the chill of winter was in the air. Jennifer fed a roaring fire in the big stove and snuggled under a heavy sweater as she hunched over her desk. The office, now outfitted with new furniture, looked more like a professional business office than a newspaper office. The press sat under a white sheet, unused and forgotten. A new issue of the *Advertiser* hadn't come out in weeks. Jennifer's newly found wealth took up her efforts and time. Her passion for writing wasn't dead; it just sat in a dark corner of her thoughts. But her daily affairs left little time to pursue such thoughts—the days were simply too short.

By the light of a flickering, heart-shaped flame in the kerosene lamp, she reviewed the figures from the Wild Horse production. Profits were still increasing, and by now she was worth a million and a half dollars in liquid assets. Emmitt Tugs was doing well at around four million. Jason had around a million at his immediate disposal for investment purposes and had carried a letter from the bank to back any deals he might make in Leadville.

Hearing the noise of movement outside, Jennifer walked over to the newly hung curtains and pushed them back. There was a lacquered black carriage parked out front, and the driver was hitching the horses. Two brass lanterns cast a silvery light at its sides as the man opened the carriage door to allow Mr. Tugs to exit. Emmitt took his time, using his fancy walking stick, then told the driver something and headed up the boardwalk. Jennifer moved to the door and opened it.

"Good evening," Emmitt announced, his ever-present smile showing his missing teeth. He hobbled in wearing a new black suit and a top hat to match.

"Hello, Emmitt. Nice of you to drop by. Can I get you something to drink?" Jennifer had grown fond of Emmitt. He was almost a father figure to her.

"No, thanks. I think I'll just sit in front of this nice fire you have going. Warm my old bones some." He pulled up a new reproduction of an old Victorian chair and sat down with a groan, staring into the flames.

Jennifer waited, wondering if the visit was business or pleasure. Emmitt seemed to have forgotten why he had come. "Emmitt, is there something wrong?"

"Wrong?" Emmitt came out of the fog a bit. "Why, no, nothing's wrong. Why would you think something's wrong?"

"Well," Jennifer began, "you just came in, and—well, sort of sat down and didn't say anything, so I thought maybe there was a problem."

"The only problem I got is too much money and no real friends," Emmitt said tiredly. "I mean, I can't go anywhere and find a place where all the people aren't suddenly my friends." He stopped and squinted at Jennifer, making sure she was following him. "The only problem is, I don't have any *real* friends 'cept for maybe you," he stated sadly. Craning his neck and leaning over, Emmitt spat a long stream of tobacco juice into the fire. It hissed back at him.

Grabbing a matching chair, Jennifer pulled it up beside Emmitt and sat down. "What are you saying, Emmitt?"

"Oh, I been out and about this evening, and everywhere I go they treat me somethin' special. But if I wasn't so rich they wouldn't even let me in one of them fancy places. My happiness is store-bought, I tell you. No real friends. These people is a friend of my money, and that's about all there is to it."

His back was slightly hunched over from years of hard labor, and Jennifer gave his shoulder a reassuring pat. "You're always welcome here where you have some real friends."

"I know—that's why I come over here." Emmitt turned to Jennifer and looked her in the face. "You don't mind, do you?"

"Of course not. You're always welcome here. Are you sure I can't get you anything? Are you hungry?"

"Naw. I had steak and oysters for dinner. You know what I did last week? I went over to see Pete at the stable—I cain't have him with me all the time—and he carried on somethin' fierce, hollerin' and bellowin' and all."

"Why don't you just sell him? Seems all he does is cause you grief," Jennifer said.

"He ain't much use, that's for sure. He's got pancake hooves and trips over things, and he's swaybacked and can't carry a load without tossing it to one side. And sometimes he throws his load no matter how good it's rigged. Then he gets to carryin' on in the middle of the night and wakes me up so I have to sleep near him. Nothin' wrong with him—he's just bein' ornery. Worst of all is when he used to wander off—all the time wandering off. I got lost once lookin' for him, and we like to never got back to where we started." Emmitt sighed. "I've had him for seventeen years now, but . . ."

It was becoming apparent to Jennifer that Emmitt was lonely, and being separated from his faithful animal much of the time had upset him. "Can't you go by and visit with him again?"

"Naw, he's mad at me now. Besides, sometimes he don't even recognize me. Might be these new duds, but he ought to know me anyway 'cause I still smell the same."

Leaning back in the glow of the fire, Jennifer studied Emmitt. He wasn't used to being a financial success and probably found it a bit intimidating. "Emmitt, why don't you get back into your old clothes and take Pete for a stroll through the mountains, just like the old days? Pete doesn't know if you're rich or poor—he just knows the old Emmitt, whom he doesn't see anymore."

Perking up, Emmitt's eyes brightened. "Now ain't that a thought! I reckon he don't know the difference. Everybody else thinks I need to act rich, which I am, but old Pete, he don't know nothin'."

Smiling, Jennifer was glad she could be some help to her good friend. Part of the problem was, Emmitt had worked himself out of a job and had little to do but watch the money roll in. They had hired professionals to oversee the works at the mine. Emmitt no longer needed to actually work there. He even felt like he was in the way, for the mine had turned into a big operation with new, modern gadgets he didn't understand. Acting rich around town had been fun at first but soon grew old and boring.

"I could be gone for a while if I did that," Emmitt said, thinking it through. "Might do me some good to get back outdoors, sleeping under the moon with old Pete nearby. Never know, I might even make another discovery."

"You could," Jennifer agreed. "Take a vacation, Emmitt—you deserve it. Everything is under control here."

"You pretty young thing," Emmitt said, coming to his feet. Jennifer stood also. He gave her a thankful hug as a smile played across his face. "Leave it to a pretty woman to find the answer." As he made his way for the door he added, "If'n anyone was to ask, just tell them I'm out doing a little lookin' around at some other property. You know, I sure like discoverin' gold, but the money, well, it don't mean all that much to me anymore. I was happier without it. Old Pete'll be happy to see me like I used to be. He'll be glad to get back up on them trails and screamin' his lungs out at the mountain. Good night, Miss Jenny."

"Good night, Emmitt," Jennifer called behind him. Soon the carriage was gone, and the place was quiet again. The flames flickered on the wall as Jennifer returned to her desk. *Strange*, she thought, *the man is a multimillionaire but wants to return to his rough, almost primitive ways, scrounging around a mountainside with a rebellious burro. At least he knows what he wants, he knows where his happiness is, and that's more than I can honestly say.*

～

The next morning was Sunday, and Jennifer and Abby were smartly dressed for church. Grant was in his suit and ready to drive them in a carriage up the hill to the church. It was a foggy and misty morning but not cold at all. Once up the ridge, they couldn't see where they had come from.

It appeared to Abby that they had ascended the clouds to attend church, but that made sense to her since heaven was somewhere up above. She wasn't quite as mad at God as she used to be, for He had redeemed Himself a little by giving them the gold strike. But her true reason for going to church was to dress up in her fine clothes so all the young men would adore her.

Jennifer and her children found a pew near the front as a choir of four women sang like angels. She was feeling guilty, for lately they had missed more services than they'd attended. "More important" matters had for the most part shoved prayer and church aside. "Dear

Lord, forgive me," she mumbled with her eyes closed. "Seems I only come running to You when things aren't going right. Right now I don't even know what the problem is. I pray for Your guidance. Help me make right decisions. Show me the way."

"Mother!" Abby whispered, giving her mother a poke with her elbow. "Wait until church starts before you get carried away with prayin'."

Jennifer smiled. But she meant what she'd said in her prayer. She clearly felt a need for guidance.

In Reverend Blackburn's sermon on faith and works, he quoted Hebrews 13:5 by mistake: "'Let your conversation be without covetousness; and be content with such things as ye have: for he hath said, I will never leave thee, nor forsake thee.'"

This comforted Jennifer. It was just the Bible truth she most needed to hear. She felt a little better after the service, her hopes renewed.

～

Over the next few days Emmitt's comments weighed heavily on Jennifer's mind. Besides Abby and Lita, and of course her children, she didn't have any real friends in Black Hawk or Central City either. The closest thing she'd had to a good friend had been Baby Doe, who frequently came by, usually in the mornings, to chat over coffee. Jennifer found Baby Doe's personality refreshing and uplifting. Though Jennifer didn't approve of everything in Baby Doe's life, she valued their friendship.

Today rays of morning sun came through the windows and radiated across the polished wooden floor. Jennifer sat at her desk with her coffee, wishing Baby Doe was still around, wishing she had someone to talk to about current affairs and the dubious society of Central City. She remembered one morning when Baby Doe had knocked gently on the front door, eased it open, and called in her soft voice, "Jennifer, are you in?"

"Over here, Lizzie," Jennifer had answered. "Lita, could you bring Mrs. Doe some coffee?"

Baby Doe's shaky walk exhibited excitement and anticipation.

Her blue eyes twinkled, and her smile was genuine, the curls in her blonde hair bouncing with life. "I was over this way and thought I'd drop in. How are things?" she had said as she sat down, holding her purse in her lap.

Jennifer was happy to report, "What we thought was a little gold mine has turned out to be more than I ever dreamed possible. I hardly ever see Jason anymore—he practically lives up there at the mine."

"He's so handsome," Baby Doe said dreamily. "It must be wonderful to have a good man who cares about you and loves you. It's all so obvious every time you two are together."

"Yes," Jennifer agreed as she propped her elbow on the desk and rested her jaw on the back of her hand. "He's wonderful."

"You two should marry. You're rich now—there's no reason why you couldn't." Before Jennifer could respond to the touchy subject, Baby Doe rambled on, "I dream about marrying a rich man someday—I just know I will."

Lita came in carrying a silver tray of coffee cups with a pot of coffee and confections. "Good mornin', Miss Lizzie."

"Thank you, Lita," she said. "I feel good too."

"I'm happy for you," Lita added as she left the room.

"What about Jake, Lizzie? Anybody can see he's crazy about you, and he's a good businessman," Jennifer suggested. "He's very nice looking too."

"Jake?" Lizzie responded, waving him away with a sweep of her hand. "He's so sweet, and he's looked after me through some hard times. I adore him, Jennifer, like a close friend, but I'm not in love with him. But he is going to send for me soon, and I'll be moving up to Leadville. I can't wait. There's so much happening there—lots of mines and millionaires."

Jennifer tried to hold back her smile so her friend wouldn't think she was laughing at her. "It does sound like you're out to land a rich man for yourself."

"To me," Baby Doe continued, "men are like bank accounts. Without a lot of money they don't generate much interest."

Both women's laughter was beautiful, almost musical. "That's a good one," Jennifer said. "What will you do up in Leadville?"

"I can always work for Jake, but I have my sights set much higher." Pausing for a moment, she delicately took a sip of her coffee. She knew how men flocked to her, and the thought of an exciting romance lifted her spirits even higher. Then her expression changed and grew more serious. "Jennifer, why don't you go there too? You and Jason could both come, and we would have a wonderful time."

Jennifer could tell from the way Baby Doe talked and conducted herself that she had been raised by a proper family. She also recognized from the dreamy gaze in her friend's eyes that she was hoping for a fairy-tale romance that might or might not exist. She said, "I think Jason is going soon, looking for investments, but I don't know if I want to live in a new mining camp again. I've done that before, and such a town can be a wild place—not very sanitary either. But then again, that doesn't mean I can't come visit, Lizzie."

"I hope you do," Baby Doe said with an urgent appeal in her soft voice. She reached over and touched Jennifer's hand. "You're the closest friend I have. I'm going to miss you."

Although Baby Doe was several years younger than Jennifer and had the unrealistic expectations typical of her generation, their shared emotional turmoil and hopeful outlooks had created a bond between them. Their unlikely friendship had become a special friendship.

Awaking from her daydream, Jennifer realized that was the last time she had spoken to Baby Doe. She had to give the sweet young woman credit, for she was one of the most honest women she'd ever met, never hiding anything and never fearing anything including hard work. She wished the woman had a greater commitment to what the Bible said about right and wrong, but nevertheless she considered Baby Doe a true friend.

She missed Jason, and she missed Baby Doe. Surely Jason would soon let her know what was happening.

∼

Abe Washington kept busy day to day remodeling and adding on to his small church. Jennifer had made it all possible with a huge donation that he accepted bashfully but with great appreciation. The money had changed the lives of those closest to him drastically, and not always in positive ways; but he was determined to stick to his own scruples. Early morning was still his favorite time of day, for it was then that he visited with Lita and expressed his deepest feelings.

"I feel it in my bones," he said while he sat at the table one morning watching Lita prepare his breakfast. The totally remodeled kitchen was warm and comfortable, but he still missed the old kitchen with the wood stove. Lita even looked different in her new white attire—pressed cotton dresses that fit her rather snugly. "All this money—it isn't true wealth. Seems it got everybody hoppin' in different directions."

"Nobody asked you what you thought," Lita remarked, half teasing. "I notice you don't mind fixing up the church with that money Miss Jenny give you."

Befuddled, Abe often found it difficult to express his thoughts when Lita began to tease. "What I mean is, I love these people, but there could be sad happenin's comin'."

Lita knew he was right. She understood that the wealth from a gold mine could lead folks astray. "If the Lord's in it, they'll be all right."

"Amen," Abe added. A fire-and-brimstone preacher, he could put fear into the souls of most people who heard his sermons. But he wanted to preach God's love as well and usually reserved that for last. Right now he wanted to think of God's mercies, not His judgments. "I don't suppose there's any way I could warn Miss Jenny or Jason— I reckon they'll just have to find out for themselves."

"You worry too much," Lita scolded as she set a plate of fried eggs and sliced ham in front of her husband. "They got God in their souls, and He'll look out for them, mark my word."

"I just hope they listen to Him, Lita," Abe mumbled as he dug in. "I sure hope so."

CHAPTER

∼ 10 ∼

A Blaze of Glory

After writing a brief letter to Jennifer telling her he was safe and that he missed her and was looking for solid investments, Jason busily began checking out the potential investment opportunities in Leadville. Using the information he'd received from Horace Tabor and Jake Sands, he was soon walking through cold, dripping tunnels in mines that were for sale, mostly small operations with a limited budget for expansion. Tabor happily accompanied Jason as they looked over a poorly run operation known as the Baron mine, named after the similar-sounding word *barren*. One of Tabor's superintendents accompanied them, offering his expert advice. Henry Talbot was not only a man with much mining experience but was well-schooled in recognizing formations and discerning the quality of ore samples.

After a bucket ride down several hundred feet, the men depended on the lights of candles and lanterns. Water in the mine dripped with a depressing rhythm as the men plodded along in a wet stream. A steam engine chug-chugged up above, running a pump that slurped up the collecting water. The five-man day crew was all that worked the hole, and they had gone above for lunch, leaving the speculators to have a look for themselves.

"Ain't nothin' down here," Talbot said disgustedly as he picked up some of the muck and studied it. "These here signs of silver are planted—come from somewhere else. I don't see none of it in the drifts. Ain't even no vein to follow; they're just groping down here."

Jason was despondent. The depressing mine screamed from neglect. "Well, no sense wasting time here."

"Hold on," Tabor said, almost shouting. "How deep are we, Henry?"

"Oh, I'd say 200 feet or a little better."

Tabor looked at Jason, his eyes sparkling in the lantern light. "This is perfect, Jason. Most of the mines here don't hit any pay dirt until they at least reach 200 feet. They've already got a good start here for you. And with no pay dirt yet, they certainly can't be asking much for it. Take my word, son, buy it!"

"But it's salted," Jason argued.

"That's even better. We'll tell them we know, but we're still interested. That'll give us a good haggling point. What you need to do is hire a full crew of shifts around the clock. Sell off this old equipment, and put in some bigger, better, more modern pumps and engines. By golly, put in an elevator so these men can do their job. I'm telling you, this is a steal." Tabor grew even more excited as he explained his theory of how mining work was properly done. His excitement was contagious.

Turning to Henry, Jason asked, "What do you think, Henry? You think Mr. Tabor knows what he's talking about?"

Henry laughed, and his voice echoed through the shafts. "If Tabor says it'll work, believe me, it'll work. Everything he touches turns to gold—I mean silver."

Tabor laughed at his friend and at the occasion. For him, every situation was a joyful one. Earlier Jason had caught up with Tabor as the man made his way down Chestnut with a group of followers. His generosity made him an easy target for beggars, and his good-natured affluence made others want to hang around him in hopes some of his good luck would rub off on them. He was a sincere, busy man who often forgot half of his responsibilities; making an appointment with him was all but impossible. His nightlife habitually reached into the early-morning hours, but that never kept him from rising at 6 A.M.

"I don't know," Jason said uncertainly. "Could be an expensive roll of the dice."

"My good man!" Tabor said forcefully. "Any mine is a gamble! But I'm telling you, this is a sure thing. There's silver here—I can smell it. Buy this place and get it into full operation as quickly as you can. Why, I'll even loan you old Henry here, let him be in charge until things get underway and you're counting your money. A good businessman can't pass up an offer like that, now can he?"

That did it. Jason was sold. He'd heard about men who bought run-down operations and made a success of them. He'd seen George Hearst do that very thing back in Virginia City. "All right, I'll buy it. How long do you think it will take to get this thing in shape?"

"A few weeks at the most!" Tabor said. "There's equipment for sale in town that'll take care of this mine—let's go see about it right now."

Off they went, putting together the deal as they walked. The mine owner was more than happy to unload the Baron for $6,000. But the equipment and hiring a crew ran a bit more, though still mere peanuts for a millionaire. Within five days the mine was underway with a new pump and healthy steam engine. A new shaft house was built, and an elevator.

Jason waited in the shaft house as they all listened for the first blast. Tabor and Talbot stood next to him, silent and slightly stooped as if bending over would help them hear better. A muffled rumble came from below, and Tabor clapped his hands. "Hallelujah!" He reached behind him and picked up a bottle of champagne. Opening it, he sent the cork ricocheting around the room. "Where are those glasses?" he asked. Henry placed the glasses on a bench, and Tabor filled them jubilantly. "For my good friend Jason Stone! Welcome to the city of silver and wealth!" He drank a gulp, then lowered his glass. "Well, take a sip, man!"

"I'm sorry, I can't drink," Jason said apologetically. "Makes me sick."

"What a cryin' shame," Tabor scoffed. "Well, Henry, looks like we'll have to drink his share. May Lady Luck be with you, Stone!"

⌒

That was only the first mine Jason purchased in Leadville. He also bought two other shafts that were in sad shape, the Birdsong and the Water Pit. The Birdsong was several miles from town toward Fremont Pass, near the origin of the Arkansas River. It had always showed promise but had never produced enough to pay for the operation. Jason had approached it with the attitude he'd seen in Horace Tabor—throw enough money at it and anything would work. He liked the Birdsong because the air rushing through it sounded like a bird.

The Water Pit was exactly what its name implied. After studying ore samples, Jason found the mine to be rich in lead carbonate of silver. After he purchased it, he ventured to the shaft's edge. He dropped a rock, and as he'd feared, it splashed into water not far below.

"If you're the man that bought this, you done bought a good water well, even if the water ain't fit to drink."

Jason spun around to see a whiskered man standing behind him leaning on a shovel. "Who are you?"

"My name's Levi, so that's what folks call me." The man looked older than he actually was, weathered and silvered by hard times. He had an easygoing way of talking as he limped closer, using the shovel for a cane. Jason realized he had a wooden leg. His face was crowded with wrinkles, but his eyes were alert and responsive, his shoulders big and strong.

"You know about this mine?" Jason asked.

"I ought to—I dug it," Levi replied.

"I'm Jason Stone. I just bought this mine, read the assayer reports, and saw some samples that came out of it. Looks like it might have been a producer. What's with the water?"

"It's like we hit an underground river," Levi reported with great despair. "The outfit that hired me to run this mine . . . well, they made good money for a while until we hit a gusher of water. The hole filled up so fast, we almost didn't get out in time. I suspect there're several fortunes to be made down there, but it's all underwater."

For the next few moments Jason walked around, his head hung

low while kicking rocks with the toe of his boot. He had that miserable feeling of being taken. He had paid good money for this particular mine, but in his eagerness to become even richer than he already was, he had looked at samples and reports but had never viewed the actual shaft.

A sudden insight gave him new hope. "Do you live around here, Levi?"

"Sure do—right over there in that shack with the little smokestack out the side of it."

"You want to get another crack at this hole?"

Levi stared closely at Jason to see if the man in front of him was serious. He answered in a low tone, "Sure, I do, but I don't know how you'd do it."

"What about pumps, big pumps?" Jason asked, his eyes fixing on Levi.

"I don't know of no pumps big enough to handle the gallons that come into this mine."

"Listen, when the pumps come, you show them where to set up, then get a crew lined up and get it going. I'll send some men out here to build a new office, and there'll be a man here to handle payroll. Next time I come out here I want to see some heavy production. Are you with me?"

"Yahoo!" Levi screamed, stomping his wooden leg around to the jolly music playing in his head. "I done got a job with a real winner! Glory to God, a man done come along with enough gumption to move mountains and rivers!" After a few minutes of elation he settled down enough to talk. "Yes, sir, Mr. Stone, we'll make us a silver mine right here!"

Later Jason found out there were pumps big and mean enough to handle almost any amount of mine water, and he ordered two of them. He also hired a group of men, each with reputable referrals, to set up camp at the Water Pit, build an office, and get a crew and payroll established. Steam engines and pumps were soon on their way from Denver by mule train. This by far was the boldest and costliest venture he'd taken on yet. He had dealt into a game with very high stakes.

~

November brought the cruelties of winter and several feet of cold, wonderful snow. Most people were so enthralled in the excitement of the town they barely noticed the changing of the seasons. One of the biggest events had been the grand opening of the Tabor Opera House, a three-story brick affair on Harrison Avenue. And for its first production Marie Kelly and her company, owned by Jack Langrishe, did a play called *The Marble Heart.*

Horace Tabor had been elected lieutenant governor of the state of Colorado in 1878 for a two-year term. The Republicans had been anxious to put his fortune to work for public service. Often Tabor was deliberately called governor, deliberately omitting his title's prefix, but there was no doubt that he was the genuine article when it came to his royal-sounding title, the Silver King. He was erecting the Tabor Building at 16th and Larimer Streets in Denver with stone imported from Ohio and had bought the Henry P. Brown house on Broadway in Denver as his residence. But he continued to spend most of his time in Leadville, a place he loved.

Out of sheer willpower and the power of money, Jason Stone had made all three mines show a glorious profit in a very short time, and now even more money was rolling in. As he apprenticed under Tabor in the ways and management of big money, the two became close friends. Jason did all of his financial business out of Tabor's bank in Leadville.

Late one evening the curtains fell on *Two Orphans,* the theatrical performance currently running at Tabor's Opera House. Jason, Tabor, and the theater manager, Bill Bush, shared a box seat. Some compared Bush to the moss that lives on the side of a tree, the tree being Tabor. He'd bob his potato-like head and laugh at Tabor's antics.

"You know, Jason," Tabor boasted, "that Marie Kelly is one of the finest actresses I've ever seen, and if she's anything like she is on stage, she's a live one! I envy you, my young man—I certainly do!"

"Horace," Jason argued stubbornly, "if I've told you once, I've told you a hundred times—I'm engaged to another woman. There's nothing between me and Marie—we're just friends!"

"Just friends!" Tabor mocked as he elbowed his friend Bill Bush. "Why, of course. I see him having late dinners with her, I see them walking down the street together while every man in town wishes he was in Jason's shoes, but they're just friends."

Tabor and Bush laughed contemptuously as Jason fumed. Finally Tabor slapped Jason on the back. "No harm meant, Jason. We're just having a good time. I'm starved—how about you two? Let's step over to the Saddle Rock Cafe and get something to eat. I'll buy."

Though it was late and cold, the streets were jammed with festive people of all sorts. The three made their way through the crowd to the popular cafe and were quickly seated at the most prominent table, reserved especially for the governor. Jason had quickly grown fond of being treated with the dignity that came with his fortune and his wealthy acquaintants.

Once seated, Tabor ordered a bottle of champagne as usual. "You don't know what you're missing, Jason. This is not only the fruit of the grape but the fruit of life. I don't understand why you persist in drinking water."

"It keeps my complexion young," Jason joked. But he *had* taken a liking to a good cigar and promptly lit one. He was in every way a new Jason. Life had changed so drastically that he even carried himself differently, wearing the finest clothes Jake Sands could order and living the best life money could buy in Leadville. Every single one of his business moves had been a winner. The three mines in Leadville dwarfed the production of the Wild Horse back in Black Hawk, though they were very expensive to operate. Jason knew he had to watch his expenses closely.

Tabor's attention was locked somewhere across the cafe, his eyes dark and piercing. "My heavens, who is that gorgeous creature sitting by herself?" He quickly removed pen and paper from inside his jacket and began to scribble something.

Turning around in his chair, Jason could see that Tabor was referring to Baby Doe, who sat alone.

"Bill, take this note over to that lovely young woman. I'd like to ask her to join us," Tabor said, folding the paper and handing it to Bush.

"Nonsense!" Jason huffed. "I know her—that's Baby Doe. I'll go ask her to come over." Rising from his chair, Jason moved through the crowded tables.

Tabor shook his head. "That Jason must know every good-looking woman this side of Denver. How's he do it?"

"I don't know," said Bill, "but I wish I did."

Jason approached Baby Doe, and she immediately recognized him. "Jason, how are you?" she asked in her high-pitched, innocent voice.

"Fine, Lizzie. The governor would appreciate your company at his table!"

"Oh dear!" Baby Doe uttered nervously. "He's such a handsome man—I've been watching him. I saw you all come in." She offered her hand to Jason as she rose from her seat, and he escorted her over to Tabor's table.

"Horace, this is Lizzie Doe. Many refer to her as Baby Doe. Lizzie, this is Governor Horace Tabor and his theater manager, Bill Bush." Jason was the perfect gentleman.

Both Tabor and Bush jumped to their feet. "My pleasure," Tabor said, taking Baby Doe's hand. "You must be the Baby Doe of Central City I've heard so much about. Why, all of the miners here know of you. Please, sit down."

The group sat. Tabor was obviously captivated by Baby Doe. "Order anything on the menu you'd like," he offered generously. "There's no point in returning to the show when we can sit here and entertain as pretty a young lady as you, is there, Bill, Jason? Here's a little lady I'd like to get to know. Tell me all about yourself."

Jason noticed that the blood had rushed to Baby Doe's face, making her cheeks rosy. She had that love-at-first-sight look in her eyes. Soon she and Tabor were chattering like old friends. After a while Jason and Bush exchanged glances. They were both as obviously out of place as a diamond pendant hanging from a goat's neck.

"I have to be going," Jason said, rising and placing his linen napkin on his plate.

"Me too," Bush said, standing.

"Gentleman, I'll see you tomorrow," Tabor said pleasantly.

"Forgive me, but I'm afraid this beautiful young lady has cast a spell over me."

"Good night, Lizzie," Jason said as he turned to leave.

Bush walked beside him and leaned over to whisper in Jason's ear, "Look out! He's got a live one. We're in for a ride now!"

"Yeah," Jason chuckled. He saw it too.

~

Now living in the Clarendon Hotel, Jason found that business hours for the wealthy started after a late breakfast and ended in the middle of the afternoon. If you couldn't get your business handled during those hours, he'd learned from Tabor, you simply hired someone to do it. This left plenty of free time, and Marie Kelly took advantage of that fact by being forever present as a pleasant nuisance, constantly at Jason's elbow, accompanying him almost everywhere he went.

Usually up late, Jason had gotten in the habit of sleeping late during the short December days. One morning the bright winter sun blasted through his hotel window and brought him out of a deep sleep. The clock on the wall chimed nine times. Blurry-eyed, Jason crawled out of his soft double bed, shaved, and got dressed in one of his many fine suits. *Another day—another several thousand dollars*, he thought with delight.

Downstairs, he ordered coffee in the restaurant as he looked over the newspaper. His main interest lay in the mining reports, noting especially the current status of the company he had established and its productions. Since the Wild Horse mine had been his beginning, he'd named the company the Wild Horse Mining Company. Influenced by Tabor, Jason was thinking of selling stocks in his company, a move that could be manipulated for even more profits.

Just the day before, he had mailed Jennifer another complete financial report along with a personal letter reassuring her that all was well. As always, he'd told her in the last paragraph how much he missed her and how much he loved her. But sadly, her letters to him were rarely anything close to romantic and only mentioned money and business. This bothered him. He'd even invited her to come to Leadville to see the new mining works, but she'd replied that the trip was too risky in the winter—maybe next spring. Besides, someone needed to be around to look over the Wild Horse mine. She had told him about Emmitt and his despair and that Emmitt hadn't been seen for months.

"Good morning, stranger," Marie said as she plopped down at the table with Jason. "Have you ordered yet?"

"No," Jason replied dryly. Marie's showing up at precisely the right time to join Jason had become routine.

"What's got your goat?" Marie asked, teasing him with her sweet voice.

"Oh, nothing," Jason mumbled. "Just thinking about my business concerns. I'm thinking of going public, selling stocks."

"Whatever," Marie said, shrugging her shoulders. She always dressed in a most becoming way, with a splash of red and ruffles to accent her figure. This morning she wore her wavy black hair up in the current fashion, her neck showing white and soft under the ebony curls. "You take all of this too seriously, my love."

Setting his newspaper down, Jason said, "Marie, don't call me that. We're not lovers."

"Well, honey, somebody needs to love you. Looks to me like this woman you're engaged to doesn't care a lick. If she did, she'd be here."

Marie was blunt and had a way of summing up things correctly. Though in some ways she tried his patience, Jason had not only grown used to her presence but looked forward to it. Never had he known a woman who spoke her mind so easily, who pointed out the obvious in the most difficult matters, the kinds of situations others only spoke of in whispered tones. Yet she also knew how to remain mysterious and alluring in a romantic way, tantalizing and sweet. Though he well knew her kind and her tricks, he found himself growing more and more fond of her.

Jason knew she could have her pick of any man in town. After every show she was buried in sprays of roses and other expensive flowers sent to her dressing room, all accompanied by notes begging for her company. She graciously refused. She was a woman who accomplished her goals with rigid tenacity under a veil of sugar-coated kindness. She'd found Jason resistant, but his defenses were breaking down. She could see the changing look in his slate-blue eyes and often caught him staring at her.

"Jason?" Her voice had the soft and innocent sound of a young daughter getting ready to ask her father for money. "I earn a good living, but things are so expensive here . . . Do you think you could make me a small loan?"

The thoughts of business scrambled out of Jason's mind. "Are you in trouble, Marie?" His face exhibited definite concern.

"No," she said meekly. "It's just that I have an appearance to keep up—I want to look my best, especially for you. And I can't afford to keep up with women's fashions." She rolled her eyes melodramatically. "Do you think you could?"

"Loan?" Jason repeated. He liked being in this position. For once she was at his mercy. But this wasn't a moment he was going to let slide by without getting some pleasure out of it. He leaned back in his chair, their eyes locked for a long time. Her expression never wavered. Finally he smiled and said, "I'm not about to make you any loan. Just go get what you need and tell them to send me the bill."

Happiness showed in Marie's face as she shifted anxiously in her chair. Jason was so unlike other men, the common parasites she'd known in the past. Her body language flamboyant and expressive, she quickly regained control of her emotions. "But I don't know how much . . . Even one dress is rather expensive. I'm afraid I might offend you if I spend too much."

Jason wallowed in the gratification he was feeling. "I don't care," he said casually. "Spend what you want—I have more money than I know what to do with."

Dashing around the table, Marie took Jason's face in her small hands and smothered him with kisses. He alertly grabbed the small newspaper and comically swatted at her like an annoying fly. "Stop it!" he protested without much sincerity. "Go away!"

"I'll kiss you if I want," she said in between the loud smacks she was planting on his cheeks.

They both felt the close and imposing presence, and neither

minded. Jason looked past Marie to see a tall, lean waiter hovering over them. He wore a long face of bored impatience. "Shall I come back?" he asked soberly.

Something about the man struck Marie as hilarious, and she collapsed into Jason's lap in a fit of hysterical laughter. For some reason Jason thought this funny as well and let laughter get the best of him too. The waiter stood and stared, never cracking the slightest hint of a smile, his drooping face waiting for an answer. Finally, with Marie hanging all over him, Jason found his voice. "Yes, come back."

Jason and Marie looked at each other, and the contagious laughter overcame them again. By now everyone in the restaurant was staring, but neither Jason nor Marie cared. Jason gave the actress a gentle hug. Like a stalking cat, she quickly let her lips slide across his cheek to his mouth, where she stole a warm kiss. Her mouth lingered, teased, and tempted. She let him seek and find. Weakened by months of greed and denial, he couldn't find the strength to push her away. He saw a vision of Jennifer in his mind but quickly shoved the remorseful thought into a shadowy corner of his mind, shunning the resentment and guilt.

CHAPTER

~ 11 ~

The Upper Crust

P oor Jason, he must be working so hard," Jennifer said to herself as she glanced over his most recent letter. It was accompanied by a financial report of the many thousands being earned through the three different mines he'd purchased and got running. "I bet he hardly has time to sleep," she mumbled, feeling guilty. Folding the letter, she stuck it in a desk drawer. *I'll have to write him soon. Maybe he can break away and come here for Christmas,* she thought. Her feelings for Jason hadn't changed. She still loved him in a quiet sort of way, a way that was hard to communicate in a letter. She longed to see him. His presence had been like a cornerstone in her life of confusion, and now she realized it more than ever. But the huge sums of money she'd received occupied her thoughts most of the time. Her wealth had subtly become top priority in her affections.

Today she would leave for Denver, where she and Abby planned to spend a few days. The climate in Denver would be a warm and welcome relief from the biting, cold winds of Black Hawk. Since Grant was working full-time at the assayer's office, he'd declined the invitation to join his mother and sister on their trip. As for school, neither Grant nor Abby attended any longer, having completed enough to satisfy personal and community expectations. But Jennifer had insisted on buying books of further learning that she insisted her children read and study. With Grant, this was no problem, for he had a hungry mind. Abby was another story.

"I can't believe you bought me a mathematics book!" she'd said gruffly. "You know I hate math."

"It's for your own good," Jennifer had insisted. "Read a chapter; then we can go over the problems at the end of the chapter together."

"That sounds wonderful! I can't wait to do that!" Abby had said sarcastically. "This has fractions, and they're just plain stupid! I don't think *anyone* understands them!"

But at the same time Abby wasn't nearly the anxious young girl she'd once been. Her brooding had subsided, giving way to a more cheerful life of extravagance. Her expensive dresses and new hairstyles made her resemble a young, upper-class woman with means. It didn't take her long to realize there was no room for childish fits and mannerisms if she wanted to impress the upper class.

"What time does the train leave?" Abby now asked pleasantly, trying to hide her excitement.

"At ten o'clock," Jennifer answered. "Are you all packed?"

"I can't wait," Abby readily admitted. "I'm sick of this town. Denver has so many nice things, and I can't wait to see them."

Nodding, Jennifer smiled. Abby seemed to have grown up overnight. Her radiant and youthful beauty astonished Jennifer every time she looked at her. Jennifer hoped she could guide Abby so she would avoid the heartaches Jennifer had known in her own previous relationships. Now that the relationship between mother and daughter had deepened, they talked freely about even the most sensitive issues. Jennifer felt hope, and Abby had found a close friend.

∾

"Lita, we're off," Jennifer said hurriedly as she checked her handbag to make sure all was in order. The luggage sat piled at the front door as they waited for a carriage to take them to the train station.

"Miss Jenny, you be careful now. That's a big city," Lita warned.

"I'm sure we'll be perfectly fine. We should be back in a few weeks—don't you worry."

Turning away, Lita grabbed a brown paper sack with grease stains near the bottom. "This here is just in case you get hungry. I fried some apple pies." She handed Jennifer the heavy little sack. Making sure everyone stayed fed was her way of showing affection.

Understanding this, Jennifer accepted the sack with gratitude. "Thank you, Lita. We'll miss you."

"I'll miss ya'll too, honey," Lita said as she wrapped her arms around Jennifer's neck and patted her on the back. "All this big money done got everyone going in every which direction." She backed away. "Don't forget to read your Bible."

"Oh, I almost forgot it. Abby, would you run up to my room and get it for me? It's beside my bed," Jennifer asked, turning to Abby.

As Abby scampered away, Jennifer again looked at Lita. "Is there anything I can get for you in Denver?"

"Oh no, ma'am," Lita cried. "There's more than I can keep up with around here now with all this new stuff. Ya'll go on and have a good time. We'll be all right."

A carriage pulled up out front, and Jennifer opened the door. It was a bright day, and a cool breeze rushed through the opening. Holding her head high, she enjoyed the anticipation of the trip to Denver.

As she watched the carriage pull away a few minutes later, Lita stood on the front porch wringing her hands. "Lord, watch after Your children," she whispered mournfully. "Keep 'em thinkin' 'bout You, Lord!"

∽

Robust, high-living Denver, playground of Colorado's wealthiest and Europe's most bored society, gave an outward impression of, "All that is wanted is available here." The hotels, theaters, and nightlife were surpassed by no other. In fact, Denver's transformation from raw frontier town to metropolitan society had made the front pages of Eastern newspapers. And the local newspapers, the *Rocky Mountain News* and the *Denver Post*, reported almost daily on the exciting adventures of the well-to-do, monitoring their every move.

Arriving at the stately new Windsor Hotel, Jennifer and Abby disembarked carrying frilly parasols and entered a reception area decorated with modern lavishness. She began to introduce herself to a man behind the main desk when she was rudely interrupted.

"Miss DeSpain," a young man cried, waving his hand at her. He approached quickly. "I'm Eric Dawson, *Rocky Mountain News*. May I ask you a few questions?"

Baffled by this young man's interest, Jennifer stopped in the lobby, Abby beside her. "Well, I suppose so. What sort of questions?"

Dawson ran his hand over his shiny black hair in nervous excitement. Usually the rich brushed him off, but fortunately he'd found a novice. "Just the usual questions for the society page. I heard you were coming, and I'd like to welcome you to Denver."

The little man removed a pencil from behind his ear, produced a tablet from inside his coat pocket, and began to scribble. "Are you staying long? Is this your daughter? Will you be attending any of the parties—I mean, social affairs? Are you here to buy land for a house here in Denver? Are you . . . ?"

"Slow down!" Jennifer entreated. "I can only answer one question at a time. Abby and I decided to visit, that's all. We might do a little shopping, maybe even go to the theater. I'm not sure." The attention from a major newspaper brought a lovely smile to her face. She watched the excited little man write as fast as he could.

"I take it this is a trip of leisure then?" he asked, glancing up, unaware he was staring at her friendly smile.

"No, we came down here to chop firewood," Abby said sarcastically.

"Ha ha," the man said, smiling and pointing his pencil at Abby. "That's very funny."

Abby turned the other way, not a hint of a smile on her face. This nervous little man annoyed her.

Moving on, Jennifer tried to get around the reporter so she could turn back to the desk to check in. She didn't want to be rude and run him off, and detecting this, he kept up with his stupid questions while Jennifer registered and had a bellboy take their luggage. She finally said, "We'll be going up to our room now."

"Look for this article in tomorrow's paper," Dawson shouted as Jennifer and Abby walked off.

"What a pest!" Abby remarked.

Not listening, Jennifer's head was in the clouds. "I'd never have thought the society page would be interested in us."

"Who cares?" Abby said.

~

Along with Denver's rapid growth and desire for affluence and fortune came new types of criminals—the swindler, the confidence man, the bunco steerer. Jefferson Randolph Smith had come to Cherry Creek looking for riches. His game in the beginning involved bars of soap. Setting up his box on a street corner, Smith drew a curious crowd as he picked up a bar of soap, appeared to wrap around it a twenty dollar, fifty dollar, or one hundred dollar bill, and then quickly enclosed the currency-wrapped soap in plain blue paper. He'd call to the onlookers, "Come on, gentlemen, cleanliness is next to godliness—buy a cake of soap and maybe get the richest bath you ever had. Five dollars can get you a hundred! Step up and clean up!" In a few minutes one onlooker would push through the crowd and lay down his five dollars. Carefully selecting his cake of soap from the pile, he'd rip off the paper and triumphantly hold aloft a crisp hundred dollar bill. The suckers bit, buying all the merchandise—and finding nothing but a five cent bar of soap.

Having just returned from Leadville where he had expanded his operations, "Soapy" Smith sat reading the morning newspaper in his hotel suite with his sidekick, Joe Simmons. Soapy had a friendly and likable face that assured his victims of his sincerity and honesty. His slight, dancing eyebrows and simple, expressive eyes shone convincingly above his black beard and mustache.

"Say, Joe, did you see this in the morning paper?" Soapy asked as he continued to read. "Says here that a Jennifer DeSpain and her daughter Abby are visiting our fair city. Says her newly found riches from a gold mine up in Black Hawk have made her a society wonder in that she's friendly but mysterious. She won't say what her business here is." He laid the paper in his lap as he sat on a plush, feather-filled chair. "Sounds like a woman who needs my financial services, doesn't it, Banker Joe?"

Joe laughed. "What are you going to do, offer to take all of that money off her hands?"

"Of course. I'll offer the best interest rates available and dividends for certificates that nobody can match. Get one of the boys to follow her and keep me posted. When she and her daughter have dinner, be sure to get me the table beside them."

"This ought to be good," Joe commented as he put his coat on and left.

"Oh, I'm good all right," Soapy mumbled as his mind began calculating.

~

That evening Jennifer and Abby were enjoying their meal in the hotel restaurant after a whirlwind day of shopping and sightseeing.

"I hope we can go on one of those fancy carriage rides tomorrow," Abby said as she gorged herself on cold shrimp set in a dish of fresh lettuce and cocktail sauce. "These things are good." The excitement of the day had made her hungry.

"I used to think nothing of having shrimp when I was your age," Jennifer observed. "Shrimp in New Orleans is like beef in Texas. I wonder how they get them up here and keep them fresh?"

The man at the very next table stood and approached Jennifer. He had a black beard and young, friendly eyes; a smile accented his face. He held up the newspaper in his hand and asked, "Might you be Miss DeSpain, and is this your daughter Abby?"

"Yes," Jennifer replied, surprised.

"Allow me—I'm Jefferson Smith of Smith Bank and Trust. I couldn't help but notice you." He held up the newspaper. "I was just reading about you. I must say, the author of this article forgot to mention how lovely you are."

Slightly blushing, Jennifer dabbed her mouth with a white napkin. "Thank you. I'm afraid the article was a bit too flattering. We're just here to visit and have a little fun."

"Please, may I join you for a moment, Miss DeSpain?" Pulling out a chair, Soapy sat down, eager to spill his information. "I've read so much about you in the newspapers, I feel as if I know you. That must be some mine you have up there! I hear it's the prettiest gold ore in these parts."

Reluctant to offer information to this bold character, Jennifer said hastily, "It pays the bills."

"And then some, I imagine!" Soapy added happily. "I was wondering, have you thought of investing with any banks? I offer the best rates going right now. We even sell certificates, and nobody can match the interest I'm offering." Suddenly Soapy slapped his palm against his forehead as if reprimanding himself. "Where are my manners! Disturbing a beautiful lady and her lovely daughter at the dinner table with boring business talk! Maybe we can talk later; perhaps you'd be interested in what I have to offer." The seed was planted.

"Oh, that's all right," Jennifer said. "You're not imposing. Actually, most of our efforts are being invested in mining in Leadville right now."

"Is that right?" Soapy said, acting surprised. "I've just returned from Leadville—opened some offices there. It's a fine place, and I'm sure you won't regret your ventures there. Have you had the chance to go to Leadville yourself?"

"Not yet," Jennifer said. "I hear it's a wild and woolly place."

"That it is," Soapy agreed. He noticed Abby was staring at him. "A pretty young lady like you—why, you ought to be on stage entertaining!"

Abby smiled at the thought. However, she didn't know what she would do to "entertain."

"So, Mr. Smith, do you have a bank here in Denver?" Jennifer continued.

"Yes, but maybe not like you picture. We're investment bankers. We don't have tellers and windows."

"Interesting," Jennifer said. Out of the corner of her eye she could see that a tall man with receding black hair and a black walrus mustache was moving toward her table. There was a resolute gait in his step, his dark eyes beaming at the man sitting across from her.

He arrived at the table and placed a firm hand on Mr. Smith's shoulder.

"Soapy, I'll not have you swindling my guest in my hotel!" he said intensely.

"But, Governor Tabor, you know I run a legitimate operation!" Soapy asserted.

"Then you won't mind taking your legitimate business elsewhere, will you?"

Standing, Soapy rapped the folded newspaper into the clenched fist of his other hand. "Tabor, you shouldn't be interfering—it's not right," he said contemptuously. "Besides, you don't own this hotel."

"I lease it!" Tabor sneered. "I'm asking you to leave politely, Soapy. Don't make me call the house detective."

Pulling his mouth into a tight line, Soapy glared at Tabor. Finally he backed down and dropped his angry expression like a hot potato, then turned and smiled at Jennifer. "So nice to have met you, Miss DeSpain. Perhaps some other time." He turned and left hurriedly.

Tabor placed both his hands on the table and leaned over close so as not to be overheard. "That man is Soapy Smith, con artist and swindler. You'd do well to stay clear of him."

Jennifer was so amazed that the lieutenant governor of the state, Horace Tabor, had so dramatically stepped in and kept her from possible future grief that she hardly knew what to say. "I'm most grateful, Governor Tabor," she said wistfully.

"I didn't see what was wrong with him," Abby blurted out. "He seemed like a nice man."

Tabor kindly said, "That's right—that's how these unscrupulous men work. They gain your confidence and trust, and the next thing you know they've double-crossed you. It's an old game."

"Thank you again," Jennifer said.

"You are most welcome, madam," Tabor said, offering her his hand. "I'm sorry, I didn't get your name."

"DeSpain. Jennifer DeSpain."

"So pleased to have met you. Perhaps you'd care to join me in my box at the theater sometime—I'll be in touch," Tabor said, then graciously walked back to his table to join a stolid, long-faced woman with dark hair. When Tabor sat down, the woman expressed a fiery displeasure.

"Wonder what's wrong with her?" Abby said, making a face as she watched the woman scold Tabor. "He's a real nice man."

Jennifer rolled her eyes away from Tabor, still mesmerized by what had happened. "Must be his wife," she said. "Some women are possessive."

"I'd say she's mean," Abby observed with a keen eye. "Maybe he should get a new wife."

"Maybe he will," Jennifer said jokingly.

~

Grant was completely happy with his world, except for some old questions that still annoyed him. The evening had settled on Black Hawk like an old tarp; a layer of winter clouds had moved in from the north. After dinner with Abe and Lita, he retired to his room to bury himself in his books. He loved books. With Jason, Jennifer, and Abby gone, the place was sort of lonely, but he kept himself busy to hold the loneliness at bay. He figured the books, like the rocks at the assayer's office, might hold some clues as to why people went crazy over gold and silver and riches. In the past, working at the newspaper had given him insights into people, but now he was pursuing answers in different ways.

He had learned that the ore attracted another sort of character to the frontier mining camps as well—outlaws who became famous for their evil exploits. To learn more about them, Grant had purchased a handful of dime novels describing the notorious gunmen. He shuffled through the stack of books until he came to one that struck his interest, *The Adventures of Jesse James.* Flipping through the pages in the dank light of his kerosene lantern, he skimmed over the story. Within moments Grant was absorbed in the tale of the James brothers and their outlaw ways.

Grant heard the shuffling of feet before someone knocked on his door. "Grant, honey?" Lita inquired tentatively.

"Come in, Lita," Grant said, setting the book down.

Lita showed her face in the crack of the door, then let herself in.

"Me and Abe was wonderin' . . . it's kind of lonely 'round here . . . we thought you might want to join us down at the kitchen table for some Bible readin'. Might be a piece of pie down there somewhere too."

"Sure, Lita," Grant said as he sprang off the bed.

Lita was continually surprised at how fast Grant was growing. He seemed to have gained another inch since she'd noticed last. His face had the shadow of a day's growth. Almost sixteen, his shoulders were wide and strong, his waist narrow. Trying to fill him with food was like trying to fill an open mine shaft. His full head of wavy auburn hair had reddened, and his eyes were as striking as his mother's but in a manly sort of way. Lita was proud of him—he was becoming a responsible, respectable young man with character.

Down in the kitchen, Abe sat at the new oak dinner table by the light of a candle, his Bible open. He wore a small pair of spectacles as he read silently. Old age had crept up on him like darkness at the dusk of day. His hair had whitened, and his big, strong shoulders had a slight stoop. He moved more slowly but with more assurance; the old timid Abe had long departed. The new Abe was a confident man who taught about the Gospel of Christ with authority.

"Come on in here, Grant," Abe said, pulling out a chair for him. He gazed up at him as he sat down. "You're a young man now—things gonna change for you."

"They already are," Grant mumbled.

Lita filed in behind Grant and checked the coffeepot to see how full it was. She cut some pie to go with it. "Anybody like some coffee?"

"Just a sip," Grant replied, his eyes sparkling in the candlelight.

"But there's one thing that always stays the same, and you can depend on it," Abe said, addressing Grant.

"What's that, Abe?"

"Folks are creatures of habit, and they don't like change none, but things change. The only thing that stays the same and never changes is the Lord. He is the only one we can depend on."

Grant thought about this in connection with how changed people were by the silver and gold they mined. The Lord's never changing was good, a foundation to build his life on. "How come people change so much, Abe? What's in the rocks that makes them lose all their common sense?"

Abe knew the answer, but he had to think about how to explain it so Grant could understand. "I reckon it comes from man's sin nature. It must come from things like lust and greed and covetousness, things like that."

"I can see that, but it still doesn't make any sense to me. People sell everything they have and bring their families out here expecting a life of luxury, but once they're here their life is terrible. Can't they see this ahead of time?"

"I reckon not," Abe said, removing his small glasses and wiping his eyes with his big fingers. He replaced his glasses carefully on his wide nose. The candle reflection shone off his forehead as he thumbed through his Bible.

"This might help you understand, Grant. In Luke 12:15 Jesus says, 'Take heed, and beware of covetousness: for a man's life consisteth not in the abundance of the things which he possesseth.' That's the mistake right there—folks think life is about their possessions." He quickly fanned through more pages in his worn Bible until he came to the passage he was looking for. He studied it, then said, "In Mark 8:36 Jesus says, 'For what shall it profit a man, if he shall gain the whole world, and lose his own soul?'"

"That's right," Lita said as she sat at the table with her hands in her lap. "Ain't nobody gonna take it with them when they die."

Grant swallowed a piece of pie and frowned as a question came to mind. "The Bible has the answers and the warnings, but nobody listens. People risk their lives to get in on the riches in these mining towns. Maybe it's the appeal of money that I don't understand—it never meant that much to me. Sooner or later the things you buy wear out. Nothing lasts forever."

"Things in the heart can last," Lita agreed gently. "Especially love."

"That's right," Abe said. "And love is from God."

Grant recognized the truth of all this, but it didn't satisfy his curiosity. The mystery was only partly solved.

"We don't always know what the right thing to do is," Lita said sleepily. "That's why we have to read God's Word and trust Him to guide us." She glanced at Abe. "Say a prayer, honey."

After an uplifting prayer, Abe shut his Bible and said, "Amen. See you in the morning, Grant."

"Good night, Abe. Good night, Lita," Grant said. He left the kitchen, softly closing the door behind him.

"There's a lot of good in that young man," Abe commented as he removed his glasses and set them on the table. "He's a searcher, and he ain't gonna quit until he finds the answers."

"We best keep asking the Lord to help him find his callin'," Lita added. "We best keep prayin'."

Misplaced Affection

Baby Doe sat at her usual table having her usual late lunch in the Saddle Rock Cafe—all of her expenses now taken care of by Horace Tabor. She found that Tabor was all she thought of; and as for poor Jake Sands, well, Tabor had been most astute in helping her write a letter to inform Sands that Baby Doe no longer had an interest in him. Tabor had even offered Sands a check to repay him for his trouble, but Jake wouldn't accept it.

Usually wearing a huge, dazzling diamond on his long finger and diamond cuff links, Tabor made one fortune after another. The constant trips between Leadville and Denver left Baby Doe in a whirlwind of despair and joy. The problem was, Tabor was still married, and that gave Denver's society plenty to talk about. He was busy with mining properties in Aspen, Rico, and Ouray and was building the Tabor Grand Opera in Denver, the most stylish theater west of the Mississippi. This made Baby Doe feel like she was only a small part of the great man's life, and she resented that. Some even referred to her as his mistress, which offended her since there was so much more to their relationship—she was in love with Tabor and he with her.

Above the low roar of the restaurant crowd Baby Doe heard the giggling and laughing of what sounded like a young girl. But when she looked up, she saw Jason Stone and Marie Kelly acting like a couple of adolescent schoolchildren, carrying on like they hadn't a trouble in the world.

She's sure got a hook in him! Baby Doe thought with remorse. *Poor Jennifer. If she only knew, maybe she could do something about it.* At the same time, as she watched the couple she envied their carefree happiness. A vague jealousy gave rise to envy toward the attractive young Marie Kelly. *I think I'll write Jennifer a letter. I don't have to tell her everything, just enough to give her something to think about.* But then Baby Doe realized that she was in a similar situation with Horace Tabor. What if someone were to write Augusta, Tabor's wife, informing her of the way Baby Doe and Horace were carrying on in Leadville? But news of the great man traveled quickly anyway. She'd been told that Tabor's wife was already aware of Baby Doe and that she readily ridiculed him, even in public places. Her round blue eyes squinted at the woman who was showing such affection for Jason.

~

In December Jason decided he needed to make a brief trip back to Black Hawk. Unsettled feelings deep in his chest kept him awake at night, and he had to get some things settled. Jennifer hadn't written him much lately, and apparently she and Abby were spending quite a bit of time in Denver. He worried that she might be drifting away, that he might lose her to some Lance Rivers type who came swooping down like a predatory bird.

Of course, he also wrestled with his feelings for Marie Kelly. The shapely gold digger had wormed her way into his life, and he couldn't deny he loved her attention. She was so attentive and affectionate, so thoroughly enticing . . . She was the opposite of the reserved Jennifer, who preferred to remain behind her protective wall. And yet Jennifer had what Marie didn't—class and character. She was a woman of depth, the kind of woman a man would want for his wife.

"I have to go back to Black Hawk—but only briefly," Jason told Marie one day. They were sitting in the lobby of the Clarendon Hotel, where they both stayed in fancy suites. Jason removed a cigar from his satin vest pocket and lit it in a showy way.

Marie's eyes glared with the ferocity of a building on fire. "You're going back to see *her*, aren't you?" She had a temper like dynamite with a short fuse. "What does that fickle woman care about you?"

Making a face of complete disgust, Jason took a long puff on the cigar and blew the smoke high above them. "You don't know her, Marie, so don't say anything. If I want to go see her, I will!" Wealth and power had turned Jason into a man who did as he pleased. He answered to no one, especially to a manipulator like Marie Kelly.

Marie realized that her grasp on Jason was slipping, and she was willing to do anything to regain her dominance. "If you go," she said tenaciously, "I might not be here for you when you come back."

"Suit yourself," Jason said, just as determined and stubborn as she was for once. At the same time, though he wouldn't admit it, he felt a twinge of regret. He did not want to lose Jennifer, but he also did not wish to lose Marie. Not yet.

Glaring, she sat with her mouth pulled into a tight frown. This was a standoff, and she knew it; a mistake now could be fatal. Seeing that her temper would do her no good in this situation, she decided on a different line of attack. "Jason," she said softly, the sparkle coming back into her eyes as she pressed closer, "there's something I must tell you. I had hoped to wait, but now . . ." She drew her face close to his. "I love you, Jason Stone, and I don't want to lose you. I love you so much that I just want you to be happy, even if it means losing you to another woman. You can't imagine how difficult it is for me to say this."

Jason felt weak and remorseful. Perhaps he'd misjudged Marie.

"I'll always wait for you," she continued, her eyes glossy and her voice low. "I've never been in love before. I had no idea something so wonderful could be so painful." She dropped her glance and reached in her purse for something to dab at her tearful eyes.

Jason felt terrible. Unable to think of any appropriate words, he tapped his cigar over a nearby ashtray. The situation had become a little too intense for anything contrived, so he did the only thing he could think of—speak in complete honesty. "Marie," he said softly, setting down the cigar and taking her by her small shoulders, "this is something I have to do. If I don't, I will never know if I did the right thing. I wouldn't expect anything less of you if you were in the same situation." He stared into her lovely eyes. Her expression reflected deep inner pain, and that pierced him.

"All right," she agreed, apparently hurt. She stood to leave, as if the pain was too much for her. "I hope you'll be back soon."

"I will," Jason said, standing and looking down at her. He reached for her, but she walked off. As he watched her leave, he felt ashamed for hurting her.

That did the trick! she thought as she walked away, still dabbing at her already dry eyes.

～

The winter ride over the mountains was decent for December but nevertheless rough and bone-jarring. Jason expected to surprise Jennifer since he was arriving unannounced. He thought she would throw herself into his arms and all would be well. He couldn't wait to see her, smell her, feel her touch.

The hired carriage pulled up in front of the remodeled office, and Jason dragged the luggage onto the boardwalk. He quickly threw a coin to the driver.

"Thanks, Mr. Stone!" the driver called in appreciation for the excellent tip.

Jason jiggled the front doorknob in his hand, trying to get it open. Surely Jennifer was just inside and was already rushing for the door. His heart fluttered; he couldn't wait to feel the warmth of her kiss. Somebody was on the other side of the doorknob, unlatching the lock, and he felt the door pull and open. "Jennifer!"

But it was Lita. "Why, Mister Jason, what you doin' here?"

"Lita!" Jason said excitedly, some disappointment in his voice. Nevertheless he was glad to see her and hugged her enthusiastically. She smelled like fried chicken—the best fried chicken ever. "Where's Jennifer?"

Backing away so she could see Jason better, Lita announced sadly. "She and Abby gone to Denver."

"Do you know when she'll be back?"

"Said maybe in a week or so," Lita guessed.

"Oh no! That's just great!" Jason said, exasperated and exhausted.

"You get on in here and rest up. I got some chicken fryin', and Mister Grant will be home soon. Ain't no sense in frustratin' yourself."

Jason looked like somebody had knocked the wind out of him. "You're right, Lita. I'll grab my things and go clean up."

Lita turned, watching Jason lug his bags past her. His disappointment was obvious. She felt sorry for him; he'd expected to surprise his love.

At dinner Jason was in much better spirits as he told the others about grand and glorious Leadville. Jason loved to tell the story of fortune and fame and his personal success with three different mines. He had Grant's total interest. Even Abe and Lita enjoyed hearing about the big boomtown above the clouds.

"And that Governor Tabor's a sight," Jason was saying with unyielding enthusiasm. "He's got so much silver and money that they call him the Silver King."

"Well, Mister Jason, how's Miss Lizzie doin'? You see her up there, don't you?" Lita asked. Her concern was genuine, for she'd grown fond of the humble young lady when she visited Jennifer.

A mischievous smile turned Jason's lips. "I dare say, Lita, I believe Baby Doe has found her a man."

Lita clapped her hands in good-hearted surprise. "Good for her," she said. "She need a good man." Then her tone changed. "Is he a *good* man, Mister Jason?"

By now Jason was finding it hard to restrain his laughter. "I should say so—he's the lieutenant governor of the state!"

"Oh my!" Lita exclaimed, turning to Abe who was listening closely. "But . . . that'd be Governor Tabor, and he's married!"

"I'm afraid that's right, Lita. But who knows? Their relationship may not be ill-fated. Horace told me he and his wife haven't gotten along in years, long before he met Lizzie. He said the only reason his wife wanted to stay with him was because he'd hit it big and made a lot of money." Jason reached for another chicken breast.

"That don't make it right," Lita concluded. "If God ain't in it, nothin' good can come of it. Miss Baby Doe could get herself in a mess of trouble."

"Amen," Abe said. "I done lived long enough to see that."

"So are you going to Denver to look for Mother?" Grant asked, wanting to change the subject.

"Yeah. I guess I'll go in the morning," Jason said. "I didn't come all of this way not to see her."

"Care if I go?" Grant asked.

"You're more than welcome," Jason answered. "We have a lot to catch up on, and good company always makes the trip more enjoyable."

"I know she'll be glad to see you," Lita stated. "If she'd know'd you were comin' I'm sure she would've been here."

"I'm sure she would," Jason agreed, though he wasn't really so sure.

~

The train's brakes squealed all the way down Clear Creek as Grant filled Jason in on his growing abilities as an assayer. Grant was proud to again be with Jason; it was like the reunion of long-lost friends. But soon Jason was hypnotized by the grand view from his window and became lost in memories. Noticing this, Grant grew silent.

It seemed like a hundred years ago, and seemed like only a matter of days, since they'd first made their venture up Clear Creek to Black Hawk. Things had looked so promising at that time. Then came the torturous winter with its affliction and pain. He quickly put aside those memories and thought of more pleasant ones. Images of Jennifer's smiling face invaded his thoughts and filled him with anticipation. "You're sure they're staying at the Windsor Hotel?" he asked Grant. The sound of overworked brakes pierced the air again.

"That's where she always stays," Grant answered.

"I forgot how beautiful it is in these parts," Jason said, turning again to the window.

"Yeah," Grant agreed flatly. Jason's previous quietness and tension made him feel uncomfortable, but he didn't know how to verbalize it.

Arriving at the Windsor Hotel, Jason tipped a boy to handle

their luggage as he rushed to the clerk, a snippy little man with quick movements and heavy glasses. "Is a Jennifer DeSpain registered here?"

The man looked at him cross-eyed through his thick spectacles. "I'm sorry, sir, we don't give out that information."

Jason sighed with disgust. "She's my fiancée."

"And she's my mother!" Grant protested.

"It's against policy," the stubborn desk clerk said, obviously distrusting the curious men.

Jason sighed with disgust, then suddenly lightened. He removed his vest wallet and pulled out a twenty dollar bill, then stuffed it in the man's vest pocket. "Now, what room did you say they were in."

The man studied the ledger and said, "Room 221."

"Can you put us in an adjacent room?" Jason inquired.

"Of course, sir," he said, spinning the register around. "Sign here please."

After Jason and Grant got their things settled in their room, they returned to the lobby and waited for Jennifer, not realizing how long they would have to wait.

The sun had reached the distant mountains when Jennifer and Abby finally appeared, a porter carrying many boxes behind them. Jason jumped to his feet and grabbed her shoulders with both hands. Jennifer, tired and unsuspecting, was startled. She stared at him until her apprehension gave way to recognition. "Jason!" They fell into an immediate embrace.

Abby watched impatiently, then gave Grant an irritated glance. "You'd think they could behave in public."

Grant smiled. He liked what he saw.

Jennifer hugged him again. "I didn't know you were coming—we've been out shopping." She drank in his handsome face, her eyes taking in every feature. "I'm so glad you're here."

If Jason had had any doubts about their relationship, they now rapidly disappeared. He'd forgotten how gorgeous she was, and he didn't want to stop holding her as they moved across the lobby. "How about a big dinner? I'm buying," he announced.

"Oh, well . . ." Jennifer said as though she'd forgotten something.

"We have plans—Abby and I have been invited to the theater, and we shouldn't disappoint our host."

"Must be somebody very important," Jason said, disappointed but trying to be patient.

"I should say so—it's the governor . . . Well, actually, I guess, the lieutenant governor!"

"Horace Tabor?" Jason laughed. "Well, Grant and I will get into our fancy duds and join you and your governor, Mrs. DeSpain!" He howled with laughter, enough to cause people in the lobby to stare with disapproval.

Jennifer's face showed her confusion. "But he has a private box. Wouldn't bringing additional guests be bad manners?"

"Trust me," Jason said. "When are we supposed to meet the governor?"

"At seven o'clock," Jennifer answered, studying Jason skeptically. Perhaps he'd lost his common sense in his fairy-tale journey to wealth.

With renewed energy, Jason headed for his room to change clothes and freshen up for the evening. He couldn't have been happier.

"Is he all right?" Jennifer asked Grant, certain he would inform her of any ill health.

"That's just Jason," was Grant's reply as he marched off, following him.

Abby sighed, "Men! They never grow up."

❧

Once again loitering in the lobby, this time dressed in their fanciest suits, Grant and Jason looked like two penguins. Jason checked his gold pocket watch, then slipped a cigar from his vest and lit it.

"I didn't know you smoked cigars," Grant observed curiously.

"Not just any cigar," Jason said, puffing on the black cheroot. "These are imported, the best money can buy."

"Oh," Grant mumbled. A sudden thought occurred to him. Was he seeing the crazy change in Jason, the kind of change that gold and silver did to people? That prospect frightened him.

After a while the women showed up dressed in new styles Jason had never seen before. Jennifer's dress was the boldest thing he'd ever seen her wear, a low-cut gown with a lot of lace. She wore a fur over her bare shoulders and a small hat on her head. His heart skipped a beat, and he felt a lump in his throat. *She's so beautiful!*

Abby looked pretty too. Her movements were those of a young woman, not a little girl. The way she batted her eyes, her pouting lips, the slight hint of a smile—she would certainly catch the attention of all the young men who saw her. Grant couldn't believe this was the same rude and obnoxious Abby he'd grown up with. But he was glad she was growing up and was proud to be seen with her.

Jason took Jennifer's arm, and Grant took Abby's as he stared at her. "Still want to be a dance hall girl?" he asked, but his smile made it clear he was teasing.

Abby made a face at Grant, then let her expression go back to that of innocent beauty. "I prefer being a lady," she answered.

In the dining room the four waited for Governor Tabor. When he finally arrived, Jason had his back to the approaching man and tried to hide a child's mischievous smile as he hunched down so as not to be recognized.

"I'll introduce you," Jennifer said, her sincere smile having now been replaced by uneasy apprehension.

As Tabor came closer, he extended his hand toward Jennifer as if asking her to dance. "Miss DeSpain and Abby, good evening!" His sharp eyes quickly darted to Grant and then to the back of the head of the other man at the table.

"Governor, I want to introduce you to my fiancé," Jennifer said.

Jason turned around and came to his feet with his hand extended for a shake. "So pleased to meet you, Governor!"

Tabor leaned back and howled with unrestrained laughter, and Jason joined in. Then Tabor threw an arm around Jason and slapped him again and again on the back. "You rascal! I thought you were up to your eyeballs in silver ore!"

"I am, Horace—practically buried in it. I take it you've already met my fiancée, Jennifer."

Tabor was still laughing but now felt a little confused as well. His thoughts swiftly shifted back to Leadville where he'd grown used to seeing Jason with Marie. Searching for the proper thing to say, a look of consternation appeared on his face.

Jennifer wondered at the look on Tabor's face. "Shall we?" Tabor asked, suggesting with a wave of his hand that they depart.

"How do you know each other?" Jennifer asked. "From Leadville?"

"Jason has been the perfect understudy, and I'm sure he'll inhabit my perch someday," Tabor said joyfully. "He's a good one, Jennifer. Better hang on to him."

Jason happily escorted Jennifer, pleased with his clever surprise and overjoyed at once again enjoying Jennifer's company.

Meanwhile, Jennifer wrestled with the little cry of warning she'd discerned in what Tabor had said: *"Better hang on to him." What'd he mean by that? Is there a chance I could lose Jason?*

~

The grand sights and sounds of Denver were left behind on the plains as they all returned to Black Hawk. Their conversation had now shifted to business and money, investments and fortunes to be made. The Wild Horse mine was continuing to make a substantial profit, and Jason needed to return to Leadville to check their investments there.

"Why don't you come with me, Jennifer? We can celebrate Christmas in Leadville." Jason wanted Jennifer to return with him, though he feared the complication of the temptress, Marie Kelly.

"I'm not up to that kind of trip in a stage over the mountains in the winter. And I'm not particularly interested in staying in a new boomtown where things aren't very sanitary yet. Why don't you stay here and spend Christmas with us, then go back afterwards?"

"I guess I worry too much," Jason explained. "We have a lot invested there, and I'm afraid if I'm gone too long I might return to find it's all been stolen from me somehow or other. You know how things are in a place like that. I've hired men I can trust, but with so much money at their fingertips . . ."

"Maybe Abby and I can come up there this spring when the heavy snows are finished," Jennifer said unhappily.

Jason didn't like the idea of their being apart all winter. "The trip is long and hard this time of year, but I might be able to sneak back between winter storms."

Jennifer leaned heavily on Jason's shoulder. "Why don't we sell everything and move away from here? We can do anything, go anywhere."

This sounded like a proposal to Jason, and he spun around to face her. "Does this mean we'll get married?" he asked, afraid she'd say no.

Still in love with Jason, and yet still afraid of a permanent commitment, Jennifer wasn't sure what to say. "There's so much happening right now . . . We know how we feel about each other, and yet we're managing mines on different sides of the mountains." She hesitated, thinking, then looked Jason in the eye. "I'm sorry . . . I don't mean to . . . I don't know what I'm trying to say. Perhaps we can plan on something more definite next spring."

Quickly taking her in his arms, Jason asked, "Do you mean it? Can we set a date for next spring?"

"Yes . . . next spring," she said quietly, content to be in his arms.

"Jennifer DeSpain," Jason said happily, "I love you!" He gave her a jubilant kiss.

Jennifer enjoyed the moment, even as she hoped she wasn't making another mistake.

⁓

After their return home, Grant announced he wanted to go to Leadville with Jason. Everyone agreed that the skills he'd learned in the assayer's office would come in handy. "You'll like it there," Jason had said. "It's a wild place, but there's plenty of work to do."

When Grant had informed Mr. Potter he'd be leaving, the old man dejectedly ran his wrinkled hand over his bald head. "I'm going to miss you, Grant. I've grown fond of you. You've got a good head— use it wisely." He took Grant's hand and slowly pumped it two or three times.

"Thanks for everything, Mr. Potter. You've been a good teacher, you've taught me a lot, and I'll always remember you."

The old man smiled as Grant left.

Before Jason and Grant left for Leadville, the family attended church together. Reverend Blackburn's sermon on the evils of temptation made Jason feel guilty and unfit to be in God's house. *I haven't even thought about God lately,* Jason thought regretfully. He bowed his head and prayed for God's forgiveness and grace. Most of all, he thanked God for Jennifer and promised to stay true to her.

Later, after one of Lita's wonderful Sunday dinners, it was time for Jason and Grant to depart. "I hate this," he told Jennifer as he held her in his arms. "I wish you'd come with me."

She looked forlorn and wistful. Without Jason around, her life had been nothing but busily doing this and that, a life without much purpose or satisfaction. "I'm afraid the winter months will keep us apart."

"We'll see," Jason answered. "We'll come back to visit when we can."

Jennifer turned her attention to Grant, now taller than she was, and gave him a motherly kiss. "You be careful. You know how boomtowns are."

"That's all I know, Mother, remember?"

Smiling, Jennifer realized that was true. "You be careful anyway."

Once the stage was on its bouncy way, Jason smiled. His faith had been restored and his love renewed.

Meanwhile, back in town Jennifer struggled with regrets and self-doubt. Maybe she should have gone with him after all. Their wealth had demanded their attention and had split them apart. Was it worth it?

~

PART THREE

A New World

The Letter

The wearisome stagecoach ride left Jason and Grant jostled and sore, but the excitement of arriving in Leadville gave them a second wind.

As he and Jason got off the stage, Grant remarked, "It's bigger than I thought—and look at all the people!"

"Second biggest city in Colorado," Jason stated proudly. He tipped a man at the stage house and told him where to deliver their luggage. Striking a match and cupping his hands around a fine cigar, he lit it, then tossed the match away. He adjusted his thick-brimmed derby and glanced over at Grant, whose eyes were as wide as saucers.

"It's really something, isn't it?"

"What a sight!" Grant said with astonishment as he gazed at the mountains in the distance. It was a clear and crisp afternoon, and the sun was brilliant.

"Just wait. You haven't seen anything yet."

Jason led Grant through the crowd to his suite at the Clarendon Hotel. Grant hadn't seen this kind of excitement since their early days in Virginia City.

In their room, Jason showed Grant the extra bed where he would sleep and the drawers where he could put his things. Jason marveled at how Grant had gone from being a boy to a man seemingly overnight. "Interested in girls yet?" he asked playfully.

This was a touchy subject, and Grant turned to make sure Jason was smiling. "Sure, but I don't have any idea how to talk to them."

"It'll come in time. Don't worry about it," Jason advised.

"I noticed there's a lot of good-looking women around here," Grant said shyly.

"Not the kind you want to get mixed up with," Jason said as he poured water from the pitcher into the washbasin and washed his face. He grabbed a towel and dried himself as he spoke. "These women are heartbreakers. They'll promise you the world but leave you broke."

Nodding, Grant copied Jason and went to the washbowl. "How do you know a good one from a bad one?"

"Experience," Jason said with authority as he changed into a fresh shirt. It was a relief to shed the grit from the stage ride. "I can spot a dishonest woman a mile away."

Grant stored all of this away for future reference.

"Once you're cleaned up, we'll go grab a bite," Jason said as he changed boots.

Grant slipped out of his shirt and found a cleaner one, then went to the window overlooking Harrison Avenue. He stood there buttoning his shirt, watching the people below. They hurried, they laughed, some worked, some strolled, but all had the appearance of having something important to do. The forces that brought these people here, the ambitions they had—this is what intrigued Grant.

"Okay," Jason said, shaking Grant from his thoughts, "let's go."

Downstairs Grant sat with Jason at a small round table and studied the menu, though Jason had already ordered for them both. "What kind of fish is a mignon?" Grant questioned, his brow furrowed.

"Never heard of it. What's it say?"

"It says filet mignon."

Jason slapped the table with his palm and let out a hoot of laughter. "Grant, I don't know how you can be so funny without even trying. That's a steak, a filet cut of beef."

"Oh," Grant said, his face red. He wasn't used to the upper class and their ways. Maybe he would seem more intelligent if he didn't ask questions but just kept his mouth shut and waited for the answers to reveal themselves. In a way he wanted to go ahead and laugh at his own stupidity, but he kept quiet.

Soon two sizzling steaks were brought out to the hungry men. "This is the best beef steak I ever ate," Grant soon said with a full mouth.

Jason smiled. "Actually it's not beef steak—it's elk."

Grant's mouth stopped in mid-bite. He'd seen the great animals of the Rockies with their huge antlers. Some were as big as a horse. But he'd never considered eating one, especially without even being told what he was eating. Slowly he began chewing again and came to the same conclusion—it was the best steak he'd ever had. "It's delicious!" he exclaimed.

Glancing up, Grant noticed a pretty young woman hurrying their way. Her bright blue eyes shone like jewels. He couldn't help but notice her tight-waisted, low-cut, red dress. The way she walked and swayed first struck him as offensive and then as alluring.

Seated with his back to the girl, Jason didn't see her coming. Without warning she was beside him and touched him lightly on the shoulder. "I'm so glad you're back!" Marie said cheerfully as she moved to the chair between Grant and Jason. "I hope you got every-thing straightened out."

"Yeah, I did," Jason answered, not smiling, determined to tell her the bad news but afraid of her reaction.

Unaware of what was to come, Marie politely smiled and said, "I really missed you—it just isn't the same without you around." She glanced at Grant and then back at Jason as she rearranged herself in the spindle-back chair, then shifted again, trying to get comfortable.

Jason couldn't help but feel some of his old feelings for her, but he was determined to tell her that they were through, that he would be marrying someone else. "Marie," he said firmly. "I have to tell you—"

"Who's this handsome young man?" Marie interrupted. She gave Grant a captivating stare. "Aren't you going to introduce me, Jason?"

"Uh, this is Grant DeSpain. Grant, this is Marie Kelly. You

might remember her from when we went to the theater in Central City some time ago. She played Little Red Riding Hood."

Grant stared. Everything about her had his full attention.

"He doesn't say much," Marie teased, finally moving her eyes back to Jason and breaking the hypnotic spell she held over Grant.

"Marie—" Jason tried again, his voice more firm.

Quickly standing, Marie seemed suddenly preoccupied with other worries. "I'm sorry, honey, but I have to run. We're starting a new production tonight, and I've got to rehearse. See you tonight!" She darted away but spun around instantly to wave good-bye with her petite hand. "Nice to have met you, Grant." Then, like a whirl-wind, she was gone.

Grant had an odd look on his face as he stared at Jason. The young man's hands were motionless above his plate. He was confused and seemed about to ask a hundred questions. *Did she call Jason "honey"?*

Jason waved his hand in front of his face, apparently about to defend himself. "It isn't what you think, Grant. She doesn't mean anything to me. She's just a . . . well, like one of the girls we were talking about earlier. A gold digger, that's what she is. She's been a pest to me—I can't seem to keep her away from me."

"I'll take her!" Grant said without thinking.

Recognizing his dilemma, Jason couldn't resist a chuckle. "She *is* quite attractive," he admitted.

"Jason, she's the most beautiful woman I've ever seen," Grant said honestly. Upon further reflection, he added, "You two seem to know each other real well."

"Well, I guess . . ." Jason said guiltily. "Listen, I want you to know, I'm in love with your mother, and if she'll have me, we'll get mar-ried. End of story. As for Marie, she's sort of a—" He stopped and frowned. "I don't know what she is, Grant."

"I don't know how any man could resist her." Grant started eat-ing again, but by now the steak had lost its appeal.

"Welcome to the real world where men think they make the decisions, but in actual fact the women are in charge," Jason philosophized.

~

As her social importance rose, so did the amount of mail Jennifer received. Most of it was from firms seeking investors and guaranteeing more wealth. There were also reports from investors who were doing all they could to squeeze another dollar out of everything the Wild Horse Company had invested in—stocks and certificates, bank bonds, savings account statements. It was all business and more business, numbers and more numbers. But one day a scented letter with flowing handwriting dropped from the stack of dull business mail.

Jennifer was delighted to see it was from her friend, Lizzie Doe, in Leadville. She sliced it open with a pearl-handled letter opener and unfolded the gold-gilded stationery.

> December 15, 1879
> Dear Jennifer,
>
> I'm hopelessly in love! I met Horace Tabor, thanks to Jason, and he's been the kindest, most considerate man I've ever known—not to mention, very handsome. I know he's married, but he says he and Augusta were finished before I ever came along.
>
> Now I'm hoping that someday Horace and I will be married and have a family. I know it's a long way off, but I believe it will happen.
>
> There are many wealthy men here, and some are nice-looking, decent men. The girls are after them with a vigor! Jennifer, one more thing . . . well, all I can say is, if you love Jason, you'd better rescue him before it's too late!
>
> Your loving friend,
> Lizzie

"Jason?" Jennifer mumbled. "After all this time he's talked about being in love with me, surely he'd never look at another woman." She moved across the office with the letter in her hand, searching for answers.

She felt the dull pain of heartache at the possibility of losing Jason. *I've put him off forever, I've refused to consent to a specific marriage date, and he's been patient with my fickle behavior for years.* She sighed. *What am I doing letting a wealthy and good-looking man like Jason live up there in Leadville by himself? Of course the women are trying to win his affection—why wouldn't they?*

The letter fell to the floor as Jennifer hastened to make plans for a trip. Excuses no longer mattered—she and Abby were headed for Leadville!

~

Robert Jones, a middle-aged assayer, was fed up with the trade in Leadville. "Black muck and tons of silver!" he spat disgustingly. "That's all I see!" He was tall, lean, and unshaven. He had alert, small eyes, a wispy head of graying hair, and unusually large ears. With his severely stooped shoulders he resembled an old tree bent and withered by severe weather.

"Two thousand and that's my final offer," Jason said, unworried as he glanced out the window of the assayer's small shop and into the busy street.

"These fools!" Jones declared. "I tell them of the abundance of other minerals, but what do they care? Copper and nickel and lead and tons of other valuable ores, but all they want is to get rich quick. It's plundering! Can't even build a privy without hitting the stuff!" He stopped fuming for a moment, then said to Jason, "I'll take it, and good riddance to this place. I'm out of here on the first stage tomorrow!"

The paperwork was routine, and the next day Grant and Jason entered the small assayer's offices. "Well, here you are, Grant. If there's anything else you need, let me know and we'll order it."

Busying himself with the inventory, Grant found things in amazingly good order. "Looks like everything is here as far as I can tell."

There were assayers all over town, and Grant had no intention of competing with them. He would collect ore samples from Jason's three mines and figure out percentages of silver per ton, just to be sure everything was being handled honestly.

Grant was excited about this new opportunity. He would be well paid for an easy job. He only wished he had Midnight with him for his rides to the mines. But he knew Abe was taking good care of both his and Jason's horses.

"Lock her up, and let's go get some ore samples. I'll introduce you to the men in charge."

All of this was like a dream come true for Grant. He would be his own boss without any motherly supervision, although he did miss Jennifer. This wasn't really that new because since he hadn't been a troublemaker, his mother had let him follow his own instincts and rarely intruded on his decision-making. But now he would have even more freedom to search for the answers he'd sought for so long. Only one thing complicated his life—his new affinity for the opposite sex.

Jason and Grant decided to temporarily rent a couple of horses from the Dalton brothers, Bob, Emmett, and Gratton, who operated a corral on the corner of Pine and Front Streets. Bob Dalton, a young man, explained, "It's all I can do to keep a horse to rent, and what I got ain't much. But if you're goin' to need somethin' on a regular basis I'll see what I can do."

"Grant here will need a horse he can depend on. I'll pay for him or however you want to work it," Jason said.

"I'll get him somethin' regular in the next day or so," Bob said, happily accepting the money from Jason. "Say, you got some mining claims?"

"Certainly do," Jason bragged.

Jason and Grant were soon on their horses riding out of town.

"That Bob Dalton had a wild look about him, didn't he?" Grant asked.

"Oh, I don't know," Jason said, pulling out a cigar. "Looked harmless enough—they're Kansas hayseeds out here trying to make a living like the rest of us."

The first mine they rode out to was the Baron, where operations were steady and productive. Earnest Smith, or Smitty as he was called, was the superintendent. He had one good eye and wore a patch over the other. "So this here's our assayer," he said, shaking hands with Grant. "He's a fine-looking young man, Mr. Stone."

"Take care of him, Smitty. Anything he wants, you see to it he gets it. My orders."

"Yes, sir, Mr. Stone. Anything he wants. You got my word."

On their way to the Birdsong, Grant leaned over to watch the unsure feet of the nag he'd rented from the stable. "This horse might as well have frying pans for hooves, the way it stumbles."

"I'm sure Dalton can find you something better," Jason said confidently. "You've got an expense account—use it."

Grant liked the way things were going. But he did have one question. "Don't you think some of your superintendents might think you're being distrustful? It's like I'm checking up on them to make sure no high grading is going on."

"It's all part of the game, and they know that. I pay them well, so they won't complain much."

Grant noticed that Jason now spoke with an air of authority he'd never had before.

When they reached the Birdsong, Jason wasn't so easy on the superintendent, Ray Henderson, a small, aging man who reminded Grant of a bantam rooster.

After checking the charts, Jason complained, "What's happening here, Ray? Two nights in a row and no work getting done."

"I'm doin' all I can," Ray fired back. "We ain't got no relief crew, and that leaves a shift open. I'm advertising for help, but so far nobody's showed up looking for work." He wasn't a bashful man by any standards, and his fiery temper turned his pate red. He pulled what appeared to be a short piece of rope from a desk drawer and cut a section off. It was rope tobacco, and after biting off a plug, he stuck the remaining piece in his front coveralls pocket for future use.

"Give the men some incentive, Ray. Tell them I'm going to figure in a little profit sharing. The more production, the more they make. I'll bring you back some figures tomorrow." Jason was getting better and better at this business all the time.

"I'll do it, Mr. Stone. I ain't never heard of nothing like that before, but it sounds like a good idea all right."

Most impressive to Grant were the tremendous works at the Water Pit mine. Huge engines, hoists, and pumps shook the ground. Two main shafts descended into the depths, and the water being pumped out made a powerful river in a nearby gully. One-legged Levi was quick to meet Jason and Grant, for he had a grand view from the tower over the shaft house and could see someone coming for miles.

Levi was waiting outside to greet his visitors. "Mr. Stone, I guess you heard, the only mine that's outproducing us right now is Tabor's Matchless."

"That's good news, Levi. But I doubt Tabor has the expenses at the Matchless that we have here, so it's easier for them to produce more."

"Well, yeah," Levi agreed, stroking his beard. He was proud of Jason and proud of the Water Pit mine. "Who's your partner?"

"This is Grant, Levi. He'll be doing the assay work from now on. If he needs anything, you take care of it."

"That I'll do," Levi agreed happily as he stumped along on his wooden peg beside Jason and Grant. "Good to know you, Grant."

Grant shook the man's firm and rough hand. "That's the biggest flywheel I've ever seen," Grant shouted in amazement, staring up at the thirty tons of spinning steel.

"There's two of them," Levi shouted over the steam engines. "Each one has her own shaft—I call 'em Sarah and Linda."

"Why women's names?" Grant shouted.

"Because they're of about the same temperament—they change moods every day." Levi smiled. He loved his monstrous steam engines.

On the way back to town, Grant was quiet, impressed by the mining works he'd seen.

"How about we take in the theater tonight," Jason said, figuring Grant might enjoy the live entertainment. "You heard Marie— they're putting on a new play."

"Sure," Grant answered, trying not to let his excitement show. He couldn't think of anything he wanted to do more than go watch Marie on stage. Without realizing it, he gave the nag he was riding an eager kick to urge her on.

～

That evening at the Tabor Opera House, in all of its splendid grandeur, Grant and Jason waited impatiently for the curtains to rise on the new production, A Heart of Silver. Marie would play a jilted mistress. Jason Stone laughed inwardly at the fact that the part she would be playing was strangely close to the truth at hand, although Marie thus far was unsuspecting.

Grant fidgeted, impatient for the show to begin. The theater was packed, and a roar of conversation filled the air. "When's it going to start?" he asked.

"They do this on purpose—it builds anticipation," Jason said knowingly. He smiled. "What's your hurry?"

"I don't know," Grant said, irritated. He wasn't sure how to deal with the new emotions stirring within him.

"I don't know why you're so excited. It's only a play."

Grant cut short his response as lamps dimmed.

The heavy, massive curtains parted and lifted, and there before them sat a man and his wife in a luxurious den with gaudy furniture. The tall man with a hearty voice reassured his wife he was a man of virtue and was true only to her. He was a silver baron who'd found his riches in Leadville.

A few moments later a small stringed orchestra played a mellow tune, taking the audience into scene 2, where the silver baron was found with his mistress, played by Marie. She looked like a store-bought china doll in a full dress with red cheeks and red lips. Jason noticed Grant leaning forward, his neck craned high to see all he could.

The man tenderly promised to leave his wife for the other woman. Marie sang a song of joy at the end of the scene, her voice angelic and hopeful.

Then in scene 3 trouble came. The baron had been found out, and his lovely wife was determined to leave him. He sang from his knees, begging her with all his heart to forgive him, promising her the world. She agreed on one condition, that he tell the mistress he would see her no more.

Grant and Jason found the plot predictable but were nevertheless anxious to see what Marie would do. There was a solemn silence except for the melancholy crying of a single violin.

In scene 4, the tall, handsome, wealthy baron sat on a small bridge with Marie. The bridge arced over a babbling brook of blue and green tinsel. The sad violin died off as the man said, "Darling, my love for you will never die, but I cannot see you again."

Marie jumped up and argued that love can never be buried or hidden away. Then she broke into a mournful and tragic plea, holding the back of her wrist pathetically over her brow.

The man stood to take her in his arms, but she pulled away.

Then something strange happened. The audience sensed it but couldn't identify exactly what was wrong. Marie began to cry, and her grief grew until it reached a distress that could not be ignored. Everyone wondered whether this was part of the act or if the actress herself was distraught. Apparently unable to regain her composure, Marie dashed from the stage, leaving the actor alone to fend for himself.

After an eternity of silence, the man stood and bowed, as if this had all been planned. About that time he had to duck quickly to dodge a well-thrown apple core. Then came a barrage of various objects as he scrambled from the stage under jeers of, "How could you do that to her!" and "You skunk!" and "Get out of town, you coward!" The curtains quickly fell, and the lamps came to full brightness.

Jason turned to an embarrassed Grant, who swiftly wiped his wet eyes. "I wonder what's wrong with Marie," Jason said.

"I don't know," Grant mumbled shakily. Unaccustomed to drama, Grant had been drawn deeply into the play. He seldom lost control of his emotions, and he hated doing it now, thinking it a sign of weakness.

"Let's get out of here," Jason said as he jumped to his feet.

Grant had a hard time keeping up as he followed Jason. They went around to the back of the theater where a man who looked like a gorilla in a suit said, "I'm sorry, gents. Can't go any further."

"I need to see Marie!" Jason said impatiently

"Who doesn't?" he taunted.

Unwilling to submit, Jason tried to push him aside. The bruiser politely grabbed Jason by the scruff of the neck and gave him a little toss that sent him sliding across the ground.

Seeing a fire in Jason's eye that scared him, Grant grabbed Jason in a bear hug. "Are you crazy?" Grant pleaded. He turned Jason around so they could walk away.

"I'll have your job for this!" Jason threatened with a pointed finger.

"You can have it," the bulky man chided. "It don't pay nothin' anyhow."

CHAPTER

~ 14 ~

A Question of Love

Jason spent the entire next day worrying about Marie Kelly. With Grant busy taking care of his new responsibilities, Jason rambled around speculating on this and that but finally realized he was getting nothing accomplished. "I've got to see her," he mumbled as he moved through the crowded street. It was a warm day for December, the smells of the busy city hanging in the mountain air. The sun never seemed to climb very high this time of year.

Jason made his way to the Clarendon to see her and found her in the dining room sitting by herself, overcome with despair. He made his way to her table, slid out a chair, and sat down. "Marie, about last night . . . what happened?"

Refusing to look him in the eye, she continued to eat as if she were thinking of something deep and dreadful. She finally turned back to Jason. "I lost my confidence—I couldn't stand to be in front of all those people." Her shoulders sagged a little more. "That's never happened to me before."

Jason didn't know what to say. "I'm sorry," he finally said softly. "Do you have any idea what the problem was? I felt so sorry for you. I even tried to see you, but some ape wouldn't let me in."

She tried to smile but was obviously still upset. "Don't you see?" she asked, her voice sounding hopeless. "The play . . . the play was too real. I could see it really happening to me." She stopped, fighting her emotions. "I could see you coming to me to tell me we could never see each other again."

Jason placed his hands on the table, leaned back, and sighed heavily. "Marie, I never intended for things to get close between us. I told you I was engaged, but you pretended it wasn't true, and I didn't fight it like I should have. I love my fiancée—she's a wonderful person, and I'm going to marry her."

Marie was finally beginning to accept the truth. "I understand," she said almost whispering. "It's you who can't understand."

A look of astonishment twisted Jason's face. "Understand what?"

"See? You don't understand at all." She placed her napkin and silverware neatly on the table, brought her small hands up in front of her, and clasped them. "You said you can't help how you feel about your fiancée. Well, I can't help how I feel about you. Jason, I've grown so fond of you, I can't simply turn away and give you up." As she spoke, her voice became more determined and self-confident. "I'll wait for you to come back to me—I'll always be here for you. I can't help how I feel."

What have I gotten myself into? Jason wondered as he stared into Marie's eyes. "That's crazy, Marie. I'm nothing special—you'll get over me."

A flash of anger came into Marie's turquoise eyes and then quickly vanished. "You can't tell my heart who to love any more than I can. It's not something we have control over. I don't even know this woman, but I know I could make you happy all of your life, happier than she can!"

Jason shook his head and let out a sick little laugh. "You sure are persistent," he said awkwardly, trying to smile but failing. "I don't know what else to tell you. We've set wedding plans for this spring."

The anger flashed again, except this time it stayed for several moments. Her pupils shrank to black pinholes; her eyes squinted, and her mouth tightened. Then the rage gave way, and her face became soft again. The sudden changes frightened Jason.

"I'll never give up hope," Marie said confidently. "And until you're married I still have a fighting chance." She stood abruptly and glared down at Jason with a confidence he found bewildering. "I've never given up on anything, and I'm not about to start now!" she scolded mildly, then hurried away.

Watching her walk, he admired her stubborn willpower though he knew their attachment was over. *Maybe she'll get over it*, he hoped. Then he smiled, thinking, *Who am I kidding?* He was glad he'd finally told her the truth, though he knew Marie was the kind of woman he couldn't easily banish from his thoughts.

～

Tom Cooper, a renowned driver of the Walt & Witter stage line, reined the team to a halt and stepped on the brake of the big Concord coach. The passengers grumbled at his rough ways, but he had something he wanted to do. Jumping from the height of his driver's seat, he landed agilely on his feet and opened the coach door. "Ladies first," he announced with some authority.

Abby stepped down the steps with Jennifer right behind her, both dressed in fancy traveling apparel, complete with hats and colorful feathers.

"It's been my pleasure to bring two of the prettiest ladies I've ever seen to Leadville," Tom said with proud enthusiasm.

"Thank you, Mr. Cooper," Jennifer said, her eyes roving over the surroundings in awe of the town. "This is a busy place."

A loud whistle shrilled from a passing wagon load of miners. "My darlings, I love you!" a miner sang theatrically with his hands over his heart and then fell back into his boisterous group of laughing friends.

"Don't mind them none," said Tom. "They're good, hard-working men and would do anything to help you."

"I'm familiar with their sort," Jennifer said, smiling.

But Abby had taken it personally. She was slowly coming to realize the effect her beauty had on men, a fact she would store away for use later.

"Is this a good hotel?" Jennifer asked Tom.

"Yes, ma'am," Tom answered, glancing at Walsh's Grand Hotel.

"Will you see to it our trunks are taken care of?"

"Be glad to, ma'am."

Abby and Jennifer were exhausted. The day's ride had consisted of wind, dust, and the smells of sweaty horses and wild sage. The only thing they wanted now was a warm bath; everything else could wait.

∼

In his new surroundings, Grant worked with a happy fervor. He had gathered samples and was meticulously performing his analyses of the black chunks. It was late afternoon, but he was determined to gain his results before he left the small assayer's shop.

Someone tapped on the door. *Funny*, Grant thought, knowing there was nothing to indicate this place was open to the public. *Must be Jason, or somebody's confused.* He set his utensils down and came around the counter to the locked door. As soon as he opened it, two men pushed their way in.

They were lean men with hollows under their dark, cold, dangerous eyes. Each carried a big pistol slung within easy reach.

"Where's the assayer?" one asked coldly.

"I'm the assayer," Grant replied, trying not to show his worried concern.

"A mite young, ain't you?"

"Maybe," Grant replied coolly. The man's face looked familiar, but he couldn't place it. "Actually, I'm only the assayer for the Wild Horse Company—this office isn't open to the public."

"That's good," the taller man said matter-of-factly. His partner was scanning the shop like he was memorizing it. "I'm looking for an assayer who can keep his mouth shut." He took three golden double eagles and clanged them on a countertop in front of Grant.

The three coins shined up at Grant with the lure of pure gold. Grant slowly lifted his eyes to meet the piercing glare of the strange man.

The man removed a bag he had hanging under his coat and set it down gently beside the gold coins. "I can trust you not to say a word about where this ore came from, can't I?"

"Yes, sir," Grant said, his voice growing shaky.

"You know anything about any of the claims out near Soda Springs, about five miles out?"

"I just got here yesterday," Grant said. "I don't know anything about any of the claims. All I'm supposed to do is assay the three mines the company owns."

"How long will it take you to assay these ore samples?"

Grant picked up the bag and dumped its contents on a tabletop. It looked like the same ore he had gathered. "I can have it done by tomorrow afternoon."

"We'll be back. C'mon, Frank, let's go." They disappeared like ghosts, leaving the coins to pay for Grant's work.

I've seen him before, Grant thought. *They sure acted suspicious*. But he didn't mind earning some extra money, so he smiled and put the heavy coins in his pocket. They gave him a sense of approaching prosperity.

Later, as the sun sank over Mount Elbert and Mount Massive, the sky reflected varied hues of blue and orange until it reached a deep purple, all in the five or ten minutes it took Grant to walk back to the room at the Clarendon. He found Jason changing into more lively attire for the evening.

Grant told him about the two men and held out the three brilliant coins.

"Not bad!" Jason said as he fixed his tie. "If you want to make a little on the side, that's fine with me."

Grant had brought a box of his books with him so he'd have something to read and now rushed over to where he had it stored. Squatting down, he grabbed books from the box until he came to the stack of dime novels. Flashing through them, he stopped, holding one up to see it in better light. He stared for a long time. "Jason, the two men who came in today—they . . . they were Frank and Jesse James!"

That got Jason's attention now, and he came closer and saw Grant looking at a sketch of Jesse on the front cover. "Are you sure?"

"I heard him say, 'C'mon, Frank.'"

Jason pondered all this, thinking about what to tell Grant to do. "I guess you'd better do what they say. We don't want any trouble."

"That's what I was thinking," Grant agreed. "They're still wanted in some states, and there's no lawman to tell this to. Besides, we don't know that they've done anything against the law to get their silver ore."

~

If there was one thing Jennifer had learned, it was how to spend money. Staying at Walsh's Grand Hotel was roughing it in her opinion, and as soon as she located Jason, she and Abby would find more suitable quarters. She carried a wad of bills in her purse just for such an occasion. "Send someone up to my room who can locate somebody for me," she'd told the desk clerk.

"Yes, ma'am, Mrs. DeSpain. I'll send a boy up as soon as I can."

After a brief rest and washing up, Jennifer and Abby dressed for an evening out. They were determined to have an elegant meal after their harsh ride, whether they found Jason or not. A knock sounded at the door, and Jennifer opened it to see a buck-toothed boy of about fifteen standing there. His pants were too short, like he was expecting high water, and his red hair stood up like the comb on a rooster. Freckles covered his face, but his smile was friendly.

"I'm Sam Gooten—I work for the newspaper. The desk clerk said you need to find someone. If they're in this town, I can find 'em. I can find out anything you want to know about what goes on in this town."

"Newspaper, huh? Do you write?"

"No, ma'am. I just find people and discover what's goin' on, then I tell somebody who can write it down."

"I see," Jennifer said. Abby stood curiously at her side. "I need you to find a man for me."

All of a sudden the boy's face turned flame-red. "Beggin' your pardon, ma'am, but a woman as pretty as you, why, all you got to do is step out on the street and every man around would be at your service." He swallowed hard.

An uncontrollable giggle escaped both Jennifer and Abby. "No, you don't understand. I want you to find a certain man. His name is Jason Stone."

"Oh," Sam gawked, now thoroughly embarrassed. "Yes'm. I can find him."

Without hesitation, Jennifer grabbed her purse and fished out the wad of bills. She peeled off two and handed them to the boy. His eyes grew big. "Yes, ma'am—I'll find him right away, and I'll be right back!" He hurried off at a full run.

"What a strange boy," Abby said as Jennifer closed the door.

"It takes all kinds to make the world go around," Jennifer said pleasantly. "Looks like he's found his place, and I bet he's good at what he does. I'll have to keep him in mind."

"I think he's got mush in his head," Abby said with a giggle.

~

True to his word, Sam Gooten was back in a jiffy to inform Jennifer that Jason Stone was registered at the Clarendon over on Harrison Avenue. Furthermore, a dinner table was reserved for him for six o'clock.

"Well, I must say you're very efficient, Sam," Jennifer said. She took another bill from her purse. "Now, do you think you could get us a carriage to take us over there?"

"Yes, ma'am!" Sam cried as he ran off again.

"Are you ready, Abby?"

"Yes, but don't you think it's going to look kind of funny, us inviting ourselves to dinner unannounced? That's not ladylike."

"Don't be silly. Jason will be happy to see me, I'm sure." Checking herself in the mirror, she tidied her hair. "And I'm anxious to see Jason," she said happily. "Let's be on our way."

For Abby, being in the newest, biggest, and richest boomtown of the West was a great adventure. She would enjoy putting on a show for all the watching and hungry eyes.

As Jennifer and Abby rode down the dusty and fire-lit streets of Leadville in the carriage, they had a good look at the growing town. In many ways it was overdone with its excessive wealth. Dusk brought out street revelers who would spend the night in singing, dancing, and heavy drinking. The saloons and dance halls overflowed with music and laughter, and people swarmed everywhere.

"This is a happy place," Abby decided. At first she had been against coming to Leadville. She preferred the high life of Denver.

But Denver was nowhere near this festive. And Leadville was a rich place, thanks to the likes of Walsh and Tabor and now Jason Stone.

When they arrived at the Clarendon, a porter helped them from the carriage and showed them inside. Upon entering the dining room, Jennifer and Abby spotted Jason and Grant at a table for four. When Jennifer suddenly stood before Jason, the big black cigar almost fell from his mouth.

"Jennifer!" he said between clenched teeth.

"Mother!" Grant exclaimed, just as surprised, though also happy. "Abby, sit down." He jumped to his feet and pulled out a chair for his pretty sister.

"What are you doing smoking that hideous thing?" Jennifer asked Jason.

Jason placed the cigar in an ashtray and stood to hug Jennifer. "This is a wonderful surprise! You decided to come after all! I couldn't be happier to see you." He moved to kiss her, but she turned her head away.

"Jason, I can still smell that cigar on your breath!" She smiled an irritated smile, then sat down as Jason scooted the chair under her.

"Had I known you were coming I wouldn't have smoked a cigar," he said.

"Since when did you start smoking them anyway?"

"I don't know—some time back," Jason said defensively. Without realizing it, Jennifer had taken the joy out of her surprise, and Jason reacted with inner anger. Grant and Abby sensed the discord immediately.

"So how was your trip?" Jason asked, trying to get things back on track.

"Uneventful and long," Jennifer reported, still irritated.

"We haven't ordered yet," Jason said, maintaining his smile. "What do you think of Leadville?"

"It's bigger than I thought," Abby answered. "How'd it get so big so fast?"

"Money," Jason answered proudly. "There's lots and lots of money here."

That definitely appealed to Abby.

"Our hotel leaves something to be desired," Jennifer complained mildly.

"Where are you staying?"

"The Grand Hotel."

"I'll send for your things right after dinner and get you a room here," Jason said confidently. "Grant and I share a suite upstairs."

Jennifer finally began to smile.

Detecting the change, Jason excitedly began to ramble on about their three mines. "I want to take you out to see them," he said. "I want to show you the whole town."

"That sounds fine," Jennifer replied without much enthusiasm. "Jason, I don't want to go inside any mine shafts. When you've seen one, you've seen them all."

"I'll show you the works then. We own some impressive equipment, like the twin steam engines out at the Water Pit. I bet you've never seen a flywheel as big as these!"

Actually Jennifer didn't care to see many of these things, just the town and its refined features such as restaurants and theaters. As far as she was concerned, the only thing that really mattered about the mines were the profits. She had made this trip only to keep any other woman from stealing Jason away from her. Her sour mood had come out of nowhere, and as she thought about it she realized that Jason's cigar had reminded her of Lance Rivers, a man who had deceived and hurt her. She took a breath and calmed down.

"I'd love to see the town. Have you seen Jake lately? How about Lizzie?"

"Not lately," Jason answered. "But I'm sure they won't be too hard to find."

At that moment a fragrance of expensive perfume interrupted their conversation, and Jason glanced up to see Marie standing over him and Jennifer. She wore a revealing dress, and she had the same big smile she used on stage. "Hello, Jason," she said in her sweet voice. "Who's your friend?" She swung her eyes over to Jennifer and gave her a threatening look.

Stunned but remaining calm, Jason said, "Marie, this is Jennifer

DeSpain, my fiancée. Jennifer, this is Marie Kelly. She's an actress. She played Little Red Riding Hood, remember?"

Jealousy ran through Jennifer like a lightning bolt. She could barely keep her voice civil. "Nice to meet you," she said. "I saw you on stage in Central City."

"How nice," Marie said, her face cheerful but the tone in her voice ominous. She hovered over Jason much too close, Jennifer noticed.

Marie despised Jennifer from the first moment she saw her. She was beautiful, though of course not as beautiful as she herself was. But Jennifer had something Marie didn't have and never would have—charm and class. Marie resented this but was determined to remain patient and find any flaw she could take advantage of.

"Are you planning on attending the show tonight?"

"Certainly," Jason answered.

"Have a nice evening," Marie said. She strutted off as if she didn't have a care in the world.

Once she was out of sight, Jennifer leaned over to Jason and said, "Seems to me you two are pretty good friends."

The last thing Jason wanted was for Jennifer to question his faithfulness. He could see that Grant and Abby had watched the whole scene as if it were a play. "She's an acquaintance, and that's all."

So this is the woman that Lizzie wrote me about, Jennifer thought. Not wanting her fear to show, Jennifer remained pleasant and kind, but after dinner when it came time to go to Marie Kelly's performance, she informed Jason she was exhausted from the trip and was too tired to go to the theater. A short walk was all she could manage, she said.

Grant and Abby went upstairs to catch up on gossip as Jason escorted Jennifer outdoors. The refreshing high mountain air smelled of pine, spruce, and wood smoke. They walked along the crowded boardwalk and continued onward toward the edge of town where the crowd thinned and the lighted streets grew dimmer.

"Does that woman mean anything to you?" Jennifer asked abruptly.

Jason was glad Jennifer asked the question. He wanted everything out in the open. "There's something about her—it's hard to explain. Yes, Jennifer, she's most appealing, but I promise you, I've remained a gentleman and true to you."

Jennifer felt relieved and smiled. She loved Jason's honesty. "I trust you, but knowing human nature . . . she's gorgeous and young, and I'm sure if she wanted to, she could make any man pay attention."

"I can't say there's been no temptation, but I'm in love with you," Jason stated.

Jennifer stopped walking, and Jason put his arm around her. After a moment they continued strolling.

"I think June 13 would make a wonderful wedding date," Jennifer announced proudly.

Jennifer was bolder than Jason remembered, and he liked the change.

"A big wedding?" he asked enthusiastically.

"Yes, of course—in Denver. We'll invite everybody."

Jennifer was finally ready to get married, and Jason couldn't have been happier. They moved along hand in hand, dreamily discussing their future.

Suddenly two men dashed out of a dark alley, guns drawn. "Over here," one growled, motioning with his pistol for the couple to duck into the alley.

Frightened, Jennifer clung to Jason as they moved slowly into the dark alley. Jason had a small pistol in his coat pocket but wondered if he dared use it. *I can pretend I'm going for my wallet and pull out the gun,* he thought. *But what if shots are fired and Jennifer is hit?*

"Give me your money—all of it!" one of the robbers ordered. He was a grubby man with a dirty, unshaven face and long stringy hair protruding in clumps from under his hat.

The other robber looked much the same, his clothes worn-out and his teeth rotten. He held the short barrel of his six-shooter in Jason's ribs. "No funny business," he mumbled, glancing over his shoulder toward the street to make sure nobody had seen them.

Slowly Jason removed his wallet. It only had about $500 in it. Jennifer carefully pulled her roll of bills from her purse as well.

"I'll take that diamond ring too," the man said, glaring at her.

"But that's my engagement ring," Jennifer whined, almost in tears.

Common sense told Jason to let the men have whatever they wanted, but he was on the verge of losing his temper. Despite his fear, his hand gradually moved toward the pocket with the gun.

"It'd be a good idea for you gentlemen to put them smokestacks away!" a voice loudly commanded from behind them.

The robbers turned to see who was speaking, and the man at the front of the alley looked like something of a prankster. He wore a black tailor-made suit and a smart bowler hat with a high-curled brim. He was a good-looking man with a pleasant face and a carefully barbered mustache. The man smiled at the robbers and pushed his coat back to reveal two huge, silver-plated, ivory-handled pistols in a heavy gun belt.

The robbers nervously glanced at each other. One whispered to his friend, "That's Bat Masterson!"

Ever so slowly the robbers holstered their pistols and handed the stolen money and goods back to Jason and Jennifer. Then they slowly backed deeper into the dark alley with their hands held high until they got far enough away to break into a run.

Jennifer sighed with relief and began to shake. Jason held her tightly. "It's all right, darling. Everything's all right now."

She clung to him tightly.

Bat walked up to the couple, still wearing his mischievous smile. "Is she going to be all right?" he asked Jason.

"I think so," Jason said. He held out his hand. "I'm Jason Stone, and this is my fiancée, Jennifer DeSpain."

She turned now to look at the man who had rescued them. "I thought I heard one of those men say you're Bat Masterson."

"At your service," Bat said, touching the brim of his hat. He had a carefree way about him.

"I thought you were sheriff of Dodge City," Jason said.

"Oh," Bat sighed, "I lost the election, so here I am."

"Would you have shot those two men?" Jennifer inquired nervously.

"Quicker than I'd shoot a snake," Bat boasted honestly.

"You must let me repay you," Jason said, counting the bills he still held in his hand.

"Forget it!" Bat insisted, placing his hand over Jason's fumbling fingers. "I saw those men force you into the alley, and I couldn't stand to see the likes of them bothering a fine-looking couple like your-selves—especially a woman as lovely as you, Miss DeSpain."

The three moved back to the street and started down the board-walk toward the busy area of town, talking like old friends.

"Well, we do appreciate your assistance. How about joining us for dinner tomorrow at the Clarendon Hotel? Jennifer has a son who would love to meet you—he's read all about you," Jason explained.

"Please, Mr. Masterson," Jennifer said. "We were in the newspa-per business for many years and received most of the stories on famous lawmen and gunmen—like the time you caught those train robbers in a driving blizzard."

Bat replied, "I'll tell you more interesting stories than that one over dinner tomorrow. But I must be going now." He stepped down from the boardwalk and turned to wink at Jennifer before getting lost in the crowd.

"Amazing," Jason said. "We're being robbed and Bat Masterson comes along to save the day. Who'd ever believe a story like that?"

For the first time in a long time Jennifer remembered the spiri-tual world she'd all but abandoned. "Thank God for Mr. Masterson," she said.

"Thank God and those two pearl-handled Colts," Jason added.

CHAPTER
~ 15 ~

Happy Holidays

The Christmas season in Leadville was like everything else in that boomtown—big and glorious, haughty and wild. Decorations hung along the streets, and wreaths adorned every door. Windows were bright with candles, and bells jingled as horses pulled their carriages and sleighs. A fresh foot of powdery snow covered the town as people rushed about.

The bars, dance halls, and restaurants were warm with cheer and heat from the glowing stoves. Tabor had returned to Leadville and was enthused with the holiday spirit. "I'm going to host a big party," he said one day. "I'll have the best of everything—the best money can buy."

The group at the table with Tabor was anxious to hear more. Jason and Jennifer wanted to participate in the planning, as did Baby Doe, who said, "We can have the musicians from the theater play all night, so we can dance into the early hours of the morning." She hung on Tabor's arm.

Tabor smiled from under his walrus mustache, his eyes twinkling with excitement, as they almost always did. "We'll make the first floor of the hotel into a ballroom."

"We'll have to send out invitations," Jennifer said. "Lizzie and I can do that."

"We'll invite everybody who's somebody," Tabor said as he took another sip of champagne.

"I'll make arrangements for a spread of food never seen before in Leadville," Jason added.

"This will be a Christmas party nobody will forget," Tabor added happily.

∽

Several days before the Christmas party, Jennifer and Baby Doe sat at the small table in the parlor of Baby Doe's suite. The little table was stacked high with invitations as they discussed the elite guest list over steaming cups of tea.

"We must have 200 people," Baby Doe said as she copied another name from the list onto an invitation, then folded it over and dripped wax on it from a red candle. She then sealed it with one of Tabor's wax stamps.

Sitting with her quill poised, Jennifer remarked, "I don't know any of these people."

"But you will," Baby Doe said happily. "I can't wait. We'll have such a wonderful time."

Her suite smelled of boxwood, cedar, and roasted almonds, due to many special gifts from Horace Tabor. The big bed had a lace-trimmed bedspread and a colorful handmade quilt folded at the bottom. Huge, fluffy pillows sat at attention beneath a headboard of carved walnut. Thick oriental rugs nearly covered a polished oak floor. Jennifer glanced across the room to see her reflection in a huge bevel-edged mirror above the bureau.

"What about the theatrical company?"

Baby Doe stopped her writing and looked up. "You mean Marie Kelly? We can hardly invite the company and not invite her. I know how you must feel, but I think it will be all right."

"I don't like the way she looks at Jason."

"Oh, she's on the prowl—no doubt about that. That's why I wrote you that letter," Baby Doe said with some certainty. "But at the same time you can't stand guard over him forever. Someday you'll have to really trust him or you won't have anything to build a relationship on."

"Yes, I suppose that's true," Jennifer mused. "I think Jason is a good man, and a strong one. But I can see where she's quite tempting. She's very attractive."

"So are you," Baby Doe complimented. "If Jason can't figure out what's right, you're not to blame."

Jennifer looked worried. "All this time, all these years, I've put Jason off, and he's been ever true, always at my side. He's a good man. I should have married him a long time ago."

Baby Doe finished another invitation and set it in a pile. "Horace is the most wonderful man I've ever met, and I love him with all my heart. I think he loves me as much as a man can, but . . . he's married. At least you don't have that problem. I think one day everything will work out and we'll be married and have children. But until then I have plenty to worry about. But you know what? I trust Horace. That's what you have to do—trust Jason."

Jennifer sighed as she gazed at the overcast, gray clouds right outside the window. She recognized bits of truth in Baby Doe's words. She would have to let go of Jason in order to have him. That reminded her of something she'd read in the Bible. Jesus said, "Whoever wishes to save his life shall lose it, but whoever loses his life for my sake will save it." She would need to put the situation with Marie Kelly in God's hands and trust Him to help Jason keep making right choices.

It would be easy to be critical of Baby Doe and the relationship she was having with Tabor. Sometimes, at those rare moments when she began to think about the Lord again, Jennifer wished she knew how to explain to her friend about right and wrong, about the Lord and His love for her. But Jennifer couldn't quite find the words to say.

～

Jennifer and Abby attended a ladies' Christmas gathering given by Baby Doe, leaving Jason and Grant to fend for themselves for the evening.

"I have a friend I want you to meet," Jason said, slightly boasting. "We'll meet him at Charlie Lowe's saloon and have a bite to eat."

Grant asked, "All right. Who is it?"

"You'll see soon enough." Jason smiled, bundling up in his overcoat.

Outside the two leaned into a hard, bitter, mountain-cold winter wind as they wound their way over to State Street. With his hat pulled low over his eyes and his heavy coat collar turned up, Grant yelled into the wind, "It must be like this at the North Pole."

"Probably." Jason grimaced against the biting cold and flying snow that felt like shards of glass.

Jason and Grant found the saloon to be warm, cozy, and full of low-talking men. Dusting the snow from their coats, they made their way into the crowd, passing several gambling tables of faro and poker until they came to a few empty tables in the back.

"Let's sit over here," Jason said, indicating an out-of-the-way table.

A smoky haze had settled over the room, and the sweet smell of alcohol mixed with the tangy-bitter aroma of cigars. Jason quickly brought out one of the black cheroots he liked and lit it.

A red and yellow glow flashed from behind the mica glass of a wood-burning stove, right across from where the men sat. Grant gazed into it, momentarily captivated by the flickering light.

"What can I get for you?" a young girl asked. Grant looked at her and then at Jason. He'd never sat in a bar before and wasn't sure what to tell her.

"I'll have a tall water," Jason said, expecting a reaction from the waitress for ordering water in a bar. "Bring a sarsaparilla for my friend."

The young girl had long, straight blonde hair and pretty blue eyes, but her features were gaunt, as if she were undernourished. "A couple of heavy drinkers, I see," she said with a hint of a smile before she moved away.

The place had a homey atmosphere, and Grant found himself

enjoying their private outing. "They serve food here?" Grant questioned.

"Not much, but they serve something you'll like."

"Good 'cause I'm hungry," Grant replied. "I'm always hungry," he added.

Jason chuckled around the black cigar. "If I recall, I was at your age too. I guess all growing boys eat like that."

Grant was at an awkward age, and he was sensitive about it. But he had an answer this time. "I'm a big fella, Jason—I can't starve myself."

Nodding, Jason agreed. Grant was indeed growing fast; he was already as big as Jason. "I bet you aren't through growing yet."

Grant knew this was true. He was outgrowing boots before he could wear them out. And often he'd slip on one of his favorite old coats and find his arms sticking too far out of the sleeves.

The girl came back with their drinks and placed them on the table. "Anything else?" she asked politely.

"Bring us something to eat please—your famous smoked meat and homemade bread."

"I sure will," she said and walked away.

Grant noticed that Jason was staring across the saloon, and he turned to see what Jason was looking at. All he saw was a bunch of men, most of them heavy in conversation over a draft beer or a whiskey. But Jason kept watching, and soon one of the men spotted him and raised a hand, then came over, bringing his heavy mug of beer with him.

Standing, Jason greeted the dapper, well-dressed man wearing a bowler. Grant noticed that the man's waistcoat protruded on both sides, indicating he was carrying not one but two pistols.

"Grant, I want you to meet Bat Masterson." Jason enjoyed watching the total surprise in Grant's expression. Grant came to his feet to shake hands with the famous gentleman.

"Bat, this is Grant DeSpain, Jennifer's boy," Jason said as he sat back down.

Shaking Grant's hand heartily, Bat took a seat himself. "So

you're the one who reads the dime novels," Bat said, his face pleasant and lively.

"Yes, s-sir," Grant said, stuttering a bit.

"Don't place much heed in them," Bat suggested. "Those writers couldn't tell a true story if their life depended on it. Most of that is just plain made up—all lies, or at least exaggerations."

"But you *were* the sheriff of Dodge City," Grant proclaimed, "and you did have gunfights on the street."

"Well, yeah, but that ain't nothin'," Bat said. "Most sheriffs are going to have to shoot a man or get shot before it's over with."

"The dime novel said you've killed a man for every year of your life," Grant said, his eyes big with curiosity.

"Could be. I've never counted," Bat said as he took a sip of his beer. "But I never killed a man who wasn't trying to kill me first."

"He's read about all the famous and infamous gunmen of the wild West," Jason put in. "But I think you're the first he's actually met."

"Not really. I met Jesse James," Grant said and then realized he'd made a serious mistake. "I mean—"

"It's all right—I know Jesse's here," Bat said, to Grant's relief. "Him and Frank's got a claim outside of town. They're laying low. Some lawmen have come here snooping around, but they didn't have the gumption to accuse them of being the James brothers. Probably a wise move. Good way to stay alive anyway." By now Bat had smelled Jason's cigar long enough and pulled out his own and lit it.

"They say you can shoot just as good with either hand," Grant said curiously.

"That's a fact, but that doesn't come easily. Anybody good with a gun has to practice constantly," Bat said knowingly.

This brought back memories of the only shooting lesson Grant had ever had and the fact that Lance Rivers had said sort of the same thing. "You ever know an outlaw named Lance Rivers?"

This caught Bat's mind, and he thought it through before he answered. "Why, yes, I know him. He owes me $200 from a game of poker. I've still got the marker."

"You might have a hard time collecting," Jason said.

"Oh? Why's that?"

"Rivers is dead. Died about three years ago—shot in the back during a holdup attempt," Jason informed Masterson.

Bat shook his head sadly and said, "I'd warned him that a man can't do that kind of living forever. It always has the same ending."

The house specialty showed up on two big plates, and Grant dug in. The meat was tender and smoked, and the bread had a unique but good flavor.

"Buffalo and sour dough," Bat said. "Might keep a man going forever."

"What?" Grant said around the wad in his mouth.

"Buffalo and sour dough—that's what you're eatin'. I said it was hard to beat," Bat said lightly, realizing that Grant had thought he was eating something else.

Grant chewed the buffalo meat slowly and finally decided it tasted a little gamy but was all right. "Jason, I wish you'd quit doing that to me."

"Doing what?" Jason chided. "You didn't ask."

Bat joined in, "Reminds me of the first time I ate possum. That's a greasy critter if I ever ate one. Jason, let me buy you and Grant another round."

"Just water for me. Alcohol and me have parted company."

"Sorry to hear about that. Grant, how about you?"

"Yeah, I'll have another sarsaparilla."

That was the beginning of a long evening of storytelling. Grant got to tell the story of Jason and Big Ned back in Virginia City, which fascinated Bat. But Bat had his stories too, stories of poker and gunplay and unexpected outcomes. Grant noticed Bat had a way with words and knew how to make a story come alive. Grant enjoyed the man-to-man camaraderie. The three soon lost track of time.

~

The Christmas party brought together every person of any known stature in Leadville. All were expecting the very best, for Tabor was known for splurging and overindulging in his all-night parties. The first floor of the Clarendon Hotel was highly decorated with seasonal decorations, candles, and colorful lamps. A long table piled high with exotic treats sat waiting for the guests. Jason had been in charge of the food and spared no expense. The chefs and their staff kept the table brimming with delicacies throughout the night so the guests might dine whenever they pleased. Sugar-cured hams, honey-roasted breast of pheasant, and raw oysters were just a few of the items that tempted the taste buds of Tabor's guests.

Hired guards welcomed the guests and kept out the riffraff. They were under orders to be servants to all guests no matter how rowdy they might get.

By the low light of scented candles, an eight-piece orchestra broke into a Christmas tune to warm up their instruments. Jennifer and Baby Doe wore colorful dresses as they greeted guests at the entrance. Tabor and Jason stood some distance away in their tuxedos, discussing final details to ensure everything was in order.

"The kitchen will keep the tables overflowing. I've spoken with the chefs, and they're ready for anything," Jason said confidently to Tabor. "I doubt our guests can eat everything I've got lined up."

"Oh, you'd be surprised," Tabor chuckled, already sipping from his small glass of champagne. "Even these wealthy folks act like starving livestock when the food's free."

"It's always better when it's free," Jason added with a smile.

"I have enough champagne to float a ship," Tabor boasted. "If they drink that much, they won't be able to remain standing."

One of the town's most respected couples approached the welcoming committee of Baby Doe and Jennifer DeSpain. "Jennifer, I want you to meet Thomas Walsh," Baby Doe said cheerfully. "Thomas owns the Grand Hotel and is a well-respected prospector in these parts. This is his wife, Carrie."

"How are you?" Jennifer said, extending her hand to the Walshes. She already knew of Thomas and his wife and their increasing wealth from his sharp business dealings. These were the kind of people she was pleased to be introduced to.

"Likewise," Walsh said, rubbing his mustache. "I've heard a lot about you and Jason Stone. He doesn't waste any time, does he? Jumped right in with the best of them."

"Yes, he's quite ambitious," Jennifer admitted.

"Do tell!" Carrie Walsh said vehemently, taking Jennifer's hand in greeting. "*All* these men are ambitious, and don't let them tell you any different." She had a round but pleasant face and dark hair. Her dress was lavender satin with a huge red bow tied in the front. "Come," she said, pulling Jennifer away. "Show me where the champagne is."

Flattered by the woman's friendly nature, Jennifer escorted her over to the white linen table where two men poured the bubbly drink. Once Mrs. Walsh had a sip of the effervescent liquid, she said, "Tabor always has the best champagne money can buy."

"I find him charming, and so generous," Jennifer said.

"I could tell you a few things," Carrie said, taking Jennifer into her confidence. "All this big money that blew in from these mines— I know it seems like there's no end to it. But you know, this big money leads to expensive tastes, and before you know it, your daily living expense is more than most people make in a year. If something were to happen, if the mines dry up . . . well, not only would over half the wealthy people at this party be broke, they'd be deep in debt!"

Jennifer was about to respond, but Carrie was just getting started. "You take the Odells. He was a pauper and found a gold strike that made him a millionaire in a matter of months. But he and his wife took to the most lavish of tastes, buying a mansion in Denver, another in San Francisco, and he invested in all sorts of things. But he wasn't a wise man when it came to business. Next thing he knew, his investments were failing, and his gold mine dried up. But the expensive tastes didn't dry up—no sir. They kept right on spending until they were in the hole so far he couldn't show his face. Mrs. Odell went back to where she came from—St. Louis or Pittsburgh, somewhere like that. And he ran off and disappeared—nobody knows what happened to him. I oversee every dime Tom invests, and we use our heads. There's no fortune that can't be squandered." Carrie had a subtle but delightful way of speaking, her voice rhythmic and melodious. Although her story sounded a bit like gossip,

Jennifer understood the moral to the story, though she was sure such a terrible fate would never befall her and Jason.

"I'll admit, we're rather new to the arena of the world of wealth. But Jason and I try to do the right thing. I don't think it's gone to our heads."

"You're obviously a pretty and clever woman," Carrie said, laying her hand on Jennifer's arm like she was an old friend. "It's the men that worry me. I hear that Horace laughed about losing $10,000 in a poker game. I know he's rich, but it's that kind of living that I disapprove of. You make sure you keep your head about you. That way if your man ever loses his, you'll be able to tell."

"Jason's been a hard worker. I think I can trust him."

"Good for you, dearie. You two make a fine-looking couple." Carrie turned to see what a sudden commotion was about and saw the theatrical company entering in their expected provocative attire. The men wore top hats and shiny tuxedos, and the women, having taken off their coats, wore low-cut, flaming red dresses.

"Would you look at them!" Carrie said distastefully. "You'd think they were the cream of the crop, all decked out like that. Look at that Marie Kelly. She's a beautiful girl and a very good actress, I might add. But why does she wear a dress like that? Honey, unless that dress was stitched by a saddle maker, I bet she busts out of that tight thing before the night's over."

Jennifer agreed. "If she wanted to be the center of attention, she's doing a good job."

"Yes, but a woman like that doesn't have the fortitude to stick it out through tough times," Carrie said frankly. "I've seen it before. There's more to a woman than her looks."

Jennifer watched everyone move closer to greet the bold actress. "She certainly isn't bashful," Jennifer observed.

Taking another sip of her champagne, Carrie agreed, "No, she isn't bashful. I know her kind."

"There you are," Jason said, coming up to the women.

"Jason, you know Carrie Walsh, don't you?"

"Of course," Jason said, taking her hand lightly. "How are you, Carrie?"

"You know me," Carrie answered. "Couldn't be better."

"May I have this dance, Jennifer?" Jason asked, taking her away.

"Yes," Jennifer said as Jason led her to the open floor where others were already dancing to the music of stringed instruments.

As they danced across the floor, Jason whispered, "Carrie's a talker—I thought I'd rescue you."

"You can rescue me anytime," Jennifer said happily.

～

The party ran almost to dawn, and hardly anyone left. The more the men drank, the louder they talked, and the talk ran from business propositions to everyday gossip. Food and drink flowed as if from a magical cornucopia. The night was wonderful and the party a huge success.

No matter where Jason was, no matter what he was doing, every time he glanced up, he saw Marie. Her turquoise eyes followed his every move. Other than a brief hello, they hadn't spoken. But her eyes said enough, making him uncomfortable.

The music played all night, but at 4 A.M. the party finally began to end. "Another success," Horace Tabor said tiredly to Jason.

"Yeah," Jason yawned.

"At least we don't have to clean up the mess. Lizzie, my lovely dear, shall we retire?"

"Horace," Baby Doe giggled, "you're so funny when you're drunk."

Jason watched the two stagger away. He looked for Jennifer and found her telling some of the guests good night. "I'm exhausted, Jennifer. I came to say good night."

"You can walk me up to my room. I'm tired out too," Jennifer said wearily. "What a party. I've never talked so much."

Upstairs, at the door of her suite, Jason watched Jennifer unlock the latch.

"I'll have to be quiet so as not to disturb Abby."

"Don't I get a kiss?" Jason questioned.

"Oh, I almost forgot." Jennifer turned back, threw her arms around Jason's neck and gave him a healthy kiss." Stepping back, she said, "I'll see you tomorrow." She thought a moment, then added, "Oh, it is tomorrow. I'll see you later." She slipped inside her room and closed the door.

Unloosening his tie, Jason shuffled toward his room, reviewing all that had happened at the gala event. Jennifer had been wonderful. Together they had explored the world of the wealthy, and they both liked it very much. Unlocking his door, he smiled, thinking of Jennifer and how much he adored her. But then he recalled the conspicuous stares from Marie. In his tired state he wondered if he had the backbone to resist her.

CHAPTER

~ 16 ~

Blizzard

Pressing onward, Grant fought the powerful winds that hampered his progress. When he accepted his new job, he hadn't counted on fighting the weather to get around to the Wild Horse Company mines. Today, the day before Christmas, was clear and cold, and the sun's reflection off the white snow was blinding. The wind gusted hard, throwing icy snow in his face and frightening his horse. The superintendents of the mines were cooperative enough, allowing him to collect whatever samples he wanted and offering a hot cup of coffee to warm him up.

"You never know," said Ray Henderson, superintendent of the Birdsong. "The weather here is likely to change from one extreme to the other in under an hour. You be careful now—a man caught in a blizzard gets lost real easy. Might not find him 'til next spring."

Grant looked at Ray strangely. The hat he wore was the stupidest looking thing Grant had ever seen. "What kind of hat is that, Ray?"

"This thing?" Ray answered, removing it from his balding head and handing it to Grant for closer inspection. "It come all the way from Siberia. It's warm too, I tell ya. Now you take those Siberian winters, they make this high country look like a stroll on a beach in Florida. Them fellas over there have to stay warm or drop dead. You see them furry flaps? You turn 'em down and tie 'em under your chin.

I don't know what kind of fur it is, but it keeps my old naked head warm." Ray cut off a piece of his rope tobacco and shoved it into the back of his cheek.

"It makes you look crazy," Grant said, smiling as he handed the hat back.

Ray wiggled the cap back onto his head. "That ain't nothin' new—I been called a lot worse than crazy. Could be I am a little crazy, but it suits me fine; takes an ornery cuss to get by up here."

Grant couldn't help but like Ray, a little man full of big talk. Ray knew about people and getting along, and that was how he survived.

Grant could tell Ray was getting ready to start one of his little lectures. "I think you're a fine young man, Grant. But you listen to me, boy—when you see them clouds rolling in, you find cover. You need to have provisions along with you too; got to have respect for these mountains, 'specially this time of year. Wasn't long ago they found a man froze to death 'cause a blizzard hit all of a sudden. When they went to dig him out, they found his horse under him—the man was still in the saddle."

It was hard to tell when Ray was spinning a big one, but his point was clear. "I'll get me some things to carry along," Grant said.

"You do that," Ray said with the caring authority of a grandfather.

Later that day Grant made his last stop at the Baron mine and began the few miles back to town. The wind had been howling in his face all day. The short December day was getting dark, but he didn't realize it was too early to be getting so dark. *I'll have to get me a watch—must've fooled around too long talking,* Grant thought.

Next thing Grant knew, snowflakes were whirling around him, and in a matter of minutes they were coming down so heavy he couldn't see ten yards. He knew he was close to town but had grown disoriented, the road having disappeared under several feet of new snow. On an ordinary day the commotion from town would have led him in the right direction, but the snow snuffed out sound like a cotton blanket.

The horse stopped, and Grant kicked him on again into a stumbling trot. "C'mon, boy! Giddap!" But his horse wasn't sure where he was stepping, the snow now being past his knees. Bundling up tighter in his snow-covered coat, Grant felt nauseous with fear.

Soon Grant's horse refused to go any farther, since its eyes were caked with snow. The depth of the white stuff was increasing faster than Grant could have imagined. He looked in every direction, but visibility was so limited, he had no idea which way to go. "I might as well try to keep moving," he sighed. He dismounted and began leading his horse through snow almost waist-deep, nearly falling forward with every step. He hoped he was going in the right direction.

An hour passed, and the light began to disappear. If anything, it was snowing heavier than ever. Worse, Grant's legs were growing numb. The leather boots did little to keep his feet warm. He began to feel even more disoriented. Soon he didn't notice the cold as much but instead felt a deep sleep pulling at him.

Suddenly his horse neighed, and another horse answered back. "What's this?" a man's voice sounded through the blowing snow.

Grant felt strong arms lifting him up. "You awake, son?" Grant mumbled something unintelligible.

"Frank, give me a hand," the voice said, and Grant felt himself being lifted up into a saddle. He felt the rocking of a horse and saddle under him. A man rode behind him and held him on the saddle, but Grant barely knew it.

The next thing Grant knew, he was waking up beside a potbellied stove glowing red with heat. His boots and socks were off, and his aching feet were propped up near the stove.

"You give us a scare, boy," a man's voice said from the darkness.

It was a few minutes before Grant realized he was in his own assayer's office. Two men sat in chairs in front of him. One was carving an apple; the other simply stared at Grant.

"How'd I get here?" Grant uttered weakly.

"Found you under your horse—you'd a been a goner if we hadn't come along just then."

His eyes slowly focusing in the firelight of the office, Grant recognized the two men, Frank and Jesse James. They had saved his life!

"Thanks," Grant said. It took great effort just to speak.

"We couldn't let you die out there," Frank said. "After all, we already paid you for your assayer work and we ain't even got the results yet."

"It's good," Grant croaked. "Your samples showed good."

Frank slapped Jesse on the back, his mood improved. "See, I told you. I knew we had a good claim."

Jesse didn't seem so happy. Being a realistic man, he knew the effort it would take to get the ore out and hauled in to sell. "Well, if the winter don't improve, we won't be hauling much ore."

"How'd we get in here?" Grant asked.

"Gettin' in was easy, but gettin' out will be . . . Well, we ain't goin' nowhere for a little while," Jesse said, smiling. "Snow's chest-deep outside. They got ropes running from building to building so somebody don't get lost. We're going to have to ride it out right here in your office. You want something to eat?" He slid a saddlebag across the floor to Grant. "Eat some jerky—you probably need somethin'."

Fishing around in the old leather bag, Grant found cubes of smoked meat and stuck one in his mouth. It had a strong taste, but he was so hungry he didn't care.

"You know what that is?" Jesse asked, his smile giving away his intentions.

"I don't want to know," Grant answered.

Frank looked at Jesse and said, "He's a smart boy."

"Yeah," Jesse agreed. "You got to admire a man that don't turn his nose up at mountain goat."

~

"You haven't heard from Grant?" Jennifer asked, sitting at the plush dinner table in the hotel with Jason and Abby.

"He was gone when I got up," Jason said. "That's not so strange—I didn't get up until noon."

"I'm worried, Jason, considering this blizzard and all. What if he got stranded out there somewhere?"

"I'm sure he's holed up somewhere," Jason comforted. "Grant's got a good head—he'll be all right."

Abby sure hoped so. She dearly loved her brother. Besides,

Grant was her only true confidant. "He better be all right," she asserted.

"I can't see him missing Christmas Eve with us," Jennifer continued. "Something's wrong."

Jason waved his arm toward the outdoors. "Jennifer, people are going to be digging tunnels between the buildings soon. Nobody can get around tonight even if they wanted to. There's nothing we can do except wait."

"He better not be dead or I'll kill him," Abby remarked, her fear making her talk like a young child. "He might've frozen on his horse riding from mine to mine."

Abby's blunt way of stating things seldom failed to grasp her listeners. "Don't talk like that," Jennifer scolded as she pecked at her food.

"Why not?" Abby protested. "You're sitting here thinking the worst and worrying yourself to death about him—why can't I just go ahead and say it and get it over with?"

"She's right, you know," Jason said plainly.

"We're all scared for him. I just hope he's not in any danger," Jennifer added for her own sake.

The evening went on until the three were tired of sitting in the hotel restaurant. "I'd hoped for a happier Christmas Eve," Jennifer said, taking her last sip of coffee.

"We can't go anywhere, but neither can anyone else," Abby thought out loud.

Jason smiled, happily fed and growing sleepy. "One last thing," he said, removing a small gift-wrapped box from the inside pocket of his tailored suit. He handed it to Abby.

"For me?" she squealed, unwrapping the colorful paper. She got down to the fine little box and opened it. It was a heavy gold necklace. "It's beautiful," she said happily as she tried it on. "I've never had anything like this."

"It's lovely," Jennifer said admiringly. "Just the right length."

"Thank you, Jason," Abby said with a sparkle in her blue eyes.

"It's made from gold from the Wild Horse mine. Thought you might like that." Jason smiled.

Abby was rubbing the heavy gold between her fingers. She was all smiles.

"And this is for you," Jason said proudly, handing Jennifer an even smaller gift-wrapped package.

Perplexed, Jennifer reluctantly took the present. She wasn't good at receiving gifts and was never quite sure how to act. "What could it be?" she said childishly. Slowly she peeled away the paper and opened a small box. Multifaceted diamonds glinted with blue and gold sparkles, all arranged in a becoming design on a golden ring. Breathless, Jennifer slipped it on her finger and held her hand out, admiring the twinkling gems.

"Not bad, is it?" Jason said complacently.

"It's stunning," Jennifer sighed, finding it hard to believe she was actually wearing such a ring. "It must have cost a fortune."

"I have the money," Jason was glad to report. "I wanted to do it for you."

Leaning over, Jennifer hugged Jason. "I've never owned anything this beautiful or special. I'll have to be careful with it. Thank you, my love."

Then she remembered something. "Abby, would you run up to our room and get Jason's gift out of my bureau drawer?"

Abby made a face of disapproval but got up and left.

"This is so lovely, Jason. It means so much." She scooted her chair closer to him, her hand on his.

Loving every minute of this, Jason wallowed in the wealth of attention. "That ring came all the way from New York," he said. "Jake Sands was kind enough to bring it back for me. I designed it myself, had a jeweler make it. There's no other like it."

By now Jennifer was looking at Jason with a warmth that made her eyes a deep green, the smile on her face inviting. She moved closer to Jason, put her hand on his chest, and let it lie there. In the low light of the single candle she suddenly kissed him, her lips warm and full of love.

Pulling back, Jennifer said, "I hope that says something special."

"Jennifer, we should already be married. Moments like these drive me crazy."

Neither one of them noticed as Abby came back to the table and set the package before her mother. "Uh . . . I'm back," she said impatiently.

Turning, Jennifer addressed Abby in a soft voice. "Thank you, dear." She handed the gift to Jason. "This is for you. Merry Christmas."

Savoring the moment, to Abby's consternation, Jason slowly opened the small gift. Finally he eased the little box open. It was a gold pocket watch with a diamond fob. He flipped the watch open, and it played a sweet melody. Inscribed on the inner lid he read: *Love Always, Jennifer.*

"It's wonderful," Jason whispered. His other pocket watch was also gold, but pitifully average. "I'll always carry it," he promised. He pulled out his old watch, which was almost shameful by comparison. "I wonder if Grant could use this?"

"I wanted to give you something special, something to help you think of me when we're apart," she said softly.

"I'll always think of you," Jason replied. "Merry Christmas."

"Merry Christmas," Jennifer repeated.

"I'm leaving," Abby said with a hint of disgust. "I can't sit here and watch you two any longer."

Standing, Jason took Jennifer's hand and helped her up. "I'll walk you upstairs."

The snow-muffled evening in Leadville was indeed a silent night as the heavy clouds and white blanket tucked in the town cozily for the night.

As he went to bed, Jason stood at the ice-frosted window and looked out. He could hardly see a thing for the snowfall. "I hope Grant's all right," he mumbled worriedly, then turned away from the window to prepare for bed.

Despite all their joy, in spite of all their concern for Grant, it did not occur to either Jason or Jennifer to pray.

∼

Christmas Day was brought in with joyous cheer. Hundreds of miners armed with shovels took to the streets singing the songs of the season as they cleared paths on the streets and boardwalks. The sun blasted its way from behind the last of the clouds and brightened the day, shedding its warmth on the muscular backs of the burly miners.

Grant felt fine, although he was tired and ready for a bath. Jesse and Frank warmed up something to eat on the small stove before leaving.

"I reckon you know who we are," Frank said as they collected their gear from the office floor. "We don't mean no harm to nobody—just trying our luck at diggin'."

"What he means," Jesse said, "is we'd appreciate it if you'd keep it quiet about us—about our diggings."

"You saved my life . Of course I'll be loyal," Grant stated. "I don't have any reason to betray you."

Frank nodded. "He's a good boy, Jesse. I don't think we got nothin' to worry about."

Jesse cast a hard eye on Grant, sizing him up. "Why, he ain't no boy, Frank—he's a young man. Look at the size of those feet." He chuckled at his own thoughts. "We're obliged to ya for assayin' our rocks. Maybe we'll be back." He tossed his saddlebags over his shoulder and stuck out his hand. "We'll be seein' ya around, Grant."

Grant shook Jesse's hand and then Frank's as they left the small office. Now that he knew them better, Grant didn't feel as excited as before. They had treated him decently, though he knew they had done wrong deeds on other occasions.

∼

Late Christmas morning a good part of the crowd that stayed at the Clarendon waited on the front walk for the miners to shovel the last bit of snow from a path they'd made, then cheered at their success. Jennifer and Jason had eagerly been waiting, anxious to see what they could find out about Grant.

A group of miners stood aside as a young man pushed through to get to the hotel.

Jennifer saw him first and rushed forward. Stopping before him, she instantly noticed his disheveled appearance and sensed something askew. "Grant, what happened? Are you all right?"

"It's nothing, Mother. I had to stay down at the assayer's office last night, that's all."

"You poor thing," she said, pulling him along. "Are you hungry?"

"I'm always hungry," he answered.

Jason was beside them now. "You didn't get stuck out in the blizzard, did you?"

"Not really," Grant sighed tiredly.

"They thought you were dead," Abby bluntly stated. "But I knew you weren't." She pulled up close to Grant and walked beside him, holding his arm. "I really did—I knew you were all right." She was trying harder to convince herself than anyone else.

"What's all the fuss?" Grant complained. "I'm just tired, that's all."

"I told you there was nothing to worry about," Jason reminded her. "Women worry too much."

"Jason, stay with him for a while and see to it he comes down later. I want us all to be together—it's Christmas."

"That's a fine idea," Jason agreed. "You and Abby do whatever you want. We'll catch up with you later."

Hurrying off, Jason and Grant went upstairs, where the young man sluggishly got out of his clothes. "What happened out there, pardner?"

"You wouldn't believe it," Grant muttered miserably. "I got caught in that storm—thought I was done for. I was barely able to keep walking when Jesse and Frank James found me. Guess they were headed into town." He paused and fell back on the bed, half undressed, but kept talking. "They brought me on in. We stayed at the assayer's office."

Hovering over Grant, Jason showed concern. "You mean to say you almost died out there?"

"I thought I was a goner. Like I said, if it hadn't been for Frank and Jesse, I would be dead."

"Incredible," Jason stammered. He thought for a moment. "You know, Grant, you don't have to keep this job."

"I like it," Grant argued. "It's a great job. Ray Henderson warned me this could happen. From now on I'll always take supplies along with me."

"Are you sure?" Jason asked. "I had no idea this work could be so dangerous."

Lifting a hand, Grant waved it a little as he spoke. "Don't worry about it—you sound like my mother."

By now Jason was feeling proud of Grant. He was indeed growing up. "Anything I can get for you?"

"Set up a hot bath for me," Grant said. "I'll be fine. By the way, don't mention Frank and Jesse. I promised them."

"You have my word, Grant." Jason came over by the boy again. "Say, we got you some Christmas gifts, but this isn't one of them." He held out his old gold pocket watch. "Could you use a watch?"

Grant laughed. He remembered saying he needed one. "Yeah, thanks. I could use one for sure."

"Well, I'll go get you a bath lined up. Meet us downstairs later," Jason said. "And Merry Christmas."

"Right," Grant said, sitting up. "Merry Christmas."

~

New Year's was another reason to celebrate, and the parties were on again. In fact, it seemed that all Jason and Jennifer did was go to parties, every single night. And every time it was the same guests and the same talk and more expensive food for the well-dressed elite of Leadville.

But Horace Tabor never wavered, always his jolly and gracious self. His energy was tireless, and Baby Doe constantly hovered at his side.

One day the theater had just completed its last performance for the evening, a play called *Two Belles*. Marie Kelly had been the star of the show as usual. Jason and Jennifer accompanied Tabor and Baby Doe out to the lobby afterward. Grant and Abby had begged to come along and were delighted with the performance. Lighting a fine cigar, Tabor offered to buy a late dinner for all. He then focused his attention on Grant. "I hear you had a close call with the blizzard."

"Yes, sir," Grant said. He was wearing an uncomfortable suit and had his hair brushed back.

"I suppose you've received plenty of advice," Tabor suspected.

"Everybody has told me something about surviving a blizzard, if that's what you mean, Mr. Tabor."

Tabor placed his arm around Grant's big shoulders and pulled him aside. "Let me give you the best advice, Grant, and I'm speaking from experience. I've done a lot of dumb things myself. But if you can wait until you get older, you can do dumb things and nobody will say nothin'."

Quickly glancing at Tabor, Grant didn't know what to say. He didn't know if Tabor was serious or joking.

"Oh, I'm not kidding," Tabor said, sensing Grant's reluctance to hear him out. "Nobody will say anything."

"Thanks, Mr. Tabor," Grant said.

As the group crossed Harrison, Jason and Jennifer were approached by an old, hunched-over woman carrying a cloth-covered basket. "Waffle?" she asked.

"What?" Jason said.

"Waffle?" she said a little louder. "Fresh, hot waffles."

"Thank you, but we're going over to the cafe."

The old woman moved on along. "That's strange," Jason said to Jennifer, "a little old woman out at this time of night selling waffles."

"These towns never fail to amaze me," Jennifer observed. "All kinds of people from all sorts of places doing all sorts of odd things."

～

The new year 1880 came to Leadville with fireworks and gunfire and drunks yelling in the streets. Apparently every soul in Leadville was out to celebrate the coming of the new decade. It took days for things to settle back to the usual rowdiness and roar of everyday Leadville.

It wasn't unusual in that part of the country for January to have warm and splendid weather, often referred to as Indian summer, and this was the case high on the mountain in Leadville.

"Abby and I must return to Black Hawk," Jennifer said mildly one day. "It might be wise for us to go while the weather is mild."

Jason sat on a sofa in the comfortable lobby of the Clarendon next to Jennifer. After the holidays—sponsoring many parties and buying expensive gifts—the guilt of overspending was urging him to return to work and earn back the losses. "You don't have to go," he said.

"Somebody needs to," Jennifer assured him. "There must be a ton of book-work to check over. Somebody needs to make sure everything is doing well at the Wild Horse mine, and I'm sure Lita wouldn't mind some company either."

Jason raised his eyebrows, pondering. He hated to see Jennifer go, but she was right. The thought of being away from her saddened him, and there was so much he wanted to express . . . He'd probably think of all the things he should say after she was gone.

The Chevalier

From her window high up in the Clarendon Hotel, Marie Kelly watched Jason embrace Jennifer as she boarded the stage with her daughter. It was a pleasant day for wintertime, the sun bright as a chilly breeze stirred the dust on the street below. And for Marie, it was especially a grand day. She smiled as the stage pulled away, watching Jason as he observed its departure. She could now approach Jason freely without fearing Jennifer's opposition.

Marie moved away from the window to prepare herself for the day. Top priority was always to look her very best before she left the room. As she brushed her long and wavy dark hair, she sensed the excitement a child feels when engaging in some mysterious and mischievous action. *He'll take notice of me now*, she reassured herself, glancing at the mirror.

~

The long stagecoach ride was a test of endurance for both Jennifer and Abby, the bouncing and jostling putting them both in irritable spirits. Arriving late in Black Hawk, they greeted a happy Lita, ate a light dinner, and went to bed. Minor aches and pains combined with fatigue lulled Jennifer into a dreamless sleep.

The next morning an annoying wind whistled at the window. Rising, Jennifer pulled the curtains closer together and put on a heavy robe. She pinned her hair up and went downstairs to the kitchen, fighting off the lingering deep sleep. Lita sat at the kitchen table rewriting an old recipe she'd copied from a cornmeal carton.

"Miss Jenny, you look a sight," Lita said as she glanced up. "Let me get you some coffee and get you awake."

Rubbing her eyes, Jennifer sat down at the table as Lita placed the coffee before her. Since it had been setting on the stove where a good fire was burning, it was too hot to drink for the moment. She stirred the liquid with a small spoon, watching the fragrant steam drift upward. After a while she said, "Leadville isn't like any town I've ever seen."

Lita pretended to be interested. "What's different about it?"

"I don't know exactly—it's so high up in the mountains, it's like a town in a fairy tale. It has nice, big buildings made of stone, and the streets are wide and long. The people we met are wonderful, all of them so kind." Jennifer spoke like someone in a daze. "I never had so much fun—all the parties."

Lita thought it odd she hadn't mentioned Jason, but she continued to listen.

"I never thought I'd actually be on top of the world, but that's what I felt like in Leadville."

"You want somethin' to eat, Miss Jenny?" Lita asked, rising from her chair. "I got some smoked bacon from earlier. You want me to scramble you some eggs too?"

"That'll be fine, Lita," Jennifer mumbled as she began to sip her cooling coffee.

After breakfast Jennifer poured another cup of coffee and went to her big desk where she discovered a stack of paperwork from the Wild Horse mine. She sat down and began to study the figures. In a short few moments she was jolted out of her morning daze so abruptly she felt like she'd been splashed with cold water. Her breathing raced as she set her coffee down and held the pages closer to her face. The Wild Horse production figures had taken a sharp decline and had then dwindled down practically to nothing. The operating costs overran any profits. The shock of this news swept through her.

As she leaned back in her chair, Jennifer felt a paralyzing fear and found herself unable to accept the news before her. *There must be an explanation*, she thought desperately. *I've been gone for several weeks, and the mine's already dried up? That's just not possible.* She rushed upstairs to get dressed. She would get some answers!

It was a cold, gray, and windy day in Black Hawk as Jennifer stepped into the frosty wind, rushing toward the business district. The streets had the normal business traffic, but the boardwalks were almost vacant. Evidently most people had the good sense to stay indoors by a fire. Hurrying along, she wanted to talk with the banker first and see where she stood financially. She couldn't put the thought out of her mind that she was being cheated or robbed in some way.

At the bank the only person who could help her was a young assistant named Clifton. "These are all the files," he said, laying them on a table for her inspection. He seemed a little nervous, for the bosses were out and he wasn't used to being in charge.

In a matter of minutes Jennifer realized she already had duplicates of everything she was looking at. "This is useless!" she protested, turning to the young man.

"Yes, ma'am," he said.

"When will somebody be back who knows more about the situation?" Jennifer questioned impatiently.

"Well, Mr. Boggs will be here this afternoon," Clifton muttered.

Turning, Jennifer picked up her handbag and headed out without saying anything more. Back on the cold street, she decided she would have to hire a carriage to take her up to the mine. *Can't leave anything unattended or trust anyone*, she thought angrily.

A burro hee-hawed loudly over the wind, causing Jennifer to turn and glance toward the sound. She saw Emmitt Tugs pulling Pete along the muddy street, the wind mashing his old hat flat against his forehead.

Jennifer rushed out into the mud in her fancy shoes. "Emmitt!" she shouted. "Emmitt!"

"Hi, Missy!" he called, waving his stubby hand, showing his usual smile.

As she sloshed closer, Jennifer said, "Emmitt, what do you know about the mine? What's happening there? Something's wrong."

"Now, calm down, Miss Jenny," Emmitt said. "Why don't we get inside and I'll tell you." Turning, he tugged at Pete who bellowed, then followed. Taking his sweet time, the old miner tied the burro to a hitching post and stepped up the plank steps to the boardwalk. "In here," he said, indicating a saloon.

Jennifer was a bit uncomfortable but followed old Emmitt inside anyway. The heat was welcome as they sat at a small table near the entrance. Across the floor some miners were drinking and carrying on with the ladies, casting questioning eyes at Jennifer.

"I been up there," Emmitt said. "Looked it over good."

"What happened?" Jennifer demanded, short on patience.

"It played out," Emmitt announced with a smile, "just like it played in."

"But that can't be," Jennifer argued. "I leave town for a couple of weeks and the thing just quits? I don't believe it."

"We done good," Emmitt reminded her. "Made millions. I'd say you ought to be happy."

Jennifer was beside herself, her face showing the gloom of despair. "Can't we tunnel further in? Surely there must be more."

"We can," Emmitt said, "but it's a costly venture. When you ain't got nothin' comin' in to support the expenses, things get backwards in a hurry. My advice would be to let her go, be happy with what we got."

Things seemed to be closing in on Jennifer. She sat straight-shouldered, her features locked in a state of worry.

Emmitt wished dearly he could promise her something. Her cheeks were glowing red from the harsh cold wind. "I can tell them to carry on. Maybe we'll find somethin', but it's been my experience that when a vein dries up, you might have to tunnel purty near to the next county before you find anythin' again."

"Tell them to keep digging," Jennifer said hopefully, newly found promise in her eyes. "There must be more."

"I'll do it, Miss Jenny," Emmitt said hesitantly. He didn't have the heart to tell her the dream was over. Personally, he had plenty of money and didn't care about making more. But he did want her to be happy. "I'll tell them to work it for a couple of weeks," Emmitt agreed. "But after that, Miss Jenny, I think I'm going back up into the high country. That's where I like it best. You may not see me again for a long time."

Sad-eyed, Jennifer knew what Emmitt was saying—he would work the mine for her a little while to make her happy. But he no longer believed in it and was anxious to get back to his simpler life of prospecting and living with Pete. "You've been kind, Emmitt. You're a good man, and we'll miss you."

He scratched his ear, a bit embarrassed. "I'll miss you too, Miss Jenny. If'n I was only younger—"

Jennifer knew this was a farewell, and for a moment the fondness she felt for Emmitt was more important than the mine drying up. It had been a sad day.

Rushing off with a sense of urgency, Jennifer made her way back to the office, where she hurriedly wrote Jason a long, sad letter.

～

Grant had a dark tan on his face from the sunny rides he took daily out to the mines. Jason had a brown face too, for he'd been outdoors as well, traveling to each mine and overseeing operational procedures in an effort to minimize costs and maximize profits. And his work had paid off. In the recent months in Leadville the mines had showed $600,000 in profits.

When he returned to the hotel, the clerk caught Jason's attention and handed him a letter. The mine owner glanced at the envelope and saw it was from Jennifer. He was sure it was a love letter saying how much she missed him and how much she loved him. In his room he opened the letter and quickly felt disappointment.

January 12, 1880
My Dear Jason,

The Wild Horse mine has dried up. Emmitt says it's hopeless, but I insisted they keep on searching a little longer. His heart isn't in it, and I'm afraid he's leaving for places unknown. I don't even know if I'll ever see him again.

I've never felt so disappointed in my life. It's like receiving a great gift and then having it taken away. There's a good deal of money here in the bank, but I'd rather not use it for mining ventures. I'm afraid the money you have for Leadville investments is all there is for that, so I hope business is going well.

Love,
Jennifer

Jason read the letter again in disbelief. The Wild Horse coming to its end was in one sense awful news, but why was it so upsetting to her? *We have millions!* Jason thought. *And I'm making another fortune here in Leadville. What's she worried about? And she didn't even mention our relationship or our wedding.*

The letter had hurt deeply. There were times when he thought their relationship was perfect, only to be let down by things like this. Jason felt at times he must be about as important to Jennifer as an old shoe. "There must be something I can do," he mumbled. Putting the letter away, he decided to talk to Horace Tabor about an idea he had.

The afternoon sun grew huge as it settled over the western horizon of snow-capped peaks. When Tabor was in Leadville, he was easy enough to find. Jason located him and Baby Doe at one of their favorite hangouts, the Saddle Rock Cafe.

"Hi, Jason," Baby Doe called when she saw Jason enter. "Come join us."

Jason saw that Tabor and Baby Doe had begun celebrating the evening early with expensive champagne. "Won't you come with us tonight?" Tabor insisted. "Marie is opening a new performance—you can't miss it."

"I guess," Jason said. "Governor, I need to talk to you."

Glancing at Baby Doe, Tabor said, "I keep no secrets from Lizzie. Go ahead and say what's on your mind."

"Well," Jason began, "I want to buy a gold mine. A good one."

Immediately Tabor laughed and said, "Who doesn't?" Then he and Baby Doe both laughed, making Jason feel small and unimportant.

"Jason, you're so silly," Baby Doe said. "I can never tell when you're serious and when you're pulling our leg."

Jason rolled his eyes in disgust.

"Wait a minute," Tabor said, noticing Jason's expression. "You're serious."

"Yes, I'm serious," Jason responded impatiently.

Taking out a cigar, Tabor lit it, his mind engaged in serious thought. His eyes suddenly lit up. "Tom Walsh and I are looking at some diggings over in Ouray. We're thinking about buying a piece of land a few miles outside of town that shows good promise."

"Count me in," Jason said.

"I'll talk to Tom—he'll listen to me," Tabor promised. "You know me—everything I touch turns to money."

Relieved, Jason smiled. Now he'd be able to give Jennifer another gold mine. He reached for one of his black cigars, and Tabor struck a match for him. "Thanks, Governor," Jason said happily.

"Oh, there's Marie," Baby Doe said as she waved at the young woman just entering.

There was an empty chair at the table, so Marie came and sat down. She did most of her socializing at these hours of the early evening, for she wouldn't have another chance until after the last performance, which was after midnight.

"Hello, Jason," Marie said softly, her eyes and smile inviting. "Coming to the show tonight?"

"Ah, yes," Jason answered hesitantly.

Reaching over, Baby Doe placed a gentle hand on Marie's and said, "I hear the new play is another love story. I just love it when you do plays like that."

"Lizzie, you shouldn't flatter me so. I'm only an actress—this is not real life," Marie said smiling. "I think you would be a good actress."

"Me?" Baby Doe said, filled with delight. "I'd get stage fright."

Observant, Jason surmised that Marie and Baby Doe had apparently come to be quite close. But Marie turned her attention to Jason, making him a little nervous.

"Where's Grant? You still working him like a slave?"

"He's probably down at the assayer's office running his tests," Jason answered. "And I don't overwork him, Marie—he likes his work."

She smiled. "Be sure and tell him I said hello."

"I will," Jason assured her. Marie had gone out of her way to be kind to Grant, speaking to him at length every time she saw him. Grant had readily admitted to Jason that he thought Marie was the most wonderful woman in the world.

"Care to have a late dinner with me?" Marie asked. "After the show?" She asked the question as if it were merely a passing thought, which of course it most certainly was not.

"I'd better not," Jason said, fighting temptation. "I have to go out to one of the mines early in the morning."

Casually shrugging her shoulders, Marie acted as if it made no difference one way or another to her, which of course it most certainly did. "Well," she said, getting up to leave, "I'll see you at the show."

"Good night, my dear," Tabor said, saluting her with his glass of champagne. He took a sip and said, "She's one of the most pleasant women I've ever met—and not bad looking either."

Catching his playful remark, Baby Doe good-naturedly poked him in the side with her elbow. "You better not be looking at her too hard. Besides, she is most definitely interested in Jason. Isn't that right, Jason?"

"I don't know," Jason said, not wanting to discuss the subject.

"A man could do worse," Tabor said. "He definitely could do a lot worse."

Jason felt as if he needed to escape. "I'll be going back to Black Hawk in a few days," he said. "Jennifer needs some help there."

"Be sure and tell her I said hello," Baby Doe said pleasantly.

"Anything I can do for you while you're gone?" Tabor offered.

"Yes. If Grant needs anything, you might help him out, keep an eye on him. He's staying here."

"Consider it done," Tabor said. "Let's get a bite to eat. The show will be starting before long."

"I can't wait," Baby Doe said. "It's such a treat to watch Marie perform."

Yes, it is, Jason thought with mixed emotions.

~

Jason dreaded the long stage ride but endured it well. The weather remained tolerable, though March would be coming soon enough—the worst month of winter. He arrived in Black Hawk one late afternoon and hitched a ride over to the office with a freighter. Sometimes a carriage was available, but in his excitement to see Jennifer, Jason didn't even ask.

Finding the front door open, Jason let himself in, carrying his luggage a few feet and setting it down. "Jennifer!" he called. There was no answer. Then Lita appeared in the back door of the office.

"Master Jason," she said happily, "what you doin' here? You lookin' good, all dark from the sun."

"Good to see you too," Jason said happily. "What's for supper?"

"Somethin' good, you know that," she replied.

"Where's Jennifer?"

Lita's expression changed to one of concern. "She's upstairs in her room layin' down. Master Jason, I'm worried. She ain't felt good in days. And she won't see a doctor."

"I'll talk with her," Jason muttered as he headed for the stairs.

Coming to Jennifer's door, Jason tapped lightly.

"Come in," Jennifer said weakly.

The room was dark, with the shades pulled down and the curtains closed. "Jennifer?" Jason whispered, his eyes unaccustomed to the darkness.

"Jason?" Jennifer asked in turn, a note of enthusiasm in her voice. She quickly sat up, having been lying on top of the covers fully clothed. She came to him and put her arms around his neck. He smelled of the fresh mountain air. "I'm so glad you're here. I've missed you."

Jason returned her hug, then pulled back. "Lita says you've been ill. What's the matter?"

"Oh," she said hesitantly, "I don't know. I haven't felt like doing anything." She thought a minute. "Of course, I don't really have much to do now that the mine isn't producing anyway—just figure out the daily losses. I don't think it's ever going to produce again," she sighed.

Jennifer was obviously bored and depressed. On his long ride he'd come up with some ideas, and now, he thought, would be a good time to tell her about them. "Listen, there's no reason you should live in this place any longer. I did some looking around—there's a house in Denver, and I want to go look at it. What do you say?"

Jason could see her eyes light up in the dim room. "A house?" she repeated. "You mean a house for us to live in?"

"Why not?" Jason said joyfully. "I can afford it. The weather is warmer there, and there's much more for you and Abby to do. After all, we're millionaires—why shouldn't we buy our own house?"

"What about the Wild Horse Mine?" Jennifer inquired.

"We'll shut it down," Jason said confidently. He came closer, put his arms around her small waist, and pulled her close to him. In the shadows her face smelled warm. "Anyway, I bought you a new gold mine, over in Ouray."

Jennifer's mouth opened in surprise as she stared up at Jason. "But . . . but how can you buy a good gold mine? Who'd want to sell it?"

"It's not a mine yet. I'm buying a goldfield with Tabor and Walsh. It'll take some money, but we'll be the ones to open it up."

"So it's another high-risk project?" she asked, worried it could mean more financial loss.

"Have you ever known Walsh or Tabor not to make a fortune in their ventures?"

Thinking a moment, Jennifer realized Jason was right. Both men had shown uncanny foresight in their money-making schemes. "Oh, Jason," she said, almost whimpering, "you never let me down. You always bring me back from the most awful places that I drift off to." She kissed him, holding him snugly.

The time apart had made Jason appreciate her kisses more than ever, and now he returned her feelings passionately. He was no longer alone, and that made all the difference in the world. He had been weary but no longer. He felt once more that old hope, that old flare of excitement, that came from their relationship.

After holding each other for a few minutes, Jason thought of more practical concerns, especially for Jennifer's sake. "Lita says she's fixing something good to eat. Let's go downstairs," Jason said, happy he had come back.

"I'm a mess," Jennifer said, ruffling her hair. "I'll be down in a bit."

Smiling, Jason pulled the door shut after him. Like many times before, he wondered what made her think she was a mess. To him she was as beautiful as an angel.

~

Wasting no time, Jason and Jennifer left for Denver the next morning. A curious Abby tagged along; she loved to go to Denver.

"Is it a big house?" Abby asked Jason. Her expressive blue eyes were a woman's, but the present excitement in them was a child's.

"I don't know," Jason said. "I've never seen it."

"I hope it's a big one," Abby said dreamily.

When they arrived at the Windsor Hotel, Jason left word at the desk for a Mr. Fellows, the man in charge of selling the estate. He had been informed they would be staying there.

After they were settled in, Jason freshened up and changed into an evening suit with vest and tie. He wore a new black bowler hat, similar to the one Bat Masterson wore.

Feeling dapper, he made his way to Jennifer's suite and knocked on the door. Abby opened it, then stared at Jason. "Every time I see you, you're wearing a new outfit."

"Only the best," Jason said cheerfully. He noticed Abby's new dress and the new way she wore her hair. She was a lovely young lady, sweet and innocent. "I pity the boys who'll be after you," he said jokingly.

"Why?" Abby asked, not a hint of a smile on her face.

"Uh . . . I was only kidding," Jason said, trying to escape any confrontation. "Are you both ready?"

"Almost," Jennifer said, coming up behind Abby as she put on an earring. Jason noticed she was wearing the sparkling diamond ring he'd given her. "Jennifer, you could stop a train in that outfit."

"What? You don't like it?"

"What I meant was, you look lovely."

"Let me get my purse," she said as she turned out the lamp.

Jason was glad the sparkle had returned to Jennifer's eyes. They again had the gleam of emeralds, their color full and intense.

Downstairs in the dining room, the group sat at the linen-covered table full of anticipation. They talked about their affluent future in Denver, where the wealthy thrived and controlled business affairs throughout the state.

A small gentlemen with crisp manners approached Jason. "Mr. Stone? I'm Mr. Fellows."

"Great," Jason said, half standing. "Have a seat," he said, indicating a chair. "We've been waiting for you."

Mr. Fellows was an Englishman who represented the Worthington estate. The Worthingtons were a family of old money from England who owned estates all over the world. Unfortunately, the aging Mr. Worthington was no longer able to make the trip to Denver and had instructed Mr. Fellows to sell his estate.

"I say, Mr. Stone, it is a pleasure to meet you. And who might this be?" His eyes looked admiringly at Jennifer.

"This is my future wife, Jennifer," Jason announced. "We'll be getting married soon."

"Wonderful," Mr. Fellows said, smiling. Then his smile disappeared, and he focused on Jason. "Before we continue, I'm obligated to inform you that the estate for sale is worth a tidy sum. I've shown it more than once, only to discover the interested party couldn't afford to make the purchase. Pardon me if I seem rude, but there's no sense in wasting my time or yours."

"Tidy sum?" Jason questioned.

"Yes, my good sir. The price is $300,000."

Jennifer gasped, but Jason calmly said, "I see. When can we look at it?"

After a long pause Mr. Fellows smiled. His fine gray hair was cut short and plastered down; his eyes were calm, his attire frugal. He was obviously a professional servant who took great pride in his occupation. The desires of the Worthington family came first, his personal needs and wishes last.

"Very well," Mr. Fellows said, deciding Jason Stone was sincere, "we can view the estate in the morning. I'll have a carriage ready and shall pick you up, say, at 10?"

"That'll be fine," Jason said, trying to hide his excitement.

Mr. Fellows stood formally. "Good evening, sir, and a good evening to you, ladies." He walked calmly away.

"Those English people are strange," Abby observed.

"Always calm and well-mannered," Jason said. "He's undoubtedly from a long line of servants. His father and grandfather were probably butlers for the Worthingtons. I'm sure he can be trusted completely, for his dedication to the Worthingtons is his life."

Jennifer was still somewhat uneasy. Spending $300,000 made her uneasy. "Jason, I don't know—" She fidgeted with her hands, mildly distressed. "That's an awful lot of money."

Jason felt her distress but was determined to go forward, which meant convincing her everything would be all right. "It's not just a home we can live in—it's an investment. The value will always be there and can be turned into money again whenever we need it. This is a no-risk investment, unlike the risks of mining."

This eased Jennifer's worries to some degree but not entirely. "I just hate to pull that much out of the earnings from the Wild Horse mine."

"I wasn't thinking of doing any such thing," Jason said proudly. "*I'll* pay for it. I've made a lot more than that from the mines in Leadville."

Jennifer relaxed and began to smile. It made her feel good that Jason had thought it all through and was so considerate, always thinking of what was best for her. She took a deep breath to clear her thoughts. "I'm so proud of you, Jason, my love. I can't wait to see the house."

The next morning, exactly on time, Mr. Fellows waited for Jason and Jennifer at the hotel entrance.

"Good morning, Mr. Fellows," Jason said as they approached.

"It is a lovely day," Mr. Fellows responded. "Shall we be off?"

The carriage made its way through town and out Broadway. It was a cloudless winter day, the mountains clear in the distance. The air was crisp, clean, and thin and smelled slightly of cottonwood. Mr. Fellows sat rigid, his head high, a trained smile on his face. Soon the carriage was passing the *haute-monde* estates of Denver.

Abby held her face in the window gawking at the spacious mansions. Jennifer kept her lips pulled tight in a heart shape, her face comfortable under the bonnet she wore, her hands relaxed across her lap. But inside she was tense, still nervous about spending such a fortune.

The carriage turned into a long drive that circled in front of a white three-story mansion. Huge pillars rose the full three stories along the front; one-story wings spread to each side. A white board fence ran around the place, and massive cottonwoods reached for the skies.

When the carriage stopped, Mr. Fellows stepped out, then turned to help the ladies. Jason exited and looked up at the tall house in front of him. Its massiveness and architecture communicated a sense of awesome money and power.

Jennifer and Abby both stood perfectly still with eyes and mouths open.

"Welcome to Chevalier," Mr. Fellows said. "If you'll follow me . . ." He moved briskly up the red brick steps to the double front doors, huge doors of glass and coffee-colored walnut.

A maid in a full white dress and laced white cap opened one of the doors for Mr. Fellows. "Good morning, Betty," he said. "Would you be kind enough to prepare tea for our guests?"

"Yes, Mr. Fellows," she said and rushed away.

The prospective buyers noticed the house was full of exquisite furniture and exotic rugs; fine paintings adorned the walls. Yellow flames lapped gently in the wide fireplace.

"Do the Worthingtons still live here?" Jennifer asked.

"They never lived here," Mr. Fellows said. "They used to visit for several weeks in the warmer months, but they haven't come west in years."

"But all of the furniture, the servants, and the horses I saw . . . will they be moving these things out once the house is sold?" Jennifer was already worried about furnishing such a large mansion.

It was all Mr. Fellows could do to hold back his smile. These newly rich Americans amused him. "Oh no, madam, it's all part of the estate. Everything you see—the furniture, the servants, the head butler, Raymond, the horses—it's all part of the estate known as Chevalier, with the exception of myself, of course."

Jennifer was already in love with the place, and she hadn't even toured the house, much less the other buildings out back, which included stables and servants' quarters. Abby had no interest in looking any further; they could do that later, after they bought the place.

But Jason wanted to make a day of it and show Jennifer that he was introducing her to life at its very best, and that they would live that way forever. "This is grand," Jason said, studying the painting of a retriever with a mallard in his mouth above the fireplace. "Give us the tour, Mr. Fellows."

"Certainly, sir."

For the next three hours Mr. Fellows pointed out items of interest and great value, some historically important. It was like following a curator through a museum. The butler, Raymond, caught up with them in the third-floor parlor that overlooked the front of the estate, a view that looked west between the cottonwoods, with a ridged line of snow-capped mountains in the distance.

"Tea is served, sir," Raymond announced, a tray in his hands. He was a tall, lean man with a drawn, expressionless face of stone. His head was bald with the exception of a few thinning gray hairs. Seeing him in his tuxedo with that face, Abby thought he resembled a corpse.

Sitting down in petite, hand-carved chairs, Jennifer and Abby mixed sugar in their china teacups and took in the view from the tall windows. Jason wanted to light one of his black cigars and tell Mr. Fellows he would make the purchase, but there was no hurry. He was enjoying the tour and Mr. Fellows's abundant knowledge about the estate and its trappings.

Later, in the stables, Mr. Fellows opened two wide doors to reveal a black-lacquered victoria carriage with brass bells, lanterns, and fittings. A pair of matched black thoroughbreds and a pair of matched whites would pull the coaches. "Mr. Worthington always preferred white horses on Sundays," Mr. Fellows told them.

When a young servant girl caught up with the group, Mr. Fellows bent over. She whispered something in his ear and then hurried away. He turned to face the group, smiled, and announced, "Dinner is served."

The dining room was not typical of English tradition, for the room was open and had tall windows running the full length of the long room. It was very bright from the outside light and most cheerful, having its own fireplace in the long wall opposite the windows. The group sat clustered at one end of the long dining table so they could talk without raising their voices.

"What do you think, Jennifer?" Jason asked, though he was sure he already knew.

Jennifer couldn't have restrained her expression if her life depended on it. Her face was all smiles and lit up like a child's face at Christmas. "It's magnificent," she said softly.

"Abby, do you think you could live here?" Jason asked.

Abby smiled. "If you force me to, I could get used to it," she said smartly.

Mr. Fellows smiled at Abby's wit.

Dinner was served—three meats, ham and turkey and roast beef, along with many vegetables and fresh breads. Two servants rushed about the table and in and out of the kitchen. Dessert was fresh-made chocolates and cream pie.

Jason leaned back in his tall-backed spindle chair. The time was right. "I'll take it, Mr. Fellows. When can we make the arrangements?"

"Tomorrow, sir. We'll need a reputable attorney and banker. You may chose your own, or I have two at my disposal."

"Very good," Jason said, shaking Mr. Fellow's hand. "We have a deal."

CHAPTER
～ 18 ～

Friends

Once back at Black Hawk, Jason and Jennifer frantically wrapped up their affairs, anxious to take residence in their new home. Jason had agreed to help get her moved in, but then he'd have to get back to Leadville to see about his business affairs there. They would be leaving Black Hawk entirely.

In the kitchen that had served so many family meals and had been the place of so much close and personal conversation over the years, Jennifer sat at the dining table with Lita, telling her all about the Chevalier.

"It has twelve bedrooms, every single one decorated in its own individual way—no two are alike, Lita." Jennifer took a quick sip of her coffee. "You're going to love it there. It has the best of kitchens, big and modern—and all the help you could ever hope for. Can you believe that servants come with the place? I've never heard of anything like that. The servants' quarters are nicer than anything I've ever lived in. You and Abe will be so happy there. The horses and stables and a complete blacksmith shop—I know Abe will love it."

Lita sat with her elbow on the table, her expression one of despair as she listened to Jennifer ramble on and on. She had known this day would come, and she had dreaded it.

"Miss Jenny," Lita said, "it sounds like a wonderful place, big and nice and all. I knew all that money would sooner or later take you away from here. The Lord knows, I pray for your happiness. But, Miss Jenny, I . . . I can't go with you this time."

Jennifer stared at Lita in amazement. "I know it's hard to move," she reasoned. "But once you get used to it, everything will be fine."

"No, Miss Jenny," Lita said, her eyes big and sad. "Abe has a church to lead here. They're just about through building the parsonage, and Abe and I will be movin' there to live for the rest of our lives."

"You can't be serious," Jennifer protested, her voice thick with emotion. "After all these years? You and Abe are like family—we always stick together. Why would you want to live in a little parsonage when you can live in a mansion?"

"I'm getting old," Lita admitted tiredly. "The children are about grown. Why, Grant, he already gone. Miss Abby, she don't need me no more. Jason, he's busy here, there, and everywhere. And you, Miss Jenny, you have all them young servants helpin' you. No, Miss Jenny, me and Abe, we're happy right here in Black Hawk. And you know how much I help Aunt Clara and her good cause, helpin' freed slaves adjust to their new lives and all."

Now frowning, Jennifer couldn't believe what she was hearing. "Lita," she said firmly, "I'll pay you whatever you want, and Abe too, to live with us. I can't bear the idea of you not coming. What's here for you?"

"The church and the Lord's work," Lita replied, "and that's what makes us happy—not money."

Memories stirred within Jennifer, and she gave them her attention for a moment. She reflected on the hard times they'd had, their growing closeness to the Lord, and the Lord's material blessings. Suddenly she realized that since the gold strike, things had changed—*they'd* changed. With so much else to worry about, there'd been little time for the Lord, and now she saw how far away she'd drifted from Him. She hardly ever prayed anymore, seldom went to church, hardly even gave God any thought. It was just like Lita to point this out to her tactfully now.

Jennifer sighed. "The wealth—it's been a handful. I always

thought God had blessed us and that it was our responsibility to give it our best attention and effort."

"That's right," Lita agreed. "But you shouldn't put anything before God, not even the great wealth He gave you. The Lord gives, but you got to remember, He can take it away too."

Her shoulders slumping, Jennifer felt like crying. The idea of not having Lita with her cast a shadow on her grand thoughts of living in the new home. But they had already committed themselves to the purchase, and now they had to move. But she knew that Lita was a rock, and whatever Lita decided, that's what she would do.

Like a little girl who'd missed her mother, Jennifer hugged Lita, and the tears began to fall. Words could never convey how Jennifer felt about Lita; she was like a mother who'd shown her how to live. She was always there for her, no matter what. "Will you visit us?" Jennifer asked in a shaky voice.

"You know I will, child," Lita promised, patting Jennifer's back with her wide hand.

"We've been through so much—so many years," Jennifer said, her voice barely audible.

By now huge tears were rolling down Lita's face. "I'll be prayin' for you," Lita mumbled.

Both women dried their eyes in silence. Even the remodeled old kitchen held so many memories, but before long it would be deserted. Searching for some comfort, Jennifer said, "I'll send for you, pay your way. You can come visit often and stay a while, just for me, Lita. Please."

Lita nodded, hopeful the events Jennifer described would come true but knowing that good intentions often didn't come to pass, and that tragic reality brought her grief.

∽

The actual move wasn't that much work. All of the new furniture in the Black Hawk building, except for what belonged to Lita and Abe, would be sold with the building. And Jennifer insisted Lita take anything she wanted, especially any kitchen items she'd grown attached to. This left only personal items to be moved. A moving company loaded the crates and trunks, under Jennifer's scrutinizing glares.

"Be careful with that trunk—it's full of glass. It came all the way from New Orleans," Jennifer scolded.

"Yes, ma'am," the chunky mover answered as he grunted under the weight of the big trunk.

Jason stood in the front office. With the furniture still in place but all personal items missing, the room was cold and desolate. He glanced around, thinking of their time there—mostly tough times, though there had been many good days as well. Jason turned away and walked outside. He missed running a newspaper, but millionaires didn't work in newspaper offices.

Abe and Lita had had no trouble moving into the church parsonage, a small but efficient cabin with kitchen, den, and bedroom. It had all the necessities and close comfort of a family home. During these last moments Abe and Lita stood outside on the front porch watching the last boxes being loaded, waiting to say their good-byes.

"Are you sure that's everything?" Jennifer asked worriedly.

"I told you, Mother," Abby responded, "I looked under every bed and in every drawer—there's nothing left but the furniture."

A carriage waited for Jason, Jennifer, and Abby. They would travel by train down the mountain, then get a ride straight to Chevalier.

Jason took Abe's big, powerful hand in his own and gripped it tightly. "I'm going to miss you, Abe, but I'll never forget you. I'll have to insist that you come and visit."

Abe glanced at the ground, overcome by the moment, then looked up to say, "It's been awful good knowin' ya. I trust God that we'll see ya again."

"Sure, Abe," Jason said, releasing his hand. "Lita . . ." He hugged her affectionately. "You take care of Abe now."

"Oh, I will Master Jason, I will."

Jennifer hugged the two black folks who'd been such a big part of her life and whispered her good-bye. Abby quickly did the same.

"We'll see you soon," Jennifer said, trying to sound cheerful.

As the carriage pulled away, Abby hung out the window waving to Abe and Lita. "Good-bye," she called as the carriage disappeared around the corner.

Abe stared at the empty street before he turned his gaze to Lita, who was wiping her eyes with a red kerchief. He had his big arm around her round shoulders. "I expect they'll be all right, but I don't know. I surely hate to see 'em go."

"I'm afraid for them," Lita said. "Miss Jenny got so much money, her head's all mixed up."

"Don't you worry yourself none," Abe scolded mildly, his voice confident and strong. "The Lord will look after them folks. He has a way of workin' things, you know that."

⁓

Unlike their previous residence, the Chevalier was warm, cozy, and comfortable, with no airy drafts or whistling windows or creaky floors. And every time Jennifer turned around, some servant was at her feet begging her good graces and offering to do whatever she desired.

Abby took advantage of this, frequenting the kitchen and finding out just how far her authority carried with the servant staff. She quickly found out that the well-trained servants were eager to satisfy her every wish, but if her demands were anywhere near questionable, her mother would be consulted.

"I love this place," Abby said, catching up with Jennifer as she ascended the staircase. "But these servants, they're not like Lita—you can't talk to them very much."

"Well, they don't know you yet," Jennifer said. "I'm sure they'll be more friendly in time."

The women found Jason in the main den sitting in a big comfortable chair reading the *Rocky Mountain News*. He was enjoying the role of the rich tycoon in his plush home, for he knew he'd have to return to Leadville in a few days.

"Jason?" Jennifer called pleasantly. "The wedding is only months away—I'll have to start planning very soon."

"Good," Jason said, pleased at this confirmation of their coming marriage. "I want us to have the biggest wedding in town—plan it exactly the way you want it."

"Can I be part of this?" Abby asked.

"Absolutely," Jason insisted. "Accompany your mother to the shops and make sure she gets only the very best."

Abby's face brightened with visions of grandeur.

"I'll have to find a church too," Jennifer said. "In fact, we need to join one. And where will we have the reception?"

Jason laid his paper down and waved his hand in the air as if to take in all of Chevalier. "Can you think of a better place for a reception?" he asked, smiling. "We'll have the driveway and the front of the house lighted with hundreds of lamps. We'll have the reception out back in the spring evening air, and the house will be open to all guests."

"That's an excellent idea," Jennifer agreed, excited about showing off her new home. "I have a lot of work to do to make the reception just right."

"No need to," Jason said. "You'll have so many things worrying you that you won't be able to enjoy your own wedding. Hire somebody! Let them do all the work."

Jennifer wondered why she hadn't thought of that. She was still a novice at being wealthy. "Of course," she said. "But I can't hire somebody to make a list of the people we're going to invite."

"Invite the governor—invite the President," Jason said lovingly. "Never know, they might come. But seriously, we'll invite all of the politicians from the area—it's good to rub elbows with them, as Tabor says."

"Oh my!" Abby said in disbelief. "You think they would really come?"

"Why not?" Jason argued. "We've got more money than they do, and you know how they like those campaign contributions."

Swelling with pride, Jennifer determined to make sure the wedding was opulent and impressive, one that wouldn't soon be forgotten. Her head quickly filled with delightful notions of dancing, good food, a small orchestra, and good company. Some of the more prominent guests could even stay the night; they certainly had sufficient accommodations.

After relaxing several days at the Chevalier as they planned their remarkable wedding, Jason prepared to leave. The Wild Horse Mining Company probably needed his attention by now.

"How long will you be gone?" Jennifer asked on the sunny morning of Jason's departure.

"Two or three months maybe."

"I hope I don't have to send you an invitation to remind you there's a wedding in June," Jennifer teased.

"I'll be back, and I'll drag Grant with me. We can get him to be the flower boy or something."

Abby giggled at such a notion. She liked Jason very much and would miss him dearly until the wedding.

Standing outside the front door, Jason hugged Jennifer and gave her a quick kiss when he saw the black carriage drawing near led by the twin black horses. The carriage would take him to the train depot. "Have fun with all your planning," he said and quickly kissed Jennifer again before he boarded the carriage.

"We will," Jennifer said. "Have a safe trip, and write to me."

"Bye, Jason," Abby called as the carriage pulled away. Turning to face her mother, she said, "I'm glad you're going to marry Jason. He's the nicest man ever."

"Yes, he's a good man," Jennifer agreed, watching the carriage become a small black dot in the morning sun as it disappeared down the road. She felt sad at Jason's departure.

~

A torrent of cold wind swept through the afternoon streets of Leadville as Jason's coach arrived. Clouds raced through the blue skies in rapidly changing, ghostly shapes. Holding his hat on his head, he raced over to the Clarendon. In his room, he found things in order; Grant had kept things meticulously neat.

After changing clothes, Jason raced out into the elements again, heading for Grant's office. Wind or no wind, the wide streets were always crowded with people. Jason wondered where they all slept at night.

Jason pushed on the door at the Wild Horse assayer's office, and it swung open, letting in a gust of wind and dust. Startled, Grant jumped to his feet. He had been sitting at the bench grinding ore to powder, preparing it for tests.

"Jason," he said, settling back down on his stool, "when did you get back?"

"Just a little while ago." Jason closed the door, shutting out the howling wind. He took off his hat and slapped it against his leg, knocking the fine powder off it. "How are things?"

Eager to report, Grant said, "The Water Pit is *really* producing. You should see Levi jumping around on his wooden leg—I've never seen him so excited. He's got both of those big water pumps running full-time now."

"That *is* good news. What about the Birdsong and the Baron?" Jason questioned, "How are they doing?"

"Good as ever," Grant reported happily.

"Any problems selling or shipping ore? They paying us right?"

"Couldn't be better," Grant added. "Here are all the deposit receipts." He handed him a stack of small papers.

Jason found a pencil and figured up the receipts. "This is better than anything previous. I feel like I'm not even needed around here."

Grant smiled at Jason's compliment. The young man had done a good job of overseeing things while Jason was gone. Jason stuck his hands in his back pockets and walked over to the window, where he watched clouds of dirt and dust race by the window. Then he ran his hand through his blond hair and turned to Grant.

"Tabor still in town?"

"Sure is," Grant replied as he measured chemicals. "But you never see him unless Baby Doe is with him. And Marie is always with them now too." Grant sighed and stopped what he was doing. He looked over at Jason. "Marie talks to me a lot." He paused, searching for the right words. "She doesn't make me nervous anymore. I think she's the nicest woman I've ever met."

A tangle of thoughts fought for attention in Jason's head. Not wanting to talk about Marie, he finally decided to tell Grant about Denver instead. "We bought an estate in Denver. It's a big house with horses and stables. It's like nothing you've ever seen—called the Chevalier."

"Oh?" Grant said. "What about Black Hawk?"

"Sold out and moved out," Jason replied.

"What about the horses—Midnight and Dolly?"

"I had them moved to the new estate."

"Thanks," Grant said. "I need to get Midnight sometime. These nags I ride up here aren't half the horse he is." Grant seemed unconcerned about the mansion but asked, "What do Abe and Lita think about the place?"

Jason turned and walked across the small office. "They stayed in Black Hawk. Abe and some men built a parsonage there—that's where they live now."

"Lita didn't move with Mother? I can't believe it."

"Yeah," Jason said under his breath. "Things have changed." He felt uncomfortable talking about all this. He circled back across the office, coming closer to Grant. "How much longer are you going to be? I'm starved—why don't we go get something to eat?"

"Sure thing," Grant said with some enthusiasm, for he was always hungry. "Let's go to the Saddle Rock Cafe—I'm sure the whole gang will be there."

"The gang?" Jason questioned.

"Yeah. Tabor and Baby Doe and Marie."

"Oh," Jason said.

∼

At the crowded Saddle Rock Cafe, Tabor sat at his usual table entertaining Baby Doe and Marie. Oblivious to the rest of the world, the women carried on like children at play, laughing at Tabor's clever wit. Baby Doe and Marie had obviously become the best of friends.

Marie spotted Grant and waved him over. Then she saw Jason behind him. Her face quickly assumed a knowing and inviting smile.

"Jason," Tabor said, "and Grant, my boy, do have a seat. We haven't ordered anything yet—just having a little sip before dinner."

Jason had to sit next to Marie since there were no other empty chairs at the table. Her eyes looked at him anxiously. She was pleased to detect no resentment or ill will.

"It's nice to have you back in Leadville," Marie said cheerily. "Did you bring Jennifer?"

"No, not this time."

Marie just smiled.

"How are things back in Denver?" Tabor asked. "I was told you bought an estate there."

"Yes. Word travels fast," Jason said. "It's a very handsome estate—the Chevalier. Used to belong to an Englishman named Worthington."

"Good grief!" Tabor exclaimed. "That may well be the nicest estate in the entire state. Let's celebrate!" He held up his champagne glass. "Best wishes to your future!" He and the women clinked glasses and sipped the effervescent liquid.

But behind her smile Marie was envious. She treasured the idea of living in a stately mansion, and she hadn't ruled out the possibility that her dream would come true someday.

"Did you hear what happened at the theater?" Baby Doe asked Jason. "During one of Marie's performances—it was a comedy—she got so tickled she couldn't stop laughing, right in the middle of the show. Then the rest of the cast got to giggling, and before you knew it, the entire place was laughing hysterically. I never laughed so hard in my life." Baby Doe rolled her eyes at Marie. "You always knock 'em dead, even when you make mistakes."

"That *was* funny," Tabor agreed. "Marie is the most talented young woman I've ever known."

Jason smiled, but he felt like he was an outsider in this crowd. Marie had succeeded in winning over all of his friends, even Grant.

After dinner and lively conversation, Jason said, "Well, if you'll excuse me, I'm tired. Had a long trip you know." He stood.

Marie let her hand wander to Jason's sleeve and grasped it. "Jason, would you mind walking me back to the hotel?"

Jason hesitated, then decided that as long as he was careful, there would be no harm. "Sure, Marie. Why not?"

To Jason's dismay, Marie took his arm as they exited. The wind had settled for the day, the eastern sky now mostly dark and the western sky pink as they walked slowly down the boardwalk.

"So you bought a mansion," Marie said calmly. "Is that where you'll live with her, or will you live up here?"

"I consider it home," Jason said. "But I'll still have to spend much time here overseeing the mining works."

Marie unconsciously gave Jason's arm a vague squeeze. "And you're going to marry her in June?"

"Yes." He had an idea where Marie was headed with all this, but he hoped his few words would discourage her.

There was a time in Marie's past when she would have been dramatic and obvious, maybe even throwing a tantrum. But she'd learned better ways to beguile, so now she coolly held her head high and her shoulders back. Now that she'd won over Jason's closest friends, she'd have allies in Leadville. She would choose her words carefully.

"I don't think she can make you happy," Marie stated quietly. "I watched her the whole time she was here. Jason, she's stuffy—she doesn't know how to let loose and have fun. If she can't enjoy life, how do you expect she can ever make you happy?" She shifted her eyes to check his reaction, but he just continued to stare straight ahead.

"She'll come out of it, Marie," Jason defended, though he secretly agreed with her comments. "She's been through some difficult times; sometimes it takes people a while to get over such things."

"Sometimes they never get over it. What then?"

Jason shrugged. "If I commit myself to her, I'll stay committed. That's what marriage is all about."

"You mean you'd go down with a sinking ship, throw your life away?"

"I wouldn't put it that way," Jason said, growing uneasy.

As they walked along, men turned to get a second glimpse of Marie. Suddenly she stopped and pulled Jason around so he'd have to look at her. "I just want you to know, if it doesn't work out, I'll be here. I'll always be waiting for you," she said in a soft voice, her eyes trying to hold him captive.

"Marie," Jason muttered, rolling his eyes with a hint of impatience, "let me be honest with you—I love Jennifer, and I have for a long time. But I'm only a man—I have weaknesses. And you are a temptation I find hard to resist. I thought maybe we could be friends, but if you insist upon . . ."

Marie placed her small finger over his mouth. "I just want you know I'm here for you," she said. "I know you'll come back to me someday. But we'll always be *friends*, no matter what happens."

Exasperated, Jason took her hand and pulled her along. Smiling like a naughty little girl, she followed willingly.

◇

Comfortable in her new world and jeweled future, Jennifer addressed wedding invitations with quarter-inch silver margins and engraved superscriptions, also in silver. Invitations were addressed to President Hayes, Secretary of the Interior and Mrs. Henry M. Teller, Senator and Mrs. Nathaniel P. Hill, Senator-elect Tom Bowen, Judge and Mrs. James Belford, Senator Jerome B. Chaffee, and others with Colorado affiliations. She also addressed invitations to Mr. and Mrs. Thomas Walsh and other elites she'd met in Leadville. And of course she invited Abe and Lita Washington.

"Raymond," Jennifer called, and immediately he was present, his face dour but willing.

"Yes, madam," he drawled.

"I want these delivered personally by a liveried coachman, even the ones out of town and out of state. See to it."

"Yes, madam," Raymond answered, taking the stack of heavy invitations. He turned and left.

The tall order had made no apparent difference to him than if Jennifer had asked for a glass of water. But she had to admit, having a butler and servants made things easier. She never worried herself about frivolous rhetoric; she just gave orders, and things were done, easy as that. The next task was the wedding dress, and she expected the tailor to arrive soon. She'd already talked to him once and decided on a white satin dress costing $7,000.

Jennifer reached back, unpinned her hair, and let it fall. She shook it out until it was a cascade of wavy auburn on her shoulders. Her eyes gleamed with pride.

~

PART FOUR

OPULENCE
AND
GRACE

Nuptials

The high mountain country around Leadville showed signs of spring, the longer and warmer days causing thousands of tiny wildflowers to sprout over the slopes in a variety of colors. Jason had fallen into a daily routine of managing his business and fraternizing with friends. Leadville had already become a legend, bursting at its seams with the influx of newcomers arriving to harvest the rich silver ore.

One morning while dressing, Grant said, "It should really be something, but I hate to go to Denver—I like it up here." The window was open, refreshing the hotel suite with cool air.

Jason, shirtless and standing over the washbasin shaving, dabbed at a tiny cut with a towel. Tossing the towel over his muscular shoulder, he returned to the task, this time being more careful with the straight razor. His mind was on investing in some of the business ventures he'd heard mentioned in conversation the night before. Money was the heart of his goals and ambitions. "What ought to be something?" he mumbled, looking at Grant's reflection in the mirror while he shaved.

Grant made an uneasy face at Jason. "The wedding, of course. It's only four weeks away."

"Oh, that," Jason uttered as he rinsed off his face and toweled it dry. "I bet your mother has big plans. We should leave soon, get there a couple weeks early so we can help her out."

Grant shifted uneasily. He had a high sense of responsibility to his job and didn't like the thought of neglecting it more than necessary. "I could come later," Grant said. "Get there a few days before the wedding."

"Come on, Grant!" Jason said with some irritation. "You don't need to work all the time—things are under control here. You haven't even seen Chevalier. Why not get away from the hard work for a while—take it easy, sleep late, enjoy life a little."

"I'm enjoying life right now," Grant argued.

"Nonsense," Jason insisted. "We'll have a good time in Denver. You ready?" Jason asked, buttoning his shirt. "Let's go have some breakfast."

Grant followed silently as the two left the hotel. The day smelled like spring, and that made the people of Leadville cheerful. Cold mornings, warm days, and cool evenings made a perfect atmosphere for work and play. After Grant left to take his samples so he could monitor the mines, Jason walked along the crowded boardwalk, enjoying the sunshine.

"Jason!" a voice called.

Turning, Jason saw a man waving his hand over the heads of the people in between them. The man pushed his way closer. "Jason!"

"Hello, Bat," Jason said as Masterson came within speaking distance. "How are things?"

"Could be better, I'm afraid," Bat said, no longer smiling.

"Oh? How's that?"

"Somebody found my cache and left me high and dry. Whatever you could spare, I'll pay you back. There's a big poker game tonight."

"Sure," Jason said. Gambling didn't bother him like it used to. And besides, he had so much in the bank, he could help his friend out and not miss the money. "How much do you need?"

"A thousand too much to ask for?"

"Not at all," Jason said. "Let's walk down to the bank. I'll get you the cash."

As the two made their way down the crowded street, Bat asked, "How's the mining business, Jason?"

"Couldn't be better," Jason reported. "I just invested heavily in some smelting works. I hope that pans out too."

"I don't see why it wouldn't," Bat said idly.

Once their business in the bank was finished, Bat fanned through the bills, counting them again and sticking them safely inside his coat. "A few good games of poker and I should be caught up," Bat said. "I'll pay you back then."

"I'm not worried about it," Jason said, flicking his hand to brush the thought away.

Bat nodded, and Jason turned to see Baby Doe and Marie Kelly walking up behind him. They were dressed in spring fashion, the soft pastel-colored dresses revealing their white shoulders in the clear sunlight.

"Would you look at this," Baby Doe teased happily. "A couple of bachelors with time and money on their hands."

"I'll take this one," Marie said, playing along as she took Jason's arm in her hands. "Wouldn't you gentlemen like to buy us lunch?"

"Why not?" Bat answered. "Where's that rich boyfriend of yours?" he asked Baby Doe.

"Gone to Washington," Baby Doe said with some disgust. "Always politicking. But I don't think he'll mind if you look out for me while he's gone."

"My pleasure," Bat said.

Marie saw Jason almost every day, and she was pleased that she had succeeded in strengthening their friendship, establishing a mutual trust. She figured a man and woman could remain friends for only so long.

"Isn't this weather lovely?" Marie said from under her large, stylish hat. "Makes a person want to stay outside all day long."

The atmosphere was invigorating and inviting, and the four moved on as they conversed. Marie was as carefree as the wind, holding her head high while she clutched Jason's arm.

Jason felt uncomfortable. He was confident he and Marie were only friends, but at times he questioned his motives, and hers. He thought suddenly of Jennifer, and his discomfort grew as he glanced at the actress.

"Why are you so happy?" Jason inquired idly.

"I'm always happy. You're the one who's always gloomy."

Jason nodded. "Guess you're right. I'm not very good company." An image of Jennifer leaped into his mind, and the shame that accompanied it shocked him. He knew he should pull away from Marie, but she smiled up at him, and he thrust the thought away.

~

At the Chevalier, a much lower elevation than Leadville, the cottonwoods already had their spring leaves, shading the front of the mansion and the drive leading up to it. But Jennifer had failed to notice much in the way of weather, her hair pulled up tight in a bun behind her head. The white collar of her blouse was turned up stiffly, her back rigid. She had become obsessed with having everything in perfect order.

"We'll need to scrub and polish the floors," Jennifer told the two kitchen servants, Polly and Mildred. "Then I want all of the silver polished—and we must keep it that way. The wedding reception is only weeks away. Where's Raymond?" Before either servant could answer, she was off in search of the butler with a list of things for him to do.

"She's snippy," said Mildred, an aging Englishwoman, a cook. "Me polish floors? That woman must be confused."

Polly nodded, for she disapproved as well. Mildred's niece, she had come over from England at Mildred's insistence. At the age of twenty, she liked America, but the new lady of the house grated on her nerves. She mocked, "Polish this, polish that, then when you're done, polish this and polish that." She made a sour expression of discontent. "This lady thinks we are slaves."

"She is a mite testy," Mildred agreed. "Maybe she's nervous about getting married, with so many plans and so much to worry about." She opened the huge oven door and checked the game hens as they sizzled in sweet juices. "When Mr. Stone returns, perhaps she'll turn her attention to him and let us be."

"Aye. She could do with a good spanking," Polly visualized happily. "But you know, Aunty, I like young Miss Abby. She treats us like guests instead of servants."

"She's young yet," Mildred informed Polly. "They change."

As the days had passed, Jennifer had grown even more meticulous. She kept daily records to account for every penny and filed all expenditures in the proper columns of her ledger.

"I thought we were going to town and shop," Abby said boldly one morning. "Don't you remember? You said you wanted a fountain for the punch at the wedding."

Jennifer continued working on her books for a moment, then looked at Abby. "Yes, I did. Go tell Raymond to have a driver prepare the victoria, and tell him to hook up the white horses. By the time he's done I'll be ready." She turned back to her books.

As Abby left to find Raymond, she thought with resentment about how her mother's personality had changed. *You'd think she's the queen of England*, she thought with some distaste. *She never laughs anymore and hardly even smiles. She worries all the time about dumb things, gives everybody orders, and wants everything her way.*

When Abby found Raymond dusting the sitting room, she told him of her mother's wishes. "Yes, madam," he said, his usual unexpressive self. But after Abby left, he thought, *Jolly good—they're off for the day. These Americans are a rude bunch, with no taste whatsoever.*

Later in the day, not only did Jennifer purchase a fountain for the punch, she located a man to come to the reception and take pictures with his photographic equipment.

"Yes, I can, ma'am," he said, a short man in his thirties with a dark, short-cropped beard like President Grant had worn. "But the subjects in the pictures will have to pose and be patient—it's difficult to get quality photographs. I'm afraid it's a bit expensive too, since I have to bring all of my equipment."

Jennifer responded, "Money is no object."

"Very well then," the man said, smiling.

After leaving the photographer's office, Jennifer spotted a silversmith's shop. The shop was full of fine products of sterling silver including matching server sets on wide and gleaming trays, silverware with large handles and a place for initials, candelabras, serving dishes, and utensils for fine dining.

"I love it," Jennifer sighed as she looked over the wares.

The silversmith, a man named John Wilford, came forward smiling, "The silver here all came from Leadville," he explained. His head was bald, and he had large, gray, fuzzy sideburns. He showed Jennifer everything, clasping his skilled hands in front of him.

"I own several mines in Leadville," Jennifer said, not smiling.

"Then some of this silver may have come from your own mine," Wilford said, staring at the ring Jennifer wore.

Glancing toward the rear of the shop, Abby noted a couple of young men working in leather aprons and heavy leather gloves. She smelled the heat from the forge and saw a shop filled with many tools. One of the men began pounding on an anvil, and the ring of the metal had a musical sound. She thought the workshop more interesting than the front where the products were displayed.

Mr. Wilford, a charming salesman, made Jennifer a wonderful deal. She contracted him to make new silverware bearing the initials JS and purchased an entire new set of silver serving dishes, enough for any high-society dinner. The bill ran a little over $3,000.

Jennifer and Abby left, climbing into the carriage with the help of the driver. "Wasn't that a lovely shop? And isn't Mr. Wilford the most charming little man?" Jennifer said, happily satisfied with her outing.

She was determined to give their estate her personal touch and prove she could add things of class and taste to the Chevalier. Replacing the old silverware and silver service was a personal triumph, and like many of the recent and rather expensive trips to downtown Denver, it gave her a short-lived exhilaration. Her mood, greatly improved, made her talkative.

"Did you see that teapot set, Abby? What a work of art! And the silver is from Leadville. I've never seen such tasteful craftsmanship."

Abby didn't share her mother's enthusiasm. Silverware and dishes were just silverware and dishes to her. What fascinated her was the way they turned the precious metal into usable and pretty items. "Did you see those men in the back?" Abby interjected into her mother's babbling. "They were melting the metal down and then making those wares. I saw some liquid silver—it was like water, but it was silver."

"I love that tea service," Jennifer said, ignoring Abby.

It was again evident to Abby that a change had come over Jennifer. Her mother seemed to be in another world, a world of illusion based on her frequent spending. Although Abby enjoyed spending too, she liked buying clothes or things that would improve her appearance. But it didn't matter to her mother what she purchased, as long as it was expensive. Abby felt a rift developing between her and her mother, and that made her sad.

~

To Jennifer's pleasant surprise, the letter she'd written to Reverend John L. Dyer, known simply as the Preacher, was finally answered. He said he would be more than happy to marry her and Jason. He mentioned a modest chapel in Auraria. Jennifer had wanted a big, luxurious church wedding, but she hadn't become involved with any church since moving to Denver. Fortunately, the Preacher had connections and recommended the Auraria chapel, where a friend of his preached the Word of God.

Jennifer felt guilty about her spiritual neglect. Many things of great importance were happening in her life, and she was the queen of these events. So she found it more difficult than ever to humble herself. Though she did not recognize it, her fellowship with her Maker was broken, and He longed for her return.

~

The big wedding day arrived. The lavish and historic wedding would be famous around Denver for years to come. On a warm and sunny June 13th, at one o'clock in the afternoon, the wedding party assembled at the small chapel. Carriages and coaches of all sorts were parked up and down the road. Coachmen in black suits sat in the shade of a cottonwood drinking tea and trading stories. A packed chapel left some standing, while the elite sat close to the front. President Hayes, not wanting to snub the wealthy mining industry of Colorado and wanting to court the support of Lieutenant Governor Horace Tabor, sat in a front pew with his wife and guards, and behind him in descending order of political rank sat other government servants. Horace Tabor sat in the front pew on the other side, surrounded by men of wealth. Unfortunately, his wife, Augusta, refused to attend, and Baby Doe, not wishing to hurt Horace with unfavorable national publicity, was not with Horace at the wedding either. Five or six rows behind them, refusing to take more prominent seats, were Abe and Lita Washington, special friends, more than family, to both bride and groom.

Jennifer wore her 7,000-dollar gown, a marabou-trimmed, heavily brocaded white satin dress with real lace. It was designed to show off a 20,000-dollar diamond necklace she had purchased just for the occasion. She wore long white gloves and carried a bouquet of white and red roses. Her smile was pleasant—everything in the wedding was going perfectly as planned.

Grant did the honor of giving his mother away after he walked her down the aisle to joyous music from the organ. Abby, maid of honor, stood nearby dressed in a flowing white satin gown, holding a small bouquet of red roses.

Reverend Dyer stood in front of a table richly draped in satin white cloth. It held a candelabra with ten lighted tapers that shed a subdued glow over the scene.

The silence was broken by the Preacher's resonant, deep voice. "We are gathered here today to join this man and this woman in holy matrimony here in God's house, in the name of God."

As he continued, Jennifer's hands felt cold and clammy, and her heart beat rapidly.

Jason was proud and confident. He gripped Jennifer's ice-cold hands a little more tightly, hoping to warm them. Against all odds, the day he'd yearned for so long had finally come—he and Jennifer were getting married!

Reverend Dyer paused a long time before asking the crucial questions. His eyes were piercing, as if he knew something they didn't, as if he was praying about their future. His old eyes softened as he said, "Jason, do you take this woman to be your lawfully wedded wife, through sickness and health, for richer or poorer, to love and cherish as long as you both shall live?"

"I do," Jason answered clearly.

He turned his attention to Jennifer and asked her the same. She answered nervously, "I do."

"You may place the ring on her finger," the Preacher said.

Jason turned to his best man, Bat Masterson, and Bat smiled and handed him the ring. Jason took Jennifer's delicate hand and slid the gold band into place.

"I now pronounce you man and wife," the Preacher said graciously. "You may kiss the bride, Jason."

In his heart Jason felt the fullness of life, the gratitude of answered prayers, the reward of patient waiting—a happiness like no other. He kissed Jennifer, and this kiss meant more than ever before.

For a moment Jennifer was haunted by confusion from the past, vague memories that distorted the reality around her. Her mind raced from subject to subject, never stopping on one long enough to focus. But like a summer rain the troubling thoughts soon vanished, and all became clear. Jason was now her husband. She returned his kiss joyfully.

As they turned, President Hayes stood before them. "You are a lovely bride," he said. "I'm sorry I won't be able to attend the reception—the pressures of my work, you understand."

"Of course, Mr. President," Jennifer said softly. Not every woman was complimented by the President of the United States at her wedding!

From behind his long beard, President Hayes smiled with a twinkle in his eye. "May you have a long and happy life together."

"Thank you," Jason and Jennifer said together as they resumed their walk down the aisle.

The wedding was held at an early afternoon hour so guests would have plenty of time to make their way to Chevalier. The procession followed the victoria carriage in which Mr. and Mrs. Stone rode, pulled by white horses.

At the Chevalier, the long circle drive was bordered on each side with white and red ribbons that reached from lantern pole to lantern

pole. Above the doorway was a giant bow of the same ribbon with a
large lantern in the center. All of the lanterns would be lit at the first
sign of darkness.

Inside, massive tables awaited the guests. The first long table ran
the length of the parlor and had a centerpiece six feet high. A great
silver basin of blossoms held a massive wedding bell of white roses
surrounded by a heart of red roses. At either end of the table was a
colossal treasure chest made of white camellias and blue violets. One
chest overflowed with yellow rose petals and the other with orchids
of silver and blue.

A separate table was required to support the wedding cake, over
which a canopy of flowers rested with trailing foliage. In each corner of the large room was a bower of English ivy that appeared to be
climbing the walls.

The long dinner tables shone with fine, shining silver. Violets
encircled each guest's place, and other flowers garlanded the many
champagne buckets.

A multitude of servants dressed in white rushed around. Behind
the house Raymond stood in his tuxedo over a man who was stok-
ing the smoking fires of a large pit. Inside the pit several young pigs
baked in their juices, sending off a delicious and flavorful aroma.

"This place is like fairyland," Abby said as she stood beside
Grant watching the guests pour in.

"And more," Grant added.

"What are we supposed to do now?" Abby asked.

"Walk and talk," Grant answered knowingly. "We're just supposed to chat with the guests." Grant pulled at the tight collar of his
tuxedo.

Jason and Jennifer welcomed every guest as they came in, all
bringing splendid gifts. A small orchestra played from the corner of
the open den as the party got under way. Abe and Lita had celebrated
with them at the reception for an hour or two, then left for their
return journey to Black Hawk, not feeling that they truly belonged
in the affluent setting.

"Are you two off on a honeymoon tomorrow?" Tabor asked later
while sipping his champagne.

"Oh yes," Jennifer said. "Can I tell him where we're going, Jason?"

"By all means," Jason answered happily.

"We're going to San Francisco."

"Wonderful!" Tabor exclaimed. "They have some of the finest things you'll ever see there. Who will oversee your holdings in Leadville while you're gone, Jason?"

Jason answered, "I have some good men working for me and looking after things—including Grant. He's proved to be quite an asset."

"Grant's a wonderful young man. I enjoy his company in Leadville," Tabor added. "Excuse me. I see the Senator—I need to have a chat with him."

Jason smiled at Jennifer and squeezed her hand. "This is the best day of my life," he said softly.

"Mine too," Jennifer said happily. She never dreamed life could be so wonderful.

The photographer annoyed the guests by having them stand in the same position for uncomfortable lengths of time. Jennifer did all she could to placate the guests and have perfect pictures. This went on for some time until she had a headache and told the photographer that was enough.

Supper was exquisite, and everyone celebrated with hilarity and joy. Although some left early, most stayed until midnight. Jennifer had insisted upon some of the guests staying over—there were plenty of rooms prepared for them. But to her dismay, none stayed, not wanting to impose on bride and groom. She was beginning to feel tired and disappointed.

Jason had thoroughly enjoyed the day but was also glad it was over. He was looking forward to being alone with his beautiful new bride, having dreamed of this night for many, many years.

After the last guest had left, the lanterns out front were extinguished and the lights downstairs dimmed. Exhausted, Jason loosened his tie and removed his coat. "What a day," he said happily to Jennifer. "Shall we go upstairs and retire, Mrs. Stone? Together?"

"Yes, darling."

The two of them made their way to the ornate bedroom, and Jennifer retired to the small dressing room. She put on the silk night-gown, but when she turned to the door, a strange feeling came over her. It was not fear exactly, but closely akin to it. She suddenly wanted to dress again and run away from everything. *What's wrong with me? I love Jason!* Biting her lip, she forced herself to go into the bedroom. Jason lay in bed looking up at her, his eyes bright. He turned the cover back, and after she got in beside him, he took her into his arms. "You're the most beautiful woman I've ever known, Jennifer," he whispered.

Jennifer said nothing at all, finding herself unable to respond to Jason's caresses. Jason was aware of Jennifer's internal struggles as she lay in his arms. He could see she wasn't responding to his physical expressions of love, but he attributed that to tiredness after all the many preparations for this special day and its elaborate festivities. Being exhausted himself, he soon fell asleep.

The coldness in Jennifer's heart frightened her. She loved Jason, but something was wrong. She'd always responded to her first hus-band, but now . . . She lay awake until Jason's breathing grew slow and steady; then tears rolled down her cheeks. *What's wrong with me?*

For what felt like hours Jennifer lay stiffly beside Jason. She tried to pray, but God seemed very far away. Finally she sank into an exhausted sleep, but troublesome dreams came. Several times she awoke, and each time she knew her life had somehow, somewhere taken a radically wrong turn.

CHAPTER

～ 20 ～

The Life of Luxury

While Jennifer and Jason were away on their honeymoon, Abby and Grant stayed at the Chevalier. "They look good together, but Mother still has that worried expression," Abby commented one day as they sat on the iron furniture on the front porch. It was a warm, breezy afternoon. To the south, dark thunderheads rumbled and rolled. Rain poured from the clouds but didn't make it to the ground.

Poking at his teeth with a long straw, Grant didn't say anything at first. He was enjoying the view—watching the lightning inside the clouds and the disappearing rain beneath them. Leaning back in the chair, he propped his feet on the iron railing. The Chevalier was marvelous, but he was already bored and missed Leadville.

"Yeah," he agreed. "Mother still looks like a hen when a fox is in the henhouse."

"What do you suppose she's so worried about?" Abby asked. "She has everything." She wore a light blue cotton dress and had her hair pulled back.

Grant still marveled at the metamorphosis Abby had gone through—from a rough little girl to a beautiful young woman. He adored her more than ever, but in a way he felt sorry for her. "I don't think she was ready to *really* be married. Don't get me wrong. I think

Jason is the right man and all, but she's scared of something, and I don't know what it is."

Abby absorbed this, pondering the possibilities. "Maybe she's just scared of men. Daddy wasn't so nice to her, and neither was that Charles Fitzgerald."

"Maybe," Grant said. "But she ought to be used to Jason by now; after all, he's been around for quite a while."

"Yeah," Abby mumbled. "I don't think I'll ever have that problem—being afraid of men."

Turning, Grant studied Abby. "I don't think you will either. I think it's the men who'll be afraid."

"What's that supposed to mean?" Abby demanded.

"Nothing really. I just know how it is when I'm close to a pretty woman. It makes me nervous and sort of fearful," Grant admitted honestly.

"Has that happened to you?" Abby asked, now sympathetic.

"Well . . . yes. Do you remember Marie Kelly, the actress in Leadville? She used to make me real nervous when I first met her."

Abby thought about that. She remembered the famous actress who wore extravagant clothes and had a beautiful face and gorgeous, long, wavy black hair. But most of all she recalled her piercing, turquoise-blue eyes. "I guess so!" Abby came back. "She even made *me* nervous. Her eyes are scary."

"They're not scary," Grant whispered. "They're wonderful."

Turning her chin up, Abby wished some young man would say that about her. "She doesn't scare you anymore?"

"Not really," Grant said. "We're regular friends now. I often eat at the cafe with her and Tabor and Baby Doe."

"Why do you suppose an actress ten years older than you would be friends with you?" Abby pried.

"She likes Jason," Grant said matter-of-factly. "She's become close to all of Jason's friends, including me."

Abby put the picture together instantly. "If Mom doesn't get back to acting normal, that Marie Kelly just might steal Jason." She turned to Grant, checking to see if her reasoning was correct.

"Yep," Grant said, still watching the distant clouds. "Just like Baby Doe is doing to Horace Tabor."

∽

In San Francisco Jason and Jennifer stayed at the fanciest hotel and ate at the finest restaurants. Jason discovered Jennifer was happiest when she was shopping for exclusive treasures for the Chevalier. Yet when evening came and it was time for bed, she became quiet and withdrawn. Being kind and patient, he tried to soothe her discomfort by being sympathetic and catering to her every need.

A little time—she just needs a little more time, Jason thought. *She's scared, but she'll be all right.*

Their first disagreement occurred during a shopping spree. Jennifer spotted a Chinese trunk of exquisite hardwood, trimmed in what appeared to be ivory and gold.

"I wonder how much it is," Jennifer murmured, her eyes glued to the trunk.

Jason glanced at it. It was beautiful, but he didn't care much for oriental artwork. "It's probably expensive," he said.

The Chinese gentleman who ran the store explained that the trunk had once belonged to an emperor, and the artwork was whale-bone ivory and pure gold over ebony. He smiled, squinted his eyes, and said the trunk cost $10,000.

"I want it," Jennifer said, clasping her hands in front of her as she walked around the trunk. "It's the prettiest thing I've ever seen. To think it once belonged to an emperor."

I'll bet! Jason thought skeptically. *Probably an imitation. A hundred dollars would probably be closer to the real value.*

"I must have it, Jason. It would look lovely in front of the window in the upstairs parlor."

"Maybe we should check around—we don't know what it's really worth," Jason advised.

"But I really want it," Jennifer argued.

"Well, maybe you should get somebody to look at it who knows what he's looking at. Ten thousand dollars is a lot of money," Jason suggested.

Jennifer said abruptly, "Don't tell me what to do, Jason! Nobody tells me what to do!" She spun around, went over to the Chinese man, and made arrangements to buy the chest.

Waiting outside the store, Jason walked hurriedly back and forth with his hands in his pockets. He'd never seen Jennifer like this before. What had happened to the Jennifer he thought he was marrying? *It's only money. If she likes something, let her buy it*, he tried to tell himself.

When Jennifer came out of the store, she held her mouth tight, her eyes still flashing with anger.

"I'm sorry," Jason apologized. "I don't know what came over me. If you like something that much, it's yours because I love you."

Jennifer glared a moment longer, and then her face softened. She seemed happy again. "I did not respond as I should have," she said. "I shouldn't have spoken against you."

"It's all right," Jason said, taking her arm. "Let's go have some fun, see the sights."

Strolling away, Jason couldn't help but wonder about her quickly changed mood. Anyway, now she was sweet again. But when evening came, would she withdraw again and become the stranger he didn't know?

~

After the honeymoon, life settled in at Chevalier. Summer was hot, long, and slow. For Jason and Jennifer it was a year of travel, of parties and balls, of restaurants and theaters. Abby was delighted to tag along to as many of the affairs as possible, her smile always pleasing to the men there.

"Is that your sister?" a politician asked Jennifer at a ball in Denver.

"Heavens, no. That's my daughter, Senator," Jennifer answered, her smile indicating she welcomed the flattery.

"Could have fooled me," the man said respectfully. "She's as pretty as you."

"Thank you, Senator," Jennifer said.

As Abby grew up, she had become more outgoing, her personality vibrant, her smile genuine and sincere. She had an uninhibited way of speaking her mind with frank honesty. Her observations were usually clear and unobstructed, her wit clever and challenging. Her refreshing youthful expressions conveyed a magnetism that drew young men to her.

In contrast, Jennifer retained her beauty well, but her attitude was stiff and stuffy. Her snobbishness had become arrogance; everything had to be so proper and perfect, and she had little patience for those who made errors. Daily routines were strictly adhered to; the clock was a ruling master. Lunch was served at precisely twelve o'clock, dinner at 5. Jennifer dressed like a queen every day, her posture straight, her shoulders back, her head held high. She made a habit of finding fault with the servants, who feared her and avoided her whenever possible.

"I'll not have these weeds sneaking up around the front," Jennifer complained to one of the housemaids as she pointed to the culprits shooting up from behind the bushes.

"But, madam," Polly protested, "perhaps you should tell Tom, the man who takes care of the lawn."

"You're not doing anything," Jennifer said accusingly. "Go pull them up and dispose of them."

"Yes, madam," Polly whimpered as she crowded in behind the bush and tugged at the stubborn weeds.

Jason had finally convinced Jennifer to share intimate moments with him, but they were few and far between. He found her cold and distant as she clutched tightly to her strict, refined complacency. When she did show Jason physical affection, she acted impatient and wished him away afterwards. In fact, Jason preferred to leave, for she often belittled him. She had become untouchable, a lady of such high self-conceit he often couldn't wait to get back to Leadville and the company of friends like the fun-loving Marie Kelly.

"I have to go to Leadville," Jason informed Jennifer one fall evening. "I can't expect Grant to run everything." He was sipping tea from a thin china cup that Raymond had just served him.

Raymond stood nearby like a stone statue. They sat in the front room on a stiff sofa in front of a black fireplace.

"You need to trim your mustache," Jennifer pointed out while she worked on her fingernails. "I don't know if I even like you having one."

"Did you hear me?" Jason asked impatiently. "I'll go to Leadville tomorrow."

"You can't leave tomorrow," Jennifer insisted. "We have a party to attend Friday night at the Welshire mansion."

"Jennifer," Jason said firmly, "I'm sick of parties and balls and all this high-society stuff. I have to oversee our business interests— nobody else is going to do it."

Vehemently, Jennifer came to her feet and approached Jason. She glared at him. "Good! Then I'll go to the party by myself." She turned to walk away, then spun around to face him again. "I know about you and Marie Kelly. The only reason you go to Leadville is to see her."

"That's not true!" Jason protested angrily. "We have three mines up there—where do you think all our money comes from?"

Jennifer was not about to argue with him. She had stated what she thought, and that was final.

"Jennifer?" Jason called to her as she walked away. "Fine!" he said. "Don't talk to me." He threw the teacup into the fireplace.

"More tea, sir?" Raymond asked without changing expression.

"Oh, shut up, Raymond!" Jason snapped.

At this point in his frustration, he couldn't wait to leave. The less he and Jennifer communicated, the more the distance between them increased. And when they did talk, it was like fighting fire with fire.

The next morning Jason was packed and ready to leave. The carriage waited out front. It was an overcast day of dark gray, threatening clouds. Searching the big house, Jason couldn't find Jennifer anywhere. Finally he knocked on her bedroom door.

"Jennifer? I'm leaving—I wanted to say good-bye," Jason said to the door.

For a long moment there was no reply. Finally the door opened, and Jennifer stood facing him. Her dress was blue and tight-fitting; the skirt flowed all the way to the floor. She had all the beauty of a china doll, and she was just as cold and uncaring. "How long will you be gone this time?" she demanded.

"I don't know," Jason said defensively. "You act as if because I have to work I'm doing something wrong."

"You could hire others to do it," she said.

"I can't hire somebody to do what only I can do," Jason argued, now growing angry.

"You're missing the point," Jennifer said dryly.

"Perhaps I am," Jason agreed. "Why don't you come with me?"

"Humph!" Jennifer grunted with disgust. "I'm not going to sit around bored to death in a rough old mud hole like that. What's wrong with you."

"There was a time when you didn't mind," Jason reminded her.

"That was long ago," Jennifer said conclusively, then turned away.

Watching from the door, Jason waited for her to say more, but she kept her stiff back to him. Disgusted, he stomped off.

Moments later, from her window high above, Jennifer watched the carriage turn from the long drive onto South Broadway. Clenching her fists, a seething anger ran through her. *He thinks I'll bend, but I won't!* she thought forcefully.

～

The entire year was one of turmoil for Jason and Jennifer, due to their conflicts. In contrast, by 1881 Leadville had grown from an unsanitary boomtown to the second largest city in Colorado. The Denver & Rio Grande Railroad had even stretched her curving tracks through the treacherous slopes to Leadville, to the joy of all.

Marie Kelly refused to leave Leadville with her traveling company. "Why should I depart? I'm a star here. Any show company that comes here will hire me. This is where I'm going to stay." Of course the real reason was Jason Stone. Just as she'd said, she kept hoping Jason would become hers and gave him an enthusiastic welcome every time he came back to Leadville.

Tired of hotel suites, Jason finally purchased a house on East Chestnut and hired a housekeeper, an older woman named Clara. Grant had his own private bedroom and kept a regular work schedule. He appreciated the hot meals waiting at home and having someone wash his clothes rather than having to haul them somewhere and pick them up again.

"What's this stain on your shirt?" Clara asked one day as she bent over a washtub and scrub-board with one of Grant's white shirts. She scrubbed with a vigor, the same way she approached all her cleaning chores.

"It's probably some chemical from the assaying lab," Grant said. "Don't worry about it."

"Worry? I'll not have you going about with a stain on your shirt," Clara informed him. She was small and wiry and wore her hair in a gray bun. She was also tireless. "Someone might think I was foolish or lazy, sending you out with a stain on your shirt."

Grant made a face of disgust but didn't let Clara see it. She was so meticulous, it was annoying.

"I'll be going now," Grant said, headed back to work.

"Not without the snack I made you," Clara said, jumping quickly to fetch a paper sack. "Fried meat pie." She smiled as she handed it to Grant.

"Thanks, Clara," Grant said. Her pies were excellent.

Without a doubt Grant was exactly where he wanted to be. Besides Clara, nobody bothered him. His job was even better since he'd brought his horse, Midnight, up to Leadville. He could really get around, now that he had his sure-footed, swift mount. Young women gave him the eye, but he preferred his little chats with Marie, usually over lunch or dinner.

"So tell me more," Marie said one day as she ate another spoon of hot chicken soup.

"I don't really know any more," Grant said, eating the same. The restaurant made fresh chicken soup every Wednesday.

Marie turned on her charm. "You say your mother and Jason don't talk much?"

"When they do, they just argue," Grant said. "I can't stand to be around them then. I don't know how Abby stands it."

This pleased Marie every time she heard it, and she pried it out of Grant frequently. "What do you think the problem is?"

Grant shrugged his shoulders. "I don't know. I guess my mother's become obsessed with her money or something."

"Really?" Marie asked, delighted. "Do you ever try to talk to her?"

"I gave up. I can't reach her any more than I could talk to her by yelling from Leadville to Denver. All she thinks about is the high society there and keeping everything perfect in her wonderful mansion. I can't even spit in the street there—she'd pinch my ear off."

Marie just smiled.

The train whistle sounded, and Grant glanced over at a big grandfather clock. It was one o'clock in the afternoon. "Jason should be on that train. At least that's what he said in a letter. Want to walk down to the station with me?" Grant asked.

Marie wanted to do this very much, but she didn't want her excitement to show. She hesitated, as if pondering a busy schedule, then said, "Well, I suppose I have time."

Grant wasn't fooled. He knew Marie was anxious to see Jason. They made their way down North Poplar Street to the train depot and soon saw Jason waiting for his luggage. He appeared to be in no hurry as he enjoyed one of his black cigars while leaning against a column.

"Jason?" Marie said in her sweetest voice.

Jerking around, Jason saw Marie and Grant. "Well, hello. How're you doing, Marie?"

"Very well, thank you," she said, her smile beaming.

Grant could tell Jason was happy to see Marie. It was as obvious as the nearby mountains.

"How are things going?" Jason asked Grant.

"Great, like always," Grant replied. "Thought we'd come see if you made it in."

"The train makes it easy to get to Leadville now. Sure beats the old days."

"Oh, I don't know," Marie said. "Depends on who you're riding in the coach with."

Jason smiled at the memory.

~

Frequently Jennifer allowed Abby to accompany her to evening galas. Jennifer loved wearing new dresses and jewelry. Staying in fashion was one of her dearest obsessions and accounted for her profligate spending.

"Abby, are you about ready?" Jennifer asked through the door.

Hearing a groan, Jennifer opened Abby's door to see her half-dressed and sprawled on the bed. "What's the matter, Abby?"

"That new cook you hired," Abby moaned. "She's what's the matter."

Coming closer, Jennifer could see Abby was pale white. "Are you ill?"

"Yes," Abby sighed. "I can't go tonight—my stomach hurts."

Standing over Abby, Jennifer quickly analyzed the situation in her mind. The party was being given by some neighbors, and it wouldn't be considered indecent if she went alone. "Are you sure you can't come?" Jennifer asked.

"I think I'm going to throw up," Abby said.

"Can I get you something?"

"No."

"I'll have a talk with the cook before I leave," Jennifer said as she left the room. She felt bad for her daughter, but she certainly couldn't offend the neighbors by snubbing their invitation!

Downstairs Jennifer sent for the carriage, and while she waited she found the new cook cleaning in the kitchen. She was a Southerner from Bossier City, Louisiana. Sally was the third cook Jennifer had hired in a year. She figured since Sally was from the South, she could fix meals they'd like and be well-mannered at the same time. She was a middle-aged woman with short hair and a knack for somewhat spicy foods. "Sally, I'm afraid you've prepared something improperly. Abby is sick to her stomach, and she says it was something you fixed."

"That's right," Sally said, not even turning to look at Jennifer.

"You mean to say you deliberately fixed something you knew would make somebody sick?" Jennifer flared.

"It didn't make me sick," Sally said callously.

"What was it?" Jennifer asked, now curious.

"Chocolate cake."

"Why did it make her sick but not you?"

"Because she ate the whole thing, Mrs. Stone. All I had was one piece." Sally turned to look at Jennifer, happy with the way she'd handled the inquiry.

Jennifer knew when she was bested and decided to take care of Sally—and Abby—later. She was in a hurry to get to the party; social events always took precedence over domestic affairs. But as she left the house, she felt a little guilty. She knew she was behaving badly and yet seemed unable to stop herself. The days she could fill with frenzied activity, but the nights felt long and lonely.

I wish Jason was here.

She remembered how happy the two of them had been at one time. They'd had little money, but there had been a joy in living that was now only a faint memory. "I miss those days—I wish they were back."

It was a bittersweet thought, and she knew with sudden understanding that money and the things it could buy had indeed changed her, just as Lita had tried to tell her. A sudden desire for the former simplicity came to her; she felt an overwhelming weariness of spirit. But since there was no way to go back in time or to undo what had been done, she left the house and enjoyed the party as best as she could. As had been her habit for so long, she didn't think to ask God to come to her aid.

Contention

Jason had made so many investments that he did not have an overall picture of where he stood on a day-to-day basis. Banks, theaters, buildings, and other business ventures left him in a whirlwind of confusion. In time he realized he needed a full-time accountant to oversee his investments. So he hired Dick Shaffer, a highly recommended man who kept neat ledgers.

"I don't know how you have any idea what you're doing," Shaffer said, glancing over the satchel full of documents that Jason had brought to him.

"I don't," Jason admitted. "That's why I hired you."

Dick Shaffer was a college graduate from Boston, a short and heavyset man with a heavy head of straight white hair and bushy black eyebrows. He wore thick-lensed, black-framed glasses and came across as a very serious businessman. Every suit he had was gray, except the black one he used for marriages and funerals.

"It will take me days before I can even get an idea of how to proceed," Shaffer said, a bit irritated with Jason's disorganization. "Looks like you've invested in almost everything that came along."

"Why not?" Jason said coolly. "I have plenty of money."

"If you're interested in gambling with your money, I would suggest one of the gaming halls—you can make or lose your fortune in a much shorter time," Shaffer advised.

"Are you saying my investments are like gambling?" Jason felt insulted.

"Close," Shaffer said, pushing the hair back off his forehead. "You should have me look over any future investments before you make them."

"I've done pretty well all by myself," Jason boasted. "I have three silver mines producing as much as any mine around and you call me careless?"

"Mining is a high-risk venture," Shaffer said flatly. He held up a stock certificate. "Did you ever read this?"

"Ah, no," Jason said, settling back in his chair.

"It says in plain English that if this venture doesn't gain enough capital to put it into operation by next month, all proceeds shall be forfeited by the investors. Now tell me, why would this man want to work hard to make the venture work when he can just keep your money?"

Realizing he'd been gullible and cheated, Jason's face reddened. "Anything we can do about it? I've got five thousand dollars in that."

"Let me take care of it," Shaffer replied. "I'll need you to sign some papers giving me authority to oversee some of your funds."

"Sign authority over to you? Why should I . . . ?"

"If you don't trust me, I can't help you."

Jason pondered that. Dick Shaffer had been recommended by many of his wealthy friends in Leadville. If they could trust him, Jason could too. "All right, we'll do it your way."

Shaffer rooted around for a document and slid it across the desk for Jason to sign. "Give me a week or so, and I'll let you know exactly where you stand."

"Fine," Jason said, taking out one of his cigars and lighting it.

～

The evening was light, breezy, and comfortable. Ready for the party, Jennifer was wearing some of her most expensive jewelry, the kind that made people look twice. Gold and diamonds glittered about her neck, wrists, and fingers and dangled from her ears. Her dress was a little bold, but she preferred the conversation of men to that of chatty women.

The Robinsons owned a big mansion only a few miles away and were celebrating the announcement of their daughter's wedding. Since Abby was ill, Jennifer was attending alone. After all, she was already dressed and had an expensive gift for the bride to be.

At the lavish mansion, after being let in by a servant who took her wrap and checked her name off the guest list, Jennifer was escorted to the reception area, where Mrs. Robinson and her daughter greeted the guests. Jennifer's gift was added to the neat pile behind the plain-looking girl. Mrs. Robinson went on and on about how gorgeous Jennifer was, gawking at her diamond necklace.

"Why, look at you—if you aren't the belle of the ball . . ." Mrs. Robinson complimented, her own jewelry old and outdated. Irma Robinson had married into a family of old money and a large inheritance. She wore an old heirloom, a gaudy diamond brooch that seemed obviously out of place.

"You are too kind," Jennifer pacified. "And you, Betty, you look wonderful." Jennifer wondered what poor boy was marrying her. It had to be for the money, she decided.

Moving on, Jennifer found the punch bowl and picked up a crystal goblet. Before she could reach for the dipper, a man did the honors for her, filling her glass with bright red punch. "Thank you, Mr. Baker," Jennifer said.

Mr. Baker was one of her many bankers, an aging and wealthy widower. His Denver bank was very successful, for he catered to the extremely rich. He had made his fortune because of his finesse and charm. "Anything for you, my dear," he said, toasting her glass with his own. "And where's that dashing husband of yours?"

An unintended expression of disgust flashed across Jennifer's face before she managed to show a more pleasing smile. "He's in Leadville, where he lives much of the time. Business, you know," she answered with evident disapproval.

"My lucky night," Mr. Baker said, smiling deviously. "Now that there's no dashing prince around to challenge me, maybe I can get a dance with you."

"Perhaps while we dance you can advise me on how to increase my earnings besides through that bank of yours," Jennifer answered ever so pleasantly.

For Baker, money had always been easy to come by. But lovely young women were a much more difficult commodity to capture. He took Jennifer by the hand and led her out to the dance floor, where they waltzed slowly. He smiled broadly. "Take it from me," he said kindly, "sometimes the bank is your best investment. But I'll see if I can find something profitable elsewhere for you to invest in." The heavy man was light on his feet as he gracefully swung her around.

After the dance Jennifer wandered among the guests, looking her absolute best. Many of the people she had never met. She noticed unescorted men whose eyes followed her every movement. Although she had no interest in them, it was flattering to have them fawn over her.

"Wealth becomes you, my dear," a man's voice said from behind her.

Turning around, Jennifer found herself overcome with total surprise. The handsome, dark-haired man was none other than Charles Fitzgerald.

"Charles . . ." she said, her voice trailing off. A quandary of mixed emotions and memories made it impossible for her to concentrate.

"Yes, Jennifer, it's me," Charles said. "I used to think about you all the time, and I wondered how you were doing. Now it's easy—I read about you in the newspaper. So you finally hit it rich. A gold mine in Central City, was it?"

"Yes," Jennifer said, catching her breath. She didn't like surprises like this. "It was just outside Black Hawk."

"Was?" Charles repeated.

"Yes. It dried up. But Jason went to Leadville and invested in silver mines there. We're doing quite well." She was regaining her confidence. "And we have many other investments as well," she added for spite.

"I see. Jason is your husband? The editor of your newspaper in Virginia City?"

"The same," Jennifer answered.

"He's a lucky man, Jennifer." Charles glanced around the room as he gathered enough courage to make a confession. "I haven't had much of a life since I left Virginia City. I finally got away from Hearst and have worked on my own, but it's all been one huge disappointment after another."

"Oh?" Jennifer questioned, sensing a weakness she might exploit. "You lost your money?"

"On the contrary," Charles said, a slight smile now appearing. "I'm worth millions." Then the smile disappeared as his face grew more serious. He moved closer, making her somewhat uncomfortable. "I'd gladly give every penny I have if I could do it all over, Jennifer. Now that I look back, I can see the mistakes I made, mistakes that cost me a decent life. I've never married. No woman has ever captivated me like you did. I was a young fool, pursuing wealth as if it could buy you and the world and happiness. If I had it to do over, I'd give it all up for your sake, if you would have me. I made money my god, and it's been a cruel god. It cost me you, the greatest loss I've ever endured."

Jennifer remembered how she had despised Charles for their long engagement and the harsh realities that led to the end of their relationship. She had wanted to humiliate him, to punish him, but his story now left her bewildered. And yet she still didn't trust him, so she asked, "Would you give it all away for me now?"

"In a minute," Charles said painfully. "I'd start all over for you."

"Where do you live now? Do you have a home here in Denver?"

"No," Charles said, relieved that she was even willing to converse with him. "I have a house in New York, one in San Francisco, and one in New Orleans, but none of them qualify as a home— where people live together and love each other."

Charles's honesty touched Jennifer. She knew she lacked a home as much as he did. Pursuing great riches had brought him sorrow, and it had likewise emptied her life of the happiness that had once dwelled there. She said, "You've changed."

He nodded. "Hardship can humble any man, and it doesn't matter what kind of hardship it is either." Charles attempted a smile, trying to get Jennifer to respond in kind. He wondered how things might have been different had he made different decisions so long ago. But now he was a smarter man and would jump at any chance to please her—if he could only discover the key to attracting her to him again. "Are you happy?" he asked.

Jennifer couldn't answer the question honestly because she didn't know the answer. She struggled, but words eluded her as she stared into the eyes of a man she'd once loved. She felt vulnerable, exposed, and afraid. "I'm not sure," she finally uttered.

Sensing her anxiety, Charles stated knowingly, "Life is strange. We're all searching for something, and sometimes we find what we think we want, only to discover disappointment because of our own faulty judgment. Then it turns out that what we really wanted was something we had before, or something we always had and took for granted. So we want to go back and do it over and do it right, if only we could."

"Yes, Charles," Jennifer said snobbishly, "happiness is sometimes elusive. But I have everything I wanted—I'm content with my life."

"If that's so, then you've changed too, Jennifer. The Jennifer I knew would have never accepted financial gain from the brutal, demanding labor that miners have to do just to make a simple living—*exploiting* them, as you put it so long ago."

Jennifer glared at Charles and said, "My company employs the miners, but I'm not responsible for their lives or their working conditions."

"But you do benefit from the fruits of their labor," Charles gently reminded her.

This was not a conversation Jennifer wanted to pursue. She swung her pretty head around, then brought her glance back to Charles. "Will you be staying in Denver long?"

"No. I must leave for New York tomorrow, unless of course—"

Jennifer knew what he was hinting at. "It wouldn't look good for us to be seen together, Charles. I'm married, and I wish to maintain the dignity expected of me."

Charles had hoped for a different response. But he could see that the Jennifer he loved no longer existed. Sadly, he knew he would be departing on schedule for New York.

~

Jason had so many things going on, he decided to have a central point of command. After hiring accountants and bookkeepers, he rented a two-room office and filled it with desks, cabinets, and chairs. A shingle on the front door announced: *The Wild Horse Mining Co.* and *The Wild Horse Investment Co.* He needed a permanent employee to oversee the front office. A newspaper advertisement got the attention of Miss Carolyn Daniels.

When she entered the small office, Jason was sitting over a desk stacked high with paperwork. She was young and nice-looking. She wore a sensible cotton dress; her hair was pulled back. "Are you Mr. Stone?"

"Yes, I am. How can I help you?" Jason asked curiously.

Miss Daniels removed the newspaper from under her arm and pointed to the ad. "I'm Carolyn Daniels, and I'm here to apply for the job you advertised."

Jason smiled. This woman appeared too young to be qualified. "Uh-huh," Jason muttered. "Do you have any experience, Miss Daniels?"

"Quite a bit," Carolyn answered briefly. "And I'd rather you call me Carol."

Impressed with her confidence, Jason continued, "I need somebody to organize the paperwork from three different mines I own. Can you handle the time-consuming payroll process?"

"Yes, I can," Carol answered.

"I also have an investment company. I've just hired a man who will control that, but I'm sure he'll be sending a lot of papers over here to review and file. Can you manage all that?" Jason asked forthrightly.

"It doesn't sound like a problem," Carol answered.

Jason chuckled. "You look too young to have worked in all these areas. May I ask where you gained this kind of experience?"

"I'm sure you've heard of Daniels & Fisher & Smith," she said.

"I've worked for that company for many years. Mr. Daniels is my father."

Daniels & Fisher & Smith was a huge mercantile company with stores in both Leadville and Denver. They had been pioneers and introduced immense changes into the trade. "That's impressive. But why would you quit your father's company?"

For the first time Carol Daniels seemed caught a little off guard, but she took a breath and answered the awkward question. "My father is of the old world, Mr. Stone. He insisted that I was much too dedicated to the company, that I was making it my entire life."

"He fired you for being a devoted employee?"

"Not exactly," Carol muttered. "He says I'm becoming an old maid—that I need to get away from the business world and find me a husband."

"Is that right?" Jason said, suppressing a laugh, for this young woman couldn't have been over twenty-five. Although she appeared very reserved, Jason knew she could easily be most attractive. "Your personal life is your business, Carol. If you think you can do this job, I'm willing to give you a try. I won't be in the office much of the time, and you'll have to do what you think best. Just keep things in order—checking on documents and payroll and bank balances. You can start as soon as you like."

A sweet smile appeared on Carol's face. Her smile easily drew one from him as well. "I guess I'm sitting at your desk," Jason said, rising. "My office is behind that door there." He jerked a thumb over his shoulder. "The pay is twenty-five dollars a week, Monday through Friday."

The last thing Carol Daniels had expected to find was a decent job, for most women in Leadville were either captive to hard physical labor, washing or cooking or whatever, or they were confined to what some termed the entertainment business. Neither impressed her, for she had a good business mind and preferred the challenge of that arena. She was well aware of the fact that a woman finding a job in such a position was practically unheard of, but her determination had again won out.

"I'm grateful, Mr. Stone," Carol said. "I can start right now.

Maybe you could give me an idea of what you're doing there, and I can get going."

"Sure," Jason said. In many ways Carol reminded him of Jennifer back in Virginia City. She'd been so young and simple and honest with good intentions then, her beauty half-hidden. The memory lingered, then disappeared, bringing him back to the present. The vast difference between the Jennifer he'd known and the one he'd married gave rise to a vague regret.

~

"We have problems at the Water Pit," Grant told Jason as they sat at a table in the Saddle Rock Cafe. "Levi insists it's nothing, but I suspect there's going to be trouble."

"What's the problem?" Jason asked anxiously, for the Water Pit was his best producer.

"More water," Grant said dejectedly. "He's got those two steam engines—what does he call them, Sarah and Linda?—anyway, he's got them running at full capacity. I checked the gauges, and the boilers are working right at the safety limits. I can't help but wonder how long those boilers can hold up under that kind of pressure."

"Hmm," Jason said, rubbing his chin with his hand as his eyes darted around the table. "Maybe I should get some bigger boilers in here before he blows up half of Lake County."

"That might not be a bad idea," Grant said thoughtfully, then wiped his mouth with a napkin as he stood to leave. "I'll talk to you later."

Jason sat finishing his meal, thinking about the problem. Levi was one of his best superintendents, perhaps even a little overambitious. The old man prided himself on the fact that the Water Pit was the most productive mine owned by the Wild Horse Mining Company. But his zealous efforts might prove to be dangerous. *I'll have to keep an eye on him*, Jason thought worriedly.

"Hello, stranger," Marie said. She had crept up on him. "You look worried."

"It's nothing," Jason said as he watched Marie sit down. She put her hand on his, a new physical advance between them. It had been a subtle gesture in the beginning, as if she were simply trying to hold his attention. But it had become a habit. Jason told himself it was an act of friendship, though he knew it expressed an intimacy that was inappropriate but for which he hungered.

Marie had noticed Jason talking to a young woman earlier that day. "Who was that woman you were talking to in front of your office?" she questioned, disapproval showing in her colorful eyes.

"What?" Jason said, brought back to awareness by the question. "Oh, that's Carolyn Daniels, my new clerk."

Marie didn't say anything; her expression said it all. "She's good-looking," Marie said sadly.

"That's not a crime," Jason said defensively.

This wasn't the answer Marie wanted. If she was going to persuade Jason to accept her affections, she would have to do something more drastic than touching his hand.

∼

The parties had not held the same appeal for Jennifer since her conversation with Charles Fitzgerald. His words kept coming back to her. "I'd trade it all," he'd said. She had her mansion, her servants, her exotic jewels, and her extensive wardrobe, but she was wallowing in self-pity, and her life was empty of peace and genuine happiness. Sitting in her large bedroom with the door closed, she longed for the times back in Black Hawk when they were all poor but close, when they'd had so much promise and hope.

Jennifer thought about praying, but she was so ashamed, depressed, and guilty that she couldn't humble herself enough to do so. Instead, she stared out the window, lost in her memories.

"Mrs. Stone might be ill," Sally said as she scurried around the kitchen. "She ain't hardly come out of her room for days."

"I'm glad," said Marsha, the newest house servant. "In the two months I've been here, all that woman has caused me is misery. She's bossy."

"That's what I mean," Sally said. "If she ain't bossin' she must be sick. I'll make her some fresh chicken broth, and I want you to take it up to her."

"If you say so. I hope she stays in her room though. It sure makes my life easier."

"Sally," Abby called as she blew into the kitchen like a valley wind, "have you got the picnic lunch ready yet?"

"I sure do, Miss Abby. You say this is your first outing with a boy—a picnic?"

Embarrassed, Abby defended herself. "Don't be silly," she countered. "I had a boyfriend in Black Hawk for a long time—Butch Cassidy. He was the sweetest ever."

"Oh, excuse me," Sally said, smiling. "I should have known you were no amateur. You say ya'll are going over by the river? What's his name? Lewis something?"

"Lewis Brown. He's just a neighbor, a boy from one of the mansions down the road," Abby related with a carefree attitude.

"You watch out now, Miss Abby. Them old boys are prone to try to kiss a girl as pretty as you."

Abby blushed. There had been a day not so long ago that she would have socked a boy for attempting anything so brash. But her thoughts were different now. "He'd never try anything like that— he's too bashful," Abby said regretfully.

Servitude

Days turned into weeks as Jennifer dwelled on her well-rationalized delusions of grandeur only to have them quickly shift to delusions of persecution. She preferred the solitary seclusion of her bedroom, often sitting for hours staring out the window, strange ideas battling for her attention. On occasion she became focused and carried out her ambitions with the utmost of authority, as if there were no tomorrow, but at other times she wandered down mental paths of misery and regret.

"Have a man from the mercantile hardware company come see me," she had ordered Raymond. "Tell him I have a large purchase in mind."

"Yes, madam," Raymond drawled and went about his duty.

A hardware salesman showed up tickled at the thought of a large order, until he heard what Jennifer had in mind.

"A safe that big?" he questioned, his smooth, young face now frowning. "That's not a safe—that's a vault. We don't carry anything like that."

"Well, find one," Jennifer insisted. "One like the bank uses."

"I'll try," the young man said and went on his way.

A few weeks later a huge vault with silver handles and combination locks arrived in a freighter pulled by a six-mule team. Two strong men unloaded it. "Where do you want it, lady?" one asked gruffly.

"Downstairs, behind the iron doors of the wine cellar. I've had a place cleared for it," Jennifer said.

"Wonderful," the heavy man said, throwing his hands in the air in disgust.

Jennifer looked on as the two grunted and struggled with the heavy iron safe until they got it down the stairs and into the wine cellar. They hung around expecting a tip, but all they were offered was water, which they gladly accepted.

A few days later Jennifer announced that the livery man would take her to town along with two stablemen armed with shotguns.

"She's crazy," said Joe, a horseman by trade. "She wants us to bring shotguns like we was riding on a payroll stagecoach or something."

"I wouldn't be filthy rich for all the money in the world," replied Calvin, an old man who was initially a jack of all trades. He had been reduced to tending the horse stalls and horses due to his frequent temptation to enjoy a bottle of aged whiskey. His pay wasn't much, but he had a roof and free meals, and that was all he cared about. "You take a woman like that—she's just plain ruint. All that money done got her messed up in the head. She don't know what she's doin'."

"That's true enough," Joe said as he hitched the team up to an enameled carriage. "That's right."

In town Jennifer headed for the bank, where she proceeded to cash in every investment she had in Denver, then brought the money home and put it in the big safe downstairs. Afterwards she seemed as content as a nesting hen.

"What are you doing?" Abby asked, confused and frightened by her mother's erratic behavior.

"I've put all my money in my own safe. You never know what might happen to those banks," Jennifer professed.

"What are you talking about?" Abby questioned impatiently.

"A bank might get robbed, or it might burn down, or we might get into another war, and the enemy would just take my money. This way I can keep an eye on it," Jennifer said firmly. "I don't trust banks anymore."

Rolling her eyes in disgust, Abby went on about her business. She didn't really care where the money was, as long as there was plenty of it. For the present her friends rated far higher in importance than minor worries like banks or vaults. Her happy-go-lucky friends dominated almost all of her decisions.

~

In her dimly lit bedroom, Marie Kelly laid on her plush bed propped up on three fluffed pillows. Beside her on the night stand was a group of differently shaped bottles full of medicines and potions. Although she looked sweet and innocent, the room carried an air of mournful illness as she coughed lightly, then moaned painfully. Death seemed to be lurking nearby, ready to pounce on her and take her away forever.

Word reached Jason that Marie was deathly ill and had requested his presence. "What's the matter with her?" Jason asked the messenger boy.

He shrugged. "How should I know?" Standing his ground, he awaited his tip.

Jason tossed the boy a coin. *Marie ill? She's always seemed so carefree, so happy, without a problem in the world.* Despite her bothersome advances, he had always considered her a friend. Overcome with sorrow, he rushed over to her hotel suite.

Lightly tapping on the door, Jason heard a weak cry and let himself in. An unexpected sweet fragrance greeted him; fresh flowers and cards adorned every surface. The suite was neat and colorful; the sunlight from a window made a bright square on a velvety rug that covered the floor. Marie sat propped on pillows in her four-posted bed. She looked beautiful in a pitiful sort of way.

Holding her arm up limply, Marie whispered, "Oh, Jason, thank you for coming. Please, pull up a chair and sit with me for a while."

Jason sat down and leaned close to Marie. His expression was one of grave concern. Speaking quietly, he said, "Marie, what's wrong with you?"

"If I only knew. The doctor isn't much help either. He thinks maybe it will pass, but, Jason, I know different. I feel I don't have much time left." She was sure her words were convincing. After all, she was an actress!

Jason stared at the lovely woman before him. In the past he'd had his doubts about her, and he knew she didn't have the moral standards she should have, but now, confronted with the probability of her imminent death, he felt conflicting emotions. Not knowing what to say, he finally asked, "Where are you having pain?"

Marie muttered an answer Jason couldn't understand.

He gently touched her forehead with his palm. She was rather warm to the touch but not extremely feverish.

"Hold me," Marie pleaded. "Please."

Jason put his arm around her. She felt soft and warm. Her breathing was shallow. As her big eyes closed, she gently kissed his cheek and then moaned. Her strength seemed to be dwindling. "I'm here," Jason said, trying to comfort her.

Marie weakly put her arm around Jason's neck, pulling him closer. "I don't want to die alone. Stay with me," she said pitifully.

"I'm right here, Marie," Jason whispered. He would sit with her as long as necessary.

～

Things had changed quickly at Chevalier. Deciding the house staff was too large and overly expensive, Jennifer let many of them go. She sold all of the horses except for the two paired teams and promptly deposited the money in her vault. As a result, with summer in full swing, the grounds at Chevalier rapidly became overgrown, giving the mansion a ragged and run-down appearance.

Every afternoon dark clouds marched in from the northwest foothills. Lightning sometimes flashed and boomed and sent its blinding streaks across a darkened sky. Wind whipped the cottonwoods and shimmered across the tall grass and weeds. And every day Jennifer observed the peril from an upstairs window, somehow identifying with the turmoil she was witnessing. Usually by the time the storm front came to the open plains, the winds died down, and the clouds thinned out into orange sheets reflecting the sunset. Not a drop of badly needed rain hit the ground.

Often Abby tried to speak to her mother about her strange ways, her degenerating condition. "Why don't you take a walk with me?" Abby asked in a friendly way one day. "It's a nice afternoon, and we can get in a walk before the clouds come. It would do you good."

"No thanks, I'm fine," Jennifer assured Abby.

"But you're not fine, Mother," Abby said decisively.

"I feel perfectly all right," Jennifer said with a little more emphasis.

"But you're not!" Abby argued. "You just sit up here in your room all the time. Everything around this place is run-down, and you just sit there! What are you thinking?"

Offended but uncertain how to answer, Jennifer said nothing.

"You don't go out at all. We don't go shopping—we don't do anything! You hardly talk to anybody, except to fire somebody!" Abby's temper showed itself in the color in her young face. "I'm afraid for you, Mother."

Taken aback, Jennifer simply glared at Abby. She couldn't deny the truth of what her daughter had said. "Where would you prefer we go?" she asked mockingly.

"Downtown Denver is just down the road, in case you've forgotten," Abby stated boldly. She walked closer to her mother, staring her straight in the eye, for she was now as tall as Jennifer. "Why don't we go shopping—buy some new clothes."

Jennifer just looked out the window. "I don't like to spend money anymore. Besides, we both have closets overflowing with clothes. Why do we need more?"

Abby knew what was happening and what she needed to do. Obviously her mother had some sort of degenerating illness that was growing worse each day. She regretted that her efforts to get her mother out for some exercise had failed. It had even occurred to her that her mother's problems might be spiritual. As much as she hated to admit it, perhaps God was the only one who could save her mother. For the physically ill you called a doctor. For the spiritually ill you called, whom?

"Let's go to Black Hawk," Abby recommended. "We haven't seen Abe and Lita in quite some time."

Jennifer listlessly turned to Abby. "I'm sorry, dear. I don't want to go to that drab, old place." She paused, then said, "It brings back sad memories."

"You don't want to see Abe and Lita? It's been a long time since you've even seen them. I know I'd like to spend some time with them. You and Lita were so close before."

Thinking about Lita captured Jennifer's attention, bringing her out of her lethargy. Judging from the look on her mother's face, Abby could see there was a battle going on inside her, as if she were being tormented by unseen forces.

"Don't think about it—just pack!" Abby insisted. She felt she'd better convince her mother before she had second thoughts. "Do you want me to help you pack?"

"Well . . ." Jennifer stated uncertainly.

Abby was already moving across the room to her mother's huge closet. "This dress would be nice," she said, holding up one of Jennifer's cotton outfits. "We can stay at the Teller House."

"Not that dress," Jennifer said, now paying attention. "It's too old. What about this one?"

Once Abby had her mother committed to packing, she knew she'd won the battle, though the war was far from over. If anyone could help her mother come to her senses, it was Abe and Lita.

～

Black Hawk and Central City had improved considerably. Although mining production was down, the place had a cleaner look. The streets were no longer filled with the boisterous traffic of haughty miners and mule skinners. Things were milder and more peaceful than ever now. The summer day was breezy and mild, lifting Abby's spirits.

"Come on, Mother," Abby said, coaxing her along. "You're poking."

"Poking?" Jennifer questioned.

"Yes," Abby said. "Can't you walk a little faster?"

The enjoyable walk took them along the sights they were both familiar with. Jennifer occupied herself with pleasant memories, though she found it difficult to tell if she'd lived there months earlier or a thousand years before. It felt like another person's life, not her own.

Soon the small church where Abe preached came into sight. Behind it sat a quaint little log cabin, the parsonage where Abe and Lita lived. Abby hurried up the foot path and knocked on the door. Her mother appeared to be aware of where she was, although Abby knew she could drift off without warning.

Lita opened the door, and her eyes grew as wide as saucers. "Bless the Lord! My chil'ren done come home!" She wrapped her arms around Abby's neck, now having to reach up a bit to do it. "You done grown up, honey," Lita said, her eyes running up and down Abby's frame. "You're a young woman now."

Turning her attention to Jennifer, Lita immediately knew something was wrong. Lita hugged her lovingly and invited them both in.

"Come on in here and sit at my table," Lita said, taking Jennifer by the upper arm and pulling her inside the main room where a dinner table sat with four chairs.

The cabin was filled with the mixed odors of food cooking and a fire crackling. A well-used, stained coffeepot sat on top of the stove, giving out a fragrance of burnt black coffee. An open doorway revealed a sagging bed covered with a colorful quilt. The wooden plank floors were covered with raggedy rugs, and the walls held shelves full of canned goods and miscellaneous small items. The place had a homey and pure quality about it.

To Jennifer, Lita appeared much older than she remembered. It had been a shock to get out and away from Chevalier, but seeing Lita again stirred familiar feelings of security she'd not known for some time. The cabin, small and cozy and warm, added to the effect.

After some small talk, Abby said, "Mother isn't doing well, Lita. She's so depressed. I brought her up here so you could help her."

Lita had already surmised the situation. She could see Jennifer was in trouble, though Jennifer quickly denied it.

"That's not true, Lita. We just came to visit and say hello." She swung her attention to Abby. "You shouldn't say that, dear. I'm feeling fine."

Abby made eyes at Lita, and Lita acknowledged it with a look. "Everything gonna be all right," Lita said happily. "Ya'll come in time for a good dinner. I got all kinds of good things to eat." She jumped to her feet and began working in the kitchen as she talked. "Abe be comin' home soon, and I know he'll be glad to see you."

"That sounds wonderful," Jennifer said, suddenly realizing she was hungry. "I've missed your cooking."

"Ain't nothin' special," Lita said, smiling, though she knew the food she prepared often brought others happiness.

The door opened, and Abe walked into the room. He glanced at the women at the table and stood staring. "Looky here," he said with a big white-toothed grin, "it's Miss Abby all grow'd up and Miss Jenny lookin' young as ever." He came over to the table and let his big palms rest on their backs. "The Lord has blessed this house. Thank You, Father in heaven! So how long ya'll stayin'?"

"They stayin' for dinner," Lita piped up.

"That's good. Lita always got plenty to eat," Abe said, rubbing his belly.

The conversation before and during dinner avoided Jennifer's personal problems, covering instead life at the estate and life and mining at Leadville. The problems were obvious to Abe and Lita, especially once they knew husband and wife hadn't been living together. Jennifer had not even mentioned Jason by name.

After dinner, having had enough of the phony talk, Abby said, "Mom sits in front of her window in her bedroom high up on the third floor all day long—every day. I'm scared for her."

Both Abe and Lita turned their dark faces to Jennifer and stared in amazement. "Is that right, Miss Jenny?" Abe asked.

Though embarrassed, Jennifer would not deny she had been doing some strange things. "Some days I just don't know where the time goes," she said.

Abe stood and walked away, then returned with his worn-out Bible. He placed it on the table in front of him so the kerosene lamp shone on it. "Miss Jenny, you got to open up—you got to tell us what's wrong. It'll help us pray about this."

"I don't know," Jennifer said, a little confused. "I really don't know."

"Do you still pray?" Abe asked.

"Not anymore," Jennifer admitted. "There's nothing to pray for—I have everything I could ever need."

That last statement told Abe all he needed to know. In his years as pastor of the church he had seen the likes of this fiery demon before and knew his evil ways. This would take some work.

The afternoon slipped into evening as the sun drifted lazily over the peaks, leaving a purple horizon. The firs and pines freshened the air with their scent. A long-eared black squirrel chirped outside the door, demanding that Lita feed him.

"I forgot how peaceful it could be up here in the mountains," Jennifer said longingly as she gazed out the open window near the table.

Lita had cleared the table and now tossed a few selected scraps out the front door. Abe had put his spectacles on and was studying the Bible. Abby had just finished a piece of peach pie made from canned peaches and was feeling sleepy.

"Miss Jenny, I don't think you understand how Satan works," Abe said, glancing over the top of his glasses.

"Satan?" Jennifer asked, surprised. "I'm sure he's had his hand in my affairs in the past."

"And even more now," Abe said firmly. "You're not the same, Miss Jenny, not like we knowed you before. It's like he's runnin' free in your life—I can see that."

Lita joined them at the table. "What about your marriage?" she asked. "Jason thinks the sun rises and sets on you. Why aren't ya'll together?"

Jennifer's eyes tightened, and she determined to hide the truth. "He has his business, and I have mine," She said sternly.

"That's not the right attitude, honey," Lita said, frowning. "You need to be with your man. He needs you, and you need him—that's the way the Lord meant it to be."

"I think I see the problem now," Abe said thoughtfully. "Lita, they so busy with material things they can't see the Lord's truth or love."

Jennifer began to feel uncomfortable. She wanted to get away from the questioning. "We really should be going—it's getting late," she said politely.

"You stay right where you at," Lita ordered. "You like my own child, and me and Abe is gonna help. Now you listen to him!"

Jennifer felt as if she were being pulled away from the world where she'd been hiding. She wanted to tell Abe and Lita that nothing was wrong, that everything was fine, but at the same time, deep inside she desperately wanted help.

"It's like this," Abe began, "the devil works in subtle ways, and you may not even know he's there until it's too late. First there's separation, when he gets your attention away from the Lord, gettin' in the way of your fellowship with God. In your case he used gold, makin' you think you could buy happiness. Some folks goes crazy buying things only to find out it don't work—they still unhappy. Next comes the devil's corruption, corruption of the spirit, corruption of God's ways in our lives. With the money comes power over others. Pretty soon you not even thinking of God, and what you do think ain't right."

Abe had Jennifer's full attention now. He was telling her exactly what had happened to her.

"Last comes condemnation, when we feel like no one understands, nobody cares," Abe said. "Then there's no happiness and can't be. Living by Satan's rules is what he wants, 'cause it runs against God's ways. And when a person ain't living God's way, he's a mighty unhappy, defeated person."

Abby was listening to all this too. She could see the truth in what Abe was saying, and she felt guilty herself. She hung her head.

"You're right," Jennifer sighed sadly. "There's no happiness in my life. None. And God's not in it either. All this worry with the abundance of wealth and possessions—I thought it would make us all happy. Grant is the only one who hasn't been corrupted by it."

"Praise God!" Lita said, for she saw the Jennifer she knew beginning to come back. She took Jennifer's hands into hers. "Child, open your heart, let God help you," she pleaded.

"The love and holiness of God are harsh opponents for the temptations of money," Abe said. "Can we pray over this?"

They all bowed their heads as Abe led in prayer. Jennifer's eyes welled up with tears. The shame she felt was awful, but she knew God's forgiveness was greater. Abby felt these things applied to her as well.

After his long and soulful prayer, Abe said, "Amen" and raised his eyes. "Miss Jenny, you got to get ahold of yourself. Keep the Lord in your heart—pray about this every day. It's the only way."

Feeling much better now that she'd opened her heart to the Lord again, Jennifer began to see things clearly for the first time in a long time. Her mind was clearer, and she had the unexplainable and wondrous feeling of being filled with love. The experience was absolutely remarkable, a powerful healing.

"Now," Lita said, "what about Jason?"

"I think he's interested in another woman," Jennifer confessed unhappily. "I can't blame him. I've been so cruel and unfair to him."

"Do you love him?" Lita asked directly.

Jennifer looked straight into Lita's big brown eyes. She held her gaze and then glanced away. "Yes," she said. "He's been the only real man in my life."

"He's up in Leadville?" Lita inquired, continuing her questioning.

"Yes."

"And that other woman is up there?"

"Yes."

Lita shook her head in anger and slapped her round palm on the tabletop. "Miss Jenny, you get your things together in the morning and you get yourself up there and get your man back. You hear me? He loves you, so don't let someone else take him away and make him unhappy. You better fight for what's yours!"

Though a little shocked at Lita's anger, Jennifer found it contagious. Abby did too.

290 □ Opulence and Grace

"Lita's right, Mother! You can't sit back and let Marie take Jason without a fight!"

"That's the truth," Abe added.

The fine green color was back in Jennifer's eyes, and she felt a surge of energy. Spiritual awakening had brought her out of the worst of slumbers, a slumber of the spirit. "I will!" she said determinedly. She looked at the people around her, people who loved her and cared about her. Softening some, she said, "Thank you, Abby, for your insight and courage in bringing me here. And thank you, Abe, for enlightening me. And thank you, Lita, for your honest wisdom. I thank God for all of you."

"Amen!" Lita said.

CHAPTER

~ 23 ~

Deception

Jason did all he could for Marie. The doctor had been by twice, shaking his head both times. He was very old and stooped and had a long white beard. "I don't recognize this malady," he said sorrowfully. "Could be something some physicians call cancer, a tumor."

"Is it deadly?" Jason had asked.

"Could be," the old man had said. "I sew up wounds, dig out bullets, and deliver babies. I don't know much about these kinds of things."

Marie was apparently not improving at all. She was scared and insisted on Jason's holding her. Aside from leaving to go clean up and change clothes, Jason took his meals in Marie's room. No matter how he tried, he couldn't get her to eat or take any laudanum.

"Marie, it'll kill the pain. At least you'll feel better, maybe get some sleep," he pleaded.

But Marie would just shake her head mournfully.

The days passed slowly, and Jason wondered what he would do if Marie died. He wondered if he cared for her more than he'd thought. *If there was only something I could do!*

It was August, and the weather was pleasant enough, so Jason opened the window to let in some fresh air. Occasionally visitors would bring Marie flowers, but they were just men seeking her attention, and when they saw Jason there, they'd leave right away. Talk around town was that Jason and Marie had something more between them than met the eye.

One day Marie moaned in pain as the daylight began to fade. "Jason, for once could you hold me like you loved me?" she asked sadly. "Just for once? I can't bear the thought of leaving without you ever having cared for me."

"You're not going to die," Jason said forcefully. "I won't let you, Marie."

Jason scooted his chair closer and leaned over Marie, hugging her firmly. She mustered the strength to reach her arms around him and hug him in return. "This is the only thing that makes me feel better," she said. She tried to smile, and Jason took that as a sign of improvement, at least in her attitude.

"I do care for you, Marie," Jason whispered. "I never said I didn't."

"But you never said you loved me," Marie reminded him. She was leading Jason on a path he didn't see.

"Love is something that grows and develops," Jason said knowingly.

Smiling again, Marie reached up and mussed Jason's hair. "What if I get well? What are you going to do with me then?" she asked.

Jason studied her beauty. She was much more emotional than Jennifer had been. She was fun-loving and liked to laugh, something else he liked about her. Jennifer had turned on him, and the bitter taste of rejection had been hard to swallow. But Marie had always remained true in her devotion to him. The moment grew more intimate as they looked into each other's eyes. The temptation had become too much, and he lowered his head and let his lips touch hers.

Inwardly, she was elated. She pulled him to her with a strength that surprised him, and he couldn't resist. She had finally won him over!

Just then a gentle knock came at the door, and Jason pulled away from Marie immediately. "I wonder who that could be at this hour?" he said as he stood and straightened his disheveled appearance. Moving to the door, he opened it.

"Jennifer!" he said. "What are you doing here?"

"I might ask you the same," Jennifer replied firmly.

"Marie's sick, and I've been sitting with her."

Taking a few steps inside, Jennifer peered around Jason to see for herself.

When Jason got up to answer the door, Marie decided to make it look as though she and Jason were indeed lovers. She figured whoever was at the door would be somebody close to Jason, perhaps Grant or some friend. The fact that it was Jennifer was better yet. She quickly threw the covers back and sat on the bed seductively. She smiled wickedly at Jennifer, confident of victory.

Intense anger and disappointment made Jennifer want to run from the scene, but she glanced at Jason to try to discern the truth. Seeing something was askew, Jason looked back at Marie. He stared in disbelief, knowing what his wife must think.

He turned back to Jennifer. "Darling, this is not what it appears to be." He knew now that Marie's serious illness had been a ruse.

"Tell her to go, Jason," Marie said in a flirtatious voice, "so we can get back to what we were doing."

The complete astonishment in Jennifer's face could not begin to describe the confusion in her mind. For what seemed like an eternity, she stood staring at Jason, his face ridden with sorrow. It was nearly impossible for her to think clearly, but thanks to her spiritual healing and improved mental state, she overcame her anger and looked at the situation rationally and objectively. Jennifer knew she had been a complete disappointment to Jason. How could she blame him for seeing someone else? After a quick prayer, she decided she had not come all this way only to quit as soon as things got tough.

"Let's go, Jason," Jennifer said quietly. For a split second she wondered what her husband would do. Her heart fluttered at the thought that he might not come with her. After all, why should he? She had been impossible. She waited as the moments went by ever so slowly.

To her relief and amazement, Jason's face was filled with joy. The simple thought that the Jennifer he'd married had returned gave him new hope. He smiled and said, "I think we'd better."

Jennifer took his hand and pulled him outside the door, and Jason closed it behind him.

Having lost her prize, seeing all her work and plans vanish, Marie jumped up, stomped her foot, and screamed, throwing a fit. Jason and Jennifer could hear glass smashing as they walked away.

~

Typical of a summer afternoon, a thunderstorm churned over the foothills near Denver and invaded the nearby flats with all of its lightning and fury. Sally was in the kitchen of the Chevalier but ignored the routine turbulence. "Every day the same thing," she complained. "But all the trouble is for nothing—not a drop of water. This place is as dry as an old biscuit."

A crack of lightning shook the dishes in the cupboard, making Sally jump. This irritated her further, so she threw down her rag and went to the front of the mansion to peer out at the whipping winds and the low black clouds rolling over the countryside. Parting the curtains so she could get a better view, she watched in disgust. A bright streak flashed across the black background and bit into the top of one of the giant cottonwoods immediately out front. It looked like a bright white serpent striking and squirming through the tree. A loud boom sounded, and Sally screamed.

The blazing tree split in two, half falling into the front of the mansion and crashing through the wall. The other half fell into the tall dry grass and blazed up instantly into flames fanned by the wind. Instantly the fancy home was ablaze, and Sally ran for her life, screaming with all her might, "Fire! Get out! Fire!"

Within minutes the servants were out back of the mansion watching the wind and fire consume the stately structure. The grass fire ran quickly over to the stables and servants' quarters, engulfing them. The livery man blindfolded the horses and pulled them out into the howling blast of wind and confusion.

The servant women huddled together, watching the huge fire. Even from fifty yards away the heat was almost intolerable. Raymond stood tall in his black tuxedo watching without showing emotion, the dancing fire reflected in his dull eyes.

Soon the gale passed over, and the sky cleared again except for the billowing black smoke that stretched like a long plume into the late-afternoon sky. Bells and whistles could be heard in the distance as the fire department rushed to the scene, far too late to save anything except the neighboring fields.

As the servants watched helplessly, the Chevalier caved in on itself, followed by a loud explosion. A giant ball of flames reached upward like an orange mushroom. The stables and servants' quarters had already been flattened and continued to burn vigorously.

"I've lost everything I own," Sally cried, hanging on to Raymond. "All I have is what I'm wearing. What are we going to do?"

Stoically, Raymond said, "Shall I contact the owners?"

Sally pulled away from Raymond and gazed at him in disbelief. "You old fool!" she spat. "Does nothing affect you?"

By nightfall neighbors, firemen, and onlookers were doing all they could to help. The Edingtons, who owned the next mansion, were kind enough to take in the servants. The fire had spread out hundreds of yards from the mansion in a simple grass fire and was quickly extinguished. Gloom hung over the smoldering black heap that used to be the Chevalier. Other than the servants who lost their belongings, there was no one to cry over the lost home.

～

Jennifer and Abby had checked into the Clarendon Hotel, the same place where Marie had her suite. Jason insisted they check out and come with him to his house on East Chestnut.

At the house Jason opened the front door and let Jennifer and Abby in. They walked into the clean little house that smelled of disinfectant. An old gray-haired woman on her hands and knees was scrubbing the floor with a scrub brush and a pan of hot, soapy water.

"You ladies are in the wrong place," the old woman said, looking up at the finely dressed women. "The bordellos are on down a ways."

"What?" Jennifer said, offended.

Jason had overheard and quickly came to the rescue. "Clara, these ladies are with me!"

Coming to her feet, Clara brushed her hands on her old dress, contempt on her wrinkled face. "Mr. Stone, I'll not have this kind of going on in no place where I work. I won't have it!"

Abby giggled.

"This is my wife, Clara!" Jason said. "My wife, Jennifer, and her daughter Abby! Jennifer, Abby, this is Clara, my housekeeper."

"Oh, pardon me!" Clara said apologetically. "If I'd known you were a comin' I'd've had dinner fixed."

"I told you I don't like seeing you down on your knees scrubbing," Jason said. "Why do you persist?"

"I don't know no other way to get a floor clean, Mr. Stone," Clara said peevishly. Then, more cheerfully, she said, "Watch your step and come on into the kitchen. I'll fix some tea."

"Make it coffee," both Jennifer and Jason said together. Then they looked at each other and laughed.

"I guess we're back in tune," Jason said, still smiling.

Grant came out, having heard the noise, and quickly hugged his mother. He and Abby had news to catch up on and went into another room to talk.

Clara retired for the evening, leaving Jennifer and Jason at the small kitchen table.

"You seem different somehow," Jason observed, noticing the light in Jennifer's eyes.

"Oh?" she questioned.

"Like you've been set free from something terrible," Jason added.

"Thanks to Abe and Lita's prayers and God's mercies," Jennifer said, "I'm doing much better."

Jennifer indeed felt much better and was thinking much more clearly. But there were some things she needed to say. "I know how awful I must have been," she began. "But I need to know where I stand . . . What was going on up there with you and Marie? It didn't look good at all. Do you love her?"

Jason dropped his head and played with a matchstick on the table. A candle burned between them, and his face was in shadow as he spoke. "I can see it now—I was duped. She had me believing she was deathly ill. It's almost like she knew you were coming, like she planned it all. I guess she figured after a scene like that it would be the end of you and me."

Jennifer thought it over. She knew Jason had had many problems in the past, but he'd never been guilty of lying. "But you didn't answer me—do you love her?"

Glancing up, Jennifer could see the candle flame dancing in Jason's blue eyes as he spoke. "I was developing feelings for her, I even kissed her, but I thought she was in trouble, that she was seriously ill. She's been a friend, but nothing more has happened between us. I haven't cheated on you. I love you more than I've ever loved any woman." He paused as he looked at her smooth face. "It's good to have you back."

"It's good to be back." Jennifer smiled as she reached over and took Jason's hand.

Jason smiled, then stood and pulled Jennifer to her feet. He embraced her and kissed her. She responded warmly, then backed away. Reaching back, she removed some pins from her hair and shook her head, letting her hair fall heavily over her shoulders. She smiled confidently.

The two came together with a passion that shocked them both. Jennifer clung to Jason, holding him with all her might. She thought, *This is love—this is the way it should be!*

∼

The message came at breakfast. Jason, Jennifer, Grant, and Abby were sitting at a table in a restaurant when Sam Gooten, the red-haired, bucktoothed boy who worked for the newspaper, came running in. "Mr. Stone! Mr. Stone!" he called as he ran up to the table out of breath. "An urgent message!"

Jason snatched the paper from the boy's hand and flipped it open. His eyes quickly darted across the paper, and he looked up grimly. "There's been a fire at the Chevalier. Raymond says we must come at once."

"Oh my!" Jennifer said, thinking of the safe in the wine cellar and its contents. "Does he say anything else?"

Folding his napkin and throwing it on his plate, Jason said, "We need to catch the first train out of here this morning. Grant, you take care of your sister here. Jennifer and I are going back to Denver." He stood up. "Let's be on our way, Jennifer."

Jennifer felt a sudden turmoil. Then it dawned on her that money and its power were still the primary focus of her life, and now she was faced with losing it. Where did God stand with her in this matter? How much had she really changed?

"Come on, Jennifer," Jason stated more firmly.

Lingering, Jennifer rose slowly and followed her husband. She was more frightened than she could say.

The trip back was long and agonizing as Jason and Jennifer rode on what seemed like the slowest train ever. They didn't talk at all; expectations of the worst played havoc in their minds.

Later when their rented coach neared the Chevalier, Jason and Jennifer both craned their necks to see the house, but only charred ruins remained. The tall cottonwoods that had been near the house were blackened skeletons. A dense pile of black rubble lay on the ground where the mansion used to sit. They got out of the coach and stood staring in shock.

Jennifer began to sob, then turned to lean on Jason's shoulder. Her crying quickly became hysterical.

"Well," Jason sighed, holding his wife, wanting to say something to sustain her, "it's not the end of the world."

For a long time they stood and stared at the mess. The horses snorted at the charred smell still strong in the air. A lone horseman approached, a man riding tall in the saddle and riding with an English canter. He turned into the long drive and came closer.

"It's Raymond," Jason said, releasing Jennifer.

Dismounting, Raymond walked up to Jason. He was wearing odd-fitting clothes, those of a common working man. "Good day, sir," Raymond said formally.

"Doesn't look like there's much good about it," Jason retorted. "What happened here?"

"Lightning, sir. It hit the big tree, and it fell into the house. She was gone in an hour or so."

"Anybody hurt? Where is everybody anyway?" Jason asked impatiently.

"All are well—at the Edingtons', sir," Raymond reported. When Jason had no more questions, Raymond added, "We have no clothes and no traveling money, Mr. Stone. The servants and I were wondering if you might pay us."

Jason turned and looked at the man, his mind racing. He thought for a second, then answered, "Of course. I'll see to it as soon as I can go to a bank in town."

Jennifer continued to wail uncontrollably. Jason put his arm around her and pulled her close. "Calm down, darling. Somehow everything is going to work out."

"But you don't understand—we have no money in the bank in town, not in *any* bank," Jennifer said in panic.

"What?" Jason asked. "What are you talking about?"

"I bought a vault and put everything in it—all the money and all the valuables. It was in the wine cellar."

"Are you crazy?" Jason asked furiously. "What did you do that for?"

"I don't know . . . I don't know," she lamented through her tears.

Glancing back at the rubble, Jason got an idea. "Raymond, go get some men and some shovels. We're going to dig down to that vault."

Rolling his eyes in disgust, Raymond said, "Yes, sir," then mounted his horse and trotted away.

Jason settled down some, then turned back to Jennifer. He took her in his arms and patted her back. "Why would you put everything in a safe in the wine cellar?"

"I was afraid," she sniveled. "I don't know what I was thinking. I didn't trust anybody."

"Well, we'll dig it up. Maybe everything in the vault survived the fire."

Digging down to the cellar was a tough task for the workers. Jason was soon covered with black soot as he wielded a shovel along with the other men. Hours later they came to broken bottles and melted heavy glass.

"I think we must finally be in the wine cellar," Jason observed, studying some of the charred glass. They pushed on, Jennifer help-ing by standing above them and trying to explain where the vault was located. After another fifteen minutes, a shovel clanged loudly on some metal, drawing the attention of all. "This is it, Mr. Stone," one of the hands said.

Surrounding the huge metal box, the men dug it out until they could set it upright. It was warped and tempered from the extreme heat. "Can you come down here and work the combination, Jennifer?" Jason asked. "Some of you men, help her down."

All watched patiently as Jennifer manipulated the burned metal dials, having to guess at some of the numbers since they were now so hard to read. She worked it again and again until finally there was a click.

"Stand back," Jason ordered as he inserted his shovel tip in the crack between the double doors. Prying hard, the door squealed as it opened. Two of the men grabbed it and forced it the rest of the way. All were eager to look inside.

Jennifer's heart sank when she saw nothing but ashes. Rooting through them, Jason pulled out some hard little bits of blackened and melted gold. "Must have been a very hot fire down here. Not much left of your jewelry, Jennifer."

"The wine, sir," Raymond reminded him. "There was a large ball of flame—an explosion."

"Of course," Jason said, deflated. "I'll have to send to Leadville in order to pay you. Tell the others." He crawled up out of the hole, totally filthy. "There's nothing left here for us, Jennifer. Nothing."

Upset and tired, Jennifer clung to Jason like a lost child as they stumbled out of the ruins. Uncommonly strong in the face of adver-sity, Jason held her tightly. "We'll survive," he promised. "I don't know how, but we'll be all right. I think what we could use right now is a hot bath."

Boarding the coach, they left for Denver to find a room.

⁓

Jason and Jennifer hadn't yet experienced all their afflictions. Late one night, deep in the wet shafts of the Water Pit mine, the face

of one of the drifts burst open with a gushing underground river.
Timbers crashed, and men screamed and scrambled for their lives.
Up above the lift bell rang frantically—the miners below were in
trouble! Levi came hobbling on his wooden leg as he pulled his coveralls over his long underwear. The hoist man was bringing up the
first cage of miners from what would quickly be a watery grave. When
the elevator cleared, the men piled off like drowning rats escaping a
flood. "It's like a dam broke!" one miner called. "It's flooding down
there, and there's still two more crews below! They'll drown!"

"Not if I can help it!" Levi shouted. "You get that elevator back
down and wait on their signal!" he ordered the hoist operator. As fast
as he could, Levi made his way over to the monster steam engines.
Their huge flywheels spun in unison, the engines chugging rhyth-
mically. He screamed over to the fireman standing beside the new
boiler Jason had purchased. "Load her up, boys! Give her all the coal
she can stand!"

The big coal shovels clanged as they heaped coal into the big
firebox under the huge riveted tank. Black smoke boiled out of the
chimney like a forest on fire, and the pressure rose. Levi took the
controls of the huge steam engines and swung the brass-handled
lever forward to open the throttle wide.

"All right, ladies! Sarah, Linda," Levi growled, "show 'em what
you got!"

The thirty-ton flywheels began to whir at an incredible, unsafe
speed. Steam hissed and puffed in spewing breaths. The massive
stretch of timbers that connected the pumps below groaned under
the stress. The boiler pressure gauge bounced into the red as the
steam whistle screeched scarily into the night.

"Mr. Levi!" one of the fireman yelled. "We can't stay here—this
thing's gonna blow!"

"Go on then," Levi called. "I'll do it myself." Levi, no stranger
to a coal shovel, heaped more coals into the fiery red mouth under
the boiler. He'd chained the throttles wide-open on both engines.
Water gushed out of the twelve-inch waste pipes like water through
a broken dam as Sarah and Linda churned their brute horsepower in
an effort to save the men below.

The hoist operator had brought up another group and now waited impatiently as the cage sat at the bottom of the shaft. He had to wait on the bell before he could bring the last of the men up. What was taking them so long? He wanted to get out of there but didn't want to leave the other miners behind.

The twin steam engines were now working so hard, they shook the ground. The hoist operator could see Levi shoveling coal for all he was worth. Finally, the bell rang, and he threw the lever to bring up the cage. Cables screamed under the load while the elevator ascended. At last the men reached the surface and scrambled from the floor of the cage. The hoist operator abandoned his position and broke into a run behind them. "Levi! Levi! That's the last of them! Let it go!"

But Levi couldn't hear him over the roar of the flames and the whine of heavy equipment. A rivet shot out of the boiler like a stray bullet and ricocheted off nearby steel. The big iron boiler heated tons of water at an incredible rate, driving and pounding like a giant run-away locomotive. Another rivet shot out, and then came a ground-shaking explosion. Shrapnel from the boiler caught Linda, jamming her works and breaking the huge connecting rod. The momentum of the flywheel slapped the giant metal parts around like toys, wrecking everything they contacted in a shower of sparks. Flying debris hit the spokes of the flywheel on Sarah, breaking them like matchsticks. The centrifugal force of the massive steel flywheel caused it to break free and crash through flimsy wooden buildings, splintering everything in its path for several hundred yards.

Water soon quit gushing from the twelve-inch pipes. Levi lay dead, a courageous man who had saved others at the expense of his own life. Silence hung in the still night air as a cloud of steam and smoke hung over the mining site. Slowly filling with cold water, the Water Pit mine was no longer.

∼

Early one morning about a week later, a flight of small clouds scampered along the ground. Jason kicked the debris at his feet as he surveyed the ruins of the Water Pit. He was sick with the sadness of

Levi's death, a man who had bravely died protecting Jason's business and employees. Blame sat heavily on his shoulders as he walked around; nothing appeared to be salvageable. "Dear God, what is happening? Because of my lust for wealth, a man died! Can I ever be forgiven for something like this?" he muttered under his breath. Grant poked around fifteen yards away, looking for he knew not what. The story had been big news in Leadville, with the surviving miners treated like heroes in the local taverns.

Levi's funeral had been grand, thanks to Jason. But now he lay in the cemetery with hundreds of other miners, men who left inspiring legends behind. Levi's heroics would live long in saloon conversations over whiskey and beer.

Standing below the remnants of Sarah, a once beautiful and magnificent engine, Jason stared upward at useless twisted iron. Linda sat wrecked beyond repair. They looked like the skeletons of huge black animals. "Must've been one terrible sight," Jason said as Grant came up.

Studying the mess, Grant said, "I can't imagine what kind of power could do something like this. You see the size of that metal? Looks like a sharp knife cut it."

Jason shook his head, completely befuddled. "I hope the Birdsong and the Baron can show some decent profits. Things aren't looking too good for us right now."

Grant dropped his head and stared at the ground. He had disappointing news. "Neither mine is doing that good," he said. "Not like they were."

Turning to Grant, Jason moaned, "I'm not sure what's happening, Grant. I can't figure it out."

With his hands in his front pockets, Grant shrugged his shoulders. He didn't understand either.

CHAPTER

~ 24 ~

The Wealth of Happiness

Abby made a halfhearted attempt to fix up her little bedroom in the house on East Chestnut. This was her new home—their life in a luxurious mansion was over. She had few things now; her wardrobe consisted of items newly purchased in Leadville. Although most of her new dresses were at least a little fancy, she preferred to wear something to suit her mood, a drab and common gray cotton dress. Her prized personal collections had burned in the fire, and she was angry at God once again.

Passing the doorway, Grant stuck his head in. "Abby?"

"What is it?" she asked dully.

"Oh, nothing. Just wondered how you were doing. I guess this is a lot different than what you're used to." Grant had noticed his sister's sadness and wanted to encourage her.

"You're lucky," she said. "You never got used to the good life, the rich life."

"My life's been good," Grant said convincingly. "I don't have any complaints."

"You know what I mean!" Abby argued. "I like living in a big place and having lots of money, being able to buy what I want. Now we're broke again. I don't think I can stand it."

Grant thought about what she'd said. It was true that he'd never taken advantage of their ample supply of wealth. A respectable job and decent horse were enough for him. Money wouldn't help him discover why people behaved like they did in boomtowns. Money was just a medium of exchange.

"We're not broke," he informed her. "The Wild Horse Company has plenty of investments and two more silver mines."

"Yeah, but I hear the two mines aren't doing that well. I heard Jason tell Mother he was going to try to sell the Birdsong." Abby wanted to cheer up but couldn't find any reason to feel encouraged. "Leadville isn't Denver either."

"Things will get better, Abby," Grant said hopefully. He knew Jason had invested a fortune; surely some of his investments would be successful.

Abby set a few things on her windowsill. They were impersonal items she'd bought on a recent shopping trip. None of them had any sentimental value. A wooden miner holding a pick sat and smiled. She liked his bearded face and red shirt. A silver bell with a handle had a sweet ring to it. A slim vase was too small to hold anything, but it was pretty. She arranged the objects, then shuffled them around and examined them again.

"Look at the good side of this. When was the last time you saw Mother and Jason so happy?" Grant was almost always optimistic.

"She was really confused, sick, you might say," Abby said. "I'm the one who talked her into going to see Abe and Lita. They sure helped her turn around."

"That was a smart thing to do," Grant said. "You saved a marriage and two good people."

Rolling her pretty blue eyes in appreciation for the praise, Abby finally smiled. "I still miss my things," she said.

"You can always get more things," Grant told her. "Things ain't nothing. It's people that are important."

"Yeah," Abby said, watching Grant. "I guess you're right, but I still like living a life of luxury—and I will again. Just you wait and see!"

~

"We've used up just about all of the money in the bank," Jason complained one morning. Jennifer was preparing breakfast. Clara didn't come in until later in the morning.

"Doesn't the company still have a fortune in investments? Cash in some of them," Jennifer suggested matter-of-factly.

"Sure, we can do that," Jason said. "But I hate to pull out invested money if it's got a good chance at some handsome potential earnings."

"Doesn't look like we have much of a choice if we want to keep things running." Jennifer sat down at the table with Jason. She was genuinely concerned. Although she was thinking more clearly these days, she still sometimes depended too much on money, especially when she felt afraid. She had hopes of replacing the Chevalier, except this time she wouldn't become so suspicious and fearful, she hoped.

"I'll see if I can run down Dick Shaffer today and cash something in," Jason said. "It may take a few days before I see any funds though."

"Are you going to keep operations going at the Birdsong while you're trying to sell it?" Jennifer asked. "It seems like it's going backwards. I mean, it's costing money to keep it open."

"I know," Jason agreed. These financial worries were weighing heavily upon him. But every time he looked at Jennifer, he felt renewed and energetic. It was wonderful to have her back. He loved to look at her long auburn hair on her shoulders as it surrounded her pretty face. Her fine shape filled out the plain calico dress. It was the love he shared with her that satisfied him and made him happy. He wanted to succeed at business for her sake.

"I think the mine would be harder to sell if it wasn't in operation," he said.

"Has *anybody* been interested in buying it?" Jennifer questioned.

"So far everybody that has looked at it has mining experience, and they all say the same thing—the claim's worked out." Jason sipped his coffee and set the cup down. "I may not be able to sell it."

Jason wished they could talk about something besides money and business. Though Jennifer was doing better, there was still some distance between them, something that prevented full communication and understanding. He wanted her undivided love, her complete attention, but the old wall she'd kept around her partially remained. Something still kept her from being totally free.

"Guess I'd better get going. Dick should be in his office by now," Jason said as he grabbed his hat. He opened the door, letting the sunshine in, then swiftly walked over and kissed Jennifer on the cheek. "I almost forgot."

"Bye," Jennifer said softly. For an instant she had that girlish, carefree look, but it quickly vanished.

～

Leadville had leaped from being a raucous boomtown to a civilized city, at times even having a larger population than Denver. Everything was better organized and more sophisticated now. The gas company supplied power; streetlights and telegraph poles lined the streets with their many wires. The railroad was responsible for respectable travel and the hauling of freight and ore, and also kept prices lower, there being no tariffs on the railroad. The city was in the process of establishing street cars to run up and down Harrison Avenue and Chestnut Street. Merchants were so busy, they had little leisure time.

Though times were tough, Jason still enjoyed his business roles. He had an office and a clerk to hide behind, his time being too valuable to see every caller about every little thing. Carol had been efficient in handling the office affairs, including screening callers and setting appointments.

"Good morning, Carol," Jason said as he entered the office. "Anything important?" he asked as a matter of routine.

"I'm afraid there is," Carol began, evidently a bit distressed. "Mr. Stone, I don't have enough funds to cover the payroll. You're going to have to do something."

"I am, Carol. I have to catch Dick Shaffer and turn some investments into cash. That might take a day or two."

Carol was too astute and observant to be satisfied with that answer. "Mr. Stone, is the company having problems?"

"Yes, big ones," Jason confessed reluctantly. "My house in Denver burned down with everything in it, the Water Pit exploded and filled up with water, and now the other mines aren't doing well. You might say I need to make a few . . . adjustments."

Carol nodded in understanding. "I thought so. I've sent three messages to your accounting man, Mr. Shaffer, telling him to have your portfolio ready, that you might be liquidating some stocks. But he hasn't responded."

"How intuitive of you," Jason complimented. "When did you send him the first message?"

"Three days ago, one message each day."

"Hmm," Jason said, rubbing the back of his neck with his hand. "I'd better get over there and talk with him."

Carol watched Jason rush out the door. She couldn't help but admire him. He was friendly and decent, unlike the men she had grown accustomed to in the business world. He actually cared about people—that was what made him different.

Jason hurried through the crowd until he came to Dick Shaffer's office. Dick's shingle dangled over the door advertising his services. Jason grabbed the doorknob, but the door didn't open, and he almost fell down as he bounced off it. Collecting himself, Jason cupped his hands and peered through the glass. The office was empty, *vacant.*

Jason felt nauseous. Had Dick skipped town along with all of the investments he was overseeing?

Jason glanced around, unable in his confused state to decide what he should do. Then an idea came to him. Jake Sands would know what was going on. He rushed in a state of panic to Jake's clothing store.

"That swindling carpetbagger!" Jake Sands exclaimed as he stomped around his ritzy office. "He got $20,000 from me too. One of my boys saw him boarding the train, and he had several heavy suitcases. I checked into it—we even had the sheriff open Dick's office. No paperwork—not a scrap of anything left. But they're looking for him, I assure you!" He turned to Jason, who looked ill. "How much, Jason?"

"Everything," Jason moaned sickly as he slouched in one of Jake's leather chairs. "Over a million dollars."

"You mean to say you had all your eggs in one basket?" Jake snapped.

"He came highly recommended. Even Tabor recommended him," Jason said sheepishly.

Quickly reaching in his desk drawer, Jake pulled out a bottle of brandy. "Maybe this will steady our nerves," he said.

"That won't help me a bit," Jason said. "I have to go, Jake. Thanks for the information."

"What will you do?" Jake asked as he watched Jason head for the door.

"Maybe I'll pray about it," Jason said, closing the door behind him.

∽

The news upset Jennifer so much, she became ill. Her depression surrounded her like a cloud of poisonous gas, dragging her deeper and deeper into a world of darkness where shadows surrounded her every thought. She felt like she'd been singled out and punished for every mistake she'd made. Dressed in her gown and robe, she moved slowly about the little house, overcome with fear and anxiety.

Jason had sent Clara off on errands and told Grant to take Abby somewhere and entertain her. He had to talk to Jennifer alone.

"It's not over!" Jason fumed. "The Baron mine is still producing enough for a good living. We just can't be so extravagant, that's all. Everything will be fine."

"But you can't even cover the payroll. How are you going to keep the mines in operation?" Jennifer said. Her eyes were puffy, and she looked defeated and without hope. "There's no more money right now."

"I'll borrow some from Tabor. I know he'll lend it to me."

"Is he in town?"

"Yes. Don't worry so much, Jennifer. We'll get by no matter what happens." Jason meant what he said. He'd do anything for Jennifer, down to his last dying breath.

Jason found Tabor at the Saddle Rock Cafe.

"Of course I'll lend you the money," Tabor offered proudly. "You're a dear friend in need, and I'll not stand by and watch you drown in your sorrows. How much do you need? Ten thousand?"

"I think I can get things back in order with that amount," Jason said, relieved. "I just need to cover the payroll right now."

"Consider it done." Horace Tabor removed a wallet from inside his vest and began writing out a bank draft. He handed it to Jason.

"I'll make it up to you," Jason said as he stood. "I'd better get this in my account before some of the miners start looking for me."

"I understand," Tabor said, waving his hand in the air. "I have a few employees myself, you know."

~

Jason immediately got to work. He'd have to make sure the loan was used well.

"Assay everything," Jason said to Grant. "I want to monitor things very closely—I have to know where I stand on a day-to-day basis."

"Yes, sir," Grant said enthusiastically. "I can let you know right down to the dollar per ton."

"Good. I'm going to talk with your mother again. She's still taking this real hard."

When Jason got to the house, he found Jennifer moping over a cup of coffee and staring blankly out the kitchen window at the marvelous view of the weathered wooden wall on the building next door.

"Get dressed—I want to take you somewhere," Jason informed her happily. "Tell Abby she can come too."

"What's come over you?" Jennifer asked.

"We're back in business. Horace made me a loan, and everything is going to be just fine. Now, get ready."

Jennifer hesitantly watched Jason's expression. He seemed confident and happy. "Abby is spending the evening with Baby Doe."

"Well, it's just you and me then," Jason said. "A romantic evening."

Dinner was a grand affair with Jason dressed in his tuxedo and Jennifer in a dress fit for a ball. It was like the old days of perpetual wealth, when they didn't have a worry in the world.

"Shall we attend the theater, darling?" Jason said invitingly. Just having money in the bank had relieved the overburdening stress.

"I'd love to see a play," Jennifer said, "as long as Marie isn't playing in it."

"Consider it done," Jason said, smiling. "I don't want to see her either."

They attended the Grand Central Theater and enjoyed the singing and dancing. It was a joyous affair, lasting into the late hours. Back on the street Jason escorted Jennifer proudly. As they moved along through the late crowd an old woman approached. "Waffle?" she asked.

"You're still selling waffles?" Jason asked.

"Yes," the hunched-over old woman said.

"I am a little hungry," Jason mentioned. "How about you, Jennifer?"

"A hot waffle actually sounds good," Jennifer said pleasantly.

As Jason paid the old woman he asked, "You actually make a living selling waffles?"

"Yes," the old woman said. "Business is generally best around 2 in the morning. By then the miners leaving the saloons are powerful hungry, if they're not too drunk."

"These are very good," Jason said, munching down the hot waffle. "Who are you?"

"I'm the waffle woman." She smiled as if she knew a secret. "You would never believe who I once was—nobody would." She went on her way, calling out, "Waffles. Fresh hot waffles."

"I wonder what she meant by that?" Jennifer questioned. "These are very good."

"Maybe there's a lesson here for us."

"Perhaps there is," Jennifer said.

It was a drab Monday morning when Ray Henderson showed up at the office of the Wild Horse Mining Company. Jason had just got in and hadn't reviewed any of the weekend reports.

"It ain't right, I know," Ray said, standing in front of Jason's desk with his small hat in his hand. "Things ain't going good out at the works, not either mine. The miners . . . well, they think you're bad luck—they think you're going broke. Morale is down, and they're stealing everything that ain't tied down. They don't know if they're going to have a job tomorrow."

"Nonsense!" Jason blasted. "They'll get their pay! Tell them everything is under control."

"I wouldn't be here if it was," Ray continued. "I've tried to tell them, but they won't listen." He walked in a circle around the room, obviously worried, even frightened. "The Birdsong—she ain't producing so good, and them miners know it." He paused again. "Young man, I'd like to give you some advice."

"Yeah, what's that?" Jason said, growing impatient.

"Take your losses early," Ray said.

"What's that supposed to mean?" Jason retorted.

"It means get out while the getting's good," Ray advised firmly. "At least you'll have something to get by on."

Ray had been a good man, and he knew his business, but Jason wasn't a quitter. "We'll see," Jason said. "In the meantime, tell those men to either get to work or get out."

Old Ray nodded his head. "You're the boss," he said as he left.

Within weeks profits plummeted even further. Determined, Jason kept throwing good money after bad until Carol reported, "Looks like payroll is going to be a problem."

"How can that be?" Jason screamed angrily. "I'm sick of dealing with the payroll. It's like a leech sucking all the blood out of me."

Carol didn't say a word but just watched sadly as Jason ran his hand through his hair. He looked like he'd lost his best friend.

"If I can't make payroll, I guess we'll have to shut down," he said dejectedly.

"But these men have a paycheck coming," she said earnestly. "So do I."

"I know, I know," Jason said solemnly. "I'll have to sell something. Shut everything down before they come after me. Get the word out—tell them we're through."

Heartbroken, Carol went on softly, "I'm sorry, Mr. Stone. I'm real sorry." She knew she'd be looking for a job again soon. It had been nice working for Jason, but he was too kindhearted to be an aggressive businessman in a place like Leadville, she thought to herself.

~

The two mining operations were immediately stripped of anything of value. Large equipment disappeared until there was nothing left but flimsy wooden shacks. There were no more employees and no money. The last shipments of ore quickly had a lien placed on them to cover the payroll.

"There must be some money left somewhere," Jennifer said mournfully. "There has to be something left of all our millions."

Jason just stood there quietly. Neither of them had anything to do. Grant was busy cleaning out the assayer's office and moving the supplies over to another assayer they had sold it to for a mere pittance. Abby had found a close friend in Baby Doe and was spending a lot of time with her, still preferring a life of abundance.

"I guess this is it," Jennifer said, almost in tears. "Clara came by earlier wanting her pay, and I didn't have anything to give her." She hung her head in despair.

There was nothing Jason could do to comfort her. All he could do was march around the little kitchen trying to come up with some thought that would give them hope or at least a semblance of strength. The riches, the high times, the elite stature—all was gone, leaving them with no worthy point of reference, nothing material to rely or depend on, nothing at all.

Jason's thoughts whirled back to another time of despair, another time of poverty back in Black Hawk. He thought he'd lost it all—

Jennifer, even his health. But then Lita told him, "Don't ever give up having hope. The Lord is always with you. He'll take care of you—depend on Him."

"I've been a fool," Jason said.

"What?" Jennifer asked softly, drawn by something in his voice.

"All this money for all this time, and I haven't even thought about God. No wonder the Bible says it's easier for a rich man to pass through the eye of a needle than it is for him to get into heaven. I've depended on wealth and money, and it let me down." He stared into Jennifer's eyes. "It let you down too."

"Oh, Jason," she said taking his hand as he stood over her, "you're right. Can God ever forgive us?"

"He's a loving God," Jason said, feeling stronger now. "He's done so much for us. He saved our marriage—we still have each other. Don't you think that's worth more than all the money in the world?"

"Yes," she said, her eyes filling with tears.

"We'd better get on our knees and beg His forgiveness and mercy. We haven't been faithful to Him, but He still loves us and wants to help us, I'm sure of it."

Jason and Jennifer knelt together and prayed right there on the kitchen floor of their humble home. It was a time of soul-searching and confession, a time of redemption, a time of forgiveness.

"And, Lord," Jason said, finishing the long prayer, "please find it in Your heart to help two poor fools. We've wandered away from You and served a false god of money and wealth. Now we want to walk on Your path again. Help us, please help us! In Christ's name, we pray, amen."

At that moment Jason and Jennifer rediscovered their roots and were restored in their souls. Their problems weren't gone, and they weren't suddenly perfect, but they were going in the right direction again. They had no funds in the bank, and they had few possessions, but they faced the future with renewed faith.

"I can get a job," Jennifer suggested.

Jason laughed. "I don't even want to start on that. There's only one thing in this town a woman can do and make much money."

Jennifer turned away.

"We need a business, some honest way of making enough to live on. Too bad we can't start up another newspaper," Jason said as he read the business ads in the local paper. "We know that business, and it was something we liked."

"But we just don't have the money to do it," Jennifer said.

"How about a bakery?" Jason asked teasingly. "There's one for sale."

A light came into Jennifer's eyes. "These miners do have a weakness for baked goods, a tremendous sweet tooth. And, Jason, I know how to bake delights a place like this has never seen."

"A bakery? Are you serious?"

"Why not?" Jennifer laughed happily. "We can do it. You'd look good covered in flour."

Jason hadn't seen the real Jennifer for a very long time, and he liked what he was seeing.

"Where will we get the money to buy the bakery?" Jason asked.

"We could sell this house," Jennifer suggested.

After looking at the bakery, Jason and Jennifer discovered that even if they did sell their house they would come up short.

"It was a good idea," Jason said days later as he shuffled through a stack of mail, mostly bills he couldn't pay. "You never know, maybe I could have learned how to bake."

Jennifer wasn't ready to give up. "It's not over. We must pray, and we must have faith. I don't know about you, but I never want to suffer the consequences of forgetting God again. In His kindness He removed all the money I had so I could see what I'd done."

Jason had to admit Jennifer was right. "You know," he said, "I used to not believe in miracles, special answers to prayers. But the way my life has turned out, I not only know they happen, I depend on them."

"We've seen more than a few," Jennifer agreed. "Want some more reheated coffee?"

"No, thanks," Jason said as he looked through that day's mail. "Hey, this is a package from my publisher back east." He quickly opened it. "Look, Jennifer, it's my book—the one I wrote! It looks great." It was a brown hardcover book with the title *Adventures West*,

Volume One. As he thumbed through it, a check for $500 fell out. "I can't believe it—it's my first royalties. Now we can buy the bakery! Just one more miracle from God."

Elated, Jennifer shared Jason's enthusiasm and expressed her own gratitude to God. She took the book in her hands and glanced through it. "It's very nicely done. What do they mean, 'Volume One'?"

"I don't know. Maybe they want me to write more, which is fine with me. I could certainly write a sequel after what we've been through lately."

"Sure could," Jennifer agreed. "What a story it would make—rags to riches to rags."

"Yeah. Maybe someday we can even get back into the newspaper business. I miss it," Jason said.

"One step at a time," Jennifer reminded him. "One step at a time, as God leads us, only as God leads us."

~

Weeks later Jason and Jennifer were a happy couple living in cramped quarters over a small bakery. Out of kindness, they gave Abby the bedroom on the front of the second floor. It was the best of the two, but they wanted to do whatever they could to make her happy. Business was good, enabling them to pay off their debts a little at a time. Grant had found a job with the assayer he'd sold the leftover equipment and supplies to. He even had his own rented room. Abby had become even better friends with Baby Doe. The two were like sisters and were nearly inseparable. Despite Baby Doe's confusion about what her relationship with Horace Tabor should be, the friendship between the two women seemed to be beneficial for both.

Jason quickly discovered he had a knack for work in the bakery. Even better, he loved laboring beside a new, wonderful, fun-loving Jennifer. "What are you so happy about?" Jason complained good-naturedly one day. "This is hard work."

"I'm free!" Jennifer beamed. "I've been set free from my bondage, and I've never felt better in my life. I have a good man for a husband,

and we have a bakery to support ourselves! What's your problem, mister?"

"I don't reckon I got a problem, ma'am," Jason played along. "As long as I got you and God lookin' out for us, I don't care about nothin' else. It sure is nice to be rid of all that there worry and frustration."

Jennifer had smudges of flour on her pretty face, and Jason had flour on his hands, but that didn't stop him from grabbing her and pulling her close to him. He kissed her with all the love he could muster. This was all he'd ever really wanted anyway—a happy life with the love of his life. The many possessions and riches they'd had before now seemed like silly toys.

Jennifer was no longer hiding. She liked the simple life God had given her. And she praised the Lord for Jason, for the love between them had not only survived but had blossomed. There were no longer any veils of deceit or storms of anguish or walls of hidden feelings to cause them regret and despair.

"I'm richer now than I ever was," Jason said, still holding Jennifer close to him. "The happiness I wanted, money can't buy. I have abundant life from above the clouds."

"I was just thinking of a popular saying," Jennifer teased, genuinely happy.

"What's that?" Jason asked.

"A fool and his money are soon parted," she said playfully.

"Maybe so," Jason agreed. "But a man and his woman should never be parted." He kissed her again, harder this time.

"Maybe we weren't meant to be rich—it certainly made a mess out of us," Jennifer reflected.

"I don't think that's it," Jason suggested. "I think God wants us to have abundance, but He wants us to have control over it, and not the other way around. Next time we get rich, if God wills it, we need to stay focused on our faith and not worry so much over material things."

"Oh?" Jennifer smiled. "And how are we going to get rich the next time?"

"Selling waffles," Jason teased.

The little bell over the front door jingled, announcing a customer.

"I'll get it," Jason said as he headed for the front. To his great surprise, he saw Marie Kelly looking over the delicacies inside the glass case.

"Why, Jason!" Marie said, surprised to see him. "What are you doing back there? Why are you wearing a white apron?"

"I work here," Jason announced. He wasn't overly friendly, remembering how she had pretended to be sick.

"Why on earth would you want to work here?" Marie inquired, still flirtatious.

"This place is all I have," Jason said. "I went broke."

"Broke?" Marie repeated, her expression turning hard and cruel. "How can a millionaire go broke?"

"Happens every day." Jason placed his hands on the counter and leaned forward. "Can I help you with something?"

The sweet and innocent face Marie usually wore disappeared. A hatred filled her eyes and twisted her expression. "I can't believe you're such a fool! If I'd known you were so stupid, I would have never wasted my time on you," she hissed, then spun around and pompously stomped out, slamming the door behind her, causing the little bell to jingle furiously.

"What's going on?" Jennifer asked pleasantly as she came to the front. "I thought somebody was here the way the bell was ringing."

"No one we need to concern ourselves with right now," Jason said confidently. He took her into his arms. "I love you so much, and I always will."

Jennifer kissed him back and clung to him fiercely. She felt as if she had come out of a wild storm into a calm harbor. She whispered, "I love you, too, Jason, and I always will."

Follow The Chronicles of the Golden Frontier

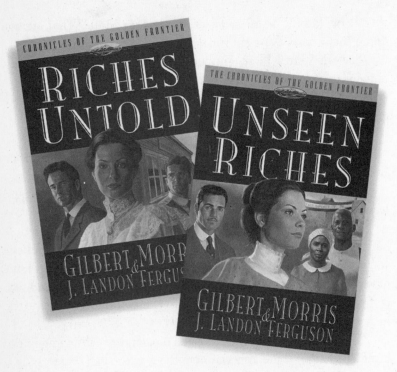

Jennifer DeSpain's life used to be quiet and dull, but that was before a whirlwind romance and marriage—and a tragedy that leaves her with only a defunct newspaper to her name. With hopes of a fresh start, Jennifer and her two children boldly move to Nevada, where she will have to resolve the challenges of poverty, newspaper publishing, a reversal of fortune—and matters of the heart—all with the help of some colorful friends and the Lord above.

Book 1: *Riches Untold*
Book 2: *Unseen Riches*